What Readers Are Saying about Karen Kingsbury's Books

Karen's book *Oceans Apart* changed my life. She has an amazing gift of bringing a reader into her stories. I can only pray she never stops writing.

Susan L.

Everyone should have the opportunity to read or listen to a book by Karen Kingsbury. It should be in the *Bill of Rights*.

Rachel S.

I want to thank Karen Kingsbury for what she is doing with the power of her storytelling—touching hearts like mine and letting God use her to change the world for Him.

Brittney N.

Karen Kingsbury's books are filled with the unshakable, remarkable, miraculous fact that God's grace is greater than our suffering. There are no words for Ms. Kingsbury's writing.

Wendie K.

Because I loaned these books to my mother, she BECAME a Christian! Thank you for a richer life here and in heaven!

Jennifer E.

When I read my first Karen Kingsbury book, I couldn't stop.... I read thirteen more in one summer!

Jamie B.

I have never read anything so uplifting and entertaining. I'm shocked as I read each new release because it's always better than the last one.

Bonnie S.

I am unable to put your books down, and I plan to read many more of them. What a wonderful spiritual message I find in each one!

Rhonda T.

I love the way Karen Kingsbury writes, and the topics she chooses to write about! Thank you so much for sharing your talent with us, your readers!

Barbara S.

My husband is equally hooked on your books. It is a family affair for us now! Can't wait for the next one.

Angie

I can't even begin to tell you what your books mean to me.... Thank you for your wonderful books and the way they touch my life again and again.

Martje L.

Every time our school buys your next new book, everybody goes crazy trying to read it first!

Roxanne

Recently I made an effort to find GOOD Christian writers, and I've hit the jackpot with Karen Kingsbury!

Linda

When Karen Kingsbury calls her books "Life-Changing Fiction™," she's merely telling the unvarnished truth. I'm still sorting through the changes in my life that have come from reading just a few of her books!

Robert M.

I must admit that I wish I was a much slower reader ... or you were a much faster writer. Either way, I can't seem to get enough of Karen Kingsbury's books!

Jillian B.

I was offered $50 one time in the airport for the fourth book in the Redemption Series. The lady's husband just couldn't understand why I wasn't interested in selling it. Through sharing Karen's books with my friends, many have decided that contemporary Christian fiction is the next best thing to the Bible. Thank you so much, Karen. It is truly a God-thing that you write the way you do.

Sue Ellen H.

Karen Kingsbury's books have made me see things in ways that I had never thought about before. I have to force myself to put them down and come up for air!

Tabitha H.

I have read many of Karen's books and I cry with every one. I feel like I actually know the people in the story, and my heart goes out to all of them when something happens!

Kathy N.

Wow, what an amazing author Karen Kingsbury is! Her stories are so heart-wrenching ... I can't wait until the next book comes out.... Karen, please don't ever lay your pen down.

Nancy T.

Karen Kingsbury's words leap off the page.... I just finished a new series last night and once again she has touched me beyond compare!

Kendra S.

Other Life-Changing Fiction™ by Karen Kingsbury

9/11 Series
One Tuesday Morning
Beyond Tuesday Morning
Every Now and Then

Lost Love Series
Even Now
Ever After

Above the Line Series
Above the Line: Take One
Above the Line: Take Two
Above the Line: Take Three
Above the Line: Take Four

Stand-Alone Titles
Oceans Apart
Between Sundays
This Side of Heaven
When Joy Came to Stay
On Every Side
Divine
Like Dandelion Dust
Where Yesterday Lives
Shades of Blue
Unlocked (Fall 2010)

Redemption Series
Redemption
Remember
Return
Rejoice
Reunion

Firstborn Series
Fame
Forgiven
Found
Family
Forever

Sunrise Series
Sunrise
Summer
Someday
Sunset

Red Glove Series
Gideon's Gift
Maggie's Miracle
Sarah's Song
Hannah's Hope

Forever Faithful Series
Waiting for Morning
Moment of Weakness
Halfway to Forever

Women of Faith Fiction Series
A Time to Dance
A Time to Embrace

Cody Gunner Series
A Thousand Tomorrows
Just Beyond the Clouds

Children's Titles
Let Me Hold You Longer
Let's Go on a Mommy Date
We Believe in Christmas
Let's Have a Daddy Day

Miracle Collections
A Treasury of Christmas Miracles
A Treasury of Miracles for Women
A Treasury of Miracles for Teens
A Treasury of Miracles for Friends
A Treasury of Adoption Miracles

Gift Books
Stay Close Little Girl
Be Safe Little Boy
*Forever Young: Ten Gifts of Faith
  for the Graduate*

KAREN
NEW YORK TIMES
BESTSELLING AUTHOR
KINGSBURY

UNLOCKED

ZONDERVAN®

ZONDERVAN.com/
AUTHORTRACKER
follow your favorite authors

ZONDERVAN

Unlocked
Copyright © 2010 by Karen Kingsbury

This title is also available as a Zondervan ebook. Visit www.zondervan.com/ebooks.

This title is also available in a Zondervan audio edition. Visit www.zondervan.fm.

Requests for information should be addressed to:
Zondervan, *Grand Rapids, Michigan* 49530

Library of Congress Cataloging-in-Publication Data

Kingsbury, Karen.
     Unlocked : a love story / Karen Kingsbury.
        p. cm.
     ISBN 978-0-310-26695-2 (softcover)
      1. Autistic children — Fiction. 2. School violence — Fiction. 3. Bullying —
Fiction. 4. Adultery — Fiction. 5. Domestic fiction. I. Title.
    PS3561.I4873U55   2010
    813'.54 — dc22
                               2010031127

Published in association with the literary agency of Alive Communications, Inc., 7680 Goddard Street, Suite 200, Colorado Springs, CO 80920. www.alivecommunications.com

Cover design: Studio Gearbox
Cover photography: Bill Tucker Studio / iStock Photo
Author photography: Dan Davis Photography

Printed in the United States of America

10 11 12 13 14 15 /DCI/ 21 20 19 18 17 16 15 14 13 12 11 10 9 8 7 6 5 4 3 2 1

DEDICATION

To Donald, my Prince Charming ...

I love that for now we can still see fall as the beginning of a new year. Summer is over, and everything wonderful about the changing of seasons is upon us. You and the boys have been working hard at football camp and now the leaves are a brilliant bouquet of golds and reds. The kids are back to school, but here's the thing: we only have so many falls like this left, so many years when back to school actually applies to us. And how can that be, when just yesterday we were bringing Kelsey home? I remember the nurse asking if we knew how to buckle her seat belt into the backseat, and you and I looked at each other. It was sort of that, "Yikes! Here we go!" sort of look, because where was the manual? The Bible... that was the only manual then, and it's the only one now. God walked us through the baby stage and the walking stage, He walked us through the off-to-school stage and now, somehow, He'll walk us through the years of letting go. All I know for sure is that I want to go through it with you, my love. I still can't believe you had a stroke nearly a year ago, or how different our lives might be if God hadn't so graciously given us a miracle back then. You are here and whole, and the heartbeat of our lives goes on. But we don't ever take a minute for granted. Play hard this fall, win big, and every now and then look for me up in the stands. I'll be taking a million mental pictures, saving every moment for that all-too-soon day when the fall isn't marked by the guttural shouts of teenage football players or the scattering of backpacks across our kitchen counter. The quiet days lie ahead, but for now, my love, hold my hand and let's run the journey together. You and our boys, making memories together. Isn't this what we always dreamed of? I love sitting back this time and letting you and God figure it out. I'll always be here—cheering for you and the team from the bleachers. But God's taught me a thing or two about being a coach's wife. He's so good that way. It's fitting that you would find varsity coaching again now—after twenty-two years of marriage. Hard to believe that as you read this, our twenty-second anniversary has come and gone. I look at you and still see the blond, blue-eyed guy who would ride his bike to my house and read the Bible with me before a movie date. You stuck with me back then and you stand by me now—when I need you more than ever. I love you, my husband, my best friend, my Prince Charming. Stay with me, by my side, and let's watch our children take wing. Always and always … The ride is breath-takingly beautiful. I pray it lasts far into our twilight years. Until then, I'll enjoy not always knowing where I end and you begin. I love you always and forever.

To Kelsey, my precious daughter …

How is it possible that you are twenty-one, my precious lit-tle girl? I still see you dancing in circles around your daddy, and carefully applying lipstick from a purse you got for Christmas when you were four. I remember listening to songs about letting kids grow up and watching them leave home and thinking, "Dear God, I'll never make it …" But there was some comfort back then, because your childhood spread before us like one long endless summer of laughter and loving and days that seemed like they'd last forever. But this fall every line of every leaving song will come rushing back as we take you to college in Southern California. Sometimes when I think about the season ahead I struggle to draw a full breath. These times will redefine for me what miss-ing someone really means. But you, sweet girl, were created to perform for Jesus. All through your childhood you would find a stage and hold your chin high, and you'd sing to whoever was listening. Well, sweetheart, more people are listening now. I'm so proud of you, and all you've become... all you stand for. Every prayer we prayed for you, God has answered. You have stood firm, holding tight to God's truth and His promises, and I know the answers will become clearer with each passing year. Remember that God walks every step of this life with us, and for those who love Him, the best is always yet to be. This fall we will watch you take wing, having worked hard to reach this point in your education. We believe in you, sweetheart, and we will be cheering for you every day. No matter where this year takes you, you'll never really leave our family. You'll always be our little girl, Kelsey. And you'll always be part of this family. Forever and ever. I'm so proud of the strength you've found. You are beautiful inside and out, and I am more convinced than ever that God has great, wonderful plans for you. Take your talents and go find your platform for Him! In the meantime, you'll be in my heart every moment. And we'll leave the porch light on. I love you, sweetheart.

To Tyler, my lasting song ...

My heart skips a beat when I think about you being a senior this year. I thought about this time as far back as you've been a part of our life, and always it seemed so far away. Even last year, I couldn't really imagine you as a senior. But here we are, right? This is where the Ferris wheel slows down; this is where you get off and make your way down the path, following God to the next season in your life. But here's the amazing part — we will always have a front row seat! This fall your first single will debut on the *Unlocked* CD, and the dreams you've had for the past couple of years will start to come true. I know God has a future in music for you, because I've seen your passion in singing and writing music for Him. I love how the music is in you, Ty... and how you seem complete when you are caught up in the process of creating. I sometimes think about your papa, and how proud he would be to watch the young man you've become. I still see him there in his favorite chair—the one by the fireplace, closest to the piano. He couldn't listen to you play and sing without getting tears in his eyes, and I can't, either. So even though I'm sad that you've reached your senior year, I'm excited too. Because this is the time of your life you've been waiting for. The world is your stage, Ty! Go stop the world for Jesus, and let your very bright light touch the lives of everyone who needs it. Thank you for the hours of joy you bring our family, and as you head into a year of lasts, I promise to stop and listen a little longer when I hear you singing. Your dad and I are proud of you, Ty. We're proud of your talent and your compassion for people and your place in our family. However your dreams unfold, we'll be in the front row to watch them happen. Hold on to Jesus, son. I love you.

To Sean, my happy sunshine...

What a thrill it is watching you—a strapping, young sophomore—take on varsity football again this year! You've worked so hard in the off season, and now you're truly ready—ready to take on the challenge of being the best receiver on the field! I'll never forget what you did last year right before the season started. You came to me and asked if I could find custom wristbands for the team. "I want them to say Philippians 4:13," you told me. You'd seen Florida University's Timmy Tebow donning that verse on his eye black before a Gator game, and now you wanted to have a similar show of faith. A week passed and another, and every few days you asked until finally I set everything aside and ordered them for the whole team. I'll never see that verse without seeing the sincerity in your eyes, the desperation, almost, that if you were going to play football, you needed to always remind yourself of the truth. You can do everything through Christ who gives you strength. And you can, Sean. You proved that this year by being the team's leading receiver. Oh, and one of the best tacklers on the team. You remain a bright sunbeam, bringing warmth to everyone around you. And now you are an example of faith as well. I'm proud of you, Sean. I love you so much. I pray God will use your dependence on Him to always make a difference in the lives around you. You're a precious gift, son. Keep smiling and keep seeking God's best for your life.

To Josh, my tenderhearted perfectionist...

You promised to work hard in the off season, and you have. Now we are here, at the beginning of your sophomore year in high school and you are ready for the challenges that face you. I don't know which records will fall or how the public will come along to see your feats on the field, but I do know this: it's so much more important that you have grown just as much in your faith. When God gives us talents, we must always remember where they come from. Who they come from. You have done this, dear son, and now you are ready to take on the world. Well, maybe not quite yet. But you're ready to take on the season, and give God the glory along the way. Josh, one memory stands out from the past year. The earthquake hit in Haiti, and you were the only one of our kids with family still in Port-au-Prince — your birth mother, Marie. At this point, we still have not heard from her and we assume that maybe she is watching you from heaven now. Maybe seated somewhere next to Papa, cheering you on. I remember you coming to me, quietly, in your unassuming way, and asking me how much money was in your birthday account. This was money you'd saved for the past eight years, and when I told you the amount you nodded and told me to send virtually all of it to World Vision. "At least then I'll know that if she's alive, and if she needs something, someone will get it to her." Yes, Josh, you may laugh a lot and tease a lot, but we know your heart and we are so proud of what we see. We have no doubt that someday we'll see your name in headlines and that—if God allows it—you'll make it to a major college team. You're that good, and everyone around you says so. Now flash back to that single moment in a broken-down Haitian orphanage. There I was meeting Sean and EJ for the first time when you walked up. You reached up with your small fingers, brushed back my bangs, and said, "Hi, Mommy. I love you." It might've taken six months of paperwork, but I knew as you said those words that you belonged with us. The picture becomes clearer all the time. Keep being a leader on the field and off. One day people will say, "Hmmm. Karen Kingsbury? Isn't she Josh's mom?" I can't wait for the day. You have an unlimited future ahead of you, son, and I'll forever be cheering on the sidelines. Keep God first in your life. I love you always.

To EJ, my chosen one ...

EJ, my jokester, you are in high school! I can't believe how fast time has flown for you and for us. The journey started a decade ago when we saw one little face on an Internet photolisting of kids up for adoption. That face was yours, but the blessing of the journey has been ours. God has brought you so far, EJ, and now you stand on the brink of becoming everything He has planned for you to become. At our Christian school you have found friends and a deeper faith, and a fire for pursuing the talents God has given you. All the things we have prayed for you! As you start high school, you are one of our top students, and we couldn't be more proud of you, EJ. But even beyond your grades and your natural way of leading your peers in the right path, we are blessed to have you in our family for so many reasons. You are wonderful with our pets—always the first to feed them and pet them and look out for them—and you are a willing worker when it comes to chores. Besides all that, you make us laugh—oftentimes right out loud. I've always believed that getting through life's little difficulties and challenges requires a lot of laughter—and I thank you for bringing that to our home. You're a wonderful boy, son, a child with such potential. I'm amazed because you're so talented in so many ways, but all of them pale in comparison to your desire to truly live for the Lord. I'm praying you'll have a strong passion to use your gifts for God as you enter high school in the fall. Because, EJ, God has great plans for you, and we want to be the first to congratulate you as you work to discover those. Thanks for your giving heart, EJ. I love you so.

To Austin, my miracle boy...

Seventh grade, and already you look like a tenth-grader! I remember this past year when you would walk up to me on your tiptoes and look me in the eyes. "It happened, Mom! I'm taller than you!" You'd celebrate a little only to realize that I was in bare feet and you were in tennis shoes. "Not quite," I'd tell you. "You're still shorter than me." But now that is no longer true. You don't walk up on your tiptoes any more because you don't have to. God has graced you with tremendous size and strength, Austin. I look at you and I see a young Timmy Tebow, a kid with an ocean of determination and leadership ability, a young man who is the first to thank his coach, the first to shake the hand of the ref, and the last one to leave the classroom because you're so busy cleaning up and expressing your gratitude to your teacher. Sure, you still struggle in a few areas, and sometimes your competitive drive can get you in trouble with your brothers. But truly, Austin, there isn't a thing you can't do as long as you keep God first. I believe you have the chance to go all the way with your dreams of playing sports, and I'm grateful to have a front-row seat. Play hard and don't ever give up, and always remember where you came from. I know I do: that hospital room when you were three weeks old and the surgeon was giving us a few minutes to say good-bye. Not every infant who goes in for emergency heart surgery comes back out again. But even then, through our tears, we were certain we'd see you somewhere—here or there. The fact that God has blessed us with the here and now is proof that He has amazing plans for you. How great that you are seizing them with everything inside you, with every breath. Keep on, precious son. We are here for you, praying for you, cheering for you. No one believes more than we do. I've said it before, and it's true: heaven has windows, and I'm convinced Papa's still cheering for you, son. Especially this season. As you soar toward your teenage years, please don't forget that or him. You're my youngest, my last, Austin. I'm holding on to every moment, for sure. Thanks for giving me so many wonderful reasons to treasure today. I thank God for you, for the miracle of your life. I love you, Austin.

And to God Almighty, the Author of Life, who has—for now—blessed me with these.

ACKNOWLEDGMENTS

NO BOOK COMES TOGETHER WITHOUT A GREAT AND TALENTED team of people making it happen. For that reason, a special thanks to my friends at Zondervan who combined efforts with a number of people who were passionate about Life-Changing Fiction™ to make *Unlocked* all it could be. A special thanks to Moe Girkins—whose commitment to excellence at Zondervan is unparalleled, and to Steve Sammons and Don Gates, who may be two of the only execs in publishing who actually get the big picture of what we're doing for the Kingdom. Also, of course, a special thanks to my dedicated and brilliant editor, Sue Brower, and to Alicia Mey, my marketing director. Thanks also to the creative teams and to the sales staff at Zondervan who work tirelessly to put this book in your hands.

Also, thanks to my amazing agent, Rick Christian, president of Alive Communications. Rick, you've always believed only the best for me. When we talk about the highest possible goals, you see them as doable, reachable. You are a brilliant manager of my career, and I thank God for you. But even with all you do for my ministry of writing, I am doubly grateful for your encouragement and prayers. Every time I finish a book, you send me a letter that deserves to be framed, and when something big happens, yours is the first call I receive. Thank you for that. But even more, the fact that you and Debbie are praying for me and my family keeps me confident every morning that God will continue to breathe life into the stories in my heart. Thank you for being so much more than a brilliant agent.

A special thank you to my husband, who puts up with me on

deadline and doesn't mind driving through Taco Bell after a football game if I've been editing all day. This wild ride wouldn't be possible without you, Donald. Your love keeps me writing; your prayers keep me believing that God has a plan in this ministry of Life-Changing Fiction™. And thanks for the hours you put in working with the guestbook entries on my website. It's a full-time job, and I am grateful for your concern for my reader friends. I look forward to that time every day when you read through them, sharing them with me and releasing them to the public, lifting up the prayer requests. Thank you, honey, and thanks to all my kids, who pull together, bringing me iced green tea and understanding my sometimes crazy schedule. I love that you know you're still first, before any deadline.

Thank you also to my mom, Anne Kingsbury, and to my sisters, Tricia and Sue. Mom, you are amazing as my assistant—working day and night sorting through the mail from my readers. I appreciate you more than you'll ever know. Traveling with you these past years for my Extraordinary Women events has given us times together we will always treasure.

Tricia, you are the best executive assistant I could ever hope to have. I treasure your loyalty and honesty, the way you include me in every decision and the daily exciting website changes. My site has been a different place since you stepped in, and the hits have grown a hundredfold. Along the way, the readers have so much more to help them in their faith, so much more than a story. Please know that I pray for God's blessings on you always, for your dedication to helping me in this season of writing, and for your wonderful son, Andrew. And aren't we having such a good time too? God works all things to the good!

Sue, I believe you should've been a counselor! From your home far from mine, you get batches of reader letters every day, and you diligently answer them using God's wisdom and His Word. When readers get a response from "Karen's sister Susan," I hope they know how carefully you've prayed for them and for the responses you give. Thank you for truly loving what you do, Sue. You're gifted with people, and I'm blessed to have you aboard.

A special thanks also to Tom McCorquodale. In this season of change, with you headed to college in California, just know that I will always be grateful for your marketing skills and ability to manage my events. You always understood the mission statement, "Do all things to love and serve our reader friends." I pray that God blesses your time at school, and that you continue to grow into an amazing man of faith—like I know you will. God's plans for you are unlimited!

And to Randy Graves, a very special thank you. Randy, you and your family have been a part of our family for more than a decade. You were a friend to my father and my brother, and you were a pall bearer when it came time to say good-bye to them. You understand the ministry of Life-Changing Fiction™ and now as my business manager and the executive director of my One Chance Foundation, you are an integral part of all we do. What a blessing to call you my friend and coworker. I pray that God always allows us to continue working together this way.

Also thanks to the newest member of our team—Peggy Rider. You have been a friend for many years, but now I feel God has brought us together for this season of working together. Your efforts in the Baxter Family Store show in every small detail. I appreciate that you care so deeply.

Thanks, too, goes to Olga Kalachik, my office assistant, who helps organize my supplies and storage areas, and who prepares our home for the marketing events and research gatherings that take place here on a regular basis. I appreciate all you're doing to make sure I have time to write. You're wonderful, Olga, and I pray God continues to bless you and your precious family.

And thanks to Will Montgomery for his watchful eye and careful attention to detail in the final editing stages of this book.

18

Glad that we're still friends, still working to further His kingdom through the power of story.

I also want to thank my friends at Premier—Roy Morgan and your team, along with my friends at Extraordinary Women —Tim and Julie Clinton, Beth Cleveland, Charles Billingsley, Angela Thomas, Matthew West, Jeremy Camp, Chonda Pierce, and so many others. How wonderful to be a part of what God is doing through all of you. Thank you for including me in your family.

And thanks to my forever friends and family, the ones who have been there and continue to be there. Your love has been a tangible source of comfort, pulling us through the tough times and making us know how very blessed we are to have you in our lives.

The greatest thanks, as always, to God Almighty. You put a story in my heart, and have a million other hearts in mind— something I could never do. I'm grateful to be a small part of what you're doing! The gift is yours. I pray I might use it for years to come in a way that will bring you honor and glory.

FOREVER IN FICTION

FOR A NUMBER OF YEARS NOW, I'VE HAD THE PRIVILEGE OF offering Forever in Fiction™* as an auction item at fundraisers across the country. So many of my more recent books have had Forever in Fiction characters that I hear from you reader friends how you look forward to this part of my novels, reading this section to see which characters in the coming pages are actually inspired by real-life people, and learning a little about their real stories. Then you enjoy looking for them in the coming pages, knowing with a smile how it must feel to their families seeing their names Forever in Fiction.

For those of you who are not familiar with Forever in Fiction, it is my way of involving you, the readers, in my stories, while raising money for charities. The winning bidder of a Forever in Fiction package has the right to have their name or the name of someone they love written into one of my novels. In this way they or their loved one will be forever in fiction. To date, Forever in Fiction has raised more than two hundred thousand dollars at charity auctions. Obviously, I am only able to donate a limited number of these each year. For that reason, I have set a fairly high minimum bid on this package so that the maximum funds are raised for charities. All money goes to the charity events.

In *Unlocked*, I bring you a very special Forever in Fiction character. That character is precious little Kate McRae, a six-year-old Arizona girl who has battled brain cancer for more than a year. Kate is the blue-eyed, blonde-haired daughter of Aaron and Holly McRae—a young pastor and his wife. The McRae family

---

* Forever in Fiction™ is a registered trademark owned by Karen Kingsbury.

has two other children—Olivia, seven, and Will, four. Life as this family knew it changed dramatically the summer day in 2009 when they noticed a tremor in Kate's hand. A simple trip to the doctor led to a myriad of tests and the diagnosis that would rock any family. Kate had an aggressive form of brain cancer.

Treatment for Kate has been both risky and uncertain. More than that, it is terribly expensive. Since Kate's mother, Holly, is one of my reader friends, I decided to do something new with Forever in Fiction. I figured we could make Kate a character in one of my books as long as enough people would come alongside me and donate at least one hundred dollars to the Kate McRae Fund. In return, I would list the names of Kate's special supporters here, in the acknowledgments of my book.

We opened up a two-month window, and during that time my hopes were wildly exceeded by your tremendous generosity. Nothing can ease the pain of cancer for a family like the McRaes. But your financial help and your tireless prayers have made it possible to withstand the storm. As I write this, Kate has finished her chemotherapy treatments and a bone-marrow transplant, along with radiation, after more than a year of almost constant time at Phoenix Children's Hospital. For now, her family, my family, and many of you must pray and wait and believe for God's miraculous touch on her life. I've followed Kate along with you through her CaringBridge site. Her mom has done a beautiful job detailing their very difficult and painful journey in a way that glorifies God at every turn.

Kate is a vibrant, gregarious little girl who loves to sing along with Hannah Montana and run around the house with her siblings. She is crazy about her goldendoodle, Patrick, and Sponge-Bob Square Pants and jumping on her hospital bed when the chemo and medications don't leave her flat on her back. "I'm a dangerous girl, Mommy," she's been known to say. And so she is. Never once has she considered anything but fighting the battle ahead of her. Even in the darkest times, her eyes provide anyone near her a window to a most precious soul.

In *Unlocked* Kate will play the sweet-natured, always believing young cousin of Holden Harris. In the book, her fictitious parents are both stationed in Iraq, serving our country. During that time, she lives with Holden's family and provides insight that can only come from a child like Kate. She is integral to Holden's world and the innocence that lies inside him.

I know Kate will be honored when she understands her place here in this special book, and I hope her family will always see a little bit of their precious Kate here in the pages of *Unlocked*, where she will remain Forever in Fiction.

Now a special thanks to the many reader friends and friends of Kate McRae who helped put her Forever in Fiction. Each of the following people donated one hundred dollars or more to the medical costs incurred by the McRae family. These special friends of Kate's include the following:

Danielle Abraham

Sarah and Jennifer Ackley

Baily Apostol

Tally Atkinson, In Memory of Marcy Knight Babcock

Beth Backus

Brandon Scott Bailey

Quint and Robin Barefoot

John R. and Marilyn F. Baxter

Beau, Michelle, Dylan, and Jack Beecher

Alison Behan

Cheri Beltramo

Marilena Benko

Rod Benson

Cheryl Bernal

Thomas and Olivia Bernards

Madeline Biddle

Melissa Bircher

Anthony and Lori Bitts

Mike Bitzer

Keith and Kathy Blum

Douglas and Lynn Bohlen

Manny and Sunghee Bote

Lynne Bottom

Papa Brian and Grandma Shirlee Bouck

Stephanie Bouck

Red and Margaret Boyles

Rebecca Brammer

Kathleen Brockhaus

Thomas Brouster

Robert Brown
Ava Nicole Buck
Pam Budinger
Mikel Bullis
Mr. and Mrs. Jonathan Burke
Kim Cain
Logan and Tuesday Calderwood
Anthony and June Kim Castellano
Elizabeth Caven
Centennial Elementary PTO
Jerry Christopherson
"Chuck"
Jessie Collins
Michael J Conte
Sharleen Copp
Kalli Corwin
Robert J. and Lori A. Cramer
Denise Cruce
Audree Davidson, In Memory
of Clint Davis
Shirley B. Delp
Alexa DenHerder
Matthew and Jenny Derr
Gwendolyn DeVaughn
Freida Marie Doebler
Jessica Dunlap
Kayla Scooby Dutra
Cole and Caden Dykstra
Steve and Julie Dykstra
Donna Efhan
Nadine Evans
Lynn Fallon
Sherry Fishbeck
Tammy Flora, In Memory of
Joseph Andrew Fox III

Mary Friesen
Virginia Friesenhahn
Sarah Gadol
Maxine Garon
Laura Garrison
Peter and Patricia Garvy
Jerry and Maria Gass
Samantha Gass
Alisha Lynn Gatchel
Drew Phineaus Gatchel
Melissa Geiger
Fin Gold
Golden Stevedoring Co.
Carolyn Goldhaber.
Larry Gott
Mary Gray
Dara Griffin
Evelyn Grace Griffin
Karen Hinton Guest, In Memory
of Jean Walker Hahn, In
Memory of Kenneth Walker
Hahn
Sheilah Hanes
Kevin and Lorna Harberts
Eddie Harlan
David Harnisch
Clarice Hartel
Libby Hedrick
Pauline Hewitt
Lisa Brigman Hicks
Darrell and Verona Highsmith
Michelle Hoffman
Bryan and Emma Hollis
Teri Honaker
Matt and Jenny Horn

Daisy Marie Howard

Colleen Howard

Denise Huett

Steve and Maggie Hull

Steve Hulsman

Jack Tucker Hunt

Sherry Hunt

Sherry and Woody Hunt

DeAnn Issac

Jennifer Jacksits

Chywan and Sonya Jackson

Jennifer Janzen

Brent Johnson

Marshella Johnson

Peggy Johnson

Jesi Jury

Ryan Jeffrey Kees

William and Linda Kelchner

Linda Kim

Robert and Louise Krough

Ashlyn E. Kullen

Lynne Kullen

Victor LaBarbera

Ann Larson

Barb Latt

Sherry Lawson

Grace Lee

Lindsay Lorraine Leavengood
Lenhoff

Sarah Levine

Angie Lien

Pat Lucas

Dolores Lyon

Albert Mallekovic

Lori Marquette

Kirk McConnell

Sharon McKinney

Grandpa Tom and Grandma
Teresa McRae

Olivia, Will, and Patrick McRae

Karen Melton

Braden, Ethan, and Nolan Metz

Deanna Miles

Charles H. and Alma W. Miller

Kimberly Mitcham

Mobile Christian School 5th
Grade

Bobbie Jean Moore

Whitney Morton

Jeanne Mosley

Christine Munn

Dr. Charles and Karon Murray

Reid and Aubrey Muscat

Debi Neale

Abby Horrell Neinast

Anne Newborn

Kirk and Joan Ney

Ginny Nixon

Susan O'Farrell

Cynthia Odum

Taylor Ogle

Abby Oldham

Charles D. Osborn

Elisa Ostropolec

Jane Owens

James and Tracy Patterson

Marcia Pecora

Ryan and Lynelle Peugh

Phyllis Podhajsky

Stephanie Poteet

AJ and Annabelle Price
Sandi (Carlson) Rasanen
Linda Wirch Reed, In Memory
   of Ramey Alana Reeves
Lisa Reinholt
Joyce Reneman
Ray Renner
Jody Ritchey
Sharon Robbins
Keith and Janell Roorbach
Sharon Rose
Marjorie Schlecht
Janet Scott
Kerry Ann Scott
Sharon Scott
Jan Scott
Great Grandma Betty Sell
Mike and Karen Shaw
Tim and Amber Sheeley, Linda
   Sheffield
Mary Shiple
Terry and Kriya Shortt
Jacki Simonds, In Memory
   of Rois Rosemary Skeates
Mary Claire Sladko
Jeff and Tammy Smith
Pamela Smith
Suzane Smith
Kristin Kay Smith
Kerry Smither.
Tammy Souza-Fairley
Gerrie Springston
Holland Stanley
Alexis Stevenson

Leslie Styler
The Slocum Family
James W. Thomas
Bethany Thompson
Esther C. Thomson
Mark, Michelle, and Marcos
   Tiderman
Stacy Fisher Timmons
Lynn Todd
Michele Trumble
Kylee Tudor
Douglas and Julie Valentine
Jeremiah and Jessica Van Dyke
Vicki Vaughn
Jim and Donna Waggoner
Gina Wallach, In Memory
   of Shawn Matthew Walsh
Tina Marie Warpool
Kimberly Weber, In Memory
   of Debbie Weeks
Merle and Barb Wickman
Jodi Wierenga
Judith Wilcox
Elaine Wilson
Nathan Wochner
Kim Wolffis
Lisa Woodley
Melissa Woodruff
Cindy Workman
Lynda S. Young
The Staff at CaringBridge
The Staff at Women's & Children's
   Unit at Thomasville Medical
   Center

UNLOCKED

PROLOGUE

TRACY HARRIS ADJUSTED HER BLUE WALMART APRON AND checked her watch. Five minutes until her shift was up. She stood a little straighter, ignoring the dull ache in her back. A smiling young mom steered her cart into Tracy's checkout lane. The customer's attention was completely taken by her toddler-age son swinging his legs from his seat in the top of the cart. Tracy let her gaze linger on the little boy, the familiar way he had about him. Then she glanced at the cart. Not too many items. This would be her last customer of the day.

"Play with me when we get home, okay, Mommy?"

The boy was maybe three, three and a half. He had sandy brown hair and he held tight to a bright yellow and blue Nerf football. His face shone, full of life.

The woman used one hand to unload her shopping cart, while she placed the other gently alongside the boy's chubby cheek. "It's a deal." She leaned close and touched her forehead to his. "But you have to eat your vegetables first."

"Mommy..." He shrugged his shoulders. "I like cookies. Daddy says he likes cookies."

"I'll bet he does." She chuckled lightly, freely—the unfettered laugh of a woman whose child was healthy and vibrant and whole.

The sound of their joy splashed a sunbeam across Tracy's afternoon. She waited until the woman turned happy eyes in her direction. "Your son ... he's darling."

"Thanks." She blew at a wisp of her bangs. "He never stops talking."

Holden used to be like that, Tracy thought. She stuffed the memory into its heart's hiding place and found her smile. "Did you find everything you needed?"

"Yes." She grinned. "All except the extra three hours I need each day, but that's okay." She lifted the last items from her cart onto the belt. "Walmart's good … but that's a lot to ask of any store."

As she entered her credit card information, the woman chatted about finding the right cabinet knobs for the cupboards they were building in their garage, and the perfect set of sheets for their guest bedroom. All the while, her son ran a sort of color commentary. "Sheets, mommy!" The boy looked right at his mother, straight into her eyes. Clear, sharp eyes the way Holden's used to look. The child pointed at the bedding. "Pretty sheets for Grandma!"

"Yes, baby." She grinned and the two locked eyes.

Tracy tried not to stare. The boy was exactly like Holden used to be.

"Cocoa Pebbles!" He raised the football over his head and giggled as two boxes of cereal slid past him toward the register. He was bright and alert, aware of every nuance his mother made, taking stock of each item she lifted from the cart. He tucked the football close against his middle. "Football after lunch, Mommy! I can jump so high … higher than you!"

"Really?" Again she laughed. "That'll be something to see!" She snagged the ball from him, then playfully tossed it in the air, caught it, and handed it back to him. "I don't know, baby. Your mom's a pretty good jumper."

"I'm a good jumper too!" Again he held both arms straight up, clinging to the ball with one hand. "Touchdown, Falcons! See that, Mommy? That's a touchdown."

"Why don't you sing your touchdown song?" She finished

the transaction, and the receipt began to print. "You love that one, remember?"

"Yay! The touchdown song!" The child swung his arms in a sort of sitting-down dance move. "Touchdown, touchdown, All the peopo' in the town, come to watch the Falcons play, and shout, 'We wanna touchdown!'" He celebrated the song for a few seconds before starting again.

As he sang, he made eye contact with his mom and held it. Eye contact. That was the hardest part about watching the customer and her son. Eye contact that shut out the world and allowed a momentary connection for just the two of them. Something Tracy missed most about Holden. The way it felt to see into his soul and know that at the very same time he was seeing into hers. Tracy let her eyes linger. Watching them was like watching home movies, the way she and Holden had played together a lifetime ago. Whatever had happened to Holden, no matter what exactly triggered the change, there had been a time when they played. When Holden laughed and sang and looked her in the eyes every time they were together.

As the woman collected her receipt, Tracy tried to stay in the moment. Young moms with little boys were always the toughest. The woman set two of her bags into her cart. "Glad there wasn't a line. My housekeeper needs to be paid." She flashed an exasperated smile. "I can't clean to save my life."

Housekeepers and home improvement projects ... a talkative child and a happy home. Tracy couldn't relate, but she smiled anyway. "Have a good day."

"Thanks." The woman grabbed the last of the bags and set them in her cart.

"Down, Mommy!" Her little boy waved the football at her. "Please, down!"

"Okay." She swept her son into her arms and kissed his cheek. He returned the kiss and squirmed free. The woman set him down beside her, took hold of his hand, and shot Tracy a wary smile. "Demanding little guy, huh?"

At least he tells you what he wants, Tracy thought. She kept her tone cheerful. "That's the age, I guess."

"For sure." They started for the front door, the little boy skipping at the woman's side. She waved at Tracy. "Have a great day."

"You too." Tracy wanted to ask the woman if her son was up to date on his immunizations. *Don't get them all at once*, she wanted to tell her. *They still use mercury in them*. But this wasn't the time or place and no one knew for sure about the mercury, anyway.

As she watched them go, Tracy wondered about the woman. She probably lived here in Roswell or in Dunwoody, even. Maybe Johns Creek. One of the suburbs of Atlanta. Somewhere with a big house and a manicured yard and a normal life. The life Tracy had planned to have back when Holden was three.

That was fifteen years ago.

Now Holden didn't laugh with her or talk to her or reach for her hand. She couldn't play with him or chat through a meal with him, and she didn't know what it felt like to be wrapped in his grown-up arms for a hug. She had no idea how or what he was feeling. Her only son never ran to her — his face lit up — and shared something about his day or his homework or his dreams for the future. Holden never sang, never played sports, never brought a friend home from school.

He never made eye contact.

Holden was autistic.

One

IF THE FIRST DAY WAS ANY INDICATION, THIS YEAR WAS GOING to be the best ever.

Quarterback Jake Collins worked his way through the crowded hallway of Fulton High School's math building until he reached the meeting spot near the stairs. A group of his buddies from the football team were already there. At the same time, a couple of blonde freshmen girls walked past and giggled, flashing flirty eyes in his direction. Jake raised his brow and winked at his buddies.

Outside the brick building, the sun shone across Johns Creek, streaming through the windows and warming the cold hallways, making the river of kids squint as they passed by.

"The gang's all here!" Jake thrust his hands into the front pockets of his jeans and swapped a laugh with the guys gathered around him. He looked back at the blonde girls now halfway down the hall. "Hotties everywhere."

"Gotta love the Fulton girls." Sam Sanders elbowed him in the ribs. Sam had been Jake's go-to guy for the past three years, one of the top receivers in the Atlanta area and Jake's best friend.

"Dude, they're gonna love *us* this year." He fist-pounded Sam. "State titles, baby. All the way. Everything we touch is gonna be gold."

"Triple threat. No class has ever done it!" Sam nodded big. "Football … basketball … track!" He strutted in a small circle, arms raised.

Jake laughed. "Girls fallin at our feet." He high-fived Sam, and the two of them chuckled, eyeing another pair of girls. "Even more than usual."

"Mmm-hmm." Sam nodded at a pretty brunette, one of the two passing by. "Best Georgia peaches in the state."

They had six minutes to get to class, but that didn't mean anything to Jake and his boys. If the group of them made a blockade in the hallway, so what? The other kids would walk around them. Jake didn't care. This was their school. They could block the hallway if they wanted to.

"Look!" Rudy Brown, another football player, laughed and pointed to an overweight kid in a wheelchair a dozen yards down the hallway. Two teachers worked to maneuver him through a classroom door. "What? He's too fat to walk?" Rudy raised his voice louder than the noise around them. Rudy was six-five, three hundred pounds. Strongest offensive lineman in the county. He was being recruited by a dozen Division I college programs.

"Hey!" Jake scowled at his teammate. "Not the wheelchair kids. They can't help it."

"Yeah." Sam kicked the big guy's shin. "Have a heart."

Commotion at the end of the hall caught Jake's attention, and he turned toward it. He shaded his eyes against the glare of the sun and realized who it was. "Well, I'll be …" He chuckled. "I thought Harris graduated."

"Who?" Sam scowled, searching the crowded sun-streaked hallway.

"That Holden Harris guy." Jake crossed his arms and watched Holden as he struggled closer. "Freak." Jake snickered. "Pretty face … you know, the queer boy."

Holden was doing that weird thing he always did when he walked to class. Hands folded, knuckles close to his chin, flapping his elbows straight out to either side. Every few steps he stopped and his eyes darted to some random spot on the ceiling. Jake sneered at him. "Freak."

Sam made a face. "Why does he do that?"

"Cause he's a sissy." Rudy chuckled. "Nothing wrong with him, 'cept that."

"Leader of the short bus." Jake laughed louder, and the others standing with him did the same.

Holden Harris didn't look like a special-needs kid. That's what bugged Jake. It was the part that really got under his skin. Holden looked perfectly normal. No, he looked better than normal. Like some Abercrombie poster kid. A pretty boy with a football player's build. Not only that, but the kid had crazy blue eyes. Eyes that made the hottest girls turn and stare—even when Holden acted like an idiot, the way he always did.

"Let's welcome him back." Jake motioned to his teammates, and they walked that direction.

"Hey, pretty boy," one of them cried out in a mock high-pitched voice. Several of the kids crowding the hall between the football players and Holden looked alarmed. They scurried to get out of the way.

Sam waved big with as much sarcasm as he could pull off. "Hey, freak … welcome back to school!"

Holden didn't seem to hear. He stopped short, clearly frustrating the kids walking behind him, and he pressed his fingers to his ears. After a few seconds, he lowered his hands and shot strange glances just above the kids passing by. Never right at them. Like he was counting them in or something.

"What's he, the welcome committee?" Jake shook his head, disgusted.

"Yeah, maybe he'll run for class president." Sam chuckled.

"Sure. President of *Special* Activities?" Rudy gave Sam a shove. "Get it? *Special* activities?"

"Yeah, that's it." Sam laughed harder and punched a few of the other players standing with them. "They don't get more *special* than that weirdo."

Jake let the others do the talking for a minute. Holden walked toward them, and as he did, he started the wing-flapping thing again. Folded hands tucked near his chin, elbows straight out and flapping at his sides.

"Maybe he thinks he can fly." Rudy sneered. He shifted so that the group of football players pretty well blocked the entire hallway. "Hey, pretty boy," he shouted. "You gonna fly home to Mama?"

Holden was only a few feet away, and he must've heard that because he lifted his chin and faced them—not exactly at them, but in their direction. His arms fell to his sides and he stopped short. Jake and his boys took up practically the whole width of the hallway, so Holden couldn't get by.

"Hey, freak." Sam gave Holden's shoulder a shove. "Why you act so weird?"

Jake waited a few seconds. "Freako, say something!" He pushed the kid's other shoulder. "You can hear us ... I know you can hear."

Holden stared to the side of Jake, like there was another person, an invisible person, standing beside him. Holden's eyes caught the light and he blinked a few times. Those ridiculously blue eyes. They searched the empty walls and rows of lockers—but never their faces—as if he couldn't understand a word they were saying. Or he didn't want to understand. He flapped his arms again and nodded a few quick times. Then he set his back-pack on the floor in front of him, unzipped it, and pulled out a thick stack of flash cards. He sorted through them, his fingers moving fast, careful not to drop a single one. He must've found what he was looking for, because he pulled out a card and handed it to Jake.

"What's this?" Jake scowled as he took it.

"Too early for Valentine's Day, right Jake, man?" Sam and a few of the guys snickered.

"Shut up." Jake glared at his friend. "You're not funny."

Jake looked at the laminated card. It had the photo of a classroom on it. In the top corner was a small picture of a clock. Beneath were the words "Class Time."

"Flash cards?" Jake flicked it back at Holden, and it fluttered to the ground. "Use your words, idiot."

Holden didn't look at them, and he didn't look at the flash card on the ground. His expression tensed, and he set his full stack of cards on his open backpack. Then he made an awkward lunge for the card on the floor. As he did, Rudy gave Holden's backpack a solid kick. The stack of cards scattered everywhere.

"There." Rudy cussed at Holden and gave him another shove, harder than anything Sam or Jake had done. "Try words next time."

Holden tried to grab the cards as they scattered, but he missed and lost his balance. He landed with a thud, sprawled out across the linoleum floor. Quickly he scrambled to his hands and knees, breathing hard, his eyes darting about at nothing in particular. Then, with a frantic intensity, he began collecting his flash cards. The crowd in the hallway had thinned out, kids making their way to class. The ones who saw Holden struggling didn't stop to help.

Jake felt a flicker of remorse. Never mind what the kid looked like or how strong he was. Holden wasn't fighting back. They'd taken it far enough. "Come on." He slapped Rudy on the shoulder. "Let's go. Coach wants us on time this year."

A murmur of snickers and agreements came from the boys, and they side-stepped Holden and his flash cards. As they did, a skinny kid walked their way. He gave the football players a look, then he called out to Harris, still crawling around on the floor. "Hey … I'll help you."

The skinny kid stayed to his side of the hallway as he passed Jake and the guys. Then he set his own backpack down and started picking up cards off the floor.

"What's this?" Sam stopped in his tracks and turned, his arms crossed. "Another guy from the short bus?" He spat the words at the kid.

The guy had stringy jet-black hair, tight straight-leg jeans, and a threadbare backpack. Another loser. The kid ignored Sam and kept gathering the cards.

"Hey, goth." Jake laughed. "You're too late. I'm pretty sure Holden already has a boyfriend."

Again the kid ignored the comment as he finished helping Holden. Jake waved his hand in their direction. "Forget 'em." Jake led the way. "We gotta get to class. It's a big day, boys."

They'd waited four years for this, the privilege to strut their stuff on the Fulton campus. Jake was about to sign a scholarship offer with one of the big Southeastern Conference colleges, and he was dating the prettiest girl on campus.

Ella Reynolds.

He'd met Ella at the pool over summer. They were both life-guards, and from the first day Jake kept one eye on the screaming kids and the other on Ella. Through the hottest days of July and August, their friendship grew. Jake had seen her around Fulton, but they never really connected until the pool. He played sweet all summer—sometimes even thought he might be turning soft. She brought that out in him. Good girl, Ella. But he was too young for good girls.

Especially now … his senior year.

Jake planned to hook up with lots of hot girls—especially the freshmen. Over summer—when he wasn't stealing kisses from Ella—he and Sam and Rudy and the guys talked constantly about the fall. This was their year, the season they'd been waiting for.

He punched Sam in the arm as they walked out of the building. "Win every game, take every title …"

"Get any girl we want." Sam finished his thought, and both of them cracked up laughing.

Everyone on campus was going to know who they were. Even the freaks like Holden Harris and the skinny goth kid, whatever his name. Because that's how it worked.

And this year they owned the school.

HOLDEN COULD HEAR THE MUSIC. BEAUTIFUL AND FULL AND sweeping through the hallways of Fulton High. Rich horns and melodic strings. A fluttering of the ivories from every key known to man. Scintillating highs and mesmerizing lows that filled his senses and carried him along, reminding him that everything was okay. Music that sang to him of Jesus and goodness and love and joy. Peace and kindness. Church music. Music that told him the truth: no matter what, he was okay. Yes, Holden could hear the music.

He just wasn't sure anyone else could hear it.

Because why would his cards be all across the floor if everyone else could hear the same song?

Holden let the question slide. He collected his special cards and sorted through them until he was sure they were all there. All seventy-three. He looked at the friend helping him. He was saying something, but the words were lost in the music. Holden sorted through the cards again, searching. It was here … it had to be. He had all seventy-three. Forty-six from the friend across from him and twenty-seven from all around his feet. Seventy-three.

Holden sorted, and the music played on. There it was! A picture of a smiling boy with his hand raised. The words on the card said "Thank you." Holden flashed it to the friend, but he didn't hand it to him.

Last time he'd handed over a card, they'd ended up scattered across the floor.

"What's that?" His friend looked at the card and smiled. "Oh. No big deal." He looked over his shoulder at the football players walking out of the building. "Stay away from those jerks."

Holden blinked and looked back at the big guys. Mixed in the music were other words, church words. He was three years old and Sunday school was in session and Holden was there again and the teacher was talking. *No, Tommy, don't call anyone a jerk. These are your classmates and this is Sunday school. We don't use that word … it's not nice. We need to pray for our friends, not call them names.*

The big guys were jerks? They were almost at the end of the hallway. Walking to the music. Teacher said to pray for people, not call them names. And that's what the sign on the wall at the church said. Pray on all occasions. Holden nodded, intense, convinced. Okay, then. He would pray. Right now before another minute ran off the clock. *Dear God, be with the guys at the end of the hall. They don't want to be jerks. Thank You, Jesus. I know You love me. Your friend, Holden Harris.*

He prayed for a few seconds, and then his new friend held out his hand.

But Holden didn't take it. The walls were closing in a little and there was too much noise, too many words. The music was very loud now. He mixed the "Thank you" card back into the deck and looked for another. One more. Harder and harder he looked. There! He pulled it out and held it up to his friend. It showed two guys giving a high five. Beneath it were the words that he wanted his friend to hear.

"You're my friend?" The guy smiled. "That's what you want to tell me?"

Holden looked out the window. This was the pretty part of the song. He swayed a little, dancing to the music.

"Anyway, I'm Michael Schwartz."

Michael Schwartz. Maybe Michael could hear the music. Maybe. Holden shuffled through his cards and then looked out the window again. He slipped the cards into his backpack and zipped it up. The music was softer again. A little more swaying and another look out the window. His mom lived out that way. But he didn't get to find her until 3:10. After 3:10 he would climb back on the bus and the bus driver would take him home.

On the other side of the window.

"Well, okay then. Gotta get to class." Michael waved. "See you around."

Holden watched him go. He would pray for Michael, too, because Teacher said to pray for friends. Michael was his friend. But he wouldn't pray right now because the clock on the wall said 9:05. And 9:05 meant Trigonometry. Trigonometry was when he could relax the most because numbers were like music. They filled his senses and reminded him of the truth. Everything was going to be okay.

He looked at the wide, open hallway and he remembered the big guys. The ones they weren't supposed to call *jerks*. Something was wrong with them. Something he didn't have a card for, not even with seventy-three cards. A sharp noise screeched through the music. What if the boys kicked his cards again or what if they kicked him? The screeching grew louder. Screeching and ... and ...

BOOM! BOOM! BOOM! The drums crashed and slammed through his head, pounding him, pushing him, hurting him. Hurting his ears. Holden covered the sides of his face, but nothing helped, nothing stopped the drums.

BOOM! CRASH! BOOM!

No! Stop the drums! Holden shouted the words, but it sounded like screaming in the music. BOOM! BOOM! BOOM! *Please, God ...* Jesus loves me, this I know ... *please* ... for the Bible tells me so ...

Holden breathed faster and faster and his eyes closed very tight. *No, not the drums! BOOM! BOOM!* Holden dropped down and lay flat on his stomach. The school floor was cool against his shirt. Quick ... very quick, he placed his hands palm down, his toes against the floor, his body stiff and flat like a board, and his daddy's voice came strong through the music.

"That's right, Holden, just like that. That's a push-up, except when you're older you'll keep your back straight. Very good ... like the big boys. If you can do that at three years old, you can do anything. Absolutely anything, Holden. Push-ups will make you big and strong like me, buddy. Thatta boy. Keep doing that and no one will mess with you ever ..."

Holden heard the words again and again and they sang out against the drumbeat. Up, down, up, down, up, down. *Keep your back straight ... push-ups will make you big and strong like me, buddy ... No one will mess with you ever ...* Up, down, up, down. Up and hold, down and hold, up and hold, down and hold. Up, down, up, down.

He breathed harder and harder, but now his breathing was the good kind. The drums were quieter now. *Boom ... boom ... boom ...*

Twenty-two push-ups, twenty-three, twenty-four ...

The drums stopped at twenty-eight push-ups. Twenty-eight. Four sevens. Fourteen twos. Holden popped back up, and the music returned to strings and winds. A couple girls walked by and laughed at him. Maybe they couldn't hear the song.

Holden grabbed his backpack and easily slung it over his shoulders. Trigonometry was at the other end of the hall and he needed to get there. While he walked, he prayed for Michael. *Thank You, God, for Michael. Jesus loves him, this I know... for the Bible tells me so... Michael helped me with my cards. And Jesus loves the girls who were laughing, because they are weak but He is strong. I know You love me. Your friend, Holden.*

As he walked into the classroom he could hear God answering him and he smiled. Because God told him exactly what he already thought.

Michael could hear the music.

Two

ELLA REYNOLDS CARRIED HER CHICKEN CAESAR SALAD AND diet Coke to a table at the center of Fulton's outdoor lunch area. Four days into the school year and still the place was packed, the laughter and voices of a thousand teens louder than usual.

"Ella! Come sit by me!" The shout came from a guy in her Algebra II class. His grin was big and goofy and he was sitting with a group of brainy kids.

"Maybe next time." She tossed him a flirty look and waved. "Right." She muttered the last word under breath, her smile intact.

"Hey, baby, over here!" Jake Collins jumped up onto the table and waved at her. He wore jeans and his football jersey, same as the other players. Jake was a big guy with a square face and a strong chin. At first she hadn't thought he was that cute, but over summer at the pool she got to know the real him. He was kind and thoughtful and romantic, more so than he'd ever show the kids at Fulton.

That was okay. Here he was charming and confident and bigger than life. Especially today. It was Friday and tonight was the first game of the football season. The local papers figured the Eagles to win it all this year, and the buzz across campus was beyond exciting.

"Can't." Ella grinned and gave a helpless shrug. She raised her voice loud enough so he could hear her. "It's game day. Just the guys, remember?"

He groaned and sank a little. A couple of his teammates — Sam and Ryan — pulled at his jersey and tugged him back down to his place around the table with them. He looked over his shoulder and winked at her. His eyes told her they might not have lunch together, but they'd hang out after the game.

Ella felt the sparkle in her eyes as she moved a few tables down and sat with a group of cheerleaders and dance team girls. They squealed her name as she set her tray down, and LaShante, her closest friend, jumped up, ran around the table, and threw her arms around Ella's neck. "You did it! I knew you could do it!"

"You know?"

"Of course I know!" LaShante let out a super-happy mock scream. "You're the lead, Ella! I mean, it's *Beauty and the Beast* and you're Belle!" She screamed again and gave Ella another quick hug. "You're perfect for it, girl."

"It's the biggest play we've ever done, right?"

"I know. It's crazy. A hundred girls must've tried out for that part." LaShante took Ella's hand and led her back to the table. The two sat next to each other, and the other girls leaned in. LaShante lowered her voice so only the group of them could hear her. "This is your *year*, girl. Jake Collins *and* the lead in the school musical!"

It was true. Everything Ella had wanted for her senior year was already happening. The auditions had been a few weeks before school started, but the news was announced this morning on the wall outside the drama room. She had the lead and she had Jake. The day after auditions, he'd asked her to be his girlfriend.

"Say yes, Ella. Make this year perfect for both of us."

She still had stars in her eyes over the way he'd kissed her that night. The way he'd kissed her a dozen times since then. Everyone at Fulton knew Jake Collins. Every guy wanted to be him, and every girl wanted to date him. But this year he belonged to her. She'd never had a serious boyfriend before. Too busy with school and singing. Plus she didn't want to feel pressured to sleep with some guy in high school. And that's what most of the other girls did, so for a lot of reasons a boyfriend never seemed like a good idea.

Until now.

"Jake's amazing." She moved in closer to the friends gathered around her at the lunch table. She didn't want anyone but these girls hearing her. "He totally lets things go at my pace."

"You told him you haven't … you know … I mean, you're a virgin. You told him, right, girl?" Nothing embarrassed LaShante. She asked whatever she wanted, any time she wanted to ask. It was one of the reasons Ella loved her so much. LaShante put her hands on her hips. "The man has to know the real you by now. Tell me he knows."

"Of course." Ella snuck a quick look at the table where the football players sat. "He said we don't have to do anything. He just likes me a lot. He doesn't want to lose me."

"I love it!" LaShante hugged Ella's neck again. "See, girls?" she snapped her fingers in the direction of the others. "Hold your ground. There's too much giving in going on at this school."

"That's right." Across the table Krissy gave Jenny a pointed look. "That's what I've been saying." Krissy nodded at a few of the other cheerleaders sitting around the table. "Too much giving in going on."

Six or seven of the girls struggled with an awkward silence for a few seconds, and then everyone giggled in Krissy's direction. Krissy took a long sip of her Coke. "Okay, okay. So it takes one to know one."

"Anyway," LaShante put her arm around Ella's shoulders and raised her eyebrows at the other girls, "we have Ella to look up to. If she can resist giving into Jake Collins, maybe the rest of us can at least try."

More laughter, and Ella wasn't sure what to say. She wasn't a role model for the abstinence club. She just wasn't ready, that's all. She was glad Jake understood, and that the girls weren't making fun of her. Still, she was grateful when they changed the subject and started talking about Mr. Jensen's history class. Ella used the diversion to take a bite of her salad.

After a few minutes, Ella checked her iPhone, looking for text messages from Jake. Hmmm. None. She glanced in his direction, but he was busy with the guys. She had ten minutes till class started, and she needed to call her mom, tell her about winning the part. She was going to play Belle! How great was that? She clicked her manicured fingernails on the table a few times and gave the girls a quick smile. "Gotta call home. I'll be right back."

She tossed her long blonde-streaked hair over her shoulder and walked quickly out of the lunch area, around the corner to where it was quieter. She pushed a few buttons and tapped the number for home. With every ring she felt her excitement drop off a little. "Come on, Mom … where are you?" She paced a few steps in one direction and then the other. "Pick up."

But the call went to voice mail, and Ella quickly tried her mother's cell. This time her mom answered on the third ring.

"Honey, I'm busy." Her voice sounded sort of stiff. "Is it important?"

"Well, yeah … I mean, wait … what are you doing?"

"Uh …" The pause that followed felt forced. "Nothing really. Just getting a little work done."

"Work?" Suddenly Ella remembered. "Botox, you mean?" Ella sighed. "I thought you were waiting longer this time."

"The mirror changed my mind." She must've been still in the chair, because her words sounded frozen, like she couldn't move her mouth muscles at all. "Really, Ella? Can it wait?"

What remained of her thrill left her heart as fast as the last days of summer. "Whatever."

"Thanks, honey." Another woman's voice sounded in the background. Her mom lowered hers to a whisper. "Gotta go."

Nice. Ella stared at the phone and watched the call disappear from the screen. Something was wrong with her parents. Her dad's team was still in the play-offs, but he sat the bench most games and his contract was up at the end of the year. When he was in town he stayed at the clubhouse most of the time, working out or whatever. Last time he was home Ella tried to find him so she could tell him about Jake, but he didn't seem to hear her. He kept saying "What?" and "Who?" and apologizing for missing major parts of her story. She gave up before she got to the point.

It didn't matter. Ella's parents were too into their own lives to care about much else. Her twin brothers were in seventh grade and playing fall baseball, busy with their friends and schedules. They passed Ella in the hall at night, barely aware she existed. The feeling was mutual.

And her mom? Her mom was acting like a crazy person. Ella was a size 2, and lately her mom seemed almost smaller. Which didn't look good. Like she was trying to be a teenager or something. Her hair was dyed super blonde and last week she actually got extensions. Her mother! They looked okay, but still … between that and all the tanning, and her addiction to Botox, she never really seemed like a mom. The only time she went out of her way to find Ella was when she needed something. "Ella, can you take the boys to practice?" Or "Ella, can you pick up groceries on the way home?" Or "Maybe you could get the boys after the game?"

Ella forced her family life from her mind. As she rounded the corner back to the lunch area, most of the tables were empty. Kids were tossing trash and collecting backpacks, heading off to class before the bell rang. Her girls were gone, but she spotted Jake and the other football players, just getting up. Jake hadn't spotted her, so she slowed her pace. Classes were this way, so maybe if she waited Jake would walk with her.

But the players gathered in a circle, laughing and giving occasional punches at each other's shoulders. As the group started to break apart, Ella saw a guy walking toward them from the other side of the lunch area. He was a strange sort of kid. Ella had seen him before, but she wasn't sure of his name. He usually hung in a group with the special-needs kids. Ella leaned her shoulder against the brick wall and watched.

Just as the guy was about to pass the football players, he stopped. It wasn't like he looked at them, but he must've known they were there because he quickly folded his hands and brought them up near his chin. He popped his elbows straight out to the sides and moved them up and down a little. Like a bird or something. He kept doing that as he tried to pass the guys.

Jake was the first one to notice. He gave Sam a shove. "Look at this." He moved to block the kid's path. "It's the freak."

"What?" Ella whispered to herself. A sick feeling spread through her stomach. That didn't sound like Jake. She inched closer. The football players had their backs to her, and Ella was glad. She didn't want Jake to notice her. Not yet, anyway. Maybe they were just playing around. When she was closer, she stopped again. Jake and his friends had created a blockade so the kid couldn't pass.

They weren't having fun. They were picking on him. She felt her heart racing within her, and anger rushed hot into her bloodstream. Why would they bug the poor kid? She studied the boy. He was tall, but not as tall as Jake. Six feet or six-one, maybe. The guy lowered his hands to his side and looked beyond the football players straight at —

Ella caught her breath. He was looking straight at her. And for the first time she could see what she hadn't seen before. Despite his strange behavior, he looked like a normal guy. Muscled arms and shoulders and a tanned, handsome face. But that wasn't why she gasped. It was his eyes. Baby blue and clearer than water around Tybee Island. His eyes were deep and pure and ... Ella blinked. Something else. They were almost familiar, like she'd looked into them this way before.

But that wasn't possible. The special-needs kids had their own building. They never mixed in, except for maybe a class or two, and even this fall the guy with the blue eyes hadn't been in any of her classes. Ella would've remembered him.

Sam and Jake must've noticed that the kid was looking at Ella. Sam took a step closer and slapped the guy on the back of his head. "Don't look at Jake's girl, freak. Stick to your own kind."

Immediately, the kid started moving his arms again, his folded hands close to his chin. Ella's anger doubled. Enough. She walked up and pushed her way through the football players until she was at Jake's side. She looked at Sam and then at Jake. "Leave him alone."

"Baby!" Jake laughed, but he sounded nervous, like he'd been caught. He looked at a few of the guys around him for approval. "What? We were just having a little fun." He raised his hands like he was innocent. "No big deal." He took a step past her and gave the kid a little push. "Just messin', right?"

The kid stopped flapping his arms. He didn't respond to Jake or act like he'd heard a word. Instead he stared at a spot in the sky just above their faces. Sam put his hands on his hips and glared at the guy. Sam was six-five and he towered over the special-needs kid. "You shouldn't walk through here at lunch time." He looked back at Ryan and Jake. "Right, guys?"

"Sam!" Ella tugged on Jake's jersey sleeve. "Come on …" She whispered near his ear. "Please, Jake. Leave him alone."

"Fine." He chuckled, as if the whole thing was nothing more than a joke. "Leave it, dude."

The group walked away with the kid standing there, breathing sort of funny. As the guys walked out of the lunch area and off to class, Ella looked back one more time, and sure enough, the kid was looking at her again. Those beautiful eyes. Ella hesitated, but only for a moment. Jake and his buddies had already forgotten the kid, and maybe he'd forgotten about them too. Maybe he never even understood that he was being picked on.

But he was certainly aware of her presence, because he wasn't flapping anymore and his eyes wouldn't look away from hers. And something else, something the kid hadn't done until just now.

He was smiling.

Three

LONG MOMENTS BETWEEN CUSTOMERS AT WALMART WERE RARE for Tracy, but this was one of them. She stared absently at the row of tabloids and movie magazines and from the mix of screaming gossip a headline caught her eye.

Hollywood Takes on Autism.

She didn't have to pick up the magazine or read the article. She already knew how the media and movie-making industries had worked to increase awareness about autism. Most days she wanted nothing more than to join them. Stage a walk for a cure or fundraise for advancements and education on the disorder. Every month she took part in events with Autism Speaks or chatted online with other mothers of autistic children. The things her husband, Dan, never did.

But right now all of that sounded exhausting. Today she only wanted Holden back, the way he was just before his third birthday.

Tracy turned her attention to her register as her relief showed up with a new cash drawer. "Slow day?" The woman had worked at Walmart as long as Tracy—four years at least.

"Very." Tracy took her drawer and moved a few steps toward the break room "Back-to-school's behind us. That has to be it." She walked to the break room, found her time card, and punched out. But before she could leave, her manager, Mr. Groves, called out to her. "Just a minute." He was tacking something onto the bulletin board of employee kids and grandkids. Above the board Mr. Groves had placed a sign that read Bragging Rights.

Tracy waited. Mr. Groves was a big guy. He'd wrestled in college, but now he split his time between working and playing with his grandkids. He finished tacking up a new photo and walked over. "How's Holden?"

Heartache welled up inside her, and Tracy felt the familiar sadness gather in her eyes. "The same." She smiled. "Thanks for asking."

"We pray for him still." Mr. Groves looked concerned. "Every week in Sunday school."

"Thank you." She pictured her manager and his wife, his peers, praying for Holden. Week after week. "We have to keep praying. The more people, the better."

"That's right." His expression lightened. "God has a plan for that boy yet!"

"Absolutely." Tracy slid her purse up onto her shoulder. "See you tomorrow."

On the way home she stopped and picked up more laminate sheets from the craft store. Holden could express himself with Picture Exchange Communication System cards. PECS cards, they were called. They were expensive, so Tracy made her own. She downloaded sets of cards from the Internet, printed them, and laminated them. Holden had responded to them better than anything else regarding his communication, and now the cards were a part of his daily therapy. It wasn't what Tracy wanted, but it was an improvement over the years of not knowing anything about what he was thinking or feeling or needing.

She set the package beside her and thought about her son. He'd be thrilled with this latest find. Tracy had stumbled onto another set of music PECS cards online—and already she'd printed them. The laminate sheets were for those. *Thank You, God ... Just what we need today.* Holden would be thrilled—even if he didn't show it.

Tracy pulled into her apartment complex and parked in

the spot closest to unit C3. Then she collected the mail from the nearby lockbox. Tired or not, she was excited about the new PECS cards. They held so many more music phrases and images. Holden had worn out the last music cards—and these were even better. Clearer pictures, better wording. He loved music, the way he had loved it before his diagnosis, back when he had been drawn to the singers and instrumentalists at church.

On more than one occasion before his diagnosis they would be at Sunday service and Holden would walk toward the front, as close as he could get to the sound. He soaked in the melodies and harmonies and he would sing. Always he would sing. Especially "Jesus Loves Me"—his favorite back then.

Tracy pictured the end of the New York City Marathon on TV, and how the runners doubled over, gasping for air at the finish line, taking in as much oxygen as they could get. Holden was that way with music. He soaked it in like his life depended on it. No question, if there was a way to reach Holden the key would involve music. Tracy and dozens of therapists had tried reaching Holden with songs and hymns—even Holden's favorites from his pre-diagnosis days.

But they still hadn't cracked the cell that so completely contained him.

Not yet, anyway.

Tracy walked down the narrow sidewalk to her front door, turned the key in the lock, and slipped inside. The apartment wasn't large—just two bedrooms—but it was newer than some. And with Dan fishing in Alaska full time, it was all the space she and Holden needed. Of course, that had changed this week. Tracy's sister, Holly, was a nurse in the army serving a tour of duty in Iraq, and next week her husband, a marine chaplain, was being shipped out too. It would be the end of the school year before Holly was back in Atlanta, so Kate would sleep on an air mattress in Tracy's room. She rode a different bus, of course, but the way it worked out she would be dropped off a few minutes after Holden each afternoon.

Tracy set the mail on the kitchen counter. The clock on the microwave read 3:10—twenty minutes until Holden came home. He rode a special bus, and even though they didn't live in the Fulton High School boundaries, the school had the best program for autistic students. The bus picked up special-needs kids like Holden all across the county.

Tracy spread out the mail. Six bills—four related to Holden's therapy. Social therapy, nutritional therapy, educational therapy —two for that. And of course a bill for his medications. At the bottom of the stack was a small envelope addressed in Dan's neat printing. Salmon season had ended in August, and Dan was out of work for two weeks after that. But last Friday he'd called to tell her he found a four-week job, harvesting shrimp on a sixty-foot shrimp boat in the freezing waters off the Alaskan Peninsula.

"It's tough." Dan sounded worn out. "Captains pay more for the permits these days, so the take's not as high. The seasons are shorter. Competition's tough."

Still Dan stayed. A few months back the weather got rough, and Tracy wondered how safe he had been. Not that he would tell her if he struggled. "We were crazy busy," was all he said when the month ended. He sent her three thousand dollars after that and a note that said the same thing every one of his notes said. She opened this envelope and pulled out a folded piece of notepaper.

For you and Holden ... with love, Dan.

The cashier's check was for just under five hundred dollars. Not a surprise, with his being out of work for a few weeks. It was like this with commercial fishing in Alaska. Some months there was money for rent, utilities, and Holden's therapy. Other months the bills had to wait.

Tracy glanced across the counter to the small, framed photo of the three of them, a picture taken back when Holden was two.

She remembered that day, how they'd arrived at the park early and played on the swings until they were all red faced and worn out. Tracy had her camera, the way she always did back then. She'd taken pictures of Holden on the swing and Holden on the slide, Dan and Holden racing across the open field, and the two of them playing in the sand near the slide.

But before it was time to go home, an older couple walked by and offered to snap a shot of the three of them. Until then Tracy hadn't thought about the fact that she wasn't in any of the pictures. Now she stared intently at the framed photograph. *I thought I had all the time in the world with that boy ... that we'd always stay just like that, every afternoon a photo opportunity.* Endless days for someone to take their picture—the three of them.

She looked at Dan, at the expression on his face, the light in his eyes. He loved Holden more than life—then and now. Tracy didn't doubt that for a moment. Dan was a good man, a man strong in his faith and convictions. It wasn't that he didn't care about Holden. He cared too much. For the first ten years after Holden's diagnosis, Dan would spend hours every day after work talking to him, reading to him, sitting near him.

Searching for him.

But after a decade when nothing worked, Dan became distant. Almost as distant as Holden. Tracy remembered one day when she'd found him sitting on the edge of their bed, his face in his hands.

"Dan?" She came to him, touched his shoulder lightly. "What is it?"

Clearly, he didn't want to look at her, but finally he lowered his hands. His eyes were red, his cheeks tear stained. "I can't do it." His eyes met hers. "I keep looking and looking, but I can't *find* him. I can't *reach* him."

Tracy tried talking to her husband, but that spring he watched *The Deadliest Catch*, and when his work at the custom cabinet shop ran out that summer, he took a flight to Alaska. Tracy didn't want him to go, but she couldn't stop him.

He came home once in the spring, again in the summer, and for Christmas — three times a year — but most days it was easier to tell herself he wasn't coming home at all. She hated to picture him sliding across the deck of an old commercial fishing boat, tossed around on towering waves in a part of the ocean where ships sank all the time. The thought could paralyze her with fear. And so she'd released him to God's care a long time ago. But even so the losses piled up.

First Holden, then the life they'd known together, and their family time the way it had been in the photograph. And finally Dan.

Tracy glanced at the microwave again. It was time to meet Holden. She peeled off her sweater and tossed it on the back of the kitchen chair. As she stepped outside, the sunshine felt warm on her shoulders. A few minutes and Holden's bus came into view. It was a short bus, of course, the kind used for special-needs kids. The size of the bus used to grate on Tracy's nerves, reminding her that something was wrong with her son. But not anymore. She was grateful for any help she could get, any efforts made in finding the boy he'd once been. Now the bus only served as a reminder that they hadn't given up.

They would never give up.

The doors of the bus opened, and Holden was quick to reach the steps, quick to bound down them. He landed on the ground with little effort, his muscled shoulders easily holding his heavy backpack. He saw her ... he had to see her. But there was no hug no greeting. None of the connecting points Tracy so desperately craved. He looked to a spot beside her and then at another spot on her other side. Then he started walking, as if she wasn't there.

"Holden, wait." She reached for his hand, but he sidestepped her attempt. Still, this was an improvement. For years he would turn away from her touch. Cry out, even. Not in words, but in shouts or grunts. He didn't do that now. Instead he seemed simply indifferent. "Kate's bus will be here in a minute. Remember?"

Holden relaxed and stayed his ground, a few feet from her. A slight humming came from him, but Tracy couldn't make out the tune. He lowered his backpack to the ground and pulled his PECS cards from inside.

"I had a good morning at Walmart," Tracy tried. She would never stop trying. "The customers were nice."

Waiting for Kate wasn't part of his routine, and Tracy had been concerned all day that the change could throw Holden into a tantrum. She watched him, studying him. So far, so good. Holden liked Kate—at least from what Tracy had seen last night when the child arrived with her things.

Tracy made small talk, telling Holden about a few of her customers, all while Holden stared at the tree line across the street. A minute later Kate's bus came into view. Relief washed over Tracy. "There it is!" She stayed at Holden's side. "Kate's bus." She smiled at him. "Kate can watch the movie with us today."

Holden swayed a little, still humming, still intent on something just out of reach.

The bus stopped and Kate scrambled out, her pale blonde hair framing her tanned face, her SpongeBob backpack almost half her size. Her face lit up when she saw them. "Aunt Tracy, hi!" She ran toward them, her eyes shining. "It was the best first day ever." She danced over to Holden and hugged him around his waist. "Hi Holden!"

Holden's posture stiffened some, but he didn't pull away or cry out. Something about Kate's childlike innocence, her youthful heart and love for people, seemed to connect with him.

Kate bounced back to Tracy. "And guess what? Teacher said it's okay that I missed last week. She's gonna help me make it up!"

"Perfect!" Tracy liked the smile in her voice. She reached for Kate's hand. "Let's get home, and I'll fix you a snack."

"Okay, and then me and Holden are watching a movie, right? That's what Mommy told me. Holden watches movies every day."

Tracy hid a ripple of laughter. "Sort of. You might get tired of it after a while." She looked over at her son. "Right, Holden?"

He moved his gaze to the ground near his feet and then up to the sky again. They started walking with Kate between them. Kate still had hold of Tracy's hand, but she seemed to know instinctively not to reach for Holden's. "Teacher says we each have a cubby with our name on it and we put our spelling in the red box and pick it up the next day in the yellow box and guess what?" Her enthusiasm was beyond refreshing.

"What?" Tracy treasured the feel of her little-girl hand, the way Kate clung to her, needing her. The moment made her realize again how much she'd missed with Holden.

"Teacher says two recesses, not one. Isn't that the best news, Aunt Tracy? Two recesses!" She giggled and skipped for a few steps. "And guess what else?"

They were almost at the apartment door. "What, sweetie?"

"Dance and music class! Every Wednesdays and Friday. That's the best news for first graders." Her expression grew serious. "Kindy-gartners don't have dance and music, even at my old school." She stopped short. "Will I ever go back to my old school?"

"Yes, honey." Tracy loved this, her niece's energy and passion. It was a tremendous change from her usual time with Holden. "Next year you'll be back."

"Okay, good. 'Cause Sarah and Tessa aren't at this school and we're bestest friends."

"I'm sure they miss you."

Kate looked sad for a few seconds, but then her eyes sparkled again. "But this 'venture will give me lots to tell them, right?"

"Right."

She looked at Holden as they walked. "Right, Holden?"

Holden shifted his gaze, but still he didn't look straight at Kate.

Kate gave him a sympathetic smile. "Holden's shy, right, Aunt Tracy?"

"He is." Tracy's heart ached at the way even little children immediately knew something was different about Holden. "He loves you very much, Kate. He just doesn't really talk much."

"That's okay." She nodded in Holden's direction. "I love you, too, Holden." She patted his arm, and again he didn't jerk away.

As they reached their apartment, Holden sorted through his PECS cards and held out the television card, the one that read "Movie." Tracy tried to take hold of it, the way she always did. But this time Holden pulled it back, keeping the card close to his chest.

Kate watched the exchange, clearly bewildered. "What's he doing?"

"Just a minute, honey …" She held up her finger to Kate, her words gentle.

Kate nodded, anxious to understand. She looked at Holden, her eyes wide, curious.

Tracy turned to her son. Had something happened at school, something that had made him less secure? "I understand, Holden." She kept her tone calm. "You don't want me to hold the card." She smiled, her voice pleasant. "That's fine. You want your movie. I understand." She didn't want to upset him. When he was upset he would drop to the ground and rattle off a string of push-ups. Something his therapists had never seen in a kid with autism. Tens and hundreds of push-ups.

That was bound to frighten Kate, so Tracy wanted to at least get the three of them inside just in case.

"Why does he have those cards?" Kate angled her head, trying to understand. "Is it like a game?"

"Yes." *Keep it simple*, she told herself. Kate didn't need more than a basic understanding of her cousin. "Holden uses cards to talk sometimes. Like a game."

"Oh!" Kate bounced around and clapped her small hands a few times. "I love games."

Holden lifted his eyes to the sky, and as always Tracy was amazed at how striking they were. Ice blue, with a depth that was almost otherworldly.

They needed to get inside. "Let's go watch our movie." She opened the door, and Holden and Kate followed.

"Can I help make snack?" Kate ran to the kitchen and set her backpack on one of the chairs. "Mommy lets me help make the snack every day."

"I'd love some help." Tracy walked with Kate to the kitchen. Holden's routine was so exact she could predict his every action. He set his backpack on the floor, kept the PECS cards tight in his hands, and crossed the room to the single sofa that stood beneath the lone window in the living room. In a series of practiced motions he stood the three sofa pillows in a perfect row and then patted out every wrinkle in all three of them. When they looked like something from a magazine, he moved to the white curtains that hung on either side of the window. Meticulously he straightened them, making sure every pleat was neat and straight.

The routine took awhile, and Kate didn't seem to notice. She was distracted by her work in the kitchen. She helped get out the string cheese and apple juice, carrots, and raisins. "I love raisins, Aunt Tracy." She giggled. "Maybe I'll live here forever."

"Maybe." Tracy loved the energy Kate brought to their small apartment. "Of course, your mom and dad would miss you an awful lot."

"True." Her smile faded for a few seconds. "I miss them so much, Aunt Tracy. So, so much. First Mommy, now Daddy."

Tracy held out her arms and Kate came to her, holding her

the way a child was supposed to hold on. Taking in all the love and comfort and support she could get. *This is what it feels like to be needed*, Tracy thought. It must kill Holly and Aaron to be away from her.

The moment passed and they made up the plates. Tracy kept Holden's diet gluten free, the way she'd been doing since he was five. She had never seen his diet make much difference, but it didn't hurt to try. Gluten-free was one of the many recommendations that had come from his nutritionist.

He finished tidying the living room and found his place at the kitchen table. Kate sat beside him with Tracy across the table. She folded her hands, her elbows spread out to either side on the small table. "Let's pray, okay?"

Kate squeezed her eyes shut, her head bowed. Holden tore his string cheese into tiny pieces and lined them along the outer edge of the plate. He didn't look at her, didn't speak.

Tracy bowed her head. "Dear God, thank you for this food. Please bless it to our bodies. Thank you that Kate can be with us for the next few months, and thank you for Holden. Let him know how much we love him. In Jesus' name, amen."

Now that his cheese pieces circled the plate, Holden made another inner circle of carrot pieces, and a third circle of raisins. Not until that task was finished did he eat the first bite. Tracy didn't have to watch to know what he would do next. He would eat his food in the exact order he'd laid it out on the plate. Not one bite out of order.

Kate noticed the pattern right off. "I like your circles. I'll eat my snack like that too." She arranged her food in circles on her plate and ate them in order, the way Holden did. Halfway through, she giggled up at him. "You're fun, Holden."

Again Tracy's heart was pierced by the child's innocent comment. Holden had no friends, no one who had ever told him he was fun. Not since he was three, anyway.

Kate chattered on about recess and lunch and how she liked the taste of milk in a cardboard carton. When she grew tired of talking, Tracy turned to Holden. "You had music today, Holden. You love music."

No response.

She remembered the new PECS cards. "And guess what? New cards, Holden! Music cards. I already printed them. I'll laminate them this afternoon." She hurried from the table to the counter and brought the package of printed cards to Holden. "Remember? Your music cards were too old, so I'm making you new ones." She set the envelope in front of him and waited, silently praying that he might pick it up on his own, be interested enough in the contents to search what was inside.

But he only looked up again, this time at a spot just above her. Kate watched, again curious at Holden's silence.

"I think he's going to like the cards, Aunt Tracy." She nodded big, her wispy blonde hair bouncing around her face. "I can tell."

"Me too." She didn't let herself feel discouraged. "Holden, those are the music cards. The ones I'm going to laminate. So they'll last longer." She pulled the new cards from the envelope and handed them to Holden. "One hundred and twenty music cards!"

"Wow… one hundred and twenty is a whole lot of cards! I never had that many cards!" Kate grinned at Holden. "Right, isn't that great?"

Holden was interested, Tracy was sure. But nothing about his expression showed it. He ignored her and Kate and the new cards and instead picked up the PECS cards he carried with him everywhere, the ones from his backpack. He sorted through them half a dozen times and after a minute he flashed her a card that read "Thank you."

Tracy's heart soared. Her son had thanked her! He'd been doing this, using the cards to communicate once in while for a few years. It was why his therapists thought he was making such progress. The therapists worked hours on end helping Holden understand what the cards meant, how the pictures matched the words, and how they could be used appropriately. There was no way to tell if Holden actually read the words, or just understood what they meant by sight familiarity. Not while he was so completely non-communicative.

That's why moments like this were such a victory—Holden using his PECS cards to thank her.

She smiled at him. "You're welcome." Then she reached slowly for the new music cards and one at a time she held them out to him, explaining their meaning, reading the words at the bottom of each one.

Kate repeated the words as they went, but eventually she finished her snack and cleared her plate to the sink. Then she pointed to the living room. "I have to read, so I'll wait out there. For the movie, okay?"

"Okay, sweetie." Tracy watched her leave. She was so sweet, so much fun and energy. But Tracy needed time alone with Holden, so this was perfect. She held up a music card, one with musical notes and a heart in the middle. "See this one?"

He didn't look. Instead he mixed through the deck he was more familiar with, intent on whichever card was on top of the stack.

"This one says 'I love music.' See? It has music notes and a heart. Hearts stand for *love*, remember?"

Holden tapped the table, his eyes fixed on nothing in particular.

Tracy moved to the next card. This one had music notes and an oversized ear. "This one says 'I can hear the music.'"

Holden blinked at that, and for half a second he looked at the card. But then, just as quickly, he looked away again.

"That's okay, Holden. I understand." She felt tears gather in her eyes, and she fought them back. "You can hear the music. I know you can."

Nothing.

She went over half the cards in the deck, but by then his snack was gone, which meant she had only a small window of time to get his movie going. She left the music cards on the table. His therapist would help him use them the right way, and in time Holden would work them into his days.

"Okay, movie time." She kept her smile in place in case he was watching. Even from his peripheral vision. There was no deciding which movie to watch. It was the same every day. If she tried something new, he would pace the living room, agitated and grunting, or drop down and rattle off thirty push-ups.

She'd made the DVD years ago on her Mac—a gift from Dan on one of his visits home after a particularly good month at sea. It was a thirty-minute movie of photos and video clips from before Holden's diagnosis. Back when he was like any other little boy. Before the nine vaccinations he received the week after this third birthday—not that anyone had officially linked vaccinations to autism. Still, Tracy couldn't help but wonder.

She walked into the living room where Kate was reading a thin paperback book, her legs sticking straight out as she sat back into the sofa. "Is it movie time?"

"Yes, honey." She wondered if Kate would be disappointed when she realized what type of movie it was.

"Where's Holden?"

She smiled. "He'll be here."

The DVD was already in the player, so she hit the power button and turned on the TV. Seconds later the loop at the beginning of the movie was on the screen, the music filling the small room. The song was one Holden used to sing with her as a little boy. *Never Be the Same* by Christopher Cross.

The music was melodic and meaningful, the message heart-wrenching.

The first notes drew Holden from the kitchen to his spot, cross-legged on the floor in front of the TV.

"Is that where we sit?" Kate hopped down from the sofa and took the spot next to Holden, their knees touching. Holden didn't acknowledge Kate, but he didn't move away, either.

This should be interesting. Tracy studied the two — small Kate, with her abundance of love and buzzing energy, and Holden — quiet and indifferent by all indications. Tracy picked up the remote control and sat in the old recliner. She knew better than to jump to the beginning of the movie. For Holden, the loop was part of the experience. So she let the song play out, let the images run across the screen.

Holden as an infant, safe in her arms … Dan standing beside them, his hand on her shoulder. Holden as a six-month-old sitting up, grinning at the camera. Holden and Ella Reynolds, eighteen months old, holding hands on the shore of Tybee Island. Holden and Ella dancing on the Reynolds' kitchen floor.

"Is that Holden?" Kate looked over her shoulder.

"Yes. Holden when he was younger."

"It looks like him." She nodded, thoughtful, and turned back to the screen. "My mom has movies of when I was little."

Tracy hid her smile and the sorrow that quickly followed. Kate was still little, of course. But already she was decades beyond Holden in her ability to relate to people.

The song reached the chorus, the part where Holden always started to rock. Not dramatically, but enough that Tracy believed this part of the song really spoke to him. She sang quietly along. "And I'll never be the same without you here. I'll live alone. Hide myself behind my tears. And I'll never be the same without your love …"

No matter how many days they sat here this way, or how

many times she heard this song or watched this movie with him, the tears came. Tracy dabbed at the corners of her eyes. She didn't want Holden to see her cry, but there was no way around the heartache that came with the home movie.

They reached the end of the song on the intro loop, and Tracy started the actual movie. This was the hardest part, seeing Holden the way he had been, watching him laugh and sing and look straight in the camera. "Hi, Mommy! See me, Mommy? I'm looking right at you!"

Kate giggled. "I like you there, Holden. You're funny!"

He didn't respond, but Kate didn't act offended. She turned her attention to the movie again.

The Reynolds family was in several of the videos because back then the two families had done everything together. The couples had been friends in high school, the best men and maids of honor for each other's weddings. They had babies at the same time, and Holden and Ella were together constantly before they could walk or talk.

Tracy and Suzanne would delight over the friendship between their children, dreaming of the day when they were older. "I can see it now," Suzanne would say. "Holden will take Ella to her senior prom and five years later they'll get married." Her laughter would lend brevity to the prediction. "We'll arrange the whole thing right now. Deal?"

Tracy's laughter would mix in. "Deal." Neither of them was serious, of course, but the possibility remained. There seemed no reason why the two wouldn't grow up together, no hint that a senior prom or even a wedding some day was out of the question.

But in the fall after Holden's third birthday, he began to slip through their fingers. Week after week he grew quieter, more withdrawn, and the visits with the Reynolds grew more infrequent. After Holden's diagnosis, Suzanne explained in a teary, awkward way that they weren't sure it was good for Ella, playing with Holden.

"He doesn't talk." Suzanne's face looked pained. "He won't look in her eyes anymore. He … he lines up their toys over and over like he's in a world all his own. Something's wrong with him, Tracy. He needs help."

She didn't say she was officially ending their friendship. She didn't have to. Her husband, Randy, was a baseball player and about that time he was called up to the majors. He played for the Mets for ten years, and when the Reynolds family moved to New York, they lost touch. Four years ago Tracy read that Randy Reynolds had been traded to the Braves, so most likely they were back in the Atlanta area.

Tracy no longer wondered what they were doing or how life had fared for them. She wouldn't think of them at all, except that here was Ella—dancing and singing with Holden on the home movie they watched every day. Ella would be a senior in high school now. She wouldn't know or remember Holden. That part didn't matter. What mattered was all she represented for Holden today.

He stared at the movie, never looking away, intent on every detail. Today Ella represented hope and possibility, the chance that someday God might grant them a miracle and Holden would find his way back. That one day he might sing and laugh and hold hands with a friend again.

Tracy had seen enough. She stood quietly and went to her bedroom. Holden was at a strange place on the autism spectrum, because other than an occasional grunt or cry or humming sound, he was completely non-communicative. Usually kids— even kids on the severe end of the spectrum—developed some language by now. Not Holden… not ever. He had the PECS cards, and that was it. Even so, the day Tracy stopped talking to him would be the day she gave up. And that wasn't going to happen.

The cool morning had given way to a hot, humid afternoon, so she slipped into a T-shirt, shorts, and flip-flops. As she did, she caught a look at herself in the mirror. Her long dark hair was pulled back in a ponytail, and her face looked thin and drawn. Back before Holden's diagnosis, people used to say she looked like Courtney Cox. But not anymore. She looked tired and sad and old. Older than her thirty-nine years, anyway.

Come on, Tracy ... where's your smile? She lifted the corners of her mouth, but the action didn't reach her eyes. She returned to the kitchen, walking softly so she didn't pull Holden or Kate from the movie, and she sat again at the kitchen table. Holden's therapy was four-thirty to six today, same as always. Kate would bring her book, and they'd read together. Otherwise, everything about her days with Holden were built around a routine. Even during summer—when all-day therapy replaced his school hours. The walk back to the apartment, the snack, the movie, the late-afternoon session.

All of it the same.

The schedule was exhausting. She looked out the kitchen window. Never mind that her view was taken up almost entirely by the apartment next door. If she looked up she could see a slice of blue, like God reminding her, *I'm still here, daughter. Still watching over you.*

But, God ... I'm so tired. I don't see progress, Father. Sometimes I don't know how to get through the days.

My child, you don't have to fight this battle ... Stand firm and see the deliverance I will give you. The battle is mine, not yours.

Tracy closed her eyes and lifted her chin. The response washed over her like an autumn breeze and she inhaled slowly, deeply. The battle belonged to the Lord. The verse was from 2 Chronicles, something Tracy had read last week in her Bible. She loved when God responded to her this way. She sat a little straighter and a new sense of strength filled her soul.

From the other room, she could hear Holden's three-year-old voice singing his favorite song back then. "Yes, Jesus loves me … yes, Jesus loves me … yes, Jesus loves me … the Bible tells me so."

Holden loved to sing back then. It was why she indulged him in this daily routine, why she was glad he wanted to watch the home movie so often. The movie fed the music inside him the music she believed was inside him.

Then she heard something else. Little Kate was singing along, her voice high and clear, the voice of an angel. She stood and returned to the living room. What she saw brought fresh tears to her eyes. Not only was Kate singing, but she'd looped her arm around Holden's elbow. She was singing along, swaying to the music. And something else — something that took Tracy's breath.

Holden wasn't look at her or singing or smiling. But he was swaying. Holden was swaying with Kate.

He was allowing physical contact, and he was sharing in her enjoyment of the song. This was something she'd never seen before. Tracy brought her hand to her mouth. *God, is this Your plan? That precious Kate would will help crack the door to Holden's private world?* The possibility was something Tracy had never considered. But what she was witnessing was extraordinary.

She sat down quietly, not wanting to interrupt the moment. As she did, she felt a renewed peace work its way through her bones. No matter how many times they watched the movie or how many hours they spent in therapy, no matter how many months or years, she would never give up on her son. Holden was in there somewhere. When they figured out how to reach the door of the prison that held him, she was pretty sure of one thing: music would be the key.

But maybe Kate would be part of that process too.

Four

OMINOUS BLACK CLOUDS AND A FRENZIED SORT OF LIGHTNING had moved in fast from the west and now the worst storm of the season was crashing in around the SS *Wicked Water*. Dan Harris braced himself, working with everything he had to pull the shrimp-laden net into the boat, but even as he worked he could tell two troubling things. First, at forty miles from shore they were too far out to get help from another boat if they needed it.

And second, Captain Charlie was worried.

"Get the nets up! Tie everything down!" The captain had both hands on the wheel, intent on getting back to shore. He didn't turn to make sure they heard him over the sound of the wind. He didn't even glance over his shoulder. His panic changed the tone on the vessel.

Dan and the crew were a step ahead of him. Cages and cables, bins and barrels, and everything with the possibility of flying off the deck was already tied down or put away. Dan and another deckhand were reeling in the last two nets.

"We got a catch!" Dan braced himself as the first storm wave hit the ship and washed over the deck.

"Let it go." The wind was howling now, and the deckhand's shouts could barely be heard above the sound. "Forget it!"

"We can't." Dan felt the weight of the net in his forearms and biceps, his shoulders and back. After weeks of poor fishing, the nets held the best take since they'd set out. "Pull harder!"

Another wave slammed the ship, and the vessel leaned hard to the left. Dan and the deckhand were no match against the force. They washed across the deck and slammed into the other side. "Get up!" he shouted at the deckhand. "Man your position."

The deckhand swore at him. Half swimming, half crawling, he headed for the hatch and when the ship rocked back the other way and the water on the deck dissipated, the guy hurried down below. If the ship capsized now—the way thirty ships did each year in these frigid waters—the guys below deck were done for.

But most deaths on Alaskan fishing boats didn't come from sinking ships. They came from the waves. Angry, fierce, frothing white waves like the ones tossing the ship around right now. One wave, one lost grip on the ship, and Dan would be swept away— never heard from again. Even in September the sea was too cold for a man to last very long, so if the roiling water didn't drown a guy, hypothermia would claim him soon enough.

Dan wiped the salt water from his eyes and squinted across the deck. The nets were still in place—both of them. He could still get the shrimp, and if he saved the catch now there could be a bonus for him. If he didn't, the nets would break off in the next couple minutes and be lost at sea. Broken nets cost a month's worth of income—money that would come out of the take and result in a lower paycheck for everyone. He clawed at the splintered deck and scrambled to the other side, back to the nets. They were heavy, but he could get them up on deck at least. Then he could tie them down and get below.

He was breathing hard, his lungs struggling to get a full breath in the violent wind. Another wave towered over the ship, and before it could crash down on top of him, Dan gritted his teeth and gripped the closest two steel rings. The water hit with ferocious force, and Dan heard both nets snap free from the boat. He wanted to breathe, needed to breathe, but the water wouldn't recede. Panic and certainty consumed him. This was it. They were under water, sinking to the ocean floor. He thought about Tracy and Holden back at home and how they'd take the news of his death. But just when he couldn't hold his breath another second, the water cleared and he was still alive, still clinging to the steel rings.

Dear God ... You see us here, right? We're in big trouble, Lord. Please protect us.

There was no loud answer, no immediate calming of the seas. In fact, the wind screamed louder than before. But Dan saw a picture in his mind: Jesus on the fishing boat with his disciples, the group of them caught in a terrible storm. The disciples terrified, sure they were about to die. And Jesus?

Jesus was sleeping.

Dan shook the freezing water from his face and the image disappeared. Bible stories were nice, but right now they needed a miracle. The ship was creaking and groaning from the intensity of the storm, and rain was falling so hard now it was impossible to draw a breath without taking in water.

Another wave, another jolt against the struggling ship. Dan couldn't make out the captain, and he wondered if the man had abandoned the wheel and gone below. No, Captain Charlie would never do that. He was a survivor. Surely he'd seen storms this bad before.

Dan held his breath again and waited for the water to run off the deck. He had one chance, one hope to get to the hatch and get below deck. He would run for it. If he made it to the hatch on time, he would survive the next few minutes. If not, if a wave hit while he was moving across the deck, he didn't stand a chance.

But then he couldn't survive another few seconds on deck either. The strain on his arms was shooting fire through his body, and he wasn't sure how many more waves he could withstand.

Again his lungs were bursting, desperate for air, when the water finally cleared. He gasped and scrambled to his feet. He could see the next wave out of the corner of his eye, approaching fast, looming toward them. *Please, God* ... He took long, lunging strides and flung himself onto the deck at the edge of the hatch.

Hurry ... come on, hurry. Please help me, Lord.

He grabbed the hatch and tried to lift it, but — what was this? Dan let out a guttural yell, a shout that came from the core of his being. The hatch wouldn't move, wouldn't budge. Jammed from the pressure the water had placed on the ship. "No! Please, God!"

The wave was like a living, breathing beast, and Dan didn't have to turn around to know it was the biggest one yet. He could feel it behind him, building and growing and ready to slam him down, ready to take his life. At the last possible second, he threw himself into a cubby built into a post at the center of the deck a few feet away. The space was for extra rope, but whatever had been there was gone now.

Just as his body slammed into the space, the wave hit. The freezing water engulfed him and he felt himself losing consciousness. Why hadn't they seen this coming? And what sort of storm moved in this fast without warning? *I'm sorry, Tracy ... I never meant for it to end this way.*

He'd been in some terrible storms since he'd started fishing in Alaska, but nothing like this. And suddenly, in the moments before death could claim him, he had to question what he was doing here, why he'd chosen a job that placed him in one dangerous situation after another.

The answer was easy.

It was because nothing out here could compare to the storm back home, the one he couldn't stand up against. The one he couldn't survive. He'd come here because maybe fighting the wind and waves would somehow teach him how to win the war he'd fought against autism for the past fifteen years.

He couldn't breathe, couldn't feel his arms or legs. Any moment now he would inhale the salt water and that would be that. Battle over ... victory to the storm. But the saddest thing, the part that made Dan want to fight a few seconds longer, was that he wasn't only losing the battle against the storm here at sea. His death would mean he'd lost the battle with Holden as well.

And then in a myriad of swirling colors and emotions, he was there again, back with Tracy in their pretty house in Dunwoody and he was the foreman of the area's best custom cabinet shop and money was as easy as the seasons. Holden was the darling of the neighborhood, drawing comments and attention wherever he went. And Ella Reynolds was his friend and they were going to grow up together, go to the prom together.

The girls had it all figured out.

And they'd go to Randy Reynolds' minor-league games and play cards back at the house later, and Holden ... Holden would sing and laugh and dance with Ella and then ... Then what happened? Was it the vaccines Tracy had read about a few years back? That must've been part of it, because he was whole and happy and here. He was so here back then.

Dan still couldn't take a breath, but his life no longer mattered. He was caught up in the past, in the calm before the storm, the one that claimed him a long time ago. No little boy was cuter than Holden. His blond hair and light-blue eyes stopped people wherever they went.

Even at the doctor's office when Holden was three. Tracy had told him that evening that the doctor felt bad. So many shots in one day. Upsetting the child when he was so happy. And Dan could see like it was yesterday the way Holden looked the next day, tired and beat up, a fever racking his little body.

"Why so many shots?" he'd asked Tracy.

The reason had made sense to everyone: his previously scheduled checkups hadn't worked out ... Holden had been sick ... or they'd been on vacation. Always something. By the time he came in that fall, he was behind on his vaccine chart. The preschool he and Ella attended wanted his immunizations up to date.

Dan had called. He'd at least done that much. When the doctor called back, Dan's tone verged on short. "He's sick. How many shots did he get?"

"Nine. But that's very normal, Mr. Harris. Kids Holden's age handle that many shots all the time."

"Nine shots!" Dan had argued with the guy, but it went nowhere. Since then they knew that a single shot contained three hundred times more mercury than the FDA considered safe in adults. Even so, the argument in favor of shots remained stronger than any opposed to them. Kids needed protection from diseases, and research on immunizations held no smoking gun.

So maybe they'd lost Holden for some other reason. Maybe the timing was nothing more than coincidence.

The water was everywhere. Dan couldn't see or hear, couldn't feel even his heartbeat anymore. He must be dead, but at least he could remember. He could spend these final moments in the place where they'd lost Holden. He could go back, the way he'd forbidden himself to go back since the day he set out for Alaska.

Holden's fever got worse before it got better, but then it went away and they waited. They waited day after day for Holden to snap out of it, for his energy to return and his smile to fill his eyes again. But the days turned into weeks and Dan could feel it. He could feel his boy slipping through their fingers and there was nothing he could do about it.

The diagnosis came six months later. Holden was autistic, but that only created in Dan a fight that raged to this day. Back then, when he wasn't at work or sleeping, he spent every possible moment with Holden — talking to him, playing with him, working with him. Raging against the storm. And he could still hear the therapist, remember the day the woman looked him straight in the face and gave him the truth. "Holden will always be like this, Mr. Harris. You can help him regain some social skills, but you will never have him back the way he was."

Never ... never the way he was.

It was the final wave in the storm that was his life, the one that buried him and suffocated him and took the breath from him. He had failed Tracy and their son. The waves had hit with a sudden force, and they'd lost everything. After that, every day with Holden was a painful reminder that the storm had won. That this new Holden would never be that boy who sang and danced with his friend Ella. Like a cruel vicious kidnapping, the storm had come upon them and taken Holden with it.

And so, he had walked away, gone off to battle this storm and others like it instead—the ones in Alaska. Because here he could actually fight the wind and waves and with every victory he could at least do one thing for his son: he could pay for therapy. The white water and deadly seas made him feel like he was still in the fight, still capable of doing some good.

But he was wrong about all of it. The therapy wasn't helping. The fierce and sudden storm that hit when Holden was three had taken their son for all time.

And now this fierce and sudden storm would take him too.

Dan had no idea how much time passed, and for most of it he was in and out of reality. Minutes, maybe, or hours. He wasn't sure. The first sign he had that he'd survived was the sound of Captain Charlie's voice.

"Harris... we thought we lost you." The guy's tone was frantic. He slapped Dan's cheek a couple times. "Get up. We gotta get you warm."

"Wh... what?" He tried to open his eyes, but they were swollen shut. "What happened?"

"You got lucky, that's what." Charlie grabbed his arm. "Come on, get up."

Dizziness swept over him, and as he lumbered to his feet he jerked to the side and threw up. Two times, then a third. He wiped at his mouth and forced himself to see through the slit in his thick eyelids. The skies were blue, the storm gone. The captain and another deckhand helped him down below the hatch, walked him to a bunk.

"Bury him in blankets. Whatever you can find." The captain stood beside him a minute longer. "You'll be okay, Harris. You're strong."

Dan felt weak and sick and feverish. But he had survived the storm, so the captain was probably right. He'd drink some bottled water and get warm and he'd be good as new in a day or so. This time, the storm wouldn't take his life.

But if it had, then what? Tracy and Holden would miss him, yes. But he was no longer a part of their lives. The truth was something Captain Charlie didn't understand: it didn't matter if Dan survived.

Because in every way that mattered, the storm had already won.

Five

ELLA WALKED BY HERSELF TO THE DRAMA ROOM. SHE SHOULD'VE been the happiest girl at Fulton High. LaShante and the girls were still celebrating for her. Telling everyone how she had won the role of Belle, and congratulating her because Jake Collins threw three touchdown passes to beat nearby Johns Creek High over the weekend.

But as Ella walked into her sixth-period drama class, she couldn't shake the cold feeling in her heart. The football game was fun, but afterward she and Jake had gone with a bunch of kids to the parking lot of Stone Mountain. Almost everyone was drinking, including Jake—which was why Ella insisted on driving home. The whole way, Jake kept tickling her and trying to touch her in places where she didn't want to be touched.

She wanted to blame her irritation on Jake's drinking, but the closer she got to home the more she remembered Jake and his buddies picking on the special-needs kid. Maybe Jake wasn't the great guy she thought he was. So, yeah, that was a problem.

Then there was the whole deal with her parents.

Her mom spent the weekend wearing dark sunglasses and a lightweight turtleneck. "I never like anyone to see the work until it's healed up," she told them. All weekend she seemed flighty and distracted, and since she never asked Ella about her news, Ella never told her. And though her dad was in town that weekend he never came home. Even her little brothers figured out something was wrong with that.

"What's up with Dad?" Alex literally had to take hold of their mom's hand and force her to stop long enough to look at him.

"Yeah." Andrew walked up, identical in looks and concern with Alex. "He should be home."

"He's busy. Lots of meetings. His contract's up at the end of the year." She smiled, but across the kitchen Ella noticed her chin was trembling. Like she was fighting tears. "He said to think good thoughts for him. This might be his year."

Think good thoughts? Ella hated that phrase.

Ella reached the classroom and set her backpack on a desk at the front. LaShante was a Christian. Well, maybe not a practicing Christian, but at least she went to church every now and then. And when something went wrong or any of the girls needed help, she was the first to offer to pray.

Prayer made sense. At least that meant asking help from a higher power. But good thoughts? Like what ... like people had the power to think something good into existence?

Ella had done a little snooping around on Sunday afternoon when her mom was out getting the color in her hair extensions adjusted. She called the clubhouse and asked for her father. The man too busy practicing baseball to come home and see them.

One of the player personnel guys answered. "He's been in the weight room all weekend." He knew Ella, and he made a few minutes of small talk. Concern leaked into the man's tone. "The boys are off Monday. I'm sure you'll see him."

"I'm sure." Ella didn't want the guy to think he'd said something wrong. He ended up being right. Her dad came home late that night and stayed home Monday. But he was distant and distracted, on the phone a lot.

Ella dropped into a classroom chair and stared blankly at the empty stage at the front of the room. Her dad needed to start hitting or he'd never be the guy he used to be. He'd done this a number of times while they were growing up, whenever he wasn't playing well. When that happened, her mom slipped into some strange insecurity. She spent every morning at the gym with a trainer and every afternoon at the spa getting one treatment or another. This time the distance between her parents seemed worse than usual.

For all Ella knew, they could be on the verge of a divorce. There was no telling.

Even LaShante noticed. She'd come home with Ella once last week and the scene was embarrassing. Ella's mom was applying mascara at the living room mirror when they walked in. She wore tight black jeans and a skintight white tank top. When the girls headed back out to Ella's car, LaShante whistled. "Your mom, Ella ... Wow."

"I know. Too far, huh?"

"She's trying awful hard." LaShante had beautiful dark-brown skin and bright brown eyes. Her hair was a spray of short braids that fit her fun personality. "I mean, I might get hair extensions. You know, sport the Jordin Sparks look." She made a concerned face. "But your mom ... I mean, wow."

It was to the point where Ella hoped both her parents would stay away from Fulton. Life was hard enough without them showing up and making a bunch of kids talk. When he was around anymore, her dad seemed like some washed-up wannabe, dressed in designer jeans and white V-necks and high-fashion jackets. And her mom ... well, LaShante said it best.

Wow.

The drama class was filling up, and Mr. Hawkins was sorting through a stack of scripts piled high on his desk. Rumor had it this might be Mr. Hawkins' last year at Fulton. He was pretty old, and he didn't have a lot of patience for the kids with nervous stage habits or the ones who had trouble memorizing their lines. If Mr. Hawkins were a character from Winnie the Pooh, he'd be Eeyore for sure.

Sixth period with Mr. Hawkins was only for the kids cast in the play. Up until now, they'd gone over basic theater and production. The turnout at auditions had been small — despite LaShante's grand ideas about a hundred girls vying for the role of Belle. Budget cuts forced the school to charge a production fee this year, so the numbers were down, and there weren't a lot of guys in the cast. The boy playing Gaston was tall and self absorbed. So that would work out. The Beast was being played by a guy with so much facial hair the costume people wouldn't have to do much.

But other than that, the townspeople all looked pretty wimpy and mild-mannered. It was hard to imagine them slamming their pitchforks against a stage shouting that it was time to "Kill the Beast!"

Oh, well. It didn't matter. The kids at Fulton High never came to the plays anyway. The theater would be maybe a quarter filled with parents and relatives. It would be a very forgiving audience. Ella figured she might not tell her mom about the play at all. That would serve her right for not asking.

"Okay, young thespians, on your feet." Mr. Hawkins sounded worn out, but he changed up his usual monotone. "First day of rehearsals. Let's warm up."

This was the way Mr. Hawkins always ran his program. Vocal warm-ups would lead to the kids learning the ensemble numbers. Once they had the music down, the blocking would begin. In the meantime, they were all responsible to learn their own lines. Two weeks into rehearsals everyone would be expected to know their part.

Mr. Hawkins took his place at an old upright piano in the front corner of the room. "Ready …" He held up one hand. "Begin."

He led them up and down a series of scales, changing the vowel sound with each set. Five minutes of that, and he motioned for the production secretary to pass out the scripts. "Turn to the first number. It's one of the biggest in the show, and it's one you're probably familiar with. In the first half hour today I want us to be comfortable with the rhythm and lyrics. Then we'll break into parts."

Ella loved this—watching a show come to life. The music started and they sang in unison, some with better vocal control than others. Ella had taken voice lessons since she was six, so the number was as simple as it was familiar, and she easily sang her several solos in the song.

"Oh … isn't this amazing … it's my favorite part because you see …" She was midway through the prettiest few lines of the song when a movement near the open classroom door caught her eye.

She kept singing, but she looked away from her music to see a line of kids walk by. It was the special-needs kids, headed to the small gym—their last class of the day. They walked past the drama wing every day at this time, but Ella never really noticed them.

He had to be there, right? The kid with the blue eyes? She kept singing, kept watching, and then there he was, last in line. He was flapping his arms again, but as he heard the music he slowed to a stop. His arms settled at his sides and he took a half step into the room, holding onto the doorframe. This time he didn't look at her the way he had in the lunch area. Instead he closed his eyes and swayed to the music.

Ella's voice died off, and the others were drawn into the interruption.

"We have to focus, people." Mr. Hawkins pushed back from the piano and cast a disappointed look at Ella. He didn't seem to notice the kid in the doorway. "I'm counting on your leadership, Miss Reynolds." His shoulders dropped a few inches and he tossed his hands. "Everyone take five. We'll pick it back up at the beginning."

Ella barely heard him. She moved from her seat, slowly, so

she wouldn't startle the boy at the door. By then he had his eyes open and he was looking at her, those piercing eyes that seemed to see straight through her. Once more she had the strangest feeling she knew him. It wasn't possible, of course. But his eyes had that sort of pull on her. As she drew closer, one of the special-ed teachers came for him, gently touching his elbow and encouraging him out into the hall again.

At first the kid looked like he might yell or throw a fit. He turned away from Ella and stared straight up at the ceiling, then down at the floor. He took a few steps toward the gym, set his backpack against the wall, and then dropped down and began doing push-ups. Perfect, military-style push-ups. Ella stepped into the hall, drawn to the boy. Why was he doing that, and how come he wouldn't talk?

"He's autistic." The teacher turned to her, her voice quiet. "He does push-ups when he gets overstimulated."

Overstimulated? "I think he liked the music." Ella had heard of autism, and she'd seen an old rerun of *Rain Man* on television last year. But she'd never known anyone who had it. "Can't he stay? So he can hear us sing?"

The woman shook her head. "He needs to be with other special-needs kids." She took a few steps closer to the guy, still on the floor doing push-ups. So many push-ups Ella was starting to worry about him.

"Maybe he'd feel better if he stayed."

Her expression grew impatient, as if Ella couldn't possibly understand someone with autism. "Not today."

The kid was getting up, his face red and sweaty. He walked a few steps toward the gym, then back their way again, but he wasn't looking at Ella the way he did before. She closed the distance between them and stopped a few feet from him. "Hi." She held out her hand. "I'm Ella Reynolds." In the classroom behind her she could hear Mr. Hawkins starting up again on the piano.

The special needs kid walked to his backpack, unzipped the top, and pulled out a large deck of flash cards. At least they looked like flash cards. He sifted through them super fast and found whatever he was looking for. Then he held up the card so Ella could see it. The card was a pair of eyes with two words written beneath them: *I see.*

"You see? You see me?" Ella looked back at the teacher. Her arms were crossed and she was clearly ready to move along. She turned her eyes to the kid again. "What's your name?"

"Holden Harris." The teacher was clearly out of patience. "His name's Holden Harris. That's his favorite card. 'I see.' It's the only way he has to communicate." She motioned dramatically to the kid. "Come on, Holden. Time to go."

"What does it mean?" Ella wanted to know. If the look in Holden's eyes was any indication, he saw a lot. More than people probably thought.

"Nothing." The teacher directed Holden to his backpack. "It's the card he shows people when he's upset, when he doesn't know what's happening around him."

"Ella!" One of the girls from the Beauty cast poked her head out the classroom door. "Hurry up. Break's over."

She was out of time. Holden was placing the card with the eyes on it back into the deck. She didn't have long. "Bye, Holden." She ignored his teacher. "Come back again, okay?"

He looked at her, but only for a few seconds. Then he lifted his backpack over his shoulder and walked quickly toward the gym. His teacher didn't say anything, just hurried after him, like she was glad to have him back on task.

Ella watched him go, and then hurried into the room. The kids were back in their seats for the most part, and Mr. Hawkins was at the piano, flipping through the score. She came to his side and lowered her voice. "Mr. Hawkins, what if there's a student who wants to sit in on our class? Would that be okay?"

Mr. Hawkins let out a heavy sigh, and ran his hand over his balding head. "Miss Reynolds, why do I think you're not serious about this production?"

"Serious?" Ella felt her expression fall. "Of course I'm serious. This has nothing to do with me. I'm talking about a kid from the special-needs group. He wanted to stay, but his teacher wouldn't let him. So next time, I just thought maybe he could—"

"Please, Miss Reynolds, you don't understand what you're asking." He shook his head, clearly discouraged. "As beleaguered as our drama department has become, I can't let it become a babysitting service." He turned to the music. "Now, if you'd please sit down …" He raised his voice. "From the beginning."

Ella wanted to scream. If Holden Harris felt like listening to them sing, what could that hurt? She moved slowly back to her seat and joined her voice with the others around her. Mr. Hawkins could at least give Holden a chance.

She focused on her solo, but even so she sang it with less passion. Not because she was angry at Mr. Hawkins or because she hadn't gotten her way, but because she couldn't stop thinking about Holden. The way he looked in the doorway, taking in the music, swaying to the song. And the words on the card he'd shown her. *I see.* Maybe he showed that card more often than others because he really could see. More than any of them knew.

The possibility grew in Ella's heart, and by the time they finished the first hour of rehearsal, she'd made up her mind. She wasn't going to give up. If Holden wanted to listen to them sing, he would get his chance.

IF THE FIRST REHEARSAL WAS ANY INDICATION OF THE SPRING production, Manny Hawkins figured he better start looking for a job. The board had called him in the week before school started and told him the situation.

"The drama department isn't bringing in enough money." Board resident Tom Banks looked like a former basketball player. Good chance Banks had never seen a musical in his life. "We've cut your budget. There will be no fall production and no winter review."

The only remaining show at Fulton this year would be the spring musical. Banks thought that would give the department a better chance of success. Manny wanted to tell him he'd have a better chance of success playing the lottery.

Fulton High was about sports, not spring productions. Football, not famous musicals. Manny couldn't fathom what it would take to hit the mark. Maybe if they brought in teen sensation Justin Bieber as the Beast or Zac Efron as Gaston. Otherwise the kids would rally around the spring production about the same way they rallied around the math lab. The only way they'd make enough on the spring musical was if they held it on the football field and promised a game for the same price.

The cast was on another break, so Manny looked over his rehearsal schedule. It might seem like they had a lot of rehearsal time, since the play wasn't until after spring break. But there were no after-school rehearsals until two weeks before the show. And they'd have to work out sets and blocking and the sound system all before then.

That meant, including breaks for Christmas and holidays, they had about a hundred and twenty hours of rehearsal time until the show opened. Not much. Especially when this was his last chance to pull off a masterpiece. On top of that, Ella Reynolds didn't seem nearly as excited as he'd hoped she'd be. She was very good, but if she didn't get passionate about her role, the show would flop for sure.

He was barely through the schedule when Ella walked up. He knew before she opened her mouth that this was about the autistic kid. He turned to face her and crossed his arms. "Yes?"

Ella lifted her chin. "I'd like you to reconsider about Holden."

"The boy with autism?"

"Yes." She pointed to the doorway. "Didn't you see him? He loved hearing us sing. Why couldn't he stay and listen?"

"I told you why. This play is very serious, Miss Reynolds. The drama department doesn't have long to prove itself."

"Maybe we prove ourselves by being kind to kids like him." Ella hesitated, as if she didn't quite understand. "I mean, how does that hurt us?"

Manny felt the fight leave him. Ella was a pretty girl, blonde hair, green eyes, with an all-American look. She had promised to dye her hair brown for the role the week before they opened. But none of that would serve the character of Belle as much as the passion in her eyes right now. "You feel very strongly about this, don't you?"

Ella's expression softened a little, but her eyes burned bright with intensity. "Yes, sir."

He thought about the autistic kid. Ella was right. He couldn't do much harm. If he became disruptive, he'd have to leave and that would be that. Otherwise, what was the difference? Short of a miracle, this was their last show anyway. He waved his hand, trying to hurry Ella on her way. "Fine. He can sit in the back, but any outbursts and he's done."

"Really?" Ella jumped up and clapped her hands. "Thank you, Mr. Hawkins. I have a feeling about this. You won't be sorry." She gave Manny a quick smile and flitted back to her desk, her steps lighter than before.

Manny returned to the script, but he felt a little better about the day. Maybe Ella was right. What harm could it bring, playing for Holden at this stage of rehearsals. The autistic kid was at least interested.

And come spring they could count on this much — at least one Fulton High student in the audience.

Six

THE DRUMBEAT STOPPED, AND THAT WAS JUST AS WELL. HOLDEN was tired of doing push-ups. Also, he didn't want to throw a ball across the gym with the other kids in his class. He'd already told the teacher that, but she wasn't listening. That's why he had to sit in a chair at the corner of the gym and work his numbers.

That was better than throwing a ball. Numbers made him feel good, and not too long from now he could go home and visit with his mom. He had so much to tell her today. Because it had finally happened! He and Ella had found their way back to each other. She was just the same, her pretty eyes and happy smile. Best of all she could still sing, just like Holden always knew she could.

Holden was bored of the numbers, finished with them. The music drew him back to the place where Ella was, and he went with it, willingly. She saw him standing at the door the way she saw him before and he went to her. He was really here and this wasn't a dream. He felt dizzy and full and happy. So happy. The edges were a little blurry and the colors weren't crisp like in therapy. But he was pretty sure what was happening was real.

He walked up to Ella. *Remember when we were kids? We laughed and played and sang all day long.*

She smiled and took his hand. *Those were the best times, Holden. And now you're here again!*

Holden looked around, but he and Ella weren't in the classroom anymore, they were on a stage and the stage was long with pretty trees and fields of green grass blowing in the breeze. *Dance with me, Ella?* He was still holding her hand, and he nodded to a bare spot on the stage.

Ella laughed, like she laughed in the movie. And they danced to the music, the way they had danced all those years ago. Holden twirled her and spun her in pretty circles and Ella sang along with the words. In the distance he could hear people clapping. Louder and longer they clapped, because this was the most beautiful thing any of them had ever seen. Ella and Holden dancing together, singing a song of the angels.

He'd spent all his life looking for her, his friend, Ella. And now she was here. *Do you know why I told you I could see you earlier?* He smiled straight into her heart. Smiling at her that way was easy. Ella's heart was wide open.

Why, Holden? She kept dancing, and her words were right to the music.

Because I could always see you. Even when you weren't here with me. I never stopped seeing you. Your soul stayed.

She did another twirl. *Your soul stayed with mine too. Because friends are like that, and you're my friend.*

Holden loved this, talking with Ella after so much silence. Now that he'd found her, they could be best friends again and he would tell her everything, how he'd been feeling and how the music played all the time and how beautiful life was. He would tell her how much he loved Fulton High and how he prayed all the time for the kids around him. Because some of the kids had sad eyes or angry voices. Most of them didn't hear the music.

But you hear the music, Ella. You always did. Just like Michael.

Ella smiled like she must've known Michael. He didn't have a lot of friends, but Holden was going to help him find some. Maybe Ella would help him too. *Michael needs our help, okay?*

Sure, Holden. They were dancing through the grass now, and the applause was quieter. *Whatever you want, that's what I'll do.*

Holden felt a tapping on his shoulder. It started light, but then it got harder and harder and he jerked away from the pain. Slicing, burning so much pain. He turned and there was Mrs. Bristowe, his teacher.

"Holden, you're supposed to be doing your math. Remember?"

His math? He was dancing with Ella across a field of pretty flowers and breezy grass. *I already did my math. Now it's time to dance with Ella.*

Mrs. Bristowe looked unhappy. "See this?" She held up the math paper. "You've been sitting here most of the hour and you've only done three problems. Either you need to get out there and play ball with the other kids, or you need to do your math, Holden. You can't just sit here staring out the window and—"

Mrs. Bristowe, I'm not staring out the window. I'm dancing with Ella, because I just found her again. She's my friend from the movies, back when we were younger. We have a lot to talk about, like the kids at this school and how come some of them seem sad. And we need to talk about Michael, because Michael needs friends. Good friends like me and Ella.

"…if you came over with the other kids and tossed a ball you might feel better about the day and—"

I feel better when I'm with Ella, because I can see her. She can see me. It's always been that way with Ella. Also maybe Michael should be here, because the jerks weren't very nice to him. Their feet sound like drumbeats. Very loud drumbeats.

"… can hear me, Holden. You need to follow instructions. Remember? That's part of your therapy and—"

The sunshine was happy and warm. Holden looked out the window and he could see Ella again. She was waiting for him outside, wanting to dance with him and talk to him and hold his hand. He'd been asking God to find Ella since she left, and now she was here! *I have to find Ella!*

Mrs. Bristowe was saying something, but the music grew louder, more intense. He couldn't hear the teacher above the song, and maybe that was just as well. Clearly, something was wrong with her, because no matter what he said, she didn't respond. Holden had a feeling she couldn't hear him at all.

His teacher looked a little angry now, and Holden closed his eyes. The drumbeats were going to start any minute, he could feel them coming. And sure enough they started right at that moment ... *Boomdity, Boom ... Boomdity, Boom ... BOOM, BOOM, BOOM.*

Pounding drums, screaming, screeching. The noise was too much, and in another heartbeat Holden was on the ground, his muscles flexing, pushing through the noise. Too much noise. This wasn't pretty like the music in his heart. Ten push-ups, fifteen. *BOOM, BOOM, Boomdity, boomdity, BOOM BOOM.* Twenty push-ups, twenty-five. When he reached thirty, the sound of the drums grew softer and faded away. Holden stood up, breathing hard.

Where is she? The song was softer now, but Mrs. Bristowe wouldn't answer him. *Where did Ella go, and why can't I go be with her?*

"Holden Harris, you're trying my patience and —"

What did I do wrong? Why did Mrs. Bristowe have to get mad? He would finish his math later. He and his mom could sit at the table like they always did and talk about his day and he would work out his math.

He needed to pray, that's what the wall at church said. *Pray on all occasions.* He could pray for Mrs. Bristowe and for Ella and for time away from math so he could dance and run through the green fields.

Dear Jesus, it's me, Holden. Why are people so angry? They have sad eyes and they don't want to hear the music ever. But right now I only want to dance with Ella. So please, Lord, could You make that happen? Please bring Ella back here so we can dance. I know You can hear me, because You let me find her. Thank You for that.

Now if we could please dance again, I would really appreciate it. I know You love me. Your friend, Holden.

The green fields were calling to him, and Ella was waiting. Today was beautiful, more beautiful than the other days. His heart was full and the sun was shining bright white and soft edges. All because he'd found Ella Reynolds.

He already explained this to Mrs. Bristowe, but she wouldn't listen. Or maybe she couldn't listen. Right now he didn't want to throw a ball or work out his math or do another push-up. He didn't want to be buried under the noise. He only wanted what he'd wanted since he was in the movies, the same thing he wanted every day when he remembered her or when he came to Fulton High.

He wanted his friend Ella.

Seven

ONCE A MONTH BEFORE SCHOOL LET OUT FOR THE DAY, TRACY met with Holden's lead teacher, Beth Bristowe. During the talk, Holden would sit in the classroom, lost in his own world, working his math problems the way he liked to do. Once he was settled, Tracy and Mrs. Bristowe would sit at her desk twenty feet away and they'd talk about Holden, how he was doing and the progress he was making.

Tracy used to look forward to the meetings, because when Holden was a freshman they introduced PECS cards to him. Back then every month seemed to show another level of progress and advancement. Another step closer to opening the doors that so firmly held her son.

The PECS cards stayed, but midway through his sophomore year, Holden hit a plateau. His therapists hoped that the PECS cards would eventually lead to verbal communication, and—for the lucky few—a return to at least a fraction of normalcy. It was what Tracy prayed for every day. But today was her first meeting with Mrs. Bristowe this school year, and Tracy had a feeling the news wouldn't be good.

At home Holden still kept his cards to himself, not trusting her to hold them. And whereas sometimes in the past she would catch a glimmer of eye contact from him, now he made none at all. He was more agitated about going to therapy, too. The only time he seemed happy and right with the world was during his movie, sitting in front of the television screen watching himself run across an open field with his father or roll on the floor laughing alongside Ella Reynolds.

Tracy could only figure he was regressing—always a possibility with autistic kids. If Mrs. Bristowe confirmed that possibility today, Tracy wasn't sure how she'd handle the news. She parked her small car amidst the Suburbans and Navigators and BMWs and headed toward the south entrance of the school. The wing for the special-needs kids.

Holden was not her only concern. Dan had called this morning sounding terrible. He was battling pneumonia and he briefly mentioned getting a little too cold in a recent storm.

"I'm fine, Tracy. Don't worry about me. Just pray." He hacked a few times, so hard it sounded like he was dying. "Everything will be okay."

But it wasn't. Dan had cheated death too many times already. One of these days the call would come from the Alaskan Coast Guard or someone from the commercial fishing industry, informing her that Dan wasn't coming home. Not ever again.

Tracy's heart thudded hard in her chest. *Please, Father ... be with me. I'm not sure how much I can take.*

I am with you, daughter. I love you, and I will fight this battle for you ... Trust me, precious child. Trust.

The answer whispered to her anxious heart and gave her something to hold onto. She couldn't imagine what the next hour would bring. *Trust God,* she told herself. *No matter how you feel, Tracy. Come on.* She peeled off her Walmart vest, tossed it on the backseat, and stepped out of the car.

She was early, so she didn't rush. Instead she soaked in everything around her—the groups of kids, their laughter and conversation. So different from the life her son was living. A pang of sadness hit her and wrapped itself around her heart. This was his senior year. Tonight these kids would go to a Fulton High football game and Holden would go to therapy. Even if something finally helped Holden step out into the light where the rest of them lived, it would be too late for any of this. Too late to experience high school.

Stop it, Tracy ...

She reached Mrs. Bristowe's classroom and peered through the window in the door. Holden was already sitting cross-legged on a pillow in the corner of the room, his eyes focused on the bare ceiling. She wanted to run to him and take him in her arms, cry out to him. *Holden, honey ... it's me, your mom. Come out of there, baby. Whatever's holding you, break away.* But she couldn't do that. She'd tried before, and it only frightened him. One time when she asked him to find his way back, he covered his face and rocked for half an hour. That was two years ago. Tracy hadn't brought up the subject since.

Please, God ... I need You. The schooling and therapy ... it isn't working, Father. How can I reach him? We need a miracle, Lord. Please.

Mrs. Bristowe must've seen her, because she came to the door and opened it. Her smile was pleasant, but she looked worn out. Not a good sign. "Hello, Mrs. Harris."

"Hello." She never knew whether to go to Holden in a moment like this. Holden rarely acknowledged her, but she was determined to treat him the way she would if he didn't have autism. So she crossed the room and crouched down to his level. "Hi, Holden. It's conference day, okay? I'll talk to Mrs. Bristowe and you do your math. Then we'll go home."

Holden rarely looked at her, and never responded. But Tracy was pretty sure he rocked a little. She smiled at him. "I'll take that as a yes." She stood again and followed Mrs. Bristowe to her desk. When they were seated, the teacher set a file with Holden's name on it squarely in front of her. "Mrs. Harris, you know that the first meeting of the school year is important. We like to assess how our students have progressed over the summer and whether we have them on the correct plan." She drew a deep breath as she opened Holden's folder. "We've definitely seen changes in Holden since last spring."

"Yes." Tracy sat rigid in her chair, her sweaty palms locked together on her lap. "He seems, I don't know ... unsettled, I guess."

"Yes." Mrs. Bristowe paused. "Definitely." She pulled a single sheet from the file and handed it to Tracy. "Here's a report from an incident the other day. I'll give you a few minutes to read over it."

Tracy glanced at Holden, but he didn't seem to be listening to them. He had his work tray on his lap and he was hunched over the paper, working trigonometry problems with as little effort as it took him to breathe. She took the report from Mrs. Bristowe and began to read.

The document told about a situation that past Monday where Holden stopped to listen to the drama production class singing a song during rehearsal. Tracy looked up at Holden's teacher. "He wanted to stay? To listen to the music?"

"Definitely." She angled her head thoughtfully. "Of course, that's a mainstream class, and Holden hasn't been approved for mainstream drama. There's no telling how he would act in that situation."

"So you didn't let him stay?"

"I couldn't. I'd need permission on a lot of levels before I could do that." She hesitated. "I'll get to that in a minute."

Tracy nodded. Why did Holden have to have a committee make a decision for him? If he wanted to hear a song, wasn't it possible to stand by him and let him listen? Everyone agreed about the importance of music, right? Even the school therapists. Tracy contained her frustration. She found her place on the page again and read how Holden had become agitated and how he'd dropped to the floor and produced a couple dozen push-ups in the hallway. Tracy felt tears brimming as she read the final line:

*When we finally reached the gym with the other special-needs kids,
Holden was completely noncompliant.*

Noncompliant? Because he wanted to listen to music? Tracy
wrestled with her frustration. She dabbed at her eyes and handed
the piece of paper back to the teacher. "What do you mean, 'noncompliant'?" She had to watch her tone. Nothing good would
come from getting angry or frustrated with the woman. After all,
Holden had been a little noncompliant for her too.

Mrs. Bristowe's expression softened, and a fresh kindness
shone in her eyes. "We have a protocol for the students. You know
that. So once I got Holden back on task and into the gym, I asked
him to participate. The kids were throwing a Nerf ball, working their large motor skills along with their ability to interact.
Holden didn't want to do that."

A Nerf ball. Tracy pictured the woman in her line at Walmart
a few weeks ago. The boy was tossing a Nerf ball, talking about
playing with his mom later that day. It was something Holden
loved to do when he was two and three. But now he was eighteen.
Maybe he didn't want to toss a Nerf ball. She forced herself to
focus.

"We never make the kids participate. As you know, we introduce an alternate activity. So I gave him a math sheet and asked
him to sit in the observation chair."

"The observation chair?"

"Yes. It's a comfortable seat in the corner of the gym where
special-needs students can observe other kids interacting.
Research shows there's benefit to observing."

Tracy wanted to scream or laugh out loud. Wasn't that all
Holden wanted to do? Observe kids in the theater room? And did
the woman really have to use all the right education words? She
could just say she had Holden sit to the side and do his school-
work. She clenched her hands and nodded. "You said he was
noncompliant."

"Yes." Her tone suggested the worst was yet to come. "Instead of working on math, he stood and turned in circles. Small circles, then larger circles, then sweeping circles until he was almost in the way of the other kids."

Circles? Holden hadn't moved in circles since he was five years old, six, maybe. Panic coursed through Tracy's veins. They'd resolved that behavior through therapy before his seventh birthday. "Did ... did he do anything else, anything that would explain why?"

"No. I spoke to him several times, but he never looked at me. He circled until finally he grew very irritable. Then he dropped down and did a series of push-ups—like always. After that he sat in his chair, but he wouldn't work on his math the rest of the day." She looked at Holden. "He's been disagreeable every day since then."

Tracy couldn't fathom why Holden would regress now, or what was at the cause of it. She prayed for him constantly, and never took a day off from therapy. This week his therapist was helping him understand the musical PECS cards. That reminded Tracy. "Usually he uses his cards? Did he have them? So he could tell you what he was thinking?"

"First ..." Mrs. Bristowe smiled patiently, "he doesn't really tell us a whole lot with the cards. There are glimpses, yes. But little more." She looked at Holden's file for a moment, then back at Tracy. "And yes, he had his cards when he stopped to listen to the drama class."

"What did he say?" Maybe there was a window here, a way to know what Holden had been thinking.

"One of the girls in the class came out to talk to him. He showed her a card he uses often." She hesitated. "The one with the pair of eyes."

"It says 'I see.'" Tracy glanced at Holden, but he was looking up again, most likely unaware of their conversation. She leaned closer, her voice lower. "What if he really meant that, Mrs. Bristowe? Maybe he could see that the class was involved in music, and he wanted to take part. Or maybe he wanted the girl to know that he saw her. Even if maybe he wasn't looking right at her."

"Sure." Mrs. Bristowe looked bewildered. "Any of those possibilities exist. And he had access to his PECS cards in the gym. But instead of using them to express himself, he turned in circles."

Tracy sighed. They were getting nowhere. She couldn't defend Holden's actions unless she knew what he was thinking. Same as anyone who worked with him. "What about his class work?"

"It's about the same as last year." She pulled a group of papers from the file. "He continues to excel in math, of course."

"You mainstreamed him this year. How's that going?" She had asked Holden, of course, but he hadn't given her any sign except one. "He started showing the cards differently after school started. He used to hand them to me, but after the first day, he stopped that." Tracy folded her arms in front of her. "Now he holds tight to the cards when he shows them to me."

"I noticed that." Mrs. Bristowe pursed her lips. "I have a sense he's getting picked on from a few of the football players." She pulled a paper from the back of the folder. "A junior, Michael Schwartz, made this report at the office that day."

Tracy felt her heart skip a beat as she took the paper. If Holden was getting picked on, then he couldn't be mainstreamed. She could hire a tutor for him, or have his therapist help him with online studies. Holden wasn't going to be the target of bullies.

She studied the report. It wasn't long. Just a fact sheet with the student's name, the date and location of the problem — in this case the math building, two doors down from the room where Holden took trig. The only details came at the bottom.

I was in the math building, and I saw a bunch of football players kick the shins of Holden Harris. I know who he is because I was a T.A. for the special-needs class last year. After they pushed him around, one of the guys kicked Holden's backpack. His flashcards scattered all over the floor and he seemed pretty upset. I thought you'd want to know.

Tracy's hands shook, and her heart raced faster than before. "The answer's right here." She had to work to keep her voice down. "No wonder he won't let go of his cards. Holden was attacked and no one told me until now."

"I wouldn't say attacked. Michael might've seen it wrong." Mrs. Bristowe took the paper and returned it to Holden's file. "But you asked about the mainstream efforts. His teacher says he doesn't act like the other kids, doesn't look at the board or talk to anyone. And he's still doing the flapping I told you about last year. But otherwise, his class work and test grades so far have been at the highest level."

Tracy leaned back in her chair. "So …" Tears brimmed in her eyes, but she fought them. "What do we do?"

"That's up to you. No one is picking on Holden in class."

"But the walk to the classroom takes him by any number of people who might." Again she forced herself to talk quieter. "Isn't that right?"

"It is." Mrs. Bristowe gave a sad shrug. "If he were my son, I'd pull him. Let him work on his trig at home."

"But if we can't mainstream him in math, then how does he ever make the transition?" The answer hit her before Holden's teacher had the chance to respond. They couldn't mainstream Holden because he wasn't making the transition. Because therapy wasn't working and change wasn't happening and Holden hadn't advanced at all since last spring. It was the whole reason Mrs. Bristowe looked discouraged.

The teacher folded her hands on her desk and looked straight at Tracy. "I have an idea."

Tracy had never felt more defeated. Sure, she was praying,

and she'd keep praying. But what reason did she have to believe anything would ever change for Holden? "What is it?"

"I mentioned it would take a committee to allow Holden into the drama room. But something has happened to expedite that process." She smiled, her eyes bright for the first time since the meeting started. "The drama student—the girl Holden showed the PECS card to the other day—has asked if Holden could observe rehearsals during sixth period. Our drama instructor Mr. Hawkins has agreed."

Tracy leaned her forearms on the desk and tried to comprehend what Mrs. Bristowe had just said. "She did that for him?"

"Yes." Mrs. Bristowe sorted through the folder and found one more piece of paper. "I've taken the idea to the team of special-needs teachers, and everyone has signed off. It's up to you now."

"Of course." Tracy made a sound that was more laugh than cry. She brought her fingers to her lips and reached for a pen in her purse. Then, with a renewed sense of hope, she signed the bottom of the page and handed it back to Mrs. Bristowe. "When ... when can he start?"

"Monday." The teacher smiled. "I know Holden loves music. We've always known that. But this is the first time he's been so proactive about it, wanting to be in the drama classroom. At the very least, he'll enjoy sitting at the back of the drama room more than tossing a Nerf ball."

"Yes." She sat a little straighter. "At the very least." No matter how small this step for Holden, it was something—a step in the right direction.

"That's all, Mrs. Harris." The teacher stood and shook her hand. She grabbed a second folder from an adjacent desk. "I made copies of everything in his file, for your records."

"Thank you." Tracy looked into the woman's eyes. "We ... we needed this." She went to Holden. "Time to go, honey. I've got your snack ready at home."

Holden took his PECS cards from his backpack and looked intently through them. Finally he pulled out a worn card, and this time she didn't reach for it. The card held an illustration of small, irregularly shaped black dots, and the word beneath that read "Raisins."

"You want raisins for a snack." Tracy grinned as Holden stood and followed her. "We'll have raisins."

They were halfway to the car when in the distance Holden seemed to spot the football field. He stopped for a few seconds, then he folded his hands tightly together, brought them to his chin, and flapped his arms. The familiar behavior lasted only a few minutes, but clearly Holden was agitated. After reading the report, Tracy understood why.

"Come on, Holden. It's okay. We're almost to the car. Kate will be home soon." She touched his arm, but he jerked away. The rest of the walk to the car, he sorted through his PECS cards. When they reached the car he showed her the card he'd been apparently looking for. It showed a TV screen and the word "Movie." Again he didn't make eye contact.

"Yes, Holden, we'll watch the movie. Of course." Tracy moved her head slightly, trying to find that sweet spot where their eyes might connect. But it didn't happen. They climbed in the car and Holden was quiet, watching out the window for the ride home.

They met up with Kate and the three of them headed inside the apartment. Tracy and Kate made the snack—and Tracy was careful to add extra raisins. Holden brought his cards to the table, but he kept his focus on the food. Intent on the process of eating. Kate chattered, all cheery and sunshine, and between bites Holden lined up his raisins around the outside of the plate and Tracy wondered if there was maybe a connection. Whatever Holden was feeling, whatever he was going through, maybe the orderliness of turning circles or lining up his raisins helped him deal with it.

There was a connection somewhere, Tracy had to believe that. A reason for everything Holden did, every quirky repetitive behavior, every silent hour. Now, like every day since Holden's diagnosis, it was a matter of finding the connection.

As Holden finished his snack, he seemed more anxious than usual, his mannerisms jerky and unsettled. Still, he took his seat on the floor and Kate took the spot beside him. It was like she had an innate understanding that something wasn't right with Holden, that he needed her companionship while he watched the movie. For whatever reason, she hadn't grown bored with the routine. Tracy was grateful. Kate was helping… even if Holden was agitated, he was aware of her presence. Lately she had even caught him looking briefly at Kate before and after the movie.

Tracy let the loop at the beginning of the DVD play through, let the song play out. *Never be the same without your love … live alone … Try so hard to rise above.* Then, like every day for as far back as she could remember, she hit the Play button and the movie began.

But today Tracy didn't want a reminder of the wonderful, communicative little boy Holden had been. The kitchen needed to be cleaned, and the laundry had to be sorted. Kate was little, but an extra child in the house had added housework and Tracy was glad for the diversion. She was on her way to Holden's room when she saw something that made her stop cold.

Holden wasn't sitting cross-legged the way he had a thousand times before today. He and Kate were on their feet, turning in circles.

The sick feeling hit like a freezing winter wind and took her breath. *No, Holden … don't go that way. You're letting it take you farther from me.* She wanted to go to him and hold his shoulders, look him in the eyes if that were possible, and beg him to stay here with her.

She had taken two steps toward him when she caught the

image on the TV screen and again she stopped, stunned too shocked to move. The scene was one where Holden and Ella were singing "Jesus Loves Me." But that wasn't all they were doing.

They were also dancing.

"Holden ..." She whispered. She no longer wanted to interrupt him.

Kate turned circles around him, her arms raised. "We're dancing, Holden!" She giggled and skipped a few steps. "I love dancing!"

Holden didn't respond, but his circles grew bigger and then smaller again. And something else was different for Holden: his eyes were closed.

Tracy looked from the dancing three-year-olds on the screen to her son and Kate and back again, and suddenly she was absolutely sure about what was happening here. What had happened the other day in gym class. So sure she wanted to call Mrs. Bristowe and ask her to come right over. The sick feeling left her, and a smile tugged at the corners of her mouth. Holden was doing something that had once given him great delight, something that had connected him to a friend and made him laugh with delight. He wasn't turning circles because he was regressing. In fact, this might even explain the way he'd turned circles when he was five and six. He wasn't being defiant or difficult or agitated or over stimulated. He was turning circles for one very simple, very beautiful reason. Somewhere in the private world where he lived, Holden was doing something he loved to do.

He was dancing with Ella.

Eight

ENGLISH CLASS WAS OVER, AND ELLA WAS ONE OF THE LAST KIDS to leave the room. As she walked out she spotted Jake and Sam, but before she reached them she saw something she could hardly believe. The guys had another kid cornered. After the incident with Holden, Ella had talked for an hour that night with Jake.

"It wasn't funny," she told him.

"I'm sorry." He touched her hair, his eyes kind and genuine again. "We didn't mean anything by it."

Ella wanted to believe him, but this time their victim was Michael Schwartz, a quiet, artsy kid who had been in a number of classes with Ella over the years. He played in the school orchestra and would probably be one of the lead flutists in the school's *Beauty and the Beast* musical. Once last year they were in the same small group in their social studies class. They had to talk about their families. She still remembered that she and Michael both seemed equally hesitant to talk about what went on at home.

"My parents are getting a divorce." Michael was quiet, not as confident as lots of kids. "I don't really talk about it."

And now here was her boyfriend—the guy who seemed so great over the summer—picking on the kid. Ella watched the way she had when the guys cornered Holden. Because she couldn't actually believe they were doing this, and she wanted to be sure it wasn't a two-way thing. Maybe Michael had picked a fight with them first.

"Hey, flower boy." Jake flicked the spot on Michael's backpack where the design included a few flowers. "What kind of wimp walks around with flowers on his backpack?"

Anger came over Ella in a flash. Whatever was happening here, Michael wasn't a part of it. Clearly the kid wanted to move along, but there was literally no way past Jake and Sam without a physical confrontation. She wanted to run up and push the guys away, but how would that look? Michael might come across as more of a victim, which could make things worse for him. Instead she seethed from her place near the classroom door.

Sam was taking a turn with him. "So what is it, fruitcake, you have something against football players?" It was Friday — game day — and he and Jake wore their uniforms. "We too manly for you, flute player?" He laughed hard. "I heard only gay guys play the flute." Sam pranced around, pretending to play an invisible flute.

Ella silently seethed. She was finished with Jake. She didn't want any part of a guy who treated other kids like this. She took a few steps toward him and Sam, but she stopped herself. Michael wasn't in danger, and again she'd only make him look weak if she tried to rescue him.

"I'm not gay." Michael peered up at Sam through his long black hair. "Get out of my face."

"Really?" Jake shoved the kid. "You're talking back to my boy Sam?"

Ella couldn't stand there another minute. She stormed toward the guys, intent on pushing Jake out of the way. At the same time, three other football players walked up, and Ella stopped herself once more. Jake's teammates seemed to understand pretty quickly what was happening, and one of them gave Jake a lighthearted shove.

"Leave the kid alone." The guy's name was Brian Brickell. He had also been in a number of Ella's classes over the years. "Come on J-Bird, pick on someone your own size."

At first Jake looked like he might blow up at his teammate. But then he slapped Sam on the back and sneered at Michael. "Stay out of my way."

Michael said nothing. He took the opportunity to escape and did so without looking over his shoulder. As he left, Sam yelled at him. "Yeah, that's right. Don't look back, queer boy. This is our hallway. No flute players got it?"

Ella watched Jake go, and she felt horrified. She wanted to tell him off right here in front of his friends, but she was too sick to her stomach to speak or move. She would break up with him later. They were finished.

She looked the opposite direction at Michael Schwartz, hurrying out of the building. For an instant, she thought about running after him and telling him she was sorry about how Jake acted. Sorry because she should've stepped in. But Jake would see her, and that would get awkward.

Instead, she turned a different direction and headed out a side door. What was wrong with the kids at Fulton High? The school needed more guys like Brian Brickell, a reminder that not all football players were like Jake and Sam.

ELLA DIDN'T SEE JAKE UNTIL TWO HOURS LATER BETWEEN classes. He walked up to her, hurt plastered across his face. "You didn't say hi after English."

She stopped and searched his eyes. "We need to talk."

He chuckled, doing his best to charm her. "About what?"

"Us." She didn't smile. "I saw the whole Michael Schwartz thing."

Jake knit his brow together, his laughter a little more nervous than before. "Who?"

"The flute player." She put her hand on her hip. "Don't act innocent, Jake. I watched the whole thing."

"That?" His smile was still in place, but his confidence was fading. "I told you, baby ... me and the guys do that." His laugh was more nervous than before. "We joke around with kids. It's no big deal."

She stared at him. "It is to me." A glance at her phone told her she needed to get to class. "We need to talk."

"Fine." Jake held up his hands in mock surrender. "We'll talk." He shrugged and started in the opposite direction. "Whatever, Ella ..."

"Yeah," she called back in his direction. "Whatever."

She hurried up the stairs and didn't give him another look. When lunchtime came she avoided the outdoor area, and went instead to the wing where the special-needs kids had their cafeteria. Holden had been given permission to sit in on their rehearsals for *Beauty and the Beast* starting Monday. Ella wondered if he understood that he'd gotten his way.

As she wandered the special-education wing, she tried to imagine what he usually did during lunch. She thought he probably wasn't in trig anymore, because she hadn't seen him in the hallway lately. If he'd dropped the class, he would have no reason to walk through the lunch area or the math building, the way he'd done the first week.

Ella reached the area's smaller cafeteria and stepped inside just long enough to find Holden. He was sitting by himself, looking through his stack of flash cards. Ella wanted to talk to him, but she didn't know what to say, didn't know how to connect with him. She went to the library instead. She'd rather study history than hang out with Jake and the rest of the kids in her crowd.

The thing was, Holden intrigued her. When he looked at her, it was like she got a glimpse of his heart. And what she saw told her that Holden was kind and good and real, like maybe he had the biggest heart of any kid on campus. She wanted to get to know him, the real him.

She thought about Holden through the afternoon and after Fulton notched another victory—this time over Duluth. After the game LaShante suggested everyone come to Ella's house, the way they often did since the group started high school. The Reynolds' basement contained a huge rec room with a pool table, comfy couches, and an enormous flat-screen TV. The perfect hang-out spot. Plus, her mom made sure everyone had lots to eat, so it was always a safer choice than hanging out in the parking lot of Stone Mountain. Usually Ella loved when people came over.

But as the party got going, Ella was sorry she'd said yes. More people came than she'd expected, and three of her friends were mad at each other because one of them had told the other something about that one's boyfriend. Or the other way around. The usual Friday-night drama, but it bugged Ella more this time. She wondered what kids like Holden or Michael Schwartz were doing tonight.

She ran upstairs to refill the chip bowl, and she expected to find Jake and his buddies in the kitchen with her mom. Jake was always talking to her mom. But Jake was missing, so she walked out back and sure enough, there he was—leaning against the balcony overlooking their manicured backyard.

Ella stepped outside. "Jake?" She took a few steps closer. This was as good a time as any to break things off with him. "What are you doing?"

"Thinking." He turned and faced her, leaning against the railing. "I'm sorry, Ella. You're right." He paused, regret written into his expression. "I've been a jerk lately." He held out his hand toward her.

Ella crossed her arms. Jake must've gotten the message, because he dropped his hand back to his side.

"I don't know … It's like being with the guys brings out the worst in me."

Images of Holden and Michael flashed in her mind. "The guys?" She held her ground. "Is that what it is?"

"Yes." His tone was marked by remorse. "It's just … I don't know, immature, I guess." He didn't pause long enough for her to respond. "I keep thinking about summer, our trip to the beach and how we sat on the sand and watched the sunset, talking about the future."

Ella remembered, but she kept her tone matter-of-fact. Her decision was made up. "I thought you were special."

He pursed his lips, clearly frustrated with himself. "I want you to see that side of me again."

For a few seconds, Ella was tempted to give in, to tell him that's what she wanted too — the Jake she'd come to care about over the summer. But before she could say anything, she pictured him and Sam, both of them sneering at Michael and making fun of him. Or the way they'd treated Holden. Ice ran through her veins and she steeled herself against his charm. "I have to tell you something."

"What, baby … anything." Jake leaned harder against the railing. He slipped his hands into his pockets, his long legs kicked slightly out in front of him. His eyes shone with kindness, and there in the moonlight he was the picture of athleticism and confidence.

"I can't do this." She refused to be moved. "The whole relationship thing."

He cocked his head, like maybe he hadn't heard her right. "If you need time, you can have it. I understand."

"No … not time." *This kindness thing is an act*, she told herself. The real Jake was the guy she'd seen at school bullying kids weaker than him. "I'm breaking up with you." She sounded more weary than angry. "It's over."

"What?"

"Come on, Jake. Don't act surprised." She took a step back

and rubbed her arms. The night air was chilly, fall well under way. Her smile felt sad, even to her. "I don't even know you."

He tried for another few minutes, and then, almost like a switch had been flipped, his mood changed and he seemed to give up. "Okay, then … I guess I'll see you around."

"Yeah." Ella stepped out of his way as he headed back to the house. "I guess."

Jake left, and a few minutes later she heard his tires squeal down her road. She kept to herself the next few hours while the party wound down. Sometime after one in the morning she went to bed, leaving her mom at the computer on Facebook. By then her brothers had come home from across the street, and Ella was almost sure she smelled alcohol on them. They were acting funny too.

Great, she thought. *The whole family's messed up.* Her dad was on a trip with the team, of course, but he hadn't been in the lineup for ten games. It was like everything around her was falling apart.

The next day wasn't much better.

Her dad's game was at one in the afternoon, and the whole family was expected to go. "What if I have homework?" Ella figured that would get her out of it.

But her mom didn't even take the time to look at her. "Homework can wait. Your father expects us all to be there." She'd gone tanning again that morning, and her blonde hair hung in long layers around her shoulders. Her Botox injections had settled down, but they left her face stiff and mask-like. She wore black jeans, high-heeled boots, and a tight low-cut T-shirt. She smiled at Ella. "How do I look?"

"Weird." Ella didn't how else to answer.

"Ella Jean, that's rude." The lines in her mother's forehead were more noticeable when she was angry.

"Fine." Ella put her hands on her hips. "You look like you're trying too hard." She turned and walked away.

"Ella, get back here this minute."

She didn't stop, didn't look back, didn't talk to her mother again until they rode with the boys to the ballpark for her father's game. "This is very important to your father," her mom explained. Her perfume filled the family's Audi. "This could be a turning point for him." She checked her lip gloss in the rearview mirror. "I'm glad you're all here."

None of them answered. Ella hated this — their family going to a ball game together like some kind of freak show. Why parade in together so everyone could see them? Randy Reynolds' beautiful family. Big deal. Ella kept her sunglasses in place. She hated everything about the circus that made up her life. The game was a dismal loss, even from their front-row first-baseline seats. Their dad played only one inning and struck out on three fastballs. He looked angry and distant as he huffed to the dugout. They were sitting right next to the home dugout, and her brothers tried clapping and encouraging him, but he didn't look their way — not once.

Ella only wanted to be home, and five hours later she got her wish. Her brothers headed across the street again, and her mom drove off to the gym for a late-night session with her trainer. Her dad, of course, would be late at the clubhouse. That left Ella alone in her family's big house. *I hate this*, she told herself. *Life's always lonely. Lonely and messed up.*

She wandered upstairs to the stretch of cabinets that ran along their spacious hallway. Mindlessly, she opened a few of them, not sure what was inside. Three cabinets down the line she found a stack of old photo albums and scrapbooks. She hadn't talked to anyone from school all day, and she had no plans for the night. So she took the stack from the cupboard and settled down on the floor, her back against the opposite wall.

She looked through a book of photos from when she was in third or fourth grade. Her brothers were little kids back then, and her mom and dad were together in most of the pictures. Ella ran her finger over the faces in the photographs. What happened to her family? They used to be happy, right? Sure, her dad traveled, but when he was home they did stuff together, weekend trips and afternoons at the park. Swimming in the backyard pool on hot summer afternoons.

So when had everything unraveled?

A few pages more and she came across an Easter picture, the three kids dressed in their Sunday best outside a beautiful church. Ella peered intently at the photos. As far back as she could remember, her parents hadn't taken them to church except on Easter and Christmas. But she had the sense that there had been a time when she believed in God — more than she had lately, anyway. Now, though, her family never talked about anything more than what was happening that day. The boys' soccer games, their hitting practice, her mom's busy schedule between the gym and the various salons. Ella and her mom never talked, not more than a handful of words each day, and those were only the necessary discussions about dinner and dishes and homework.

Ella slid the book back on the shelf and picked up an older-looking one from the stack on the floor. This one had a picture of Ella and her parents on the cover, back when Ella was maybe two or three. "Was this where we lost it?" she whispered. "Before Dad started playing pro ball?"

The first page of the book showed pictures of her parents, happy and clearly in love. Her mom's hair looked natural, and she carried a few more pounds on her hips. No big deal, just enough so she looked real. Not the plastic replica she was now.

Again Ella ran her finger over the photo. *Dear God … if You're there, could You tell me this? What happened to my family?*

There was no answer — not that Ella actually expected one.

She wasn't a praying person, anymore than anyone in her family was. But watching Brian Brickell the other day, she sort of wished she were. Brian was a Christian, she knew because he talked about his faith. He was kind and he stuck up for kids like Michael or Holden. He wrote Bible verses in his eye black the way Tim Tebow once did for the University of Florida.

Just once she wished she had that kind of certain faith in God.

She turned the next page and the layout was filled with photos from some beach day. But it wasn't just Ella's parents this time. There was another couple in the pictures, and a little boy about her age. In one picture, she and the boy were holding hands, facing the ocean. The caption beneath the photo read "Ella and Holden at Tybee Island Beach."

Ella and Holden? She pulled up her knees and brought the book closer to her face. Holden who? She and the boy were both tan and blond—adorable kids who were clearly the best of friends. Another picture showed the six of them. Her family and this Holden's family. Their parents looked happy and relaxed— the way people looked when they'd been friends for a lifetime.

Again Ella studied the images and looked intently at their faces. She didn't recognize any of them. Whoever the people were, her parents must have lost touch with them. Ella tilted her head, sad for the loss. Everyone missed out when friendships died. And this one clearly had died a long time ago, because Ella had no idea who the people were.

The next few pages were more of the same. Beneath a few of the pictures, her mother had identified the couple as Tracy and Dan—but no last name. And every other picture was another darling shot of her and this Holden kid. Whoever he was, he had huge blue eyes. Familiar eyes, almost, and Ella wondered if some part of her brain somehow remembered back that long ago.

It wasn't until a few pages more into the book that she

reached a page that consisted entirely of an enlarged photograph of her and the little boy. The picture was of the two of them dancing, and it appeared almost professional. Beneath the photo —

Ella gasped. Her feet slid forward and she nearly dropped the book. "What in the world …?"

Beneath the beautiful picture, the caption read "Ella Jean Reynolds and Holden Benjamin Harris — age 3."

Holden Harris? The same Holden Harris autistic boy at her school? It wasn't possible, right? She and her parents had lived in New York for a decade. And before that they'd been all over Atlanta. They'd moved from Dunwoody to Duluth and finally to Johns Creek four years ago. There was no way the boy in the pictures could be the same kid who walked around Fulton flapping his arms. The boy in the photographs was normal. He was smiling and playing and dancing like a regular kid. His eyes had the look of someone fully with it, fully there. Not Holden's vacant, spacey look.

But the longer she looked at his eyes, the more the truth became clear. The boy in the picture and the Holden at school had the same eyes. And slowly … like the most beautiful sunrise … the truth dawned on her. And as it did, she understood why Holden had seemed so familiar.

A lifetime ago, Holden Harris had been her friend.

She lifted the edges of the yellowed plastic protector and carefully removed one of the smaller pictures of Holden and her. She also eased from the page one of the photographs of their parents. Something was very wrong with all of this. How had their families met, and what had happened to separate them? Most of all, how come Holden looked normal in the pictures, when he was so far from it now?

Suddenly she remembered the card Holden had showed her the first day he came by her drama class. The card had two eyes and the words *I see.* He hadn't acted like he knew her, and he certainly hadn't said anything about recognizing her. But maybe there was a deeper meaning to the words on his flash card. Maybe he was trying to tell her he knew her, that he could see past the years to the little girl she'd once been. It was possible, right?

Ella had no answers. She put the photo albums back in the cupboard and found an empty folder from among her father's office supplies downstairs. She slipped the photographs inside and hurried to the closest computer. Her research could take all night, but she didn't care. She had to have answers about why Holden had changed, and how come they stopped being friends. This was one place to start. She positioned the cursor on the Google search line and typed in just one word.

Autism.

Nine

TRACY MANAGED TO ENTER AT THE BACK OF THE THEATER ROOM and find a seat without catching Holden's attention. The room held about a hundred seats and a small stage—large enough for rehearsals, but nothing more. Tracy tried to still her nerves. This was Holden's first day observing the class, and Tracy was grateful Mrs. Bristowe had granted her permission to join him. If Holden had an outburst, no one could help calm him better than she could.

She'd been looking forward to this all weekend. She'd even called Dan and told him the news. "Holden's going to watch the drama class rehearse!"

Dan's silence lasted a little too long on the other end. "Is that a good thing?" He didn't sound sarcastic, just confused.

Tracy tried not to let his response dim her enthusiasm. "Of course it's good. This is a mainstream class. Holden's therapists think that maybe by listening to the music, he might open up a little more."

"Really?" Dan must've been outside, because the wind howled in the background. "Well, then … that's great." An awkward silence slid between them. "Tell him I love him."

Their conversation didn't last long. Dan told her the shrimping still wasn't that great. Not like the salmon back in July. Storms continued to batter the region, and his pneumonia wasn't quite cleared up. By the time she told him good-bye and that she loved him, her excitement was almost forgotten.

But now that she was here and the class was about to begin, Tracy could hardly sit in her seat in very back of the room.

Holden was sitting a few rows in front of her, but still far removed from the rest of the class. Tracy was glad Holden couldn't see her. She didn't want anything to distract him from this opportunity. She was still convinced Holden wasn't merely noncompliant last week in the gym. He was dancing. Maybe in his mind he was dancing with his little friend Ella from so many years ago. He heard music in the drama class, he stopped to listen, and then a little later, with the music still in his heart, he must have started dancing.

What was so unusual about that?

She'd called that morning to tell Mrs. Bristowe her thoughts, but the woman wasn't as quick to get behind the idea. "Dancing is a very social activity." She had that tone again, the one that said her training was superior to any instinct Tracy might have as Holden's mother. "Holden is at the place on the autistic spectrum where socialization is out of the question. He is completely noncommunicative."

They'd been over this. "Except for the PECS cards."

"Yes. Except that. But it's a lot of therapy and distance from using an occasional PECS card … to understanding and wanting to dance. Turning circles, flapping … this sort of repetitive behavior is typical for students with autism."

Tracy didn't want to argue with the woman or waste time trying to explain Holden. Here, in the drama room, she could see for herself. She still had a couple of minutes, so she prayed silently for her son. *Dear Lord, this is a chance … a beginning. Maybe the miracle I've been asking for is going to start here. Right now. So please, Father, be with Holden and don't let him act out. If he does … well, if he does he won't be able to stay. So please, Lord … please help him.*

Take your position and stand firm … see the deliverance I will give you, my daughter.

The answer was strong and breathtaking. It filled her heart

and soul and mind and left her anxious with hope. God was in this. She could feel Him working. Now she only had to stand firm and watch the next hour play out.

Mr. Hawkins walked to the front of the room and announced that they were going to work again on the Belle song. "This time, we'll break into parts according to your character. You all know your roles. The baker, the bookseller, Belle ..." He looked around and discouragement colored his expression. "Where exactly is our Belle? She should be here by now."

Tracy studied the drama teacher. He seemed tired, like he doubted the kids' ability to truly pull off a great production come spring. She let the notion pass. This wasn't about the drama class, it was about Holden's response to the music. She looked at the back of his light-brown head. His hair was darker than it had been when he was little, and it held just the slightest curl. But he wore it short so most of the time it was impossible to tell. Tracy willed herself to look beyond his hair and handsome face to the boy locked inside. What was he feeling right now? Fear excitement wonder? Like always, she had no idea other than the obvious. He was here, and he had chosen to sit quite a distance from any of the other kids.

Before Mr. Hawkins began to play, a beautiful girl ran into the room and took a seat in the front row. She pulled out her script, looked back at Holden and smiled. Tracy couldn't see Holden's reaction, but he seemed to look at the girl. Straight at her.

Mr. Hawkins raised an eye in her direction. "Thank you for joining us, Belle."

"Sorry." She sounded truly upset with herself. "I had to go home for my script."

"For the last time," the teacher held her gaze.

"Yes, for the last time," she repeated, clearly sorry. She kept her attention straight ahead and opened her script.

Tracy wondered if the pretty girl was the one who had pushed for Holden to have a place in the class. Why else would she have looked back at him when she first arrived? Tracy made a point to thank the girl, whoever she was.

The students rose to their feet as the music began. The girl who'd arrived late started the song, her voice clear and beautiful. Tracy smiled. She would do a wonderful job as Belle, Tracy had no doubt. Other kids sang out their lines on cue, and Tracy was impressed. If this rehearsal was an indication, the spring production would be very professional.

Tracy could only see the backs of the students, but she was so caught up in the song she almost forgot about Holden. As she turned to him, what she saw brought tears to her eyes. It was just like she'd thought. Holden was no longer sitting in the chair looking at the ceiling or studying the empty desk in front of him, the way he might've been. He was on his feet doing something that seemed absolutely appropriate given the music that surrounded them. To anyone else, it might've looked like Holden was turning in circles, acting out even. But Tracy knew better.

Holden was dancing.

AFTER A FEW TIMES THROUGH THE SONG, MANNY GAVE HIS drama kids a quick break. He was happy with the way the earlier song sounded, and it was time to do something new. He never taught the musical numbers in order. He taught them according to difficulty. "Belle" was a tougher piece for an ensemble group, so he wanted to follow it with a less time-consuming number. Hence, "The Mob Song" would be next.

He needed another copy of the rehearsal schedule. One for the mother of Holden Harris—so she might know when he should and shouldn't observe the class. So far the boy had done pretty well. A little circling in place, but nothing too disruptive. Manny left the room and went to his private adjoining office.

He found the schedule and stopped at the window. Two stories and a hundred yards away, the football team was practicing. An announcement this morning had told the students of Fulton High that their football team was undefeated. "You can be proud, students. Very proud," the principal told them.

Manny squinted at the horizon. Just once—this one last time—he dared hope for something that hadn't happened in his tenure at Fulton:

A musical that might make the students feel the same way.

He drew a long, slow breath and stared at the rehearsal schedule in his hand, the one he'd printed for Holden. Something about the kid's presence breathed new life into him. New meaning. If his downtrodden drama program could help a kid like Holden Harris even a little, then his efforts here had to be worth something. Today, while the kids were singing "Belle," Manny even allowed himself to feel enthusiastic. Hopeful. The students sounded wonderful. So maybe they had a chance after all. Word could get out. The school would get behind them. It might happen.

Once, a long time ago, Manny had been a praying man. But his prayers hadn't done a thing to help him with his divorce or the custody battle that ensued. His girls lived in Los Angeles with their mother. They got his eyes, he liked to say, and her arms. He hadn't prayed much since then. But today, with Holden turning circles in the back row, Manny had the impulse to talk to God. A stronger impulse than he'd felt in two decades.

He closed his eyes. *Okay, Lord ... here I am. Remember me? I'm the guy you forgot about.* A pang of guilt sliced through Manny's heart. *Okay, maybe you didn't forget about me. But it felt that way. It definitely felt that way.* He struggled with the words. Lecturing never gave him reason to pause. But talking to God ... This was harder. *Anyway, Lord, ... there's this kid, Holden Harris. He loves hearing us rehearse, and I was wondering if ... if maybe*

You could help him out. He has autism, God. So maybe if the music could unlock that little world he's in, maybe he could be a different person. He felt guilty asking for the rest, but he'd committed himself. If God was really listening, Manny might as well give Him the whole list. *One last thing, God … we won't have a drama department next year if the kids don't come watch. I don't know how to make that happen, but I have a feeling You do. So if You could work that out, I'd be … well, I'd be amazed. Because both those things are going to take a miracle. Thanks for listening, God. Sorry it's been so long.*

He opened his eyes. "Amen." He took a final look out the window and returned to the classroom. "Back to your seats, loquacious youngsters." This was Manny's schtick, his *modus operandi.* Talking as if he held a Shakespearean doctorate degree. "Enough waxing on. Enough intermingling."

He caught the kids' giggles and strange looks at his word choice. He loved that, challenging them to break out of their limited vocabulary. They loved it, too, even though it had been awhile since he'd cared. He looked out over the classroom. "Remain standing." Thirty kids packed the first few rows in front of him. "How many of you know the music from this show?"

Just about everyone raised a hand.

Manny caught a quick look at Holden. He was standing, but he wasn't turning circles anymore. His eyes were focused on the ceiling just above the classroom window, but every so often Manny swore he looked at him. Like he was taking instruction, same as the other kids.

"You are now villagers. I'd say Village People, but some of you would harken back to the seventies and think I intended something I did not. So you are villagers and you fear the Beast more than any creature you've encountered." He flipped through the score on his piano. "As you sing this piece, I will hear fear and determination in your voices. Determination driven by fear. If

I do not hear this, we will sing it again. We will sing it well into December, if necessary, but we will find our inner fear."

The music was dark and foreboding, with a pulsing rhythm intended to replicate the stomping feet and slamming farm implements that would give the number its ferocity. Manny enjoyed this, getting his students to feel the emotion in the music. "Okay ... five ... six, five-six-seven-eight!"

For the most part, the students began on the same note, but they were hardly in unison. Manny stopped playing and faced them. He paused for a long beat. "Who can give me the definition of *ensemble*?"

Ella was the first to raise her hand.

"Very well, Miss Reynolds. What is the definition?"

"It means all the parts acting together as one." She gave a slightly embarrassed shrug. "I did a report on it last spring."

"Exactly." Manny was impressed. The question had often stumped his previous casts. Usually they figured *ensemble* meant everyone other than the leads. Whoever was left. Manny paced in front of the students. "All parts acting as one." He stopped and looked pointedly at the second row. "That means each word sounds like it's being sung by how many people?"

The cast looked at each other, and then sort of mumbled. "One."

Manny shook his head and rubbed at his right ear, as if he wasn't getting a clear read on their answer. "How many?"

"One." This time their answer was both loud and together.

"Very good." He walked back to the piano. "Begin again." He counted off the song and they came in much stronger. Their diction would get crisper in the coming months, but he could at least understand the lyrics. "Louder!" he shouted over the music. "Make me feel your fear!"

Their voices grew, and with the sound came the terror that was essential for the song. "It's a beast, he's got fangs, razor-sharp ones …" Then as quickly as the song built to a crescendo, it died off.

Manny stopped playing and turned around. Half the students were no longer singing, but watching Holden Harris. He was pacing up and down the side of the classroom, his hands folded near his chin, elbows straight out, pumping his arms like he was either in pain or very nervous. He looked like an anxious mallard duck, and a few of the students were giggling at him.

The thrill of the afternoon leaked from him like air from an old tire. "Okay, people. Back to your places." He looked at Holden's mother. "Can you help us?"

Tracy Harris was already making her way to her son. But Holden didn't seem to hear her. He stopped suddenly and plummeted to the floor. Then, in a display more impressive than almost anything the jugheads out on the football field could pull off, he laid into a series of perfect push-ups. Absolutely perfect.

A few of the girls backed up. "That's weird," one of them whispered loud enough for the class to hear. "Why's he doing that?"

"I don't know." Another one chuckled quietly. "But he's good at it."

There were seven minutes left in the hour, and Manny wanted desperately to get the students back on track. But now half the guys were gathered around Holden, counting off his push-ups the way they might in some locker-room machismo contest.

Holden's mother stooped down, her hand on his shoulder. After a few seconds, she stood and politely motioned for the kids to step back, to leave her son alone. "He gets nervous. He needs his space." Her tone carried an apology. "He'll be okay. Just go back to singing."

Manny was able to get the kids rallied for one last go at the "Beast" song. Holden tired of the push-ups and sat in his chair at the back of the class, breathing hard. His arm muscles pumped up, his blue eyes deep and intense, the kid was better looking than any of the guys in the cast. *He'd be perfect for the Prince,* Manny thought. The role of the transformed Beast was a brief, but important part. Manny hadn't made up his mind which of the ensemble would play the role—mainly because no one looked like a prince.

No one except Holden Harris.

If he weren't autistic, he could play the part based on his looks alone. But that wasn't going to happen, because already Holden was working his wings again. Flapping and nodding his head. Discouragement flooded his mind and heart. Why did he bother praying? They weren't going to get a miracle for the drama department, and not for Holden Harris, either. Manny embraced his disappointment. It was at least familiar. And no harm done about the hope he'd felt earlier.

He hadn't really expected prayer to work, anyway.

Ten

ELLA COULD HARDLY WAIT FOR THEATER CLASS TO END. She planned to pull Holden aside and tell him the amazing truth — they had been friends when they were little! And how great it was that they'd found each other now! But when Mr. Hawkins reached the loudest, most intense part of the song, Holden lost it. Ella watched him, helpless to do anything. Holden still didn't know who she was, after all. She couldn't just run up and expect him to find comfort in anything she might say or do.

Even now when he had to be tired from his push-ups, Holden was still moving his arms. He looked intent on something, like he was trying to accomplish a task. Ella glanced back at him several times, but Holden never let his eyes meet hers. He looked a few inches to her right or left, but never straight at her. *It's his autism*, she told herself. A lack of communication, little or no eye contact, repeated behaviors. They're locked in a world all their own, one website had explained.

Throughout the last painful minutes of class, Mr. Hawkins had everyone sing again, but a few of the guys still laughed at Holden.

"Maybe he wants to play the Beast," some kid whispered. "Next thing you know he'll do a transformation."

"Hey," Ella kept her voice low. She tapped the guy's shoulder hard enough to make a mark. "He's autistic. Give him a break."

The kid looked like he wanted to cuss at her. But he thought twice and closed his mouth. Again Mr. Hawkins stopped the song.

"Really, people? Is this your best?" He gave a sad shake of his head. "If so, this is a grand disappointment. If we cannot gather ourselves for five minutes the outcome will be dire indeed." He waited until the room was silent. " Now let's hear the fear in your voices. One voice. Ensemble." He began playing the piano. "And... begin!"

The cast was able to sing the song through without distraction this time, and when Mr. Hawkins dismissed them, Ella gathered her books and turned toward Holden. A few kids approached him, as if they intended to welcome him or ask him a question. But no matter who came close, Holden didn't respond. He looked like he might jump up and sprint from the room. But instead he hung his head, gripped the edge of the seat, and rocked hard—so hard he had to catch himself from falling to the floor a couple times. Eventually the kids gave up and went their own ways.

Ella bit her lip and took a step closer. *Here goes*, she told herself. *He'll remember me and then maybe he'll feel safe talking.* She took a deep breath, but just as she was about to walk up, she saw a familiar-looking woman in the back of the room. Ella hadn't noticed her, but she must have been here throughout class. The woman was ... Ella let out a quiet gasp. She was Holden's mother—the woman from the pictures in her parents' scrapbook.

Ella looked at Holden, but he was still staring at the floor, still rocking. So far she hadn't told anyone about her discovery—that she and Holden had been best friends when they were little. Her mother had come home too late, and the house was empty most of the next day. Ella still hadn't told her about winning the part of Belle for the spring production. She certainly wasn't ready to ask about Holden. Not until she talked to Holden's mother.

She had a feeling she would get a more honest answer from her.

Her research on autism had taught her a lot, but most of all it taught her what the old photographs already made clear. Holden wasn't born with it. Some kids showed signs of autism all their lives, from birth on. But others, like Holden, reached a certain age around two or three and then started slipping away. *Regression*, the websites called it. There were all sorts of therapies people tried with their autistic kids—therapy dealing with nutrition and motor skills, intellect and behavior. Even something called *chelation therapy*. Some of it worked, some didn't, according to the experts.

But most of the time, after a person was diagnosed with autism they never made their way back or found their way out of the world inside their mind. Never managed to unlock the doors and step into the real world again.

Mrs. Harris was talking to Mr. Hawkins, so Ella moved in closer to Holden. He wasn't rocking as badly now, and he was sitting a little straighter in his seat, even though his eyes were still downcast. She walked up slowly, so she wouldn't scare him. The other kids were all gone now, and the hallway outside the classroom was almost empty.

She practically tiptoed the final steps as she closed the distance, then she lowered herself carefully into the seat beside him. She set her backpack down without making a sound and turned to face him. "Holden?"

He stopped rocking, and looked straight ahead.

Bluest eyes I've ever seen, she thought. Shining and innocent and full of light. They caught her off guard and for a moment Ella wasn't sure what to say. Like it was enough to get a glimpse of his eyes and know at least one comforting thing—the private world of Holden Harris must be a beautiful place. Otherwise his eyes couldn't have looked like that.

She tried again. "Holden?" Her instinct was to reach out and touch his shoulder, connect with him somehow. But she remembered autistic kids need their space. She was probably close enough. The right words escaped her, but she tried anyway. "Holden?"

He didn't move, didn't look up at her.

"Holden … My name's Ella. We used to be friends a long time ago. When we were two or three years old."

Holden rocked ever so slightly, his eyes still straight ahead. Then he reached into his backpack and pulled out his stack of flash cards. With a quick, jerky motion he sifted through them, almost like he was desperate to find the one he wanted to show her. Finally, he pulled out the card. The edges looked newer than some of the others. Then, without looking at her, he showed her the card. Almost the way a magician shows a card to an audience when he wants everyone to see it, but no one to touch it.

This time the cards had a heart and music notes on it. Beneath the drawings were the words "I love music."

"I thought so." Her heart melted. She kept her words kind and gentle. "I thought so. That's why you want to be in the class, right?"

Holden slipped the card back in with the others and mixed them up a little, sifting through and sorting them as if he had a system to the way he liked them organized.

She couldn't stop thinking about the card he'd shown her. He loved music. She wanted to hug him, but again she stopped herself. At least he was opening up, even a little. She kept her hands to herself, folded on the edge of her knees. "Do you remember me, Holden? How we used to play when we were little?"

He turned his head just enough that she was certain he had heard her. But before he could look at her the way he'd done that day in the cafeteria, his mother walked up and stood on Holden's other side. "Hi." She smiled at Ella. "You must be the one who helped Holden?"

Mr. Hawkins had already left the room and returned to his adjacent office. Ella's heart pounded, but she stood and smiled.

"Yes, ma'am. I asked Mr. Hawkins to let him have a seat in class, if that's what you mean."

"It is." The woman looked older than she had in the photographs, weary and worn out around the corners of her eyes. But she was still pretty. Thin with nice cheekbones and long brown hair she wore in a simple ponytail. She put her hand on Holden's shoulder. "We need to get Holden to his after-school therapy." Her smile was warm and sincere. "Thank you again, for caring about Holden."

Ella wasn't sure if this was the time, especially if Holden and his mother were in a hurry. But she couldn't hide the truth another moment. "Do you recognize me, ma'am?"

Mrs. Harris did a double take, her smile still in place. As she did, Holden began mixing through his cards once more, his pace practically frantic. His mother didn't seem to notice. Either that, or she was just used to Holden's odd behavior. Mrs. Harris shook her head. "You do look a little familiar." She allowed a nervous laugh. "Look at me, I haven't even introduced myself." She held out her hand. "I'm Tracy Harris, Holden's mother."

"Yes, ma'am." She took the woman's hand and didn't break eye contact. "I'm Ella." She paused, letting her first name sink in for a moment. "Ella Reynolds."

The shock hit Holden's mother in stages. First with a sense of surprise and excitement, and then just as quickly her joy turned to a deep kind of sadness. She squeezed Ella's hand softly and released it as her smile dropped off. "Ella ..." Her eyes grew watery. "I never thought ... I wasn't sure I'd ever see you again."

Ella nodded. There were tears in her eyes too. "What ... what happened? To you and my parents?"

Mrs. Harris started to say something, but her chin was quivering. Instead she glanced at Holden, who was still looking through the cards. Suddenly he pulled one card from the deck and showed it to his mother, and then to her. It was the card from the other day, the one with the eyes on the top, and the words that said "I see."

"You *see*, Holden?" Mrs. Harris reached toward him like she might put her hand on his shoulder, but then she seemed to change her mind. She crossed her arms instead. "What do you see?"

Ella had to wonder. "He showed me that card the other day, the first time I noticed him watching our theater class." She didn't want to say so, but maybe the card had something to do with her, maybe even that Holden had remembered seeing her somewhere before. "So why? What happened to the four of you?" Ella lifted her eyes to Holden's mother again, and her look needed no explanation.

A horrifying feeling spread through Ella's chest. "Holden?" her voice was barely a choked whisper. "Is that why ... why you and my parents ..."

Tears pooled in the woman's eyes now. "It was a long time ago, Ella. People change." She glanced at her watch. "I'd love to talk sometime. But we have to go."

Ella nodded, her throat tight. "Yes, ma'am." She barely brushed her fingertips against Holden's elbow. His arms were solid, like those of the football players she hung out with. All the push-ups, probably. Ella's heart felt broken over the sad possibility that hung between them. "Holden ... I'm glad I found you." She dabbed at a single tear as it slid down her cheek, and she uttered a sound that tried to be more laugh than cry. "I'd like ... to be friends again."

Holden didn't say anything. He only slid the *I see* card back into the deck, and placed the deck in his backpack once more. Mrs. Harris reached for Ella's hand and gave it a brief squeeze. "Thank you ... for helping Holden. He really does love music."

Ella felt the corners of her lips lift a little. "I know."

Mrs. Harris directed Holden toward the door, and then she

took the lead into the hallway. Ella watched, unmoving, her eyes on Holden. Then, before he left the room he did something that made her believe in the impossible, in the miracle Holden Harris still needed.

He turned and looked at her.

Not through her or near her, but straight into her eyes. Never mind that as he turned around he started flapping his arms again. In that moment Ella knew whatever had happened in the past, why ever their parents' friendship had ended, and however far gone Holden had slipped into his private world of autism, this was only the beginning. Because Holden's eyes were not only full of light and innocence as he looked at her, but they shone with something that hadn't been there before.

A pure and childlike hope.

Eleven

HOLDEN COULD HARDLY WAIT TO PRAY FOR ELLA. THIS WAS why they'd found each other, after all. Because God had answered his prayers and finally ... finally, He had brought back Holden's very best friend. *Dear Jesus, thank You for a perfect day! You let me be part of the theater group, and You let me pray when everyone tried to kill the Beast. He's a nice Beast, Jesus. You know that. No one needs to kill him. You made the drums go away, and You let my mom be here with me to sing along. But most of all, You brought back Ella! Thank You for doing that, God. I know You love me ... your friend, Holden Harris.*

A feeling of joy and satisfaction worked through Holden's body. He replayed his conversation with Ella as he and his mom walked to the car. She'd come up to him, just as sweet and kind as she was in the movie every day. "Holden?"

Yes, Ella?

Her smile was the one he liked best of all. "Holden, do you remember me?"

Of course I do. I wasn't sure if you'd remember me. He liked the way she smelled. Like flowers and fresh soap. *We used to run through the fields and dance around and around and sing, remember that?*

Ella remembered. Of course she remembered.

Our favorite song was 'Jesus Loves Me.' Remember that too?

A song filled the air around them and it was rich and deep and full and it spread across the room and out the windows, so that the whole school and then the whole city and even the whole world could hear it. This time the song had words, and it was their song. The song he and Ella used to sing. *Jesus loves me, this I know ... for the Bible tells me so ... Little ones to Him belong ... they are weak but He is strong.*

Even the kids leaving school and getting on the busses could hear the song, and everyone was singing. Well, most of the people. Some kids didn't know the words yet. And he and Ella began to dance around the room and his mom watched from the side, the way she used to watch from the side when they were little. Only Ella's mom wasn't there, but somewhere ... somewhere she was singing. Holden was sure.

And then he and Ella talked about the play. *Beauty and the Beast.* Holden had to pray a lot when the people wanted to kill the Beast, because the Beast was so nice inside. He looked mean, but his heart was kind and gentle. And not everyone looked the same on the outside. Some people were like Gaston and they looked nice on the outside but on the inside they were locked up and sad. Some of the kids at school were like that. A lot of them wore the football shirts.

They were like Gaston.

But the Beast was a good person. If Holden could be in the play he would want to be the Beast, very kind like the Beast. But maybe he'd rather be the Prince at the end. Because the Prince looked on the outside the way the Beast was on the inside. Sometimes people couldn't see the inside of a person unless they liked the outside of a person. Because they hadn't learned to hear the music yet.

His mother was saying something, but the music changed and grew loud again, the strings and keyboard swirled together for the most beautiful sound. Holden sang along, dancing down the hallway and praying for Ella. This was a song he hadn't heard much of before, but maybe it would end up being his favorite song of all. Because this song was the one he'd been waiting for all his life.

A song called "Maybe Ella and I Will Have a Second Chance to be Friends."

He told his mom about it the whole way to therapy.

Twelve

ELLA COULDN'T FOCUS ON HER ALGEBRA HOMEWORK. SHE hadn't gotten all the information she wanted from Holden's mother, but the woman's eyes told her enough. The friendship between their families must have fallen apart when Holden began showing signs of autism.

The longer Ella thought about the possibility, the angrier she became. Sun streamed through the window and splashed rays of light across the kitchen counter. Ella pushed her homework aside and walked upstairs to the scrapbook that held the pictures of Holden and her. Again she sat on the floor and flipped through the pages and this time she found other pictures, enough that the reality of the situation became clearer than before. Their families weren't only good friends. They were best friends.

She found a photo where she and Holden were sitting next to each other in a double-seat swing. They had their arms around each other's shoulders and in their free hands they held what looked like chocolate ice-cream cones. Smears of chocolate were on their cheeks and shirts, and the image eased Ella's anger. She looked at Holden's little face, the way his eyes pierced the camera, the joy in his expression. The photo had definitely been snapped mid-laugh, and it was clear Holden was happy and healthy.

The longer Ella looked into Holden's three-year-old eyes the more she was convinced: what she saw there was still a part of Holden today. That fun-loving child was inside him somewhere. She'd seen a glimpse of him, when he looked back at her before he left with his mom.

From downstairs came the sound of a door opening. "Ella?" It was her mother.

Her anger burned quick and intense once more. She didn't answer. Instead she stood and tucked the scrapbook safely beneath her arm. Ever since she saw the pictures of Holden and her for the first time she'd known this moment was coming. Now, after getting a glimpse of what must've separated the two families, Ella was furious with her mother. She padded downstairs into the kitchen in time to see her mom drop her gym bag and grab a glass from the cupboard. She turned as Ella walked closer. "Oh, hey, honey. How was school?"

Like you care, she wanted to say. "Fine." She folded her arms in front of her, the scrapbook clutched to her chest. Her mom was drinking her water now, looking at her reflection in the glass door of the built-in microwave. Her Botox was completely worked into her face, so her forehead was once again very smooth. Too smooth.

"That's it?" Her mom kept her eyes on her reflection, pressing her fingers against the skin beneath her eyes and above her brow. "Just fine?" Then, as she finished her water, she laid her hand against her flat stomach, like she was checking that the workout had paid off. She glanced at Ella, and then back at her reflection.

Ella leaned her hip into the kitchen counter. She wanted to scream. Everything about her mom seemed phony and shallow, and for what? Her dad was too busy trying to hold onto yesterday. Meanwhile they'd lost friends like the Harris family. So what did the fake tan and Botox and endless workouts really amount to?

"Okay." Her mother turned and put her hands on her waist. "You're quiet. Is there a reason?"

If she didn't say something, she would explode. "I have a question." She spoke each word deliberately and controlled.

Her mom raked her pale blonde hair off her face and exhaled, more weary than tired. "Ask it."

"Why did we stop being friends with the Harris family?"

It took a few seconds for the realization to register on her mother's face. At first she opened her mouth like she might ask which Harris family, or for Ella to explain herself better. But then her lips closed again and she lifted her chin. The defensive tone in her eyes cast an awkward feeling over the moment. "You mean Holden Harris' family?"

"Of course I mean Holden Harris." She released a short burst of air. Then she thrust the scrapbook in her mother's direction. "The Holden Harris who was my best friend when I was three."

"Don't shout." Her mom filled her glass of water again. She was stalling, for sure.

"I'm not shouting, I'm asking."

"You're asking very loud."

"Because I want the answer." Ella was definitely shouting, but she was too angry to admit it. She lowered her voice. If she pushed any harder, her mom would walk away without another word. It happened all the time.

Her mother took a long sip of water and set her cup down on the black granite countertop. "What ... you were bored, so you looked through our photo albums?"

Of course I'm bored, she wanted to scream. Instead she remained motionless, desperate to keep control. "You didn't answer me. Why did we stop being friends?"

"We went different directions." She studied her manicured fingernails and barely glanced at Ella. "That happens sometimes." She crossed her arms and leveled an impatient look at Ella. "You had lots of friends growing up." The defeat was back in her tone. "How come you don't ask about them?"

"Because Holden goes to my school." There. She'd said it. She watched again while the surprise hit.

"He goes to Fulton?" For the first time that afternoon, her

mother looked concerned about something other than herself. "So he's ... he's in regular classes?"

"Of course not." She tried to keep the acid from her voice. "He's autistic."

A momentary sadness filled her eyes. She looked down at the stone floor. "I know that." She sounded embarrassed. "I just thought ..."

Ella let the statement hang uncomfortably for a long moment. "So ... answer my question." Ella waited until she had her mother's full attention. "Why did we stop being friends with them?"

The doorbell rang, and her mother snapped into action. "I told you, Ella." She jogged off toward the front door, and Ella watched her go. Her mother wasn't wearing much, as usual. Tight dance pants and a bright blue tank top. Whatever delivery guy was at the door, he was bound to be surprised.

But instead of returning to the kitchen, Ella heard her mother bound up the front stairs.

Ella thought about letting the issue slide. She already knew the answer, right? Holden slipped into autism, and the Reynolds family slipped out the back door. What else could it be?

But this time she wanted to hear the words from her mother's mouth. Or maybe from her heart. She wanted to see her mom squirm and dodge the issue until she had to face the fact that maybe Holden wasn't the only one to go through a change fifteen years ago. Ella darted up the stairs, every step intentional. Being the wife of a major-league baseball player came with certain expectations, right? Her heart hurt as the reality became even clearer. The daughter of Randy and Suzanne Reynolds couldn't possibly have an autistic friend. How would that look?

Ella walked quickly down the hall and flung open the door of the upstairs office at the west end of the house. Her mom was sitting at the computer on Facebook. Once again Ella wanted to scream. What was she doing here, when she knew Ella wanted to talk? Before she could say anything, she noticed something. Her mom had tears on her cheeks. Ella hesitated. She searched her heart and found a scrap of compassion for her mother. "Did you think," her tone was kinder than before, "I wouldn't come looking for you?"

Her mother's teary eyes looked defeated. "I thought we were finished talking."

"We weren't." Ella kept her tone level. "I still want an answer. About Holden Harris." She took a step closer, her eyes never broke contact. "Why did we stop being friends?"

Her mother opened her mouth like she might rattle off a quick answer, the kind she'd given Ella earlier. But then she dabbed at her eyes and stared out the window. A sigh came from what sounded like a very deep place in her soul. A forgotten place. When she turned to Ella again, her eyes looked softer than they had in a long time. "We loved Holden. He was ... the sweetest little boy." Her smile didn't take the pain from her eyes. "We used to talk about the two of you growing up and ..." She swallowed and gave a brief shake of her head. "None of us saw it coming, Ella. It was like ... like we lost him overnight."

Ella had guessed as much from the photos. "So why?" She lowered her voice, sad for Holden and all he'd lost. "Why aren't we friends?"

Her mother's shoulders sank. "He stopped laughing and singing. Before we knew it he wouldn't dance or play or run around with you the way he used to." Her sorrow became more of an embarrassment. "He started ... stacking things and lining up your toys when we were together."

"So you separated us?" Her anger was back, and Ella had to work to contain it. She tossed her hand in the air. "Because he was quiet? Because he stacked things?"

"It bothered you, Ella." Her voice held more passion than before. "You would ... you would walk up and tap his shoulder and try to get him to run around and play with you or sing with you." She pinched the bridge of her nose and closed her eyes, as if she might not finish her explanation. When she looked up, her expression was hard again. "I don't expect you to remember. But after a few weeks he wouldn't even ... he wouldn't look at you. He wouldn't talk at all. Not a word." She leaned back in her chair. The past was written into her expression. "Sometimes you'd cry because you wanted him ... the way he used to be."

Ella didn't understand everything about autism, but she knew this much: therapy had to start immediately. The earlier the better. "So I could've stayed in his life. We could've been part of the solution for him, but instead ... what? It was too awkward, Mom, is that it?"

Her mother pushed back from the desk and stood, clearly finished with the conversation. "Yes, it was awkward." She crossed her arms. "Is that what you want to hear? Fine. We stopped being friends because it was too awkward." She met Ella's gaze head on. "Now, if you don't mind, I'm taking a shower."

She stormed past Ella and down the hallway to her room. Ella didn't move. She looked out the window and let the truth settle. She and Holden had been best friends, but when he changed, when autism set in, things became awkward and her parents went their own way. Everything beautiful about the little boy Holden once was had been dismissed and forgotten. The way a person might forget about losing a favorite camera or a cell phone.

She reminded herself to breathe.

What ways might Holden have come out of his private world years ago if only the two of them had been allowed to continue their friendship? Certainly their connection was a strong one back then. That sort of childlike bond would've been very help-ful in reaching him, right?

Ella took hold of the back of the computer chair and looked at the Facebook page still up on the screen. Her mother spent way too much time here, looking for old friends and even guys she used to date. It was her way of escaping, Ella figured. Even on an afternoon like this when she knew Ella was trying to talk to her. Instead she'd come up here and gone looking for what? For a way to—

Her heart suddenly slammed into a strange rhythm. She stared at the Facebook search window, not believing her eyes. "There's more to the story," she whispered. "Isn't there, Mom?"

There must have been. Because for all her mother's attitude and avoidance of the topic of Holden Harris, she clearly cared. She'd been crying, after all. So maybe the loss hurt more than she wanted to let on, or maybe the separation was more difficult than she was leading Ella to believe. Something must have touched her mother's heart or moved her, and this new understanding reduced Ella's anger to an ocean of sadness. For the first time in a long time, Ella didn't hate her. Because she and Holden weren't the only friends who had lost each other fifteen years ago. The words in the search window told her that much.

Her mother had typed in "Tracy Harris."

Thirteen

TRACY MISSED THE OLD HOLDEN MOST ON FRIDAYS.

The last day of the school week, there was always some reason for her to stop by Fulton High before school let out. Paperwork in the office, or a meeting with his teacher, a quick consult with the school therapist. Something. And on those days Holden would skip the bus and drive home with her.

Tracy punched the clock in the Walmart break room and left an hour early, the way she did most Fridays. *I'm picking my son up from school,* she told herself as she walked to the back of the crowded parking lot and slipped behind the wheel of her '98 blue Honda. And for the entire ride she felt like any other mother, doing what any other mother might do. That was the problem, of course. The reason she missed him so much on Fridays.

The other days when he stepped off the special bus there was no denying her reality. Holden battled the private world of autism, Dan battled the Alaskan seas, and Tracy battled her despair before God on her knees—begging Him every day for a sign or a breakthrough. Praying that one day Holden might look at her or talk to her, or that she might hug him again or hold his hand. She missed so much about Holden, but maybe she missed his touch most of all. The touch of his smile and sparkling eyes, the feel of his little-boy, long-lost self, safe in her arms. The brush of his fingers against hers when they crossed a parking lot or read a book at night.

So much missing that usually she did better to keep herself grounded in the moment.

But on Fridays she couldn't stop herself from thinking back.

The craziest thing was that he and Ella had reconnected. Tracy had been sure they would never see each other again. There were dozens of high schools in the greater Atlanta area. Only God could've led them both to Fulton. Like some divine plan being set into motion, one Tracy couldn't fully comprehend. But something miraculous was happening, because not only were they at the same school, but Ella had actually befriended him. Gone to bat for him with Mr. Hawkins, the drama teacher. And she'd done that before she even realized they'd been friends when they were little.

Suzanne Reynolds' daughter … What were the odds?

The light turned green and she kept up with traffic. There were no harsh words or terrible fights to mark the death of her friendship with Ella's mother. It had died like so many other relationships, friendships tossed in the trash heap of life. The more days passed, the more it didn't seem right to call or contact Suzanne. And Suzanne must've felt the same way because the phone never rang.

A breeze brushed against her damp cheeks as she turned left on the main highway that led to Fulton. *Dear God, sometimes I still miss her. I miss her the way I miss Dan and Holden and everything that used to be.* She blinked back fresh tears. Most days she was too busy at Walmart or working with Holden to think about all she'd lost. But times like this the burden felt like more than she could bear. *Please, God … speak to my former friend and her husband … and thank You for her daughter.* She wiped at another tear. Ella had grown up to be very kind. Like her mama used to be when they were in high school. Seeing Ella made her miss Suzanne the way she hadn't missed her in more than a decade. She sniffed and tried to gather her emotions. She couldn't cry as she pulled into Fulton High. She had a meeting with Holden's PE teacher today. *So, Father, I don't know what You're doing, but I can feel it. Something's happening. Isn't that right, God?*

My precious daughter, I am doing a new thing! Now it springs up ... do you not perceive it ... I am making a way in the desert and streams in the wasteland. I love you, my daughter ... you are not alone. Not now or ever.

Tracy almost pulled off the road. The answer was so clear, so strong she caught herself glancing in the rearview mirror. As if the Lord were sitting in her backseat. This was the verse she'd prayed so many times over Holden. The verse from Isaiah 43:19 about God making a way through the wilderness, streams in the desert. But never — not once since she'd been praying that verse — had she ever felt the Lord speak it back to her.

Until this moment.

She was almost at the school, driving the last few miles on the highway, when a memory came to life, crisp and real from fifteen years ago. She and Suzanne were sitting in the Reynolds' kitchen drinking sweet tea and Suzanne was saying something about the lemons being better than usual and suddenly from the backyard came the sheer limitless laughter of Holden and Ella.

The memory was so real and vivid she could smell the lemon, feel the cool glass in her hand. And she could hear the laughter of their children, ringing in her heart and soul and mind, like it did that long ago day.

She and Suzanne had both turned at the sound. "Can you hear it?" Suzanne smiled and the future shone in her eyes. "That's the sound of the years flying by." She snapped her manicured fingers.

"You're right." Tracy looked at their children. "Tomorrow they'll be seniors in high school."

"They're the most precious kids." Suzanne stared out the window again. "Look at them."

Tracy looked. She was still looking, because the picture

burned a lasting impression in her heart. Holden was holding a handful of dandelions as he chased Ella around the swing set and he was catching up to her, and Ella was spinning around and they were both laughing. Always laughing. And Tracy had her best friend across from her and the sun was shining on the faces of their kids and Holden was saying, "Half for you because you're my Ella! Okay? Half for you."

And Ella was holding out her hands and telling Holden, "Okay, give me half!" Holden was separating half the dandelions out and placing them in Ella's little fingers and she was grinning at him and raising her blonde eyebrows and squealing, "Now what, Ho'den?"

"Now throw 'em!" And Holden was tossing the flowers in the air and Ella was joining in and doing the same, and they were giggling as the flowers rained down on their heads. A few dandelions stayed in their hair, and the sight hit a funny bone in both of them, because they were picking the flowers up off the ground and placing them on their heads until they looked like a couple of hippie kids. And they were laughing and laughing until they fell down on the ground, two towheads in a mix of dirty knees and dandelions.

The laughter faded first, and then the image of their faces, and finally like every other wonderful moment from the past, the memory slipped back to yesterday where it belonged. So much missing. So very much missing. Tracy ran her fingers beneath her eyes and dried her cheeks. But she could do nothing about the ache in her heart. Because yesterday only loaned out memories like that at times like this — when Tracy was doing the most absolutely normal thing.

Driving to Fulton High to pick up Holden.

Fourteen

ELLA WASN'T SURE, BUT SHE HAD A FEELING HOLDEN REMEMBERED her. He still flapped his arms in drama that afternoon, but he didn't do any push-ups. Once when Mr. Hawkins told them to take a break, Ella looked back and caught him staring at her. Not past her or through her, but right straight at her. The way he had a couple times now. His eyes shifted almost as soon as she saw him, but that didn't change the fact. By the end of their third full theater rehearsal together, Ella had a hunch about Holden.

He understood more than the kids at Fulton thought.

Class had just ended, and Ella went to Holden's side. He was still sitting, rocking slightly and looking into his backpack. Probably for his flash cards. "Holden, I'm Ella. Do you remember me?"

He stopped rocking and sat straighter. Then in a way that was slow and clearly on purpose, Holden lifted his eyes to hers. This time he didn't look away. Instead he stayed connected to her and she didn't have to hear his answer. His blue eyes told her everything she needed to know.

Yes, he remembered her.

She wasn't sure how, because fifteen years was a long time. But Holden remembered, she was sure. And standing there in Mr. Hawkins' class with the rest of the kids already gone, somehow Ella remembered him too. Not just from the photos in the scrapbook she'd brought to school that day. But him ... the heart behind his amazing eyes.

There was a noise behind her, and Ella turned toward the

sound. Holden's mother stood in the doorway. Their eyes met, and the woman smiled. But still her eyes were sad. "Hi, Ella."

"Hello, ma'am." Ella looked back at Holden. He was staring at his backpack again, the connection they'd shared a moment earlier gone. "I was just ..." Her eyes found Mrs. Harris. "I was talking to Holden. I asked if he remembers me."

"Hmmm." She didn't seem in a hurry like the other day. "You're very nice to him, Ella. I pray all the time that Holden will find a friend. I pray for a miracle for him. I just didn't think ..."

"You didn't think it would be me." Ella heard the disappointment in her voice. If only her mother would've given Holden a chance. She managed a quick smile. "I talked to my mom about it."

The news seemed to hit Mrs. Harris, because something changed in her expression. But only for a brief moment. She came closer and Ella sensed a peace within her. Like she had a special kind of faith or trust, maybe. She stopped near Holden's other side. "You asked if he remembers you." Her smile softened and she looked at Holden and then back. "He does, Ella. I know he does."

"I think so too." Ella let that thought settle in her heart for a few seconds. "He looked at me. Just before you got here." In the corner of her eye she saw Holden digging through his backpack. He pulled out his cards and started shuffling them."

"*At* you?" Mrs. Harris hesitated. "You mean in your direction? Near you?"

"No." She smiled and the slightest laugh came from her. A happy laugh. "He looked right at me. He's done that a few times. That's how come I think you're right, that he remembers me."

Holden pulled a card from the deck and then changed his mind and stuck it back in the middle somewhere. Mrs. Harris looked at him and then settled carefully in the seat beside him. "Holden, are you glad you found Ella?"

Ella expected him to look up again, but he kept sorting. After half a minute, Mrs. Harris stood again and lowered her voice. "He ... he hasn't looked right at me in a long time. And he hasn't talked since his diagnosis."

The truth hit Ella like so many fragments of broken glass. She squinted, not believing. Holden didn't look at his mother? How hard would that be, living with someone who didn't connect with you? But then ... he had definitely connected with her.

Once more Holden snagged a card from the deck and this time he held it up for them to see. Both Ella and Mrs. Harris leaned a little closer. The picture was a heart and music notes and what looked like an old-fashioned radio. Beneath it the words said, *I love this song.* As he held it, Holden didn't look at either of them. His eyes were cast upward to a distant empty spot on the classroom wall.

Ella's heart fell. When Holden looked at her, for that short time he was like any other kid. No, he was better than the other kids, because his eyes were kind and sweet and full of hope. Like no one had ever been mean to him or picked on him. Like all things in life were possible. But now ... She looked at Holden's mother. "What song?"

A helpless look warmed her expression and she smiled briefly at Holden. "I'm not sure. The music cards are new." She sighed. "Holden loves all music. It was very nice of you, Ella. Getting him in this class."

"He tried to stop and watch. When his class walked by." She shrugged one shoulder. "I thought he should be allowed to stay."

"Well ... thank you." She looked deep into Ella's face, like she was seeing the little girl she'd once been. "You were such a sweet child. I always thought you'd grow up to be a nice girl." She touched the side of Ella's face and a hint of tears sparkled in her eyes. "I wasn't sure we'd ever see you again."

Ella remembered the scrapbook. "Just a minute." It was on the other side of the classroom, and she hurried to it. Ella hadn't expected this, the connection she felt to Holden's mother. So far the woman seemed to be everything her mom was not. She talked easily, and she had a transparency about her that was refreshing. Nothing about her looked fake or bought or injected. Maybe it was the praying she'd talked about earlier. Something Ella's family never did.

As Ella returned with the scrapbook she watched Holden slide the song card back into the deck and begin sorting through them more slowly. Ella sat in a chair a few spots down from him. She motioned for Holden's mother to join her. "I brought this from home."

Mrs. Harris took the chair next to her. She stared at the scrapbook and gently touched the cover. "I remember this. We each made one." She turned her eyes to Ella. "Your mother and I."

Ella ran her hand over it. "This is how I found out about Holden. I was going to show him." She glanced at Holden. "But maybe it's too soon."

"Yes." The woman looked back at Holden. For a moment. "Maybe."

Ella opened the front cover and flipped past the first few pages to the place where the picture spreads started including the Reynolds family. "I like this one." She pointed to a photo of Holden and her sitting cross legged in what must have been the Harris' backyard. They were facing each other, blowing bubbles. "We had fun, didn't we?"

"All the time." She smiled. "I remember that day."

Another page and Ella stopped at a picture of the moms, their heads tilted in toward each other, goofy smiles on their faces. For the first time since Ella figured out her connection to Holden, something occurred to her. The friendship between Holden and her wasn't the only one lost. "You and my mom … Were you close?"

Mrs. Harris sat back in her seat a little. "Yes." A quiet sigh came from her. "Very close."

Ella studied the photo. "How did you meet?"

Holden's mother leaned close again, her eyes on the picture. "First day ... freshman year of high school. She was in three of my classes, and we both wore the same blue shirt. By the time the last class rolled around, she told the teacher we were twins." She smiled, the memory a happy one. "We were best friends from that day on."

Ella enjoyed the story, but ... best friends? She felt her smile drop off. "Like ... best, best friends?"

"Have you seen your parents' wedding album?" Holden's mother's expression was tender.

"A long time ago." She pictured the way her parents were lately, never together, never talking. She blinked, willing away the memory. "The pictures are in our china cabinet. I don't think anyone's looked at it for a while."

"I was your mother's maid of honor." She touched the faces beneath the plastic. "And she was mine. Our husbands were friends because of us. But your mother was ... Well, she was like a sister." The shiny look was back in her eyes, and her smile all but died. "I still miss her."

"Why don't you call?" Ella hated that her mother had lost a friend like Mrs. Harris. "I mean, was it that bad? How it ended?"

"We didn't fight. Nothing like that."

Holden was rocking again, not too hard or too fast, but something was irritating him. Ella wished she knew what. Did he understand them? Did he remember when their families were friends and their mothers were like sisters? She looked straight at Holden's mother again. "It was because ... because things changed, is that right?"

Mrs. Harris sighed. "The other day ... I wished I had more time with you so I could find out about your parents, how they're doing." She looked past Ella toward the cloudy afternoon sky. "There were days after our friendship died, when I wasn't sure where the pain of losing Holden stopped and the pain of losing your mother began. It all blurred together for the longest time, especially after Holden's dad left."

"Oh." Ella felt the disappointment. "You and Holden's dad are divorced?"

"No." Her smile was sad again. She glanced at Holden. If he was listening, he didn't show it. His rocking slowed down, and he was sorting through his cards again. Mrs. Harris looked at Ella. "Mr. Harris is a fisherman in Alaska. We hardly ever see him."

"Oh." Ella thought about that. She felt sorry for Holden, that his dad wasn't around. He'd lost much over the years, and now that they'd talked this much, Ella wanted to know the reason, wanted to hear it from Mrs. Harris. "So what happened? To end things between our families?"

"It was a long time ago, Ella." She didn't look like she wanted to place the blame on anyone. "Holden's diagnosis was hard on all of us."

"In what way?"

Once more the woman hesitated, as if she were weighing out how much to say. "Your mom worried about Holden … how his autism might affect you. Whether it was a learned behavior or contagious or when it might go away."

Ella could picture her mother that way—worried more about Ella becoming autistic than the fact that they'd lost Holden.

Mrs. Harris clasped her hands and stared at them for a few seconds. "I was … Well, I didn't handle your mom's questions very well. I got defensive." She raised one shoulder. "Things became distant between us, I guess."

"I'm sorry." The story was coming together. Ella imagined that eventually her mother's uneasiness about Holden drove a wedge between them bigger than Georgia. And Mrs. Harris could only defend Holden for so long without coming across as argumentative.

"I remember when it happened ... when the break became permanent." Mrs. Harris looked back at the spread of photos again. "Our phone calls were less and less frequent, our times together less often. Your parents took you to Florida for spring training." She smiled at Ella. "Your dad was hitting better than almost anyone in the league back then."

"He hasn't hit like that for a long time."

"Yes ... well, anyway, when your family came home from Florida a month later, neither of us made contact. Weeks became months ... months became years." She paused for a long time. "Five Christmases later, I took my high school yearbook outside on the back porch on Christmas Eve and cried for an hour."

Ella wasn't sure what to say. She wanted to ask the woman why she never made the first call if the loss hurt so badly, or how come the guys didn't make contact if their wives weren't speaking. But she didn't want to seem rude or too forward. She was surprised Holden's mother had opened up this much.

"I always hoped ..." She blinked back tears, her eyes lost in what seemed like long-ago memories. "No one ever took her place."

"But she wasn't sympathetic... about Holden." That part Ella could talk about.

"Some people are put off by autism ..." She brushed her fingers beneath her eyes and looked at Holden. He still held onto his cards, but he was staring out the window now. Mrs. Harris sighed. "Autism is ... Well, it's complicated."

Complicated? Holden's mother didn't have to be so kind. The real reason was ugly and hard to say out loud. Especially in front of Holden. Yes, Mrs. Harris could've placed the first phone call after so much time slipped away. But Ella's mom was the one put off by a child with autism. She could've been sympathetic or helpful or at least a listening ear for what Holden's mother must've been going through. But instead she'd run the other direction.

And how sad was that? Ella felt tears in her own eyes. She looked at the photographs again. "I don't really know my mother. She never told me about you. About your friendship."

The truth clearly hurt. Mrs. Harris struggled with her next words. "I guess some things are too sad to talk about." Her words seemed as much for herself as for Ella. This detail—her mom never mentioning this special friendship—created still more pain. It had to. Holden's mother took a deep breath and forced a bigger smile than before. "I'll say this. Your mother and I had a lot of fun." She nodded, as if she were assuring herself. "She could always make me laugh. We hung out every day. We fell in love around the same time and married our husbands the same year. Hers was a spring wedding, mine was summer."

Ella listened, amazed. She was learning more about her mother from a woman she'd just met, here in an empty classroom, than she'd ever learned before. She could've sat here all night if it meant hearing more details like this.

"A few years later ... we had our babies—just three months apart."

"Who's older?"

"He is." Mrs. Harris smiled sweetly at Holden. "Right, Holden?"

His eyes didn't focus on either of them, but he had a hopeful look. The one where all the world was ever right and good. At least that's how his expression seemed. Ella looked at the clock on the wall. "Mrs. Harris... I need to go." She had to pick up her mother's cleaning before four o'clock. It was on the list of 'this-is-the-least-you-can-do-for-me' jobs her mother asked her to do once in a while. "I want to hear more sometime, if that's okay?"

"Definitely." Again the woman's expression was sweet. "You'll have to come over. I have a home movie of the two of you."

Ella's heart warmed. "I'd like that. Thank you." She stood, and Holden's mother did the same thing. "I have a question."

"Anything." Mrs. Harris went to Holden and put her hand gently against his back. Her touch must have acted like some kind of signal because Holden put his flash cards away and stood. He swayed a little, but he didn't flap or look agitated.

"Can Holden be in the school play?" She'd been tossing the idea around since the first time she saw him stop at the classroom door. "I mean, if I can get him in?"

A nervous look tightened the woman's face a little. She cast a brief look at Holden. "He would love it, I really believe he would." Cold reality dimmed her enthusiasm. "But I'm afraid… It's a stretch for Holden to be an audience member." She didn't want to hurt Holden's feelings. That much was obvious. "You know what I mean?"

Ella had to agree, but she wasn't willing to give up. "Maybe if he's enrolled in the class, at least then if he wants to he can have a part. In the ensemble."

Holden's mother patted Ella shoulder. She looked like she might tell Ella she was wasting her time, but then she lowered her voice to a whisper. "Even if God gave us a miracle and Holden could stand on a stage without acting out, we couldn't afford the fees." She hugged Ella and placed her hand along Ella's face. "But thanks for caring about him." She smiled, searching Ella's face. "You're such a nice girl, Ella. You turned out exactly the way I knew you would."

Holden was waiting patiently, but he was turning in tight circles and his hands were folded near his chin again.

"Here," Mrs. Harris dug through her purse and pulled out a pen and a notepad. She jotted something down. "This is our phone number. I meant what I said about stopping by. Call any-time." She led Holden toward the door. "Do me a favor, Ella?"

The moment was ending too soon. She still wanted to talk to Holden and show him the scrapbook. But they were out of time. "Anything."

"Tell your mother … I said hi."

"I will." Ella gave her a final smile. Then she gathered her things and headed out the other door, the one closer to the senior parking lot. On the way out, she nearly ran into Michael Schwartz. "Oh … sorry."

"It's okay." He stepped to the side and hesitated. He was car-rying a music case—probably for his flute. The one the football players had made fun of that day in the hall. His shy eyes con-nected with hers. "What you're doing for Holden… that's really cool."

Ella was touched. Was it getting around school that Holden was hanging out in the theater room? "How did you know?"

"I keep an eye on him." A crooked grin tugged at his lips. "Those jerks would kill him otherwise. That's what they want. A school where no one's different or quiet, you know? Everyone has to be just like them."

Regret splashed like ice water against her face. Michael was one of the few kids at Fulton who stuck up for Holden Harris. But who stuck up for Michael? She pictured him cornered by Jake and his buddy and she could hear their voices again. *"You play the flute … most gay kids do … freak … this is our hallway …"* How could she ever have fallen for a guy like Jake?

"You play the flute, right?" She had never asked before, never allowed herself to be interested in a guy like Michael who was so different from her crowd.

"Yeah." He lifted his case a little. "I'm in orchestra. We're working on the spring production."

"Right. I thought so." That meant Michael would be part of

rehearsals in the weeks leading up to the April performance. "I'm in the play."

"Yeah." A quiet laugh came from him. "You're Belle. Everyone knows that."

This was the most she'd talked to Michael Schwartz in the three years they'd shared at Fulton. He was a year younger, but she'd seen him around a lot — in the halls or at lunch. In a number of her classes. But she'd never talked to him like this until today. In some ways, her handicap was worse than Holden's. What excuse did she have for not talking? For picking and choosing whom to speak with?

Ella hid her frustration with herself. "That'll be fun. Rehearsing together next semester." She wanted to find out more about Michael, where he went after school and who his friends were.

"Sure." He looked away and then back at her, like he was ready to move on. "I guess."

Ella's heart sank. Michael didn't believe her, not after three years of her pretending he didn't exist. She wanted to ask him to stay for a few minutes, but, then, she couldn't make up for the past all at once. She'd lived in the confines of her own shallow, mean-spirited crowd, unwilling to connect with kids outside her group.

But never again.

She stared at the ground for a moment, searching for the words. "Hey...".." She held tight to the straps of her backpack, shame reducing her voice to half what it had been. "I'm sorry about the other day. The way Jake and those guys treated you." She gave him an apologetic look. "They really are jerks."

"Yeah." He shrugged, but his smile faded. "It's okay. Guys like that always get what they want." He started walking, his fingers gripped tightly around the handle of his flute case. "See you, Ella."

She watched him go, not moving. "See ya, Michael." It was

the first time either of them had acknowledged that they knew each other's names.

Ella started slowly toward her car, the sun on her shoulders. Michael was right. Guys like Jake always got what they wanted. They were practically heroes because they could throw a ball or catch a touchdown pass.

But maybe this was the year Holden and Michael would finally have their turn. Michael could play the flute for the orchestra and maybe Holden would be in the play somehow and all the school would come to watch. LaShante would help her get everyone excited about it. That was possible, right?

Ella smiled at the picture in her mind. As she reached her car, she was consumed by a single thought: Mrs. Harris was praying for a miracle. So maybe miracles really did happen, and maybe they happened when people prayed. People like Mrs. Harris. If that was true, then a miracle might be in the works. For Mrs. Harris and Ella's mother and Holden. Even for Michael.

For all of them.

She thought about what Holden's mother said. Even if he could control himself enough to stand silently in the back row of an ensemble, there was no money to pay for theater fees. But there could be no miracle if Holden wasn't at least given a chance. This year the cost was nearly two hundred dollars—a hurdle Ella had never thought about. As she walked to her car she knew what she was going to do after she picked up her mother's laundry.

She was going to figure out a way to get Holden's drama fee.

Fifteen

HOLDEN PRACTICALLY DANCED HIS WAY TO HIS MOTHER'S CAR. It was like that after dancing with Ella, the way he'd danced with her in the classroom a few minutes ago. Round and round they danced, and they laughed and the beautiful song kept playing. His favorite song called "Maybe Ella and I Will Have a Second Chance to Be Friends."

Across the campus everyone who walked by was happy and kind and Holden smiled at them, but he also prayed for them. Every single one. Because some of the kids were kind on the inside but their outsides were all trapped up. Kids like the football players and some of the girls who laughed a lot. So Holden prayed the kindness inside them would come all the way to the outside where people could see it and feel it. More kindness would be good for everyone at Fulton High.

Isn't this the greatest day ever, Mom? He smiled at her as they reached the car. *What a nice talk with Ella.*

"Get in the car, Holden." His mom opened his door. "Don't forget your seatbelt."

I won't, because seatbelts make us safer. He heard the music swell, heard the strings kick in. When his mom climbed into the car he grinned again. *I'm glad you were there with me and Ella. I think all of us should be friends again — not just me and her.*

"Ella says you looked at her today." His mom kept her eyes straight ahead because she was driving them home.

Of course I looked at her. Holden felt better than he could remember feeling. *I told you, I can see Ella. And she can see me.*

We could always see each other. Through our eyes and into our hearts.

His mom was saying something, but Holden couldn't hear her as well because of the music. Pretty, soothing music without a single drumbeat. Holden took a deep breath and rested his head against the back of the seat. This was the best day in his whole grown-up life. Because Ella remembered him, and because Ella and his mom found each other again too.

His favorite part was when Ella took out the photo album. "I brought this to show you, Holden," she told him.

That's very nice of you, Ella. He saw the pictures in the book and he felt like singing. *I remember those pictures,* he told her. *Those were great times back then. Especially blowing bubbles.*

"We had fun, didn't we?" Ella looked happy, like she enjoyed remembering.

Yes, we sure did. We would play all day and laugh and sing. Right, Mom?

"All the time." His mother smiled. She was always smiling. "I remember that day."

Holden remembered too. *Ella, you were so funny that bubble day. You wanted to blow a bubble that would reach all the way to heaven, and you told me to blow one that big too. So we both kept trying and trying, and finally your eyes got really happy and you told me, "There! I think Jesus could see that one!" And so we leaned back on our hands and the grass was soft around our fingers and we watched the bubbles go up to Jesus in a long line. One bubble, then two, then three, then four ... Remember that?*

"Yes ... of course I remember." Ella said a lot more stories from when they were little, but she said them with her eyes. Her words were quiet because the music was louder. Pretty wind sounds and keys and flutes filling the classroom, filling Holden's heart and soul, and it was his favorite song. The flute was nice because it was Michael's kind of music. Michael played the flute.

I love this song, Holden told Ella and his mother. And they smiled because one thing was sure. His mom and Ella heard the music.

His heart was so full and so happy, that on the drive home Holden couldn't go another minute without praying. *Dear Jesus, thank You for this special day, and for that great time with Ella and my mom. I can see it all spread out like a painting, dear God. Me and Ella and Michael in the spring play. And my mom and Ella's mom will be friends again and everyone will love everyone and no one will ever be mean, because the kindness will be unlocked all throughout Fulton High. That will be a special time, Lord. And I know it will happen because look how wonderful today was, and that was from You. All good things are from You. Be with Ella and talk to her. Sometimes I think she needs to hear Your voice. Thanks, Jesus. I know You love me. Your friend, Holden.*

Yes, everything was going to work out because now he was going to be in the play with Ella, which was only because he'd been praying about it every day. God answered his prayers today when Ella brought it up. "Can Holden be in the play?"

And Holden's mom said, "Sure, he can be in the play. He'd be wonderful in a play. Also he loves *Beauty and the Beast.*"

So that settled it.

He and Ella were going to be in *Beauty and the Beast* together, which was one of their favorite videos when they were young. He remembered because his mom always sang the song about home being where your heart was. And that was true, but not true every single time. Right now his heart wasn't exactly at home.

In Mr. Hawkins' drama class, there in the eleventh row near the back of the room between the tall music chart with the picture of the piano keys and seven octaves and twenty-five chord types by four positions, which made a total of one hundred chords per octave with twelve different roots, which meant 1,200 chords per octave or 8,400 possible chords … There between the music poster Holden liked and the window with six squares in it, two seats from the right and four seats straight behind Ella, just beneath the classroom clock with the quiet ticking ...

That's where his heart was.

Sixteen

ELLA PAID FOR HER MOTHER'S CLEANING AND DROVE TO THE opposite side of the parking lot. She needed a quiet place to focus. Calling her dad wasn't something she ever did, so this might catch him off guard. She pulled out her phone and found his number. It wasn't listed in her favorites.

As the ringing started, Ella felt her heart slide into a strange rhythm. *Why am I so scared?* She closed her eyes, shaded her face with her free hand. *He's my dad, after all.*

He answered on the last possible ring, right before the call went to voice mail. "This is Randy."

His words hurt, but she didn't let the pain linger. So what if he didn't recognize her phone number. She wouldn't have recognized his, either. They barely talked when they were in person, let alone on the phone. "Dad ... it's Ella."

"Oh, hey, sweetheart." He sounded rushed, anxious to get the call over with. "What's up?"

In the background Ella heard a bunch of voices. "Randy, get off the phone ... Come on, you got a girl on the line or what?"

"Back off, Simmons. It's my daughter, okay?" The clang of weights rang in the background.

As pathetic as the guy's comment was, her dad's response proved one thing. He cared enough to acknowledge her as his daughter. The thought touched her long enough for her to pause.

"Ella." He sounded distracted. "Honey, I'm busy. Is there an emergency? Something you need?"

Love and conversation, a father who cares what I'm involved

in, she wanted to say. She gritted her teeth, fighting her anger. "I need money. Two hundred dollars." That was the amount for Holden's production fees if he were allowed in the play. She hated that this was the only reason she had to call him, but there was nothing else to say. She wasn't about to explain the situation with Holden.

"Honey, you're breaking up. Something about dollars?" More laughter in the background. "Can you talk a little louder?"

Suddenly Ella felt like a fool. What was she doing, trying to reach her father? What was the point? She no longer wanted to be on the phone with him another minute. However she would get the money for Holden, it wouldn't be through her father. No, this was her decision … She needed to pay for it herself. She would work, maybe. But whatever she did she would pay for it herself. Her father was waiting. "Never mind, Dad. I'll talk to you later."

"I'm sorry." He sounded defeated. Again the noise in the background was almost louder than his voice on the line. "I still can hardly hear you. We'll talk tonight, okay?"

Tears stung at her eyes. "Okay." She hung up before saying good-bye. He wouldn't hear her anyway.

She was halfway home before it hit her that she couldn't exactly get a job. She didn't have time with the play rehearsals and her homework. But before she could get too discouraged, another thought hit her. She could sell something. Her iPod Touch, maybe. She'd paid twice that for it, right? One of her friends would buy it for half price for sure.

Ella lowered the phone to her lap. Her hands were shaking but her heart soared with possibility. She could hardly wait to go through her phone and call her friends tonight. The kids at Fulton had money … Someone would buy her iPod tomorrow. Then Holden could officially be in the theater production class.

And from there, Ella believed with her whole heart, anything could happen.

Suzanne wondered if she might fall to the floor and die. Not because the shock was so great—it wasn't. But now Ella knew, and the embarrassment made it hard for her to draw a breath. She could do everything possible to stay young. She could starve herself into size-2 jeans and tan her body and get her Botox. But she couldn't force her husband to come home.

Their marriage was becoming little more than a sham.

A memory came to mind, one from twenty years earlier. When she accepted Randy's offer of marriage, her mother celebrated with her for a few minutes, and then pulled her aside. With her father and her siblings in the next room, her mom lowered her voice and gave her two pieces of advice: stay thin and look the other way. "Randy's going to the big leagues one day, mark my words. Professional athletes have a different standard."

Suzanne was sickened by her mother's supposed wisdom, so she'd turned to Tracy Harris—her best friend at the time. Her best friend ever. Tracy was a Christian, and because of that, Suzanne and Randy had started believing in God too. A year before their weddings, the couples began attending church together, and Suzanne felt something changing inside her. Randy felt it too—at least that's what he said. He even connected with the church's men's group, and for a year every Monday he and Dan Harris would make the trip to church to help each other stay strong in their faith.

Tracy's advice when Suzanne married Randy was far different from her mother's. Suzanne remembered every word, because for the first few years Tracy's wisdom worked like a charm. *Love God first, and your husband second. Remember to compliment him, because if you don't, someone else will. And always give a hundred percent. If you both do that, you'll be covered on the days when someone slips a little.*

But what exactly was a little slip? Randy's attention came when he was hitting well, when he was making the sports page and winning games. The less he played, the less he stayed home and spent time with her. Lately he didn't know she was alive—no matter how she looked.

The first four years, Randy might hit a slump and check out at home, but later he would explain himself and apologize. For a while everything would be good between them again. Especially the year he and Dan went to the men's Bible study. But times like this, when Suzanne was completely honest with herself, she had to admit that neither she nor Randy ever committed their lives to Christ. They talked about making such a decision, and they watched other people do so. But there was always a reason why they didn't. They needed more information … they wanted to be sure … they didn't understand everything the Bible taught …

But after the break in their friendship with Tracy and Dan, the Reynolds stopped going to church and what faith they once had grew cold as quick as winter. At first it didn't seem to matter. Randy was playing well, and they moved to New York, where he flourished. But even then he wasn't a great communicator, especially when the team lost or he didn't get the hits he wanted. Suzanne figured if she tried harder—worked out more, kept a better tan, stayed young looking—he would want to be home more. But now, with rumors that the Braves weren't going to resign Randy, he acted like he didn't have a wife or a home or a family whatsoever. Like he was back in college in some fraternity, always hanging out with the guys … lifting weights with the guys … going out with the guys …

Suzanne wasn't sure how much more she could take.

She walked into her room, shut the door, and locked it. Maybe it was time to admit the whole truth. Not only was her marriage a sham, her entire life had become nothing more than a charade. She had the feeling lately that people saw her as a joke, the pro athlete's wife trying to find her way back to twenty-nine, while her husband chased a dying dream.

Better to go out on top and retire than submit himself to the media scrutiny and degradation of being cut. Especially after once being so good, so highly chosen. So while Randy fought to find the game inside him, she worked overtime trying to attract his attention. But where had that gotten her?

She went to the bathroom and stared at her reflection. No matter what she did to her face, she couldn't find the look she'd had when she was younger. It wasn't her skin tone or the shade of blonde in her hair. The problem was her eyes. They were older than her years and nothing she tried ever seemed to help. It wasn't only Randy who was becoming washed up; she was right there with him. A terribly sad joke.

Her options looked back at her from the mirror. She would call him, of course, and ask him to come home earlier — the way she did once a week or so. But he would stay late, like always. He'd head to the bar and talk shop and come home after midnight. Then he'd walk through the house like she was invisible. If there were other women, Suzanne never heard about it, never found proof. She figured he was probably faithful — for the most part, anyway. But their marriage was nothing more than a formality. No wonder over time her confidence had eroded like a sandy shoreline during a storm.

Suzanne blinked, but she couldn't shake the dead look from her eyes. She would lose, of course. She was Randy Reynolds' wife. It was her identity, where she found her value and self-worth. And of course there was the other benefit: Randy's salary. Even sitting the bench, the money was always good. It kept her in Botox and beauty shops, salons and spa visits.

Disgust filled her eyes as she stared at herself. What had she allowed herself to become? A slave to her image and reputation? A woman who had sold her soul for a six-figure bank account? And now that Ella had found Holden, how hard would she have to work to avoid seeing Tracy? The loss of their friendship was awkward, and Suzanne had no idea what to say to Tracy if they ran into each other again.

But the part that made Suzanne feel worse about herself was that after twenty years of marriage, she actually lived by the horrific advice her mother had once given her. Her mother had been gone for thirteen years now—lost to a quick bout of lung cancer. But if her mother could see her now, she wouldn't feel sorry for Suzanne. She'd be proud of her. By her mother's standards, Suzanne was getting along just fine because she was still thin.

And she had absolutely mastered the art of looking the other way.

Seventeen

THE DAY FIGURED TO BE STORMY AGAIN. DAN WAS READY, hunkered in at his station on the shrimping boat. The catch had been great lately, enough that Tracy could catch up on bills and pay the therapists. Maybe even enough to pad their account a little. That way they'd be covered for the next time the seas were too rough to fish, or a boat broke down or equipment gave out.

"Looks like another monster." One of the other fishermen planted himself beside Dan and stared at the distant horizon. "Blackest clouds I've seen."

"At least we're ready." Dan remembered the last storm like this. He'd almost lost his life. He would be more careful this time, quicker to get the shrimp load up and put away, quicker to get below deck. Last week a storm had come in so hard and fast, they never made it out to sea. But this time they would have to ride it out; there wasn't enough time to get back before it hit. Besides the shrimp were plentiful right now. The bigger the catch, the greater the cut. That was the motto for guys like him.

Dan felt his cell phone vibrate in his back pocket. He kept it in a double plastic Ziploc bag, tucked in the driest part of his pants. They didn't always get service, but when they did he liked at least having the possibility of calling home. He tried to call home a few times a week, but it had been four days. The work had been almost around the clock.

"Take your call." The guy beside him returned to his station. "But keep it short. We'll need everyone on their game."

Dan figured they had ten … fifteen minutes tops. He pulled

the phone from his pocket and slipped it from the plastic bags. It was Tracy. He got a call from his parents once a month or so, but otherwise he didn't keep in touch with anyone from his old life. The life before Holden became autistic. He clicked the right button and held the phone to his ear. He covered his other one with his free hand, otherwise the wind wouldn't have let him hear a thing.

"Hello?" The mist from a rough wave brushed across his face.

"Hi." She sounded hurt, distant. "It's been awhile."

"Yeah," He dried his hand over his eyes, ignoring the sting of salt water. "Sorry … it's been busy."

"Hmmm." She allowed a brief silence. "It sounds really windy."

"A storm's coming." Dan squinted at the encroaching black clouds. "Probably seems like I'm always saying that."

"It does. But you're all right?" Concern replaced the distance in her voice. "You've got cover?"

"I'm fine." He closed his eyes for a long moment. It felt great hearing her voice. He wasn't due to go home until Christmas — three months from now — but he wondered if maybe he wouldn't head back sooner. "I miss you."

"I miss you too." An edge of excitement filled her voice. "Dan … I called because … Well, God is doing something with Holden. I'm serious."

Dan opened his eyes and stared at the rough seas surrounding their old ship. "What do you mean?" He kept control of his emotions. Holden never made significant progress.

"Earlier this week … he found Ella." She paused and the wind made it hard to hear her. "Ella Reynolds, Dan. They found each other at Fulton High."

Dan felt his enthusiasm dim. Finding an old friend was one thing. Seeing God work in Holden's life was something entirely different. "The Reynoldses." He heard his voice go flat. "It's been a long time."

"There's more to this …" Tracy began to explain how Ella had been drawn to help Holden, and how because of her Holden was allowed to sit in on rehearsals for next semester's spring musical. "And that was before she knew who he was, that we'd known each other back then."

Dan would've liked to think Holden told her. Certainly Holden remembered Ella. He watched the video of the two of them every day, after all. For more years than Dan could remember. But that wasn't possible.

The wind was blowing harder now, the storm about to bear down. He couldn't talk long, but he raised his voice so he could be heard. "How'd she make the connection?"

"A scrapbook. She was going through family pictures and saw a bunch with all of us together. Holden's name was in the caption, I guess, and Ella put it all together."

Dan remembered the tension between the families after Holden's change. "Is she… like her mother?"

Tracy hesitated. "She's like Suzanne used to be. She's kind and genuine and she wants Holden to be in the spring play. It's *Beauty and the Beast*."

Unless there was something Tracy wasn't telling him, the idea was outlandish. "Holden can barely sit through a single class without doing push-ups."

"He's trying. I have to believe his is making a difference."

"That's not the point." Dan needed to get off the phone. The storm was going to engulf them any minute. "He struggles, Tracy."

"I know that." Some of her enthusiasm faded. "But Dan, Ella said Holden looked at her. Straight into her eyes."

It was the first detail that came with even the slightest glimpse of hope. He gripped the edge of the crank in front of him. "Good. Has he looked at you? Or his therapists?"

"Not them. And not me lately." Her tone made it clear she wasn't dissuaded by the fact. "But it's a start." She barely took time for a breath. "I don't know, Dan, I feel like something's happening, like God's beginning something bigger than we could imagine."

A clap of thunder shook the sky not far from where he stood. His estimate was clearly off. The storm was bearing down and he'd only been talking eight, maybe nine minutes. "That's good, Tracy. Really. All we can do is keep praying, right?"

She didn't answer right away. "Yes. That's all we can do." Sometimes he could almost see the tears in her eyes at the end of one of their conversations. This was one of those times. "I wish you were coming home sooner."

"Me, too." *Especially now.* Lighting flashed too close for comfort. "Hey, listen. I have to go. I'll call you in a few days, okay?"

Another short pause. "I love you, Dan."

"I lo—" A fast busy signal sounded and Dan checked the phone. They'd lost connection. He slid the phone back into the plastic bags, and then into his pocket again. And suddenly he saw something he'd never seen in his five years at sea.

A wave towering twenty-five feet or more was headed straight for them.

"Rogue wave!" The shout came up across the deck from half a dozen fishermen and deckhands. "Take cover! Rogue wave! Rogue—"

That was all the time they had. The wave should've capsized them, but somehow the captain must have swung the bow just enough so they took it head on. Dan ducked beneath the crank and pushed his body against the side of the ship, grabbing whatever he could. But he was no match for the wave. It ripped him from his hiding spot and for several seconds he had no contact with the boat whatsoever. He thrashed about in the water, kicking and grabbing for any sign of the ship beneath him. The water was freezing, so cold that even if he could get his head above the wave he wasn't sure he could breathe.

How can this be happening again? *God … help me! Please …*

Just when he was sure he was lost, his body thudded hard into a post. Dan couldn't grab it with his hands, so he wrapped his body around it and held tight with his ankles. He still hadn't had a breath, and he knew it was only a matter of time. The blackout would come soon and then death would be quick.

God, if You're taking me home then so be it. I love You and I always have. But Father … if You're doing something with Holden, if You're working a miracle in his life then please let me live. The water swirled around his face and mouth. His lungs were screaming for air. Any second he would breathe in the salty seawater. *Lord, I'll stop fishing, I'll stay home and get a different job. I'll do what You want, Lord. Just please don't let me die without seeing Holden come back. Even a little, God. If he could look at me the way he looked at Ella, I would do anything to live. Please, God … please …*

Dan was just taking his first gasp of water when in a rush there was a tremendous sucking sound and the wave receded. He gasped in one breath after another, choking on the water that had started its way down his throat. What had happened? Was he really alive or was this heaven? He tried to crawl up on his hands and knees, but he was too weak, too spent from his battle with the wave. Instead he lay on the tossing ship, his body bruised and battered.

The captain pushed open the door and shouted across the deck. "Everyone down below. We need a count."

This wasn't heaven. A count meant guys were missing, right? Some of the men fishing beside him had been swept to sea in as much time as it took a single rogue wave to crash in around them. The storm was still just hitting them, the rain just starting in earnest. Dan had been this route before. He needed to get

below deck or in a few minutes they could add his name to however many men weren't accounted for.

He tried to get up again, and fell to his stomach. *Come on,
Dan ... You can do this.* As he lay there he remembered his prayer.
He had begged God to let him live if there was a chance of seeing Holden changed, if he might get even a little of his son back.
And here he was, alive! So that had to mean something, right? He
pictured Holden, going tirelessly through the days, working his
therapy and homework and never seeing progress.

The image of his son's tender heart and courageous spirit
breathed new life, new strength into him.

"Below deck now," the captain shouted. "Don't wait ...
another wave's on the horizon."

Dan pushed himself up on his hands and knees and began
to crawl. He could do this. If Holden could struggle through a
silent world of autism, Dan could make it below deck. It was the
least he could do. He pushed himself, ignoring the splinters slicing into his knees. How many times would he do this? How often
would he nearly lose a battle with the sea before he called it a day
and went home? *Push Dan*, he told himself. *Please, God ... You
spared me once. Help me get below deck. Please ...*

I am a safe tower, my son ... run to me.

The answer gave him another burst of strength. Out here at
sea, a lot of men lost touch with God, but Dan never did. He
could sense the wave looming toward them. As he lifted the hatch
and shoved his body through the hole, he could feel the shadow
of the second rogue wave, coming down on them like some crazy
monster. He hit the bunk area just as the wave smashed into the
ship. He hit his head on the leg of the nearest bed, and he held his
breath, certain the ship was going to flip.

But it didn't.

And though the storm raged and the ship tossed around the
sea, there were no more rogue waves. Dan managed to pull him-

self up onto a bunk where he didn't move for the next hour. He had seen scary waves in his days working Alaskan fishing boats. *Deadliest Catch* was right on; he'd learned that much. But no reality TV show could ever truly capture the sheer terror of being completely and utterly at the mercy of the sea.

He couldn't fight Holden's battles, so what made him think he could battle the Alaskan sea? And what about Tracy's thought that God was doing something in Holden's life? *God ... I give up. I surrender. I'm at Your mercy ...*

Be strong and courageous ... I am with you.

Exhaustion still suffocated him, his ribs still pushed against his sides as his lungs worked to catch up. But as God's words came over him, they filled him with strength and peace — a peace he hadn't known in far too long. What if — after eighteen years — he was simply done fighting? Maybe he should go home for good, find work, and get to know his wife and son again.

He learned later that two fishermen and one deckhand were lost at sea when the rogue wave hit. A series of giant rogue waves had spun off the turbulent seas, capsizing two smaller ships and sweeping their crews and seven additional men into the freezing ocean. The story made headlines across the nation and was all Fox News talked about for days. Dan called Tracy as soon as he had service again. "I'm safe. I wanted you to know," he told her. He could save the other details until later.

He still wasn't sure about leaving Alaska for good, but in the days after the storm, not a minute passed when Dan didn't feel at least a little excited. He had asked to live if God was really doing something in Holden, the way Tracy believed He was. This became more meaningful because Dan was still here, still alive. So that could only mean one thing when it came to his only child, his grown son.

Maybe ... just maybe, Tracy was right.

Eighteen

ELLA SOLD HER IPOD TO JENNY, ONE OF THE CHEERLEADERS, AND took the money to the business office Monday morning. She opened the door and walked up to the counter where Ms. Henley sat. The woman rarely smiled. She had worked at Fulton as far back as anyone could remember. Ms. Henley was typing something at her computer a few feet away. She must've heard Ella walk in, but she took another two minutes before she turned around. She checked her watch. "I'm not technically open for another five minutes."

"Okay." Ella smiled. She clutched the two hundred dollars in her hand. Nothing could take the edge off her enthusiasm today. "I can wait."

Ms. Henley choked out a frustrated sigh. "That's okay." She was heavy and slow moving. She made an exaggerated effort at getting out of her chair. "What do you need?"

Ella set the bills on the counter. "I'd like to pay theater fees for Holden Harris."

The woman raised one eyebrow and gave Ella a wary look. "Holden Harris?" She shook her head. "He's not authorized to take theater. He has autism, Miss Reynolds."

Compassion for Holden increased Ella's determination. "I know about Holden. His mom and I think he might like to be *in* the play, not just watch it come together."

Her nod was slow, sarcastic. "Is that right? You and Holden's mother?" She crossed her arms and leaned against the counter

174

behind her. "Have either of you asked Mr. Hawkins? It's his theater program."

Ella hadn't expected this much trouble. She willed herself to be calm and clear. Her eyes fell on Ms. Henley's nameplate at the edge of her desk. *Roberta Henley, Business Office Manager.* Maybe another tack. Ella took a slow breath. "The drama department needs money, right?"

"Well ..." Ms. Henley practically glared at Ella. "Yes, I suppose so. The theater department is a costly line item for Fulton High."

"So, then ..." She pushed the bills a few inches closer to the woman. "Here's the theater fee for Holden Harris. If he can get on stage and help out, fine. If not, the school can keep the fees." She smiled. "And don't worry about Mr. Hawkins. I'll tell him Holden's covered. Just in case."

"In case of what?"

"In case Holden gets his miracle." She had won! She could sense the victory at hand, and sure enough, Ms. Henley reached for the money. Ms. Henley pulled a few sheets of paper from one of her file folders and handed it to Ella. "We'll need his mother's signature."

"Yes." Ella couldn't stop smiling as she backed toward the door. "She'll sign it today."

The harsh look in Ms. Henley's eyes softened. "Miss Reynolds, I know you mean well." The woman's southern accent was as thick as stew.

"Thank you, ma'am." Ella had been a southerner all her life, and even she struggled to understand Ms. Henley.

"The truth is you're wasting your money, Miss Reynolds. Holden Harris is not going to sing on a stage. The school specialists are still trying to get him to stop flapping his arms." She gave Ella a look that was more pity than consternation. "You can throw money at the boy and wish him a place in the theater group, but that isn't going to change the fact. Holden is autistic, bless his heart. He can't connect with other kids. He will never in a million years stand up on that stage and perform in the spring musical."

"Yes, ma'am. Thank you for your concern." Ella straightened her shoulders. How sad that school officials didn't think Holden could change. What hope was there with that attitude. "Maybe Holden will never stand on the stage and perform with the rest of us. But at least he has the chance." She smiled one last time. "Good day, ma'am."

As Ella walked out the door she felt something so rich and deep and foreign, she had to stop to realize what it was. The feeling was joy—the sort of joy she hadn't felt as far back as she could remember. And she was suddenly grateful she hadn't taken her father's money, because this was the greatest gift of all—doing something for Holden.

SHE DIDN'T TELL MR. HAWKINS ABOUT HOLDEN'S DRAMA FEES that afternoon, but with each passing day, Ella came a little closer to doing so. The reason was Holden, of course. Every drama class she saw little changes in his behavior. Monday she caught him looking at her three times, and each time he held her gaze a little longer.

The next day when she turned around and found him watching her, she smiled and Holden did the same thing. At least she thought he did. He walked around with a slight sort of smile all the time—like he was the happiest kid on campus. But this was different. This time he smiled *at* her.

By Wednesday Holden was able to sit through the entire rehearsal without doing a single push-up, and twice during one of the big musical numbers Ella glanced at him and caught his lips moving silently. Like he was trying to sing the words to the song. That day after class Ella went to Mr. Hawkins' desk. "Do you see it? The change in Holden?"

"Change?" Mr. Hawkins looked up. He was studying the *Beauty* script, making notations in the margins.

Ella hid her disappointment. Maybe she only saw the changes because she was looking so closely. Or maybe she was only imagining them. "You didn't notice?"

"Hmmm … He hasn't stopped rehearsal this week, if that's what you mean?"

"He's following along. Today I looked back when we were singing and both times he was moving his lips! That's got to mean something."

Mr. Hawkins stopped short of rolling his eyes, but his body language managed the same effect. "I wouldn't expect you to be an expert on autism, Miss Reynolds. But you must know that quirky, repetitive behaviors come with the territory. Please … do not try to read too much into the eccentricities Mr. Harris provides during rehearsal time." He looked back at the script. "It's enough to say that the young man enjoys his time with us. Beyond that, I wouldn't try looking so hard."

Ella wanted to tell him that she'd paid Holden's theater fees, but this no longer seemed like the time. She backed up from his desk. "Yes, sir. Thank you for letting him stay with us."

Her teacher put his right forearm on his desk and turned so he could face her. "Can I be frank with you, Miss Reynolds?"

"Yes, sir." Maybe this was when Mr. Hawkins was going to admit to having seen the same changes in Holden. She waited, eyes wide.

"Our brief and fleeting rehearsal time must be about more than Holden Harris' advancements or lack thereof. This is, without question, the most important spring musical Fulton High has ever put on."

"Yes, sir." She hid her frustration. She already knew how much was riding on the play. But far more important was what they might do as a group for Holden Harris.

"Miss Reynolds." The slimmest degree of kindness warmed his tone. "I appreciate your philanthropic efforts on behalf of Mr. Harris, but I need your focus." He swept his arm dramatically to one side. "You are Belle, the ingénue of all ingénues. The quintessential Disney role with the potential to capture your student body and fill every seat in our theater." He paused, his eyes unblinking. "Try to remember that, will you?"

"But maybe if we—"

"Please."

She bit the inside of her lip to keep from arguing. She would need Mr. Hawkins on her side if she was ever to get Holden a spot on the stage. "Yes, sir." She nodded with as much respect as she could muster. "I'll remember. Thank you, sir."

Ella's Friday-afternoon conversation with Holden's mother had become a regular experience, and this time—after Holden's mom signed the paperwork allowing Holden to perform—she shared her frustration. "No one thinks he can perform. Not ever."

"We can't blame them." Again there was a peace about the woman that made it easy to be with her. She explained how autism varies in degrees across a spectrum of affected behaviors. "Some kids have what's called Asperger's Syndrome, or more of a high-functioning autism." Her eyes couldn't hide her sorrow. "Holden is not one of those kids. The teachers—even Mr. Hawkins—are aware of that. So they're only going with what research and evidence typically show. A student like Holden would never have the ability to perform."

Ella learned a lot about Holden during their conversations. Mrs. Harris explained that Holden didn't want to be touched. "It's common for kids at his place on the autistic spectrum." As far as anyone could tell, touch provided too much stimulus for people with significant autism, so that even a brush against his skin could send him into a panic, make him fall to the floor for a quick series of push-ups.

"I try now and then, but I haven't held his hand or hugged him since he was three," Mrs. Harris told Ella last Friday. She blinked back the tears filling her eyes.

"Never?" Ella couldn't imagine such a thing. Even her family still hugged each other once in a while.

"Well... never in the daytime. He's a light sleeper, but sometimes, if I'm quiet, I can slip into his room and sit in a chair by his bed just to be near him. Once in a while I'll touch his face or his hair. But not very often."

For Ella, this was the saddest fact of all — that Holden never let anyone touch him. She'd learned in sociology that touch was incredibly beneficial. She'd read about studies where babies in orphanages thrived or failed in direct relation to the amount of physical attention they received. After that conversation with Mrs. Harris, Ella was convinced that part of the key to reaching Holden would eventually come in the form of touch.

As the days passed, Ella felt herself more drawn to Holden. The whispered words became occasional moments of humming — right on key. Rather than staring out the window, once in a while he'd make eye contact with Mr. Hawkins. He didn't rock as much or fiddle with his PECS cards as often. Changes were happening for Holden, no matter how small, and Ella was committed to helping him. He had been well once; he could be well again. Nothing could convince her otherwise. Still, she decided to wait until Holden improved a little more before asking Mr. Hawkins if Holden could be in the play.

Over the next week Ella was careful to sing a little clearer and deliver her lines with more emphasis. If she wanted to help Holden, she had to start by delivering her best performance for Mr. Hawkins. The approach was better than fighting with him. As he grew happier with her rehearsals, he was bound to see for himself the changes in Holden.

Ella didn't have to wait long. The biggest breakthrough for

Holden came that Thursday—the third Thursday in October—almost two weeks after her meeting with the drama instructor.

The class was singing the final song in the show, the reprise of *Beauty and the Beast*'s theme, when Ella heard a new voice behind her. It wasn't as clear as the others, and it was a little too loud. But somehow the voice was familiar. She turned, expecting to see some new kid in one of the rows behind her. Instead she saw what a few other kids were noticing at the same time.

Holden Harris was singing.

He wasn't looking at any of them, not even her. His eyes were cast somewhere near the top of the room where the walls and ceiling connected. But there was no denying the obvious. Holden was singing right along with them. Ella wanted to stop the rehearsal and celebrate, but she didn't want Holden to stop. Ella kept singing, but she made a little waving motion at Mr. Hawkins.

When she finally caught his attention, she pointed discretely toward Holden. Mr. Hawkins must've heard him singing, too, because their teacher immediately turned his attention to the back of the room and kept it there. His eyes registered his shock, and the rhythm of the song fell off slightly. But he didn't look away even as he continued playing.

Ella wanted to laugh out loud in celebration or run around the room shouting the victory. But she didn't want anything to shut the window that was opening in Holden's mind. So she kept singing and waited until class was over. Then, while she was putting her script in her backpack, she secretly watched while half a dozen kids approached him.

"Hey, man." This from the guy playing Gaston. "Nice to hear you singing." He tried to give Holden a fist pound, but Holden only stared at the floor and nodded. The difference this time was that Holden didn't rock or flap his arms.

Ella narrowed her eyes, studying him. Was she imagining his

response? She watched closer, but each time one of the cast members walked up and told him "Good job" or "You sounded nice" or some other compliment, Holden did the same thing. A slight head nod at the appropriate time.

When the rest of the cast was gone, Ella walked up to him. They had a routine by now. Every day she walked him to his bus—except Fridays, when his mother met them here. Today Holden needed to catch the bus, so Ella didn't have long. She walked up and stood a foot from where he was still sitting. "That was nice, Holden. Hearing you sing."

He nodded, but this time he didn't keep his eyes on the ground. He lifted his face to hers and he smiled. Then he did something that took Ella's breath away. He opened his mouth and began to sing, "Tale as old as time, song as old as rhyme, Beauty and the Beast."

The sound that came from Ella was more laugh than cry, and her hand flew to her mouth. *Don't overreact*, she told herself. *Don't scare him away.* She stifled her excitement. "That's perfect. Just like that." She took a step toward the door. "Come on. You have to get to your bus."

Holden stood and the two of them walked out of the class. Before they left, something caught her eye and she turned back to see something that made her smile almost as much as Holden singing.

From his spot as his desk, Mr. Hawkins had seen the whole thing.

There was nothing unusual about watching Holden climb off the bus that afternoon, no signs that this would be a day Tracy would remember all her life. She agreed with Ella, of course. Holden was changing. Slowly, gradually, he seemed more connected. The hard part for Tracy was that all Holden's connecting was with Ella. So far there wasn't a single difference in the way the two of them spent their afternoons and evenings.

Kate had gone to a friend's house to play, so it was just the two of them today. Drizzle spat at them as they walked home to their apartment that afternoon, but the weather didn't change Holden's pace. He walked a few steps and then turned in a circle, walked a few more and another circle. This was something new, something that had come about since Holden had reconnected with Ella. Tracy tried to analyze why the circles, but all she could figure was that maybe he was looking for Ella. As if every few steps it occurred to him that she should be here, and she wasn't.

Whatever caused the circles, Holden seemed happy. His expression had always been pleasant, but lately he walked around with what looked like a permanent smile. Wide innocent blue eyes and a constant happy face. He seemed a lot less handicapped than some of the angry customers at Walmart.

They reached the apartment, and like every afternoon they sat at the kitchen table in silence while Holden ate his snack. Most days Tracy didn't ask questions. His lack of response was too hard on her. Instead she issued statements she assumed were true. "Math was good today, Holden. You're very good at math."

He didn't look at her, didn't respond.

"Ella says you're doing well in theater. She wants you to be in the play. I think you know that, Holden."

What Holden did next was so out of the norm, Tracy had to remind herself she wasn't dreaming. In response to her statement about theater, Holden nodded his head. He didn't make eye contact or change his expression. His eyes were still intent on the line of raisins he'd made in a circle around the edge of his plate. But that didn't change the fact. She had talked to him, and he'd nodded in response.

Ella had told her all the ways Holden had improved lately. How often he looked at her, and how he was moving his mouth like he was singing along. Since Tracy still hadn't seen that for herself, sometimes it was a little hard to believe. But now … now Holden was doing exactly what Ella said he could do. He was demonstrating an appropriate response.

He was interacting!

Dear God … it's a miracle. Whatever You're doing, please … please let it continue. Tears fell onto Tracy's cheeks like the streams in the desert she'd prayed about so many times. She wanted to rush to her son and take him in her arms, but instead she pressed her feet against the floor and refused to move. The one rule Holden's therapists had emphasized over the years was this: if he starts showing progress, don't smother him. Finding a way out of autism even in small degrees had to happen slowly.

She wiped her tears, careful not to make any sound that would tip Holden off to her emotions. Holden had a sensitive auditory system, so a moment like this required no strange or new noises. She waited until her throat wasn't so tight. "I think you'd make a very good cast member. You love music so much."

She watched, desperate for the same response and then … before she had time to pray, Holden did it again. He nodded. Then he turned his head in the general direction of the living room.

"Time for your movie, is that right?"

Another nod, his eyes wide and full of light. That new sweet smile lifting his lips. He stood and walked to the living room and she followed close behind. The movie was already cued up, like always, so Tracy sat down on the sofa, took hold of the remote, and hit the Start button.

This was usually when Holden sat on the floor a few feet from the screen and got lost in the movie. But instead he did something completely out of character—… something that made her heart skip a beat.

He sat on the couch beside her.

Not right beside her, but close enough that Tracy couldn't move or draw a breath or do anything but realize the obvious. The move was absolutely intentional. On his own, Holden had broken his routine of so many years, and he'd chosen to sit beside her. As if this time he wanted to watch the movie with her. Fresh tears flooded Tracy's eyes and again she needed all her strength to keep from shouting out loud. She'd spent the last fifteen years an arm's distance from Holden's physical body, and a million miles from his heart. Fifteen years of praying for Holden and asking God to give her some sign that her sweet Holden was still somewhere inside. Fifteen years without a hint of an answer.

Until today.

She couldn't stop the tears sliding down her cheeks, but she somehow managed to stay silent. She wouldn't have done anything to ruin this moment and she had to remind herself it was really happening. Holden was sitting beside her. He hadn't done this for fifteen years. Tracy folded her arms tight across her waist so she wouldn't reach out and hug him.

Then—when she couldn't breathe without trying—she made the only move she dared make. She put her hand on the sofa beside her, in the space between them. A minute passed, and the tears continued streaming down her cheeks. And then, at the point in the movie where Ella and Holden stood side by side and sang "Jesus Loves Me," it happened.

Without looking at her, without giving any sign that anything unusual was about to take place, Holden moved his arm closer to hers and very lightly he took hold of her fingers. Tracy could feel herself trembling, but she prayed with everything in her that Holden couldn't feel it. She closed her eyes and let the tears come—hot, cleansing tears that had built up in her heart season after season while she waited for this single moment.

The chance to hold hands with her son again.

Nineteen

HOLDEN WAS OPENING A WHOLE NEW WORLD TO ELLA. AS THEY headed into November, she started getting to school early enough to meet Holden where the bus dropped him off. Then she'd walk with him across campus to the wing where the special-needs kids had classes. After her fifth-period math class, she'd catch up with him again and they'd walk to rehearsal together.

It was the first Tuesday in November, and Ella reached the bus stop earlier than usual. From her spot, she watched Jake and his new girlfriend pull up in his Mustang and walk into school together.

LaShante kept her up to date on the kids in her former group. Apparently Jake's new girl had a bad reputation. No surprise there. Jake liked girls who couldn't say no. Apparently he'd told the guys on the football team that he'd broken up with Ella because she was boring. Whatever. She didn't care what he told people, as long as she was rid of him.

A group of cheerleaders headed inside from the far parking lot, their laughter carrying across the campus. Ella squinted in their direction. She remembered what that felt like, being part of that group. Walking around school like they owned the place, certain beyond any doubt that every guy on campus thought they were hot, and every girl wanted to be them.

LaShante was pulling away from them now too. She'd come by the drama room a couple times and she'd even heard Holden sing once. "He's so cute," she said. "I wonder if he'll ever be really, you know … normal. Like us."

Ella wasn't bothered by her friend's question. "Maybe there's no such thing as normal."

It was true. Not just where the kids at Fulton were concerned but with her own family. Her dad was staying away even more than usual. Her brothers practically lived at the house across the street, and her mother was a blur of activity—tanning and training and trips to the salon. Like everything was normal and they were a perfectly happy family.

Yeah, the longer she hung out with Holden the more normal he seemed.

She turned toward the sound of the bus and watched as it came to a stop and the door opened. Holden was always the first one off, and then he'd stand almost at attention while the other kids made their way down the steps. As soon as the first kid passed by him, he folded his hands near his chin and began flapping his arms.

The action didn't bother Ella the way it used to, but she wanted to know what he was thinking, why he did it. She had her theories. Maybe he was trying to hide his face a little from the other kids. Or maybe it was his way of saying hi. She wasn't sure, but she had decided this much: the action was intentional. It had to be, because Holden always flapped at the same times.

When he got off the bus, and when they walked across campus —if they passed a group of kids. Something about the other students at Fulton made Holden act like that, and one day ... one day Ella would figure out why. She had continued her research on autism enough to know that sometimes the therapy and dietary changes and mainstreaming resulted in a change. Sometimes something unlocked them. Yes, they would still have differences —sometimes in their mannerisms or in the way they handled social situations. But for those who emerged from the prison of autism, the change was miraculous.

The change she hoped for Holden.

He looked up and saw her—clearly saw her. Again, he would never have done that before. As he walked up she had to remind herself that he had autism. He wore jeans and a blue shirt, and his eyes connected with hers. What if he hadn't become autistic? Ella had thought about the possibility a lot. Their families would still be friends, and maybe they would still go to church. Her parents might have the most amazing marriage and she and Holden... Who could say? She and Holden might have found a love as special as the friendship they shared when they were kids.

All if Holden hadn't become autistic.

Their eyes held all the way until he reached her, but then he looked away, up at the puffy white clouds marking the early winter sky. "Hi, Holden." She always said that, even though he never answered. He would sing to her pretty easily now, sometimes even when they were walking together. The progress in Holden was remarkable by anyone's understanding.

But he still hadn't talked to her.

They were halfway to Holden's special wing when they walked past the outdoor cafeteria. Ella heard shouting and saw a few kids run toward the sound. Someone was in trouble. "Come on." She took a turn they didn't usually take so she could see—at least from a distance—what was happening. Once the building wasn't in the way, she stopped and beside her, Holden did the same thing.

"Jesus loves me, this I know." Holden sang softly as his smile faded. "For the Bible tells me so ..."

She wanted to tell him to keep his voice down. This wasn't the time to sing. But she could hardly do that when she was the one who had broken his regular order of things. And people with autism needed their routines. She shaded her eyes and stared at a group of kids clustered near one of the lunch tables. A voice yelled above the others, and Ella recognized the sound.

It was Jake.

Suddenly she had the worst feeling that maybe Jake was picking on someone again. Maybe Michael Schwartz. She hadn't seen the guy in several weeks. Her fascination with Holden had made her almost forget any other kids at school. She wanted to move closer, but Holden wouldn't want to go anywhere near the confrontation.

She decided on the safe route. "Let's go." She turned back and again Holden stayed at her side. "Time to get to class."

"Tale as old as time …" He sang the words, and then he began to hum the tune, clearly more relaxed than he'd been a minute ago. He stopped and pulled his cards from his backpack. He didn't fiddle with them the way he used to, but he still relied on them. Maybe they even made him feel like he was talking. Ella wasn't sure, but she enjoyed waiting for him to pull out just the right card.

He didn't hold onto them anymore, either. He found the card he was looking for and handed it to her. The card showed two unhappy people. Below the drawings were written the words "Is there a problem?"

His perception was perfect. "Yes." She kept her tone calm, so he wouldn't worry. "That was back there. We won't worry about it, though, okay?"

"Okay." Holden looked at her and then back at his deck of cards.

"What?" Ella laughed. She still hadn't touched Holden, but now she touched his shoulder without thinking. Her touch was light, but she hesitated in case he reacted. He didn't, so she kept her hand there. "You talked to me, Holden. Do you know that?

A fresh smile pulled at the corners of his mouth as he put the cards in his backpack and zipped the top. Then he looked at her again. "Okay."

She wanted to march Holden around to all the teachers and therapists who doubted that for Holden change was possible. But that wouldn't be good for him, so instead she walked with him to his classroom. When Holden was safely into his routine — setting his backpack with the others and finding his seat, Ella walked up to the teacher. "He talked to me." She flashed a confident smile. She'd had a few discussions with Holden's main teacher before. The woman was kind, but she seemed stifled by her belief that people on the autism spectrum couldn't experience much change.

Ella doubted she believed in miracles.

Now his teacher's brow raised a little. "He talked to you?" Doubt dripped off every word.

"Yes. I told him we were going to class, and he told me, 'Okay.'" Ella didn't have time to stay here and discuss the issue. She didn't care if the teacher believed her. She waved as she headed for the door. "Just wanted you to know."

Back outside, Ella remembered the trouble, as Holden called it. She hurried back to the place near the outdoor cafeteria, but there were only a few kids left — Jake and his buddies and... yes, it was Michael Schwartz. Whatever had happened, the first bell must've broken it up. She ran closer until the situation became clear and she stopped cold. What she saw made her furious.

There must've been a fight, because one of the football players was nursing a black eye. Maybe the original trouble hadn't been between the player and Michael. Maybe he'd just happened by ... Ella wasn't sure. The contents of Michael's backpack — dozens of loose-leaf pieces of paper, notebooks, pencils, coins — were scattered on the damp ground. Each time he bent down to pick something up, Jake kicked him. Then Jake and the jerks he hung out with would laugh like this was the funniest thing they'd ever witnessed.

"Don't come by in the middle of a fight and think we won't see you," Jake said. "You freak. This is our part of the school."

"Yeah," Sam laughed and pointed toward the special-ed wing. "You belong over there with the others."

That was it. Ella couldn't take another minute. "Hey!" She stormed the remaining ten yards that separated her from the guys. "Go to class, Jake ... Sam. Ryan."

"What?" He spun around and faced her. For a few seconds he looked like he might come after her too. Then he relaxed his posture and looked at his buddies, an angry chuckle leaking from inside him. His eyes burned with fury. He let loose a string of cuss words aimed right at her, but she didn't care.

"You make me sick," she hissed at him. Then she moved right past him to Michael. Without being asked she knelt down and started picking up pieces of paper and pencils. "Are you okay?"

Michael stood, his face pale. "What're you doing?"

"I'm helping." She stood too. From behind her, she could feel Jake and his guys moving in closer, laughing at them.

"Isn't that sweet." Jake wouldn't let up. "A couple of girl-friends helping each other."

"I said ..." Ella faced him, "get lost. Leave him alone!"

"Ella ..." Michael sounded like he might be on the verge of losing it. "I'm fine. Go on."

Before Jake could say another word, a teacher must've caught the eyes of one of his buddies, because in a rush they jogged off, still laughing. And that quickly, Michael and Ella were the only two left.

She lowered herself to her knees again and resumed the task of helping him collect his things. But Michael only stood there, staring at her. After she'd picked up a few things, she stopped and looked at him. "Is something wrong?"

"Yes." He tossed his hands in the direction Jake and his guys had run off toward. "Are you kidding me, Ella? You just rescued me in front of the worst kids at school." He paced a few steps away, and then back again. "They'll never let me live that down."

"What they did ..." Her voice was louder than she meant it to be. "It was wrong, Michael. You can't let people walk over you."

"I can do what I want." He wiped the dirt off his shirt — dirt Jake had left there with his final kick. "I survive around those guys. I keep out of their way and everything's fine."

"What about today?" Ella's voice rang with indignation. How dare Jake convince a guy like Michael that it was okay to be bullied? "Why didn't you stay out of their way today?"

"Because." Michael snagged the items from her hands and shoved them into his backpack. He dropped to the ground and collected the rest of his things in a few quick grabs. Many of them looked a little wet and dirty, but at least he could get to class now.

"Because why?"

"Just because." He slung his backpack over one shoulder. "The guy they were fighting is in orchestra with me. The mighty Eagles have decided everyone in that class is gay or a freak. I had to at least help."

Ella crossed her arms in front of herself and hung her head. Really? Was Jake that cold hearted that he would start a fight with a guy in the orchestra, all to make himself look like some big shot?

"I don't need help, okay? Not ever again." He didn't sound angry, just frightened. Because now Jake and his gang had one more reason to pick on him. "I know you meant well, Ella. But really... just leave me alone." Michael backed up a few steps, his eyes scanning the yard and the cafeteria. "I'll be fine." He held tight to his backpack and started walking again.

Ella watched him go, but before he got more than a couple steps, she called out, "Wait!"

Michael stopped and slowly turned around. He looked like he wanted to cry, but clearly he couldn't. If Jake and the guys found out, they'd hold it against him. His shoulders dropped a notch. "What?"

"Who punched Jake's friend?"

"I did." He hesitated. "I told you, I came here because someone had to stand up for the orchestra kids and the band geeks. All the rest of us who aren't Jake Collins, you know?"

"Yeah."

"Someone needed to have the guy's back." He hesitated, and after a few seconds he started walking again. "See you, Ella."

"Bye." She uttered the word too softly for him to hear. The whole situation was horrible. She wanted to walk straight to the office and report what had happened, get Jake and his group suspended, or better yet—expelled. But Michael was right. If she helped him anymore—especially if she reported what happened—her actions would only make life that much harder for him.

The old her would've felt badly about the trouble Michael was in, but she wouldn't have dreamed of saying anything. Now, as she headed for English Lit, she changed her mind. She couldn't live with herself if she didn't at least go to the office and make some kind of report. At the front of the school she walked into the main office and asked to speak to a principal. Fulton was so big they had three assistants.

One of them walked out. "Hello, Miss Reynolds." He smiled, relaxed and happy, clearly ignorant to the ways people were treated on his campus every day.

"I have something to report." She spent the next five minutes giving exact details of what happened to Michael and the other guy from orchestra. Ella was careful not to spare a detail. "But… if those guys find out I said something, they'll kill Michael. I just wanted you to know."

But even having done the right thing was hardly satisfying. Almost certainly nothing would happen to the football players, and life for the Michaels and Holdens would only get harder. Bullying was a tough thing to police because the victims never talked about what happened. If they talked, they ran the risk that next time the attack would be worse.

So they stayed silent.

Ella pictured Michael again. He looked so shocked to see her, and what he said would stay with her always: *"I'm fine ... I can handle it."* But that wasn't true. One of these days someone was going to get really hurt, all because of some peer pressure or gang mentality, and under the guise of having fun. But it wasn't fun — it was bullying and it was cruel. No, it was downright evil.

As Ella walked to class she fought tears. She couldn't control the way kids were picked on at Fulton, and she couldn't make administrators find a way to eliminate attacks like the ones on the orchestra kids this morning. She thought about Holden's mother, praying for her son every day. So why didn't she herself try praying? She didn't know how, of course, but she'd heard Mrs. Harris pray. It seemed a lot like talking. She walked slower and let her words ring silently — for her heart and God's alone.

Hi, God, this is me — Ella Reynolds. I've never talked to you before — at least not since I can remember. But we need Your help down here at Fulton. The kids are awful. You see that, right? She waited but there was no loud answer. *I want to take a stand or make a difference, but I don't know where to start. There are so many people walking around here afraid of other kids. So give me the chance to turn things around, please. God, if You're listening, show me how to stop the meanness on our campus. And help Holden keep coming out of his private world. Thanks for listening, amen.*

Something about praying made her feel good. Like she was floating or safe or something. Ella couldn't do much about the sad kids at Fulton, the ones picked on and teased. Kids like Michael. But she could keep doing what she'd been doing — being a friend to Holden Harris. She could report the bullies, and she could do this.

She could pray.

Twenty

THE FACADE WAS CRUMBLING. SUZANNE COULD SENSE THAT the same old lies weren't working anymore. It wasn't enough to have an investment plan and a BMW and a ski boat in their three-car garage. It wasn't enough to be Randy Reynolds' wife. Her life was meaningless, empty, and mechanical. She woke up wanting to scream, and she couldn't fall asleep at night without a handful of pills. Something had to give, or she'd wind up in a mental institution, strapped to a chair.

It was Sunday morning after another sleepless night. Randy hadn't been home since Tuesday. The season was over, but private training camps were in session. Randy wanted to be as ready as possible when they discussed his contract.

She stretched and felt the familiar burning in her stomach muscles. Lately she'd been taking her anger out on her ab work-out, although that didn't give her life meaning any more than anything did. She walked to the window and pressed her fore-head against the cool glass. Their front lawn was an acre, pretty and manicured even now, heading into winter. As she stood there, she remembered an old movie she and Tracy watched once when they were in high school.

The original *Stepford Wives*.

Scenes from the movie flashed in her mind. Creepy plot, the sort of story that at the time had stayed with her on dark nights and left her unsettled when she was alone in the shower. Now, the storyline consumed her again. Gradually over time, the women of Stepford had been replaced by robots, replicas of their former selves. The two women lead characters were friends, and they swore they'd never become like the others. Then one day one of them paid the other a visit looking entirely different — her dress neatly pressed, hair perfectly combed. Her face fresh and made up.

Cue the scary music, and a frantic series of questions from the unchanged woman, until finally, while chopping an onion, she accidentally stabbed her now perfect-looking friend in the hand. But there was no blood — only wires and clockwork. The friend was nothing more than a robot, a mere machine-like shell of her former self.

Suzanne blinked, and the memory lifted. That's how she felt lately. She remembered that she and Tracy had covered their teenage eyes at that scary part of the movie. Later that night they agreed they'd never be perfect, consumed with how they looked, desperate to uphold a certain image.

But that's exactly what Suzanne had become. Nothing more than a Stepford wife. No heart, no soul, no emotions. She turned from the window and headed absently into her walk-in closet. So many clothes. Every shirt and sweater and tight pair of pants a desperate attempt at… what? To hold onto an image? To keep up the act?

She slipped into a T-shirt and tight black dance pants, but as she did she caught a glimpse of herself in the mirror. What was she doing? The dance pants were something she wore when Ella's guy friends were at the house. Her way of proving she still had it, she could still turn the head of an eighteen-year-old.

The truth disgusted her. She yanked off the dance pants and shoved them back in the drawer. Sweats. Those would be better. Comfortable clothes were more appropriate for Sunday mornings. She found a pair, and when she was dressed she wandered into the upstairs hallway and a thought occurred to her. There was a time when church — not sweats — had been — more appropriate for Sunday mornings. The years when she and Tracy Harris were friends.

She walked quietly past the kids' rooms and peered in at them, first Ella, then the boys. It was only eight o'clock, which meant at least an hour before they would be up. She thought about her husband, how he hadn't been home. Training, he told the kids. But the kids could see through his lies. There was no way to avoid the truth: he didn't want to be home.

By now the kids probably all pitied her. She was a sad joke, and in time they would learn to look the other way. Then what? She'd grow old alone without the respect of the very people who were supposed to love her most? One day, Randy would leave her. He had one foot out the door already. The thought sent a shot of fear through her veins and doubled her anxiety.

The title of Randy Reynolds' wife was the only one Suzanne had ever known.

She steadied her breathing and continued down the hall to the other end, the place where a custom bookcase was built into the wall. She stared at it, half full and covered with dust. When they'd built this house, the plan was to fill the case with photo albums and scrapbooks. They would have so many happy memories one bookcase would never be enough.

A quick count told her there were twelve volumes in all — ten before Ella was four, two since then. Suzanne felt her eyes well up. The message was so loud it was deafening. All the good times, nearly every happy memory, had taken place before Ella hit kindergarten.

She came closer, studying the titles on the spines of the books. One was from high school, and another from the summer after graduation. There was a scrapbook of Randy's early baseball adventures and one titled simply "Engagement Year." The wedding took up its own book and so did their honeymoon. After that there was a fat photo book for each year until Ella was four.

The next one had a three-year span written on the edge of the book, and the last one still wasn't filled.

The glue that made them a family had lost its power some- where along the way—whether that glue was the love they'd stopped sharing or the laughter that never happened anymore. Whatever it was, Suzanne didn't see any way to make it work again.

The photo album from their second married year was the one closest to her. She pulled it out and took it across the hall into her office. With a quick turn, she shifted the office chair so she was facing the enormous picture window and their backyard. Their perfectly manicured backyard. *Best house on the block*, she told herself. *Everyone must think you really have it all.* But the truth was something different. Except for the kids, she could have walked away from it all. The idea was tempting.

She opened the photo album and there on the front page was a photo of herself with Tracy, the two of them pushing their baby strollers down the same sidewalk, iced-tea glasses raised to Dan, most likely. He was the picture-taker in the group. Certainly not Randy. When he was around, people took pictures of him, not the other way around.

There were more photos, and suddenly she wanted to see every one of them. Not just brush past them, but really look at them. She turned the page and there they were again, she and Tracy side by side on the swings, Holden in Tracy's arms, and Ella in hers. Suzanne brought the album a little closer and studied the images.

I remember that day. It was one of the first times she'd told Tracy her fears about Randy, how a good-looking pro-baseball player would struggle to be faithful.

"But you have your faith," Tracy had told her. "Stay close to Jesus, and you'll survive."

Suzanne wasn't convinced. "What about the people who say they're Christians, but they mess up anyway?"

She could still see Tracy's smile, the way she kissed the top of Holden's head, and how her voice became very gentle. "Everyone makes mistakes. It's not how we fall that defines us as Christians. It's how we get up again."

The answer grated at Suzanne. "So there's no guarantee for a happy life. Not even with God?"

Tracy thought about that for awhile. "I guess it depends how you define *happy*." She gave her swing a slight push. "With Jesus you have the guarantee of heaven … and the guarantee that God is with you, that He loves you." She slowed down, and her answer seemed to come from someplace deep within her soul. "The closer you are to Jesus, the fewer the falls." She smiled. "But when you really live for God, He helps you catch yourself before things get out of hand."

That part made sense — enough so that Suzanne had remembered her friend's words every year since then. A thick wall of Jesus around their lives and maybe they really could get through anything. But that had stopped being the case more than a decade ago. Suzanne looked intently at her face in the picture, at her eyes. They were alive and shining, full of trust. Looking into them now she could almost remember what it felt like to believe.

Her eyes moved to Tracy's, the joy and hope, the carefree way her smile shone through the photograph, as if time couldn't touch whatever happiness lived inside her. A different memory came to mind. The last time Suzanne saw Tracy, a week before spring training that year. The conversation had been short and stilted, too awkward for a long visit. By then Tracy's look was very different, closed off and protective, angry even.

The problem was Holden.

None of them had ever watched a perfectly healthy, normal child slip into some other world. How were they supposed to handle it? Suzanne turned a few more pages until she came to a close-up of Holden and Ella. He was vibrantly alive and completely with them back then, perfect eye contact, direct interaction. Of course Suzanne asked questions when the child started to change. The loss was devastating, and all Suzanne could think, all she was consumed by every time they were together after Holden's change, was one crippling question.

What if it happened to Ella?

It wasn't contagious, Suzanne understood that. But what if Ella tried to mimic Holden's behavior, or what if it was something in the air in the Harris house? The thought seemed ridiculous now, but it hadn't back then. If Holden Harris could withdraw into his own world, and leave only the shell of his body behind, then it could happen to any child.

The trouble was Tracy started taking the questions personally. Suzanne could feel the change, but she couldn't stop asking, couldn't stop being drawn to Holden and the dramatic change in him. One of the last times they were together, Suzanne and Tracy had been sitting on the sofa in Tracy's living room, silent, sipping coffee and watching the kids. At that time, Tracy was having Holden tested, but no diagnosis had been made.

Ella had a baby doll in her arms and she was talking to it, singing to it, and rocking it, chattering away in her little-girl voice. It took a few minutes to understand what Ella was saying, what she was pretending. But then they watched her set the doll down and walk over to Holden.

Holden, who was her very best friend, the one close enough to be her twin brother.

"Ho'den," that's what Ella called him back then. It was always so sweet the way she dropped the *l* whenever she said his name. Before he withdrew, Holden would know Ella's voice and the way she said his name and he would run to her. Wherever he was he would run.

But that day he was lining up his toy Hot Wheels cars near the living room window, his face pointed outward. Holden must've had three buckets of Hot Wheels cars. As Ella walked up, he didn't turn to her or look at her or acknowledge her the way he always had.

"Ho'den!" Ella touched his shoulder, desperate for him to turn around. "Play with me, Ho'den."

Nothing. No response. Holden didn't see anything but the cars in the box, or the car in his hand, for that matter. Meticulously, almost trancelike, he reached for another car and added it to the long line. Bumper to bumper in the wildest, uncanny pattern. Green car, red car, blue car, yellow car, truck ... green car, red car, blue car, yellow car, truck ... green car —

The sameness of his pattern was astonishing. Ella watched him for a few seconds then she laughed, but it sounded more like a cry, like she would do anything to get him to join her. The way he used to.

"Why doesn't he talk to her?" Suzanne couldn't understand. Holden's hearing worked. He loved Ella ... but he was ignoring her. She turned to Tracy. "Have you tried forcing him to respond? I mean, maybe this is a late case of the Terrible Twos. You know, like he's trying to exert his independence."

Suzanne remembered her words and she winced at the way they sounded replayed this many years later. But again, what could she possibly have known or understood about autism. Holden did seem rebellious or defiant, like if one of them had walked up and turned him around and ordered him to respond, then maybe he might've obeyed.

But whatever Suzanne's tone had been that day, however her words must've come across, Tracy did not take them well. Her expression iced over and her eyes flashed with an anger and intensity Suzanne hadn't seen before. "It's not like that." She stared at Holden, and her look softened. After a minute, her eyes grew watery. "He's not acting up. It's in his brain ... something's changing in his brain."

Awkwardness stood between them, so big and wide and tall neither of them could see around it so they turned their attention back to the kids, drawn to the tragedy playing out the way people are drawn to stare at car wrecks.

"Ho'den, can't you hear me?" Ella looked like she might cry, and Suzanne's heart broke for her daughter. "Play with me!"

That time when he didn't turn around, when he completely ignored her attempts, she went back to her baby doll. What she did next reduced both women to tears. Ella cradled the doll close to her face and gradually her joy returned.

"Hi, Ho'den, it's me, Ella!" Her sing-song voice was bright again. "Ho'den, let's sing a song, okay?" She rocked the baby doll a little, as if the baby were answering her. "Okay, this one. Ready?" She didn't wait for an answer. "Jesus loves me, this I know ... for the Bible tells me so ... Little ones to Him belong ..."

Tracy and Suzanne watched in silence, tears sliding down their faces. What could they say? Ella had been rejected by Holden, so she'd found a different friend. Her baby doll might not talk or sing along, but at least it looked at her.

The memory passed. Suzanne had learned more about autism since then. Obviously it wouldn't have been possible to order Holden to talk or to scold him out of his withdrawn behavior. She wasn't sure if that was the last time she and Tracy spent time with the kids, but it was one of them. She stared at the photo of Holden and Ella again, stared so long and hard that she almost believed she could will her way back to that moment.

To a time before Holden left them.

The truth was when they lost Holden, they had all lost. Of course their conversations and visits were bound to feel different and strained. It was impossible to sit on the sofa sipping coffee and laughing when their children were suffering a few feet away.

But she could've been more sensitive about how Tracy was feeling. Instead Suzanne was consumed with Ella's sadness, Ella's loss … how the situation with Holden was affecting her daughter. But had she ever just hugged Tracy and grieved with her? Suzanne couldn't remember a single time. There was an air of sadness between them always after Holden started changing. Like everyone else, Suzanne was constantly sorry. But maybe she was more sorry for herself and her daughter than for what Tracy was going through.

With no understanding of autism, Suzanne really had thought Holden was just being disobedient or sick … something correctable. She remembered another question she'd asked Tracy that day. *"Is he cutting teeth, maybe?"* She had tried to sound hopeful, because if that was it, Holden could be back to normal in a day or so.

Tracy didn't say a word for a few seconds, just looked at her with an emptiness Suzanne didn't recognize. "It's not his teeth."

"I'm just saying … some kids get moody when they're cutting teeth."

When the visit ended that day, she and Tracy exchanged no loud argument or accusations — but there was a sense about their friendship. It was over. For weeks their times together played out like that, with Suzanne occasionally asking when Holden was going to get better. In the years since, Suzanne would sometimes replay those conversations and wish for an apology from Tracy. No one knew much about autism back then, and Suzanne wasn't the only one who believed Holden's changes were merely a stage. Even Tracy's husband had felt that way. Tracy was the only one who believed Holden needed expert care or medical intervention. Even after the diagnosis, Suzanne and the guys still believed they could coax Holden back.

Only Tracy grasped the truth about her son. Tracy, who was forced to handle the loss on her own.

The reality dragged like fingernails across the chalkboard of her heart. Suzanne could've been a better friend—less concerned with her own anxiety, less worried about Ella's loss. More supportive. But once the diagnosis came, there were other reasons the friendship between her and Tracy never recovered. They would be together and Ella would say something darling or accomplish some wonderful feat like turning a somersault, and the celebration would feel stilted and forced. How could Suzanne be excited about Ella's milestones when Holden was regressing?

Whether it was Suzanne's insensitivity or Tracy's defensive spirit, the awkwardness and tension between them buried their friendship one layer at a time. During the month-long spring training that year, Ella's sadness over losing Holden seemed to lessen. She still talked about him, and her baby doll kept the name Holden. But a week after they returned home they connected with a few baseball families—all of whom had young kids. One of them had a little girl Ella's age. The void in their lives was filled and time moved them swiftly downstream from everything about the Harris family.

Suzanne missed Tracy, of course. But she missed the old Tracy, the old Holden, the old way of spending time together before ... before Holden changed. With every passing week the idea of calling Tracy seemed more overwhelming, and as the weeks became months, and the months became years, the friendship died.

A friendship that was supposed to last forever.

Suzanne turned the pages of the photo album and stopped at one final picture—a photo of her and Tracy taken at the county fair the summer before Holden's change. They wore silly tall green hats and big orange plastic sunglasses and purple feather boas. Their husbands had won the costumes throwing baseballs at a wooden board.

"Princesses Forever," the caption read.

Suzanne could still feel the hot, humid sunshine on their

faces that day, smell the heavy popcorn oil and hear the carnival barkers urging them to step right up. If there was a way back to that time, she would've taken it. And when Holden started to leave them, she would've been more sensitive. Suzanne wanted to cry, wanted to break down right here in the office while the kids were still sleeping and sob over the price they'd all paid when Holden slipped through their fingers.

This was a moment when tears should've come freely because the losses had done nothing but pile up after that. First Holden and Ella, then the time their families spent together,… the fun-loving friendship between their husbands, and a million happy moments like the one in the photograph. They had lost all of it, and finally … they had lost their faith. And it was that loss, Suzanne was sure now, that led to the next set of changes. Randy's distance, his lack of commitment to their family, her obsession with her looks, and the poor connection they had with their children. Her self-loathing and her inability to feel.

The answers to her questions all seemed clear now. The break with the Harris family had started a chain reaction she was helpless to change. There was no way to go back and undo the damage.

Suzanne began to shake a little. So much was lost along the way, she should've been weeping. That was the greatest problem, the one that made her sick to her stomach. Her life was falling apart, but even still her Botoxed eyes were dry.

Nothing but wires and clockwork.

TRACY DIDN'T ALWAYS TAKE HOLDEN TO CHURCH. HE LOVED the music, but sometimes—if the pastor got too excited or raised his voice a little louder than usual, or if too many people opened their bulletin at the same time—Holden would start to rock. And if his surroundings didn't quiet down quickly, he would find his way from the pew to the floor and start doing push-ups. The congregation was kind, the sort of church family that checked in on Tracy once in a while and kept Holden on their prayer chain. But there was a limit to the sort of distractions that could happen during Sunday service.

And Holden was often a distraction.

This Sunday, though, Holden woke up happy and humming. Yes, that was the newest change Tracy had seen in her wonderful son. He was humming. So far she'd heard him hum the theme from *Beauty and the Beast* and the song "Home" from the show. She didn't have to wonder at the source of Holden's improvements. It was the spring musical. More than that, it was Ella.

"I think we'll go to church today, Holden." She told him the news while she made herself a cup of coffee.

Holden sat at the kitchen table eating toaster waffles and sorting through his PECS cards. He still didn't respond with words, but more often now he did respond. His fork was steady in his hand as he took another bite.

She watched, willing him to answer in some way. *Please, God … I know Holden hears me … I want to take my son to church, Lord … please.* "Holden … did you hear me, honey?"

Holden set his fork down and nodded a few times, his eyes locked on the deck of cards. Quickly, almost panicky, he began moving through the cards lightning fast in search of what he wanted to say.

Tracy moved closer and took the seat beside him. "I'm here, Holden. I know you're trying to talk to me." She put her hand ever so softly on his shoulder. When he didn't flinch, she silently rejoiced. How many years had she longed for this simple moment, the chance to touch her son without the instant rejection of feeling him pull away?

Finally Holden seemed to find the card he was looking for. Without making eye contact, he handed it to her.

The card made Tracy's heart do a stutter beat. It was like

she'd always thought. Holden could understand so much more than anyone thought. He had to understand, because of the message on the card. The illustration showed a young woman. And the words simply said "The Girl."

The card didn't represent Tracy, she was sure of that. The dawning happened immediately, as soon as she looked at the card. Tenderness and clarity filled Tracy's heart. "Ella? Is that who you mean? You'd like Ella to go to church with us?"

Holden still stared at his plate, but he smiled just enough to notice. Then he hummed a little and opened his mouth and sang.

Tracy blinked, her head spinning. The line he sang was from *Beauty and the Beast*, a line about being scared and not quite ready to move on. If she hadn't been sitting down she would've fallen over. Holden understood exactly what he was asking. He wanted Ella Reynolds to go with them to church, but more than that he understood how the situation could feel a little awkward, how their nerves were bound to be somewhat jumbled.

Tracy felt a little nervous. Ella might not want to spend time with Holden outside school, and the disappointment might halt his progress. But she didn't want to keep her son waiting. "Okay." She stood and walked across the kitchen to her cell phone. "I can call her. Maybe Ella can meet us there."

Still no eye contact, but Holden nodded. He definitely nodded.

"All right, then." Tracy fought against her pounding heart. What if Ella's mother answered the phone? Or what if Suzanne got angry that Tracy was inviting her daughter to church?

I can do this ... I can do all things through Christ who gives me strength. It was another verse, another truth she clung to daily. Praying for streams in the desert, believing God would get her through even on the driest desert days when the sand scorched her feet.

She and Ella had talked a few times on the phone — times

when Ella had to share something Holden had done, or when she had an idea about how to help Holden open up more. At first his therapists didn't believe the changes were anything more than anomalies in his behavior. Quirks that didn't add up to anything significant. After all, he'd always loved music. The idea that he would enjoy rehearsals wasn't that new or advanced for Holden.

But when he started singing, his therapists and teachers and doctors all took notice. This didn't happen with all kids on the autism spectrum. It didn't happen with most. But like the rarest key in the rustiest lock, miraculously something was getting through and opening Holden's mind. Tracy had no doubt that the key was music, and Ella alone held it in her hands.

She tapped out the girl's number and waited. *Please, God . . . let her answer . . . Let her be willing . . . Don't let it be awkward . . . please, God.*

Ella answered almost immediately. "Hello?" She sounded pleasant, but tired.

"Oh, honey, I'm sorry." Tracy couldn't make her get out of bed on a Sunday. "I had an idea, but not if you're sleeping. I didn't mean to—"

"No, Mrs. Harris, I'm awake. Really." Her energy picked up some. "What's going on?"

Tracy shot a look at Holden. He was rocking a little, his eyes glued to his uneaten waffle. "Well," She closed her eyes. There was no turning back now. "Holden and I are going to church. We wondered . . . Actually, he wondered if you'd like to join us?"

Holden stopped rocking and lifted his head, his gaze straight ahead.

"Really?" She laughed, but it was clearly a show of joy, an extension of the smile that must've filled her face. "Holden wants me to go?"

"He does." She explained the story, about the PECS card and

how he nodded when she asked him if he wanted her to call Ella. "It starts in an hour."

"I'd love to go." She sounded as happy and delightful as she had when she was little.

Tracy told her where the church was and the best way to get there from Fulton High—which was near Ella's house. "So ... we'll see you there?"

Holden's smile crept a little higher on his face.

"Definitely." She paused. "Thanks for calling. That means a lot—that Holden wants me there."

"It's like you said. God is doing something big in Holden's life."

"Actually," she hesitated, her voice more emotional than before. "He's doing something big in both our lives."

As the call ended, Tracy heard Holden humming again. She turned and smiled at him. If only she could take him in her arms and hug him, celebrate with him the thrill of knowing he could ask a friend to church. The hug wasn't going to happen, but as she stood there Holden began to sing. This time the song was the same one Holden and Ella had sung so often back before. The song that rang through their home every afternoon. His voice was a little older now, but there was so much sameness, Tracy had to lean against the kitchen counter to catch her breath. Holden didn't notice. He kept staring at his eggs and rocking and singing the same sweet words over and over and over again.

"Jesus loves me, this I know ... for the Bible tells me so ... Little ones to Him belong ... they are weak, but He is strong!"

Twenty-One

THE BREAKTHROUGH HAPPENED AT CHURCH.

Ella had showered and dressed in a hurry and stopped only briefly in the kitchen to tell her mother where she was headed.

Her mother was making an egg-white omelet, and she stopped, the color fading from her cheeks. "You're going to *church*?"

"Yes." Ella resisted the urge to roll her eyes. It wouldn't be very nice to make a mockery of her mother on the way out the door to church. Besides, her mother managed to do that all on her own. "Holden wants me to go."

"Holden?" Again her mom took the news like a physical blow. "I thought he couldn't talk."

"Mom," Ella remembered to feel sorry for her. She thought about all the times her mother didn't hug her and didn't ask about her day or what she was involved in. She still didn't know about the spring musical. Ella found a reluctant smile. "Not all communication happens with words."

She waited a minute—just in case her mom might smile or say she understood or ask to come along. Something to show she cared. But she only remained motionless, her expression flat. Ella tried not to feel hurt. "Well ... see you later." With that she hurried out the door and ten minutes later she walked through the doors of Holden's church. She took a seat near the back and stared at the wooden cross that hung on the main wall. From conversations with Holden's mother Ella knew there was a time when her own family attended church every week. In her struggle to understand what had gone wrong with her parents, the fact that they'd stopped going to church seemed like at least one clear reason.

From what Ella could tell, when her parents stopped attending church, they stopped believing. She and her brothers hadn't been taught about God or praying or eternity—none of it. And she'd never imagined the other idea Mrs. Harris had talked about —having a relationship with Jesus—a friendship. As she sat down, she remembered her last phone call with Holden's mother.

"For me, I talk to Him throughout the day, and He talks to me."

"He talks to you?"

"Not out loud." Mrs. Harris laughed. She was such a nice lady, so patient with Ella. So caring. "But He talks to us through Scripture—through the Bible. And sometimes you'll hear His truth in your heart and you'll know—you'll absolutely know it's Him. Talking to you, and walking you through a difficult time. Giving you wisdom and direction."

If anyone should know it would be Mrs. Harris. So the decision to come to church was an easy one. Finding a friendship with the God of the universe, and knowing that this same mighty God wanted a friendship with her in return? Even if Holden hadn't wanted her to come, she was interested. She'd been thinking about it for weeks now.

Holden and his mother arrived, and the three of them moved to a row near the front. As they took their seats, Mrs. Harris leaned over Holden—who was sitting between them—and grinned at Ella. "We're glad you're here."

"Me too." Before she turned her attention to the people singing at the front, Holden caught her eye. The way he'd done a number of times now. Ella smiled, and before he looked away, Holden did the same thing.

The message was on being a living sacrifice, letting your life shine in such a way that it brought glory to God. By way of illustration, the pastor—Pastor Jeff—had arranged for something he called an altar to be brought into the church. It looked like a large slab of stone and it sat on six sturdy stone legs.

"It's not about the altar, the outside, the face we put on for others." Pastor Jeff was kind, his words and message clear. "It's about the sacrifice. What are you doing for God? How are you bringing Him glory?"

Ella thought about the years when she'd lived in the shadows of the cool kids, the mean crowd. She hadn't known God, but she'd known the truth about her group of friends. The way they treated other kids was terrible. She never should have hung out with them.

So what about now, she wondered. *Am I living in a way to bring You glory, God? Am I doing enough so that You'll love me?*

I love you, my daughter ... you can't earn my love.

The thought fell over her like a gentle rain, and Ella sat back in the pew. Was this what Holden's mother meant? She certainly hadn't imagined the answer, but she hadn't heard an audible voice, either. *You love me, God? Even though I never really thought about You until lately?*

The answer didn't come again, but the memory of it did. He loved her. She could do nothing to change His love, nothing to earn it. But she could try to understand Him better, and she could figure out exactly what it meant to be a Christian—to live the way Mrs. Harris and Holden lived.

At the end of the talk, Pastor Jeff called up a small boy, impish and darling with dimples and dirty blond hair. He wore jeans and a plaid flannel shirt and as soon as he was up on the stage, Pastor Jeff grinned at him. "Hi, buddy." He turned to the audience. "This is TJ. He's six years old and he's my one and only son." Pastor Jeff stooped down to the boy's level and for a long moment the two grinned at each other and the boy whispered something. His dad laughed, enjoying the private, father-son moment.

The sort of moment Ella couldn't remember ever having with her father.

Next to her, Holden folded his hands and brought them up to his chin. He wasn't looking straight at the scene playing out on the stage, but he was interested. Ella could tell. *Maybe he misses his dad, too*, she thought. For the first time she realized that they had that in common, she and Holden. In all the ways that mattered, they'd both lost their dads.

Pastor Jeff looked at the crowd again. "I love my son more than anything in this world." His eyes shone, his emotion full and rich. "I would do anything for this boy." He stood and motioned to TJ. "Okay, buddy. Go ahead."

With that, the child made a small jump to the stone altar. Then he lay down flat at the center of the stone table, his little-boy feet wiggling while he tried to stay still. Beside him, Holden raised his elbows and started moving them up and down just a little.

"It's okay," Ella whispered near his ear. "The boy's okay, Holden."

His arms stopped moving, but he kept his hands folded near his chin.

"I love my son so much." Pastor Jeff's voice was tight. "If God asked me to sacrifice him, the way He asked Abraham to sacrifice Isaac ..." He shook his head. "I'm not sure what I would say." The pastor looked at his son, and everyone in the room did the same thing.

Ella heard people around her shifting to see better. She hoped the sounds wouldn't bother Holden. She patted his hand, just so he'd know she was there.

Pastor Jeff smiled at his son. "Okay, TJ, you can get up."

The boy scrambled to his feet and grinned big as he hopped

back to his place beside his father. The pastor hugged him and roughed up his hair a little. Then he stood again, his arm still around the boy's shoulders. "The most amazing thing about God is that He won't ever ask us to do that. He didn't ask it of Abraham, and He won't ask it of you." He paused, and again the emotion in the room was powerful. Soft utterances of amen came from all around. "That's because God did it for us. He took his one and only son and laid Him down for us. And Jesus went to the cross willingly out of love for you and me." Pastor Jeff looked at the altar again. "So what is it in your life that you need to lay down? It's not your son—that's already been done. But maybe it's your time or your talents ... your treasure. You have one chance to let your lives be a sacrifice for God. Let's start today."

Ella sat up straighter. Suddenly the message was perfectly clear. God didn't just love her from a distance. He loved her enough to call upon His one and only son and give Him up for her. It was a sort of love Ella had never imagined, let alone experienced. *I want to know more, God ... Help me learn so I can follow You.* It was a beginning, Ella could feel it in her heart. The faith these people had, the faith of Holden and his mother—that's what Ella wanted too.

Pastor Jeff prayed, and Holden once more started moving his elbows and in a single instant—like a light bulb turning on —Ella understood. Holden was praying! When he brought his hands together near his chin and moved his arms, he was talking to God! Which meant ... which meant Holden talked to God all the time, for all sorts of reasons. The understanding filled her heart. She could hardly wait to talk to Holden's mother. She pictured all the times she'd seen Holden do this same motion. If she was right, Holden prayed when kids were mean, and he prayed when his friends walked off the bus. Of course he prayed. The special-needs kids needed all the prayer they could get, right?

Tears filled her eyes at the kindness of the friend beside

her. Ella had been surrounded by people who called themselves friends all her life. But never had any of them been as genuine as Holden. She thought of another time when he prayed. When their drama class sang about killing the Beast. Every time they sang that song Holden folded his hands and flapped his elbows. Maybe he was worried about the villagers. She thought about that for a few seconds and realized that couldn't be it. The villagers were on the attack in that song.

So maybe he was worried about the Beast. The misunderstood creature whose outward appearance gave no indication of the kind-hearted being inside. The possibility moved her even more, Holden's compassion and inner understanding washing over her.

When the service ended, after they'd talked to a few people and when Ella and Holden and his mother were back outside near the cars, Ella's heart was still warm with the realization about Holden praying.

"Thanks for inviting me." Ella hugged Holden's mom, and the feeling went all the way through her. It was hard to believe Mrs. Harris and her mother ever could've been best friends. They were so different. Ella smiled. "I want to know more about following Jesus. Maybe you could help me."

"I'd love that." Holden's mom looked happy. Like her eyes were windows to her soul.

Holden looked at the ground and nodded. "Jesus loves me, this I know ..."

"He's singing ..." His mother's eyes glistened, her words a shocked whisper. "I can't believe he's singing." She looked at Ella. "That was your song, the one the two of you sang most often."

She wished the tune sounded familiar, but it didn't. "He hasn't sung it to me before."

"Maybe because you're here." Mrs. Harris grinned.

Ella wasn't sure if she should talk about the prayer thing in front of Holden, but then she didn't think he would mind. He might even appreciate that finally he was being understood. "I think I figured something out." She looped her purse up onto her shoulder. The air was cool, but the sweet Georgia sky was wide and clear the way it often was in mid-November.

"About Holden?"

"Yes." She moved her elbows a few times. "You know when he does that, when he has his hands up by his chin and he moves his arms?"

"It's a sign of over-stimulation. Like the push-ups." Mrs. Harris knit her brow. "I've never really figured out a pattern. To be honest he does it more at school than at home."

"Exactly." Ella smiled at Holden, and then back to his mother. "When he does that, I think he's praying. I could tell when I was sitting by him."

"I've thought about that, but … well …" Her joy cooled some. "The kids at school … they make fun of him." A shadow fell over her eyes. "His actions seem more of a self-defense."

Ella looked from Holden to his mother. "Maybe it's both."

"… for the Bible tells me so." Holden's song was quiet and hurried. He stared at the pavement.

"Both?" Sorrow and confusion blurred together in Mrs. Harris' expression. "I'm not sure I understand."

"Maybe he prays for them … and also in self-defense." The more Ella considered the possibility, the more real it became. "It makes sense, right? Holden praying when he feels anxious or nervous."

His mom let that sink in for a long moment. She moved closer to Holden. "Is that what you do, Holden? Do you pray for people? Do you pray for your classmates?"

Holden stopped singing. He moved in quick, jerky steps to his mother's car, opened the passenger door, and removed his deck of PECS cards. He sorted through them and finally pulled one from the deck and flashed it in their direction. The picture was of a clock, and beneath it were the words "Every Hour."

Every hour! Ella put her hand to her mouth, but not before a quiet cry escaped her. She and Holden's mother exchanged a look, and Ella wasn't sure if the woman was going to break down crying or laugh out loud. This was the behavior Holden most often demonstrated, and now they understood why.

Holden didn't walk around acting like a crazy person without reason. He was praying. Today he had prayed for the little boy whose precious demonstration in church told them that the price for salvation was paid in full. Holden couldn't talk, and he could barely make eye contact. But he could do this one thing for the people in trouble around him. The exact thing Ella had only just started doing. He could pray. For the bullying jocks and his handicapped friends, and the worn-out teachers.

And yes, even for the Beast.

Twenty-Two

FOR THE NEXT TWO WEEKS ELLA WAS DRAWN TO HOLDEN, desperate to know his thoughts and hopes and dreams. Because after understanding about Holden's constant prayers, Ella was sure they'd only begun to understand the beautiful soul locked inside Holden Harris.

One afternoon before the other kids arrived at the theater room, Holden found her alone on the stage running lines. Mr. Hawkins was in his office, and class didn't officially begin for ten minutes. Holden must've finished his previous class early, because he and a teacher's aide showed up in the doorway.

"He's early." The woman looked anxious to be on her way. "I'll stay if you need me to."

Ella studied Holden, the way he directed his eyes everywhere but at the teacher's aide or at her. She smiled at the woman. "You can go." She held her spot on the stage. "I'm his friend. I'll keep an eye on him."

As soon as the word *friend* crossed Ella's lips, Holden's agitation eased. He looked at her, straight at her, and he nodded. The moment didn't last. Holden looked away and then shuffled to his seat near the back of the room. Same seat, same exact spot for his backpack. But he did something different today. He leaned forward and rested his forearms on his knees, his attention on the stage. Not her, but the stage.

He wants to perform, Ella told herself. She walked a few steps to the boom box set up on a nearby stool and hit the Play button.

Music filled the room and Holden sat up straighter, his chest full, face peaceful. As if he were getting his first fresh air all day.

Ella found her place on stage and began on cue. The song was one Belle sang after being locked in the castle by the Beast, a song about trying to find home inside her heart.

Holden stood up slowly and looked at her, straight at her.

Ella continued singing. She turned her song, her performance, entirely toward him.

They were still alone, the other kids still minutes from joining them. As the song began to build Holden walked slowly to the front of the room and climbed easily up onto the stage beside her. She was too stunned to do anything but keep singing, keep playing the role of Belle.

But now Holden was quietly singing along, and as the song reached the end, Ella somehow forgot the words, too caught up in watching the miracle play out before her. Holden wasn't only singing, he was singing in perfect pitch, his voice rich and melodic and ... well, breathtaking. And finally the room filled with the sound and Ella could do nothing but watch in wondrous awe. Holden's performance was worthy of any audience, and Ella felt weak at the knees as she took it in.

Especially the song's last few lines. "Build higher walls around me ..." Holden's blue eyes pierced her heart, her soul. He kept singing, every word and note perfect. "My heart's far, far away ... home and free."

Ella wanted the song to keep playing, but after a few bars, the music faded. Without breaking eye contact with Holden, Ella hit the Off button and stared at him. "Holden ... that was beautiful."

His performance was so real, so convincing, that Ella expected him to answer her like any other kid, like maybe suddenly and completely he was back to normal. But as soon as the music stopped, Holden stiffened and began wringing his hands.

He looked down, rocking slightly, his eyes glued to the repetitive motions of his fingers.

"Holden?"

He put both hands over his ears and jumped awkwardly off the stage. Before he reached his seat at the back of the room, he dropped to the floor and peeled off a couple dozen push-ups. Then he sat down, opened his backpack, and frantically grabbed for his flash cards.

"Holden …" Mr. Hawkins slipped into the room. His face was ashen, his eyes wide. "That was amazing."

"You heard him … I'm glad." Ella was still standing on the stage, still too amazed by what she'd witnessed to move or speak or do anything but stare in wonder at Holden. She turned to her teacher. "He was standing up here performing." She smiled even as tears filled her eyes. "I couldn't believe it."

If Mr. Hawkins hadn't heard Holden's song, Ella was sure he wouldn't have believed her. She looked at Holden again. He was staring straight down at the flash cards, silently rocking, utterly oblivious to the students starting to file into the room.

"Maybe he'll do it again." Mr. Hawkins' face was curious, as if he had to see for himself. He walked slowly toward the back of the room.

"Mr. Hawkins." Ella hopped down off the stage and followed him. "Be careful," she whispered so only her teacher could hear her. "He might not want to do it again."

The other kids didn't notice the drama playing out with Ella and Mr. Hawkins and Holden. Their voices provided a cushion of sound, so Holden wouldn't be put on the spot, whatever Mr. Hawkins was going to say. The teacher reached Holden and stopped a few feet away. "Holden … can you hear me?"

Holden didn't look up. He kept rocking, sifting the flash cards a little faster than before.

"You have a very nice voice, Holden." Ella stepped up and

put her hand on her friend's shoulder. But the touch made him recoil and again he put his hands to his ears. Ella withdrew her hand, but his reaction hurt. What was that on the stage? Hadn't they shared something special? A moment from the past, maybe? She crossed her arms tight in front of her. "Never mind." She motioned to Mr. Hawkins. "If he wants to perform, he'll let us know."

Holden lowered his hands, sifted furiously through his cards, and pulled one from the deck. He handed it to Ella—a sign that he trusted her. Ella took the card, and when she looked at it she felt fresh tears sting at the corners of her eyes. The card showed a remorseful stick figure and it read simply "I'm sorry."

Ella showed Mr. Hawkins, and the teacher nodded, a sad, defeated sort of a nod. Then he cleared his voice. "Okay, class." He strode to the front of the room, taking control of the students. "Get out your scripts."

Ella hesitated, the card still in her hand. "It's okay, Holden. I'm not mad." She spoke softly and smiled, in case he was watching her with his peripheral vision. "I liked singing with you. You were ... well, you were amazing." She handed him the card, and as she did, for a few seconds he held gently to her fingers. Then for the slightest moment he lifted his eyes to hers and again the connection was intense and immediate. Holden was in there. He was in there and he wanted to come out, wanted to connect with her and the rest of his classmates. If Ella was reading him right, Holden even wanted to perform.

Please, God, set him free. Bring him out of the place where he hides away. Her heart melted for the young man before her, for the mountain of effort it took simply for him to make eye contact. The students were taking their seats, so Ella didn't have much time. She lifted her eyes to the sky outside the classroom window. *Lord, I know You love Holden. Could You give him a miracle? Please? Thanks for listening. Amen.*

Ella sat down and opened her script, but she couldn't think about Belle or the Beast or anything other than what she'd witnessed with Holden. For a short time he was exactly who he was supposed to be—singing and performing on a stage, his song in tune, his voice something Ella would remember forever. She would spend more time with Holden, and she would create more moments like the one they'd shared before the room filled with people. If somewhere deep inside him Holden wanted to sing, then Ella would do her part, the way she'd done it today.

She would play the music.

MANNY HAWKINS COULD BARELY FOCUS ON THE REHEARSAL, because he'd seen more than he let on. When the beautiful tenor voice filled the rehearsal room before class, he set down his pen and stopped searching for dollars in the theater department's skeletal line budget. He walked to his office door and opened it just a crack. For the next minute he stared through a half-inch opening, barely able to breathe, not believing his eyes. Holden Harris? The mesmerizing voice belonged to the autistic kid? How was that even possible?

He couldn't see from his vantage point whether Holden was making eye contact with Ella, but he wasn't only singing. He was performing. That much was undeniable. He half expected Holden to bounce up from his seat and willingly take the stage for an encore round—even once the other students began filling the room. But wherever Holden had emerged from, he was lost to that place once more.

And so it was with great anticipation that for the next few weeks Manny watched through the crack in his door as Holden arrived early each day, found his place on stage with Ella, and sang through nearly every song in the show. Manny didn't talk to Ella about what he was witnessing, but he was pretty sure she knew he was watching. Sometimes before class would start she would exchange a look with him, and after a few days she approached him.

"You can hear him, right? He sings with me every day, Mr. Hawkins." Her eyes were earnest and believing. "Give him a part … please. He can handle it. Just something small."

No matter what cosmic alteration or strangely arranged miracle Manny had witnessed with Holden Harris, he was hardly ready to assign a part to a kid with autism. This was his last production. If word got around that special-needs kids were in the cast, no one would come. Kids at Fulton High weren't looking to see these kids succeed. They were looking for a good show. And if the past was any indication, they weren't even looking for that.

Manny sighed, working his hand into his thinning hair. "It's not that simple. We're under review." He waved his hand at the aging props and weathered stage. "Everything has to be perfect this time …" He held her eyes, and then shrugged, defeated. "The answer is no. I don't expect you to understand."

Ella tried again the next day. "He can sing, Mr. Hawkins. He's the best male vocalist we have … if only we can get him to work with the cast."

"That's just it." A sad laugh came from Manny. "This isn't a project, it's a play. We don't have time to teach him."

The look in Ella's eyes almost broke Manny's heart. For a minute she reminded him of his oldest daughter, the way she looked when Manny's ex-wife stopped at his apartment on her way out of the state. That day his daughter looked the same way Ella looked. Betrayed and confused, and certain that the pain she was feeling was all because of him.

After that, Ella stopped asking. Even so Manny was drawn to the metamorphosis in Holden the way he hadn't been drawn to anything in years. He waited for 2:10 each afternoon and watched Holden through the crack in his office door. At the end of the second week, on a Friday, Ella was running through the lines at the end of the play when the Beast transforms into the Prince.

Manny didn't breathe, didn't move as he watched Holden appear at the classroom door. He moved slowly toward the stage, toward the place where Ella was running her lines.

Ella had to see him, had to be aware that she was being watched. But instead of turning her attention to Holden, she slipped fully and completely into character. As if she were looking at a dying Beast, she dropped to her knees and covered her face. Her crying sounded desperate and convincing. "No! Please … please don't leave me." She looked up at a blank place on the stage. "I … I love you."

But then, instead of waiting for what would've been a time of fog and special effects where the Beast and the Prince switch places, Ella stood and purposefully started a song. Not the reprise that was supposed to happen at the end of this scene, but the entire theme song. As the music filled the room, Holden moved onto stage with the athleticism of a football player. He looked at Ella with heroic kindness as she turned to him.

"Tale as old as time … True as it can be."

Ella reached out — tentative and unwilling to make the first contact with Holden. But as if he'd never landed anywhere on the autistic spectrum, Holden took her hands and sang about finding an unexpected friendship, each word filled with meaning.

The next lines came from Ella, their hands still joined. And as the music swelled they danced in a circle, their eyes intent on each other. His words felt aimed straight at her heart. The message was fitting, about being afraid and not quite ready for this kind of friendship.

They finished the song together and Manny wished he'd thought to capture the moment on film. It was — without a doubt — one of the most beautiful duet moments that had ever graced any stage at Fulton High.

"Tale as old as time ... song as old as rhyme ... Beauty and the Beast."

Suddenly, as if Manny were seeing a vision, the pieces came together. What if Holden Harris could do this for an audience? Wouldn't even the callous, indifferent, ignorant students at Fulton line up for the chance to see what Manny had just witnessed?

The music stopped, and just this once Manny hoped the change wouldn't come, that Holden wouldn't respond as if someone had killed the lights. *Stay beside her, Holden ... Come on. Don't fade away ...*

But in the absence of horns and flutes and strings, the switch flipped sure as Friday. Holden lurched off the stage, a different person, nervous, anxious, all signs of the confident performer gone. This time he flapped his arms, his hands tucked up near his chin—something he hadn't seen Holden do for weeks.

Manny stepped back from his office door and blinked twice. What was he thinking? He could no sooner put Holden Harris in the role of Prince than he could bring in circus animals for intermission. Never mind what Holden was capable of—there was no way to reach him on a regular basis, no way to count on him. And Manny needed kids he could count on—now more than ever. Holden Harris could never be a part of the cast.

The idea was outlandish and with that Manny vowed the obvious—he wouldn't consider such a thing again.

Twenty-Three

ELLA HADN'T BEEN TO A BASKETBALL GAME ALL SEASON. SHE AND Jake weren't talking, and she rarely hung out with her old friends — even at lunch. But that Friday LaShante begged her to go. "Everyone else is meeting at Callie's house before the game and drinking." She rolled her eyes. "I'm not down with that, so come on. I need you, Ella. I don't want to go by myself."

She had thought about spending the evening at Holden's. She had stopped by a few times now — mostly to tell his mom about Holden's performances — the ones that lasted only a few minutes and took place every day lately before rehearsals. Today, his mom had even come to school to watch — through the hallway window. Holden didn't know, so when they finished singing, Ella cast a quick grin at his mom. On the other side of the glass, she was wiping tears. It wasn't that she hadn't believed Ella. But seeing Holden like this must've been like … well, like watching how Holden might've been if he'd never slipped into autism.

But tonight the idea of the high school basketball game sounded fun. She made a plan to pick up LaShante, and the whole way to the game she tried to explain the progress she'd seen in Holden. "You should hear him."

"He can sing?" LaShante collected handfuls of her fine braids and swept them into a ponytail. "Can kids with autism do that?"

"Sometimes." Ella kept her eyes on the road. "I think Holden hears the music. Maybe more than healthy kids."

"Hmmm."

"No, I mean really." Ella couldn't overstate the change in

225

Holden. "He sounds like Michael Buble or something. Seriously. He can sing, and when he does he looks straight at me. Like a melt-your-heart kind of look."

"Wow." LaShante raised one eyebrow. "If I didn't know better, I'd think you had feelings for him."

"Not like that." Ella laughed, and the sound was lighthearted. "He's my friend. He's been my friend since we were three."

"But he's cute." LaShante's eyes danced. "I mean, come on, girl, he's the hottest guy at Fulton. Weirdness and all." She pressed her lips together. "Mmmmm-hmm. And those blue eyes. Straight at you? I don't know …"

"It's not like that." Ella laughed again as she turned into the school parking lot. "But you have to hear him sing. It's like he's a different person."

"Maybe music is the key." LaShante sat up straighter and adjusted her pale blue turtleneck.

"It is. That's what I'm saying." Ella parked the car and turned to her friend. "Music brings him out, it opens him up."

"So I guess the answer is obvious." LaShante opened the car door and smiled. "Girl… you gotta find a way to keep the music going."

Ella grinned. "Exactly." She and LaShante hurried out of the car and through the parking lot to the gym. The game was a blowout—Jake and his buddies beaten soundly by the crosstown rivals. During halftime, LaShante bought popcorn and a Sprite and then once she was back in the stands she turned troubled eyes at Ella. "I have to tell you something."

Ella felt her heartbeat quicken. LaShante didn't like high school drama anymore than Ella did. Whatever was coming, it was worth talking about. Otherwise LaShante wouldn't have brought it up. "Something about Krissy or Jenny?"

"No." LaShante scowled. "About Jake. I heard it this week and

I wanted to text you. But I thought ... I thought I'd wait until I could tell you in person."

"Okay." Ella felt herself relax. She didn't care about Jake anymore. There was almost nothing LaShante could tell her that would affect her night one way or the other. "Tell me."

"He's telling everyone that you and Holden ..." She hesitated, shadows in her eyes. Very little embarrassed LaShante. Of all Ella's friends, she was the most outspoken. But here, her pretty brown eyes looked unsure about whether she could go on. "He's telling people you're hooking up with Holden." She raised her brow. "Like ... all the way, hooking up." She rolled her eyes. "So I feel terrible joking around about you and him. You know, on the way here."

A sick feeling slammed into Ella. "Why would he do that?" Ella looked out at the basketball floor. How could she ever have liked Jake Collins? The fact that he'd ever charmed her into thinking he was a good guy made her angry with herself. The Eagles were taking the court, passing the ball around and taking practice shots, warming up for the second half. Even from her place in the stands, Ella could see the cocky smile on Jake's face.

LaShante sighed, and the look on her face grew uncomfortable once again. "There's more."

Ella steeled herself. Whatever it was, she could trust LaShante. And if it meant she needed to tune out on the social scene at Fulton altogether, so be it. She'd already done that, anyway. LaShante and Holden were the only real friends she had—and graduation was only a semester away. Who cared about Jake?

Her friend crossed her arms and made a face. "He's got a bet going with Sam. Sometime before graduation, he'll sleep with you—one way or another. Otherwise he owes Sam a hundred bucks."

"A hundred bucks?" Ella wanted to throw up. Was that all she was worth to Jake and his boys? A hundred-dollar bet? Suddenly a thought occurred to her. "One way or another?"

"Yeah." Anger flashed in LaShante's eyes. "He said if Holden gets you … he wants you too. Sounds like a threat to me." She jerked her thumb in the direction of the basketball court. "Like maybe you should tell the authorities."

Jake Collins forcing himself on her? In September, Ella would've laughed at the idea. But now… a shiver ran down her arms. She would keep her distance from him. If her mom was involved in her life, she'd go home tonight and tell her, first thing. But her mom didn't even know her. No, she'd have to look out for herself. She'd keep her distance and stick to spending time with Holden and — once in a while — with LaShante.

Ella was almost glad for another reason to stay away. The longer she was away from the popular crowd of kids, the more she could see the worst of them for what they were. Cocky, arrogant bullies. Between them they had a code of ethics that required mean, mocking behavior. They sat together at lunch and called out mean names to anyone who walked by — kids who were too short or too smart or too fat. Skinny kids like Michael and kids like Holden.

Ella watched the guys run up and down the floor, watched them sub in and out of the game and argue with the coach or the refs. Did any of them wish they could break free the way she had? Wish they could live their own lives and make their own social decisions without having to impress Jake or his guys? Ella had to think so.

Holden wasn't the only one locked up inside himself.

Ella didn't see Michael Schwartz until after the game, outside on the school's front courtyard. Ella and LaShante were talking with some of the other girls, hearing about a party later that night, when Michael exited from the school's main front doors. He might've been practicing with the school band, because he had his flute case tucked under his arm and he was headed for the bike racks on the edge of the parking lot.

"So Jake's been hitting on this ugly freshman girl." Krissy was more giggly than usual. Probably the drinking beforehand. "She'll be at the party, Ella. You should totally come, girl. I mean, then you could get Jake back to his senses."

"Yeah, he's your guy." Jenny put her hands on her hips. "You two need to figure things out before Christmas break."

"I don't like Jake." Ella was patient, but she wanted to leave. She kept part of her attention on Michael. He looked lonely, troubled. She thought about excusing herself from the girls and talking to him. She remembered to smile. "The freshman girl can have him."

"Have who?"

She felt someone behind her, and she turned in time to see a freshly showered Jake strutting up. Sam and Ryan were on either side. Ella wanted to scowl at the guys, but she stopped herself. Better to leave without a lot of drama. She met his eyes briefly. "Jake ... Sam ... Ryan."

Krissy bounced into the space between them. "Good game, guys. The refs were terrible. You definitely should've won!"

"Yeah, that three-pointer was the bomb," Jenny giggled. "Right girls?"

"Yeah, you know it ... I was on tonight." Jake grinned—his arrogance like an impenetrable force around him. His eyes were on Ella, and her alone. "We'll get 'em next time."

Before the other girls could spout off another bit of empty praise, Sam nudged Jake hard in the arm. "Look," he motioned toward the parking lot. "There's that freak kid. Goth music boy, remember?"

A sick feeling started in Ella's stomach. "Leave him alone." She didn't say it loud or forcefully, but she said it.

"What's this?" Jake laughed—the mean sort of laugh that

meant he was about to pick up steam. He kicked lightly nudged Ella's white tennis shoe with his own. "Don't tell me you have feelings for Queer Boy too? Him and Holden Harris?" He chuckled louder and shoved Sam's shoulder. "You hear that?"

Sam sneered at Ella. "Coupla freaks."

Jake moved out from the crowd in Michael's direction. When he was twenty yards away, he shouted at Michael. "Hey Emo Boy ..."

Michael was bent over working on his bike lock, his flute case on the ground beside him. He must've been struggling with the combination, because it was taking too long. Once more Ella wanted to run and help him, but that wouldn't be good. Not with Jake and his gang watching.

"Didn't you hear me?" Jake's tone turned mean. Loud and mean. "What's the problem? Can't remember your combination?"

Other guys from the basketball team joined Jake, forming a group, laughing and chuckling quietly, approving his attack by their presence. "Freak," Jake yelled, "what're you doing here? Why weren't you at the game?"

"He had flute practice." Sam used a high-pitch mocking sort of voice. "Like all the gay kids."

"Hey," Ella stepped up to the guys and pushed Jake in the shoulder. "Shut up. Leave him alone."

Jake jerked away from Ella, ignoring her. "That's it, right?" he shouted, loud enough that other kids, average kids passing by could hear every word. "You're gay, right? Just come out and say it, already. Guys who play the flute are gay."

Michael finally worked the lock open and pulled his bike free. He stood and stared at Jake, and for just a moment Ella thought the quiet kid might fight back. Anger flashed in his eyes, an anger they could see clearly in the light of the parking lot. But he must've realized he didn't stand a chance against Jake and his buddies, so he picked up his flute and climbed onto his bike, the case firm against his ribs.

"You see that?" Jake laughed out loud and looked at the other guys. "Emo Boy's a queer."

"Jake!" Ella pushed him again. "Stop it."

This time LaShante separated from the girls and joined her. "You're such a loser, you know that?" She spat the words. She snapped her fingers at him, her voice loud as she looked him up and down. "On and off the court."

LaShante's outburst broke up the moment. The guys stopped laughing and stood quietly, shifting and glancing nervously at each other. Shame fell over all of them, even Jake. Ella's protest might not have made much of an impact, but LaShante had their attention. She put her hands on her hips and glared at Jake, then Sam and the others. "You oughta' be ashamed of your sorry selves." With that she motioned to Ella. "We're done."

As they walked off, Ella caught a glimpse of Michael. He was riding away on his bike, one hand on the handlebars, the other tucked in around his flute case. He made his way into the cross-walk and turned left, probably toward his house or apartment. Wherever he lived.

"Idiots." LaShante was worked up. She walked fast toward the car. "Makes me want to catch up with that kid and offer him a ride. Nobody should be treated like that."

"Wait!" Ella stopped, and then started again — moving faster than before. "That's a great idea. We could put his bike in the back."

They hurried to the car and left the parking lot quickly. Three blocks down the road they caught up to him, and a sense of desperate relief flooded Ella. It wasn't too late. They could still let the kid know someone cared. That she was sorry for Jake's behavior. She slowed her car at the next light and pushed a button to roll down the window in her Acura MDX. LaShante did the talking, since Michael was riding up on that side of the car.

"Hey ..." She stuck her head out the window, her voice friendly. "Wanna ride?"

Michael looked almost alarmed. Ella leaned over and added her approval. "Really. We can throw your bike in the back."

Other cars gathered at the stoplight, so they didn't have long. If Michael wanted a ride, he'd have to say so. LaShante tried again. "Come on ... We can pull over."

Michael's eyes darted at the other cars, as if maybe he was looking for Jake and the guys in one of the vehicles. He shook his head, his eyes wide. "That's okay." Sweat beaded up on his forehead. "I got it. I don't live far."

"You sure?" LaShante sounded disappointed. "It's no trouble."

The light turned green and Michael started pedaling. "I'm fine." He nodded once more at them and set off down the street.

LaShante powered the window back up—the breeze was cold for this time of year. "We did what we could." She shivered and folded her arms, running her hands over her sweater. "Makes me so mad, those guys." She threw her hands in the air. "Why are they like that? Bullying everyone around them?"

"They're jerks. You said it."

Ella's heart ached. Michael must feel terrible. She thought about maybe stopping and insisting that he get in her car, but then ... if Jake and the guys drove by they'd just pick on Michael all the more Monday morning. For getting a ride with a girl.

LaShante was still fuming. "Where's Jake live? We should go wait for him." She gritted her teeth, still boiling over what had happened back at the school. "I'd like to be in his driveway when he pulls in and get in his face ... let him know what's up."

But in the end they decided against that, and Ella took LaShante home. Before she climbed out of the car, LaShante tossed her ponytail of fine braids and jabbed her pointer finger into the dark night air. "If you can be a friend to Holden Harris, then I can be a friend to that Michael kid." She shook her head, disgust flooding her tone. "Forget about those jocks. They're not worth the time."

"They're not."

"Plus ... I love the flute." She smiled as she swung her feet onto the curb. "Maybe Michael will let me hear him play."

Ella liked the idea, and as she pulled away, the picture of LaShante hanging out with Michael Schwartz made her smile. Maybe Michael could actually teach her how to play. Wouldn't that be something? She and Holden in a play together, and LaShante and Michael playing the flute in the school band. Her happy thoughts faded and anger swelled inside her as she pictured Jake once more, the way he'd treated Michael. The way he was betting he'd treat her sometime before graduation. She shuddered at the idea. It was time for a change around Fulton, and if that change depended on her and LaShante, so be it.

After tonight they were both up to the challenge.

Twenty-Four

MICHAEL SCHWARTZ WAS OUT OF BREATH AND SICK TO HIS STOM-ach by the time he rode his bike into the apartment complex at the corner of Walnut and Main. His mom was at the kitchen table as he walked through the front door. She had her head in her hands, a glass of cheap wine beside her.

"You're late." She looked up, weary. Always weary. "I thought practice was over at eight."

"We had to stay longer." He still had his flute case tucked under his arm. His mom didn't like him leaving it out. She didn't like it, period. "The Christmas concert's next week. Remember?"

"Oh." She stared at the stack of mail and thumbed through the top few envelopes in the pile. With shaky hands she took a sip of wine. "I forgot." She didn't quite look up again, but her eyes found his anyway. "You thought about what I said earlier?"

"About the drums?" Michael shifted. His tennis shoes had a hole at the bottom, and he was pretty sure he had a blister.

"Yes." She adjusted her tone, less frustrated, more patient. "Your father played the drums. He'd be proud to see his boy on the drums."

"He's got a new family." Michael walked a few steps into the adjoining kitchen and poured himself a glass of water. He hated when his mom brought up the drums or his father. Hated it. "Besides…," He chugged back half a glass. "I don't like the drums. I like the flute."

"But maybe just once you could—" She stopped and hesitated for a long moment. Then she exhaled and turned back to the mail. "Never mind. The flute's nice. Play the flute, Michael."

"I will." He finished the water and set the glass down. For a long time he studied his mother. She'd been pretty once, back when his dad lived with them. When they were a family. Three years ago he came clean about an affair, and the fact that he had two babies in another part of town. Now he lived there and only called every week or so.

Michael remembered being in kindergarten and finding his father's drum set in the spare room. His dad had helped him onto the short stool and placed the sticks in his hand. "One day you'll play the drums, just like me." He could still see the smile in his father's eyes, still hear the hope in his voice.

When his father left, he didn't take much. But he took what mattered. The drums and his mom's pretty. All the pretty she had left, anyway. Michael felt sorry for her, tied down to the bills and this way of life. She didn't need any of it. If it wasn't for him she could start over again. New marriage, new family. Same as Michael's dad.

He walked over, put his hand on her shoulder, and kissed her cheek. "Need help?"

She seemed slightly startled by his question. Her tired face lifted to his. "I'll be fine." Her smile didn't reach her eyes. She still had her hospital uniform on. She was a nurse's assistant— changing bedpans and running errands for patients. "I'm working a double tomorrow. Don't wait up for me."

"Okay." He lingered, the way he almost never did. "You work too hard."

"It's life." Again her smile was weak. She squinted at him a little. "You okay? You're acting funny."

"I'm good." He flashed a smile, one that felt as foreign as it probably looked. "Hey." He gave her shoulder a tender squeeze. "Love you, Mom."

"Love you too." She was already turned back to the mail, back to the bills. It was probably borderline rocket science trying to pay for life on her salary. Especially lately. His dad had been laid off, so no money was coming in from him.

Michael headed down the hall, keenly aware of the stained threadbare carpeting and the shabby walls. They'd lived here since the divorce, and the landlord hadn't made a single upgrade. He entered his room and shut the door behind him. Maybe he'd jump rope. He did that sometimes. When he hurt so bad he couldn't stand another minute. When he was so angry he wanted to break a window or punch his fist through the wall. He would jump rope for half an hour sometimes. Until the pain subsided enough so he could breathe.

The jump rope hung across the dresser, waiting for him. His respite.

Or maybe he'd play the flute. The case was cold from the ride home, and as he set it on the end of his bed he opened the case.

For a long minute he stared at the instrument. "Play the drums …" He let his mother's words wash over him again. Like that would ever happen. He lifted the flute from its case and brought the cold metal to his lips. His favorite song from the upcoming Christmas concert was "O Holy Night." He reached into the case and pulled out the folded sheet music.

He opened it and studied the notes, soaked in the meaning of the words. Because he'd never felt that in all his life. A holy night. He blew just hard enough for quiet sounds to fill the room. No matter how quietly he played, his mom was bound to hear him. Maybe she would like the sound and come sit with him. Come listen to him play the flute. She hadn't heard him play in almost a year, not since the last Christmas concert. He practiced at school and when she was at work.

Because he didn't want her sitting in the other room wishing he was playing the drums.

The words sang softly to him as he played ... *O Holy Night ...the stars are brightly shining ... It is the night of the dear Savior's birth.* The music filled him and eased the pain. The pain that was like a towering grizzly bear, grabbing at him, clawing him. Devouring him. *Long lay the world ...in sin and error pining ...*

Was there really a Savior? Really a baby born to save the world? If so, his mom and dad had never talked about Him. They never took the family to church or gave Michael a reason to believe in God. But the song gave him hope. *O Holy Night ...* like maybe it really happened, somewhere back in time. The stars brightly shining.

Michael lowered the flute to his lap. Only gay guys played the flute? Was that really what everyone thought? He was some gay emo guy who played the flute? Like a girl or something? He laid the flute on the bed and stared out the window. It faced northwest, Michael made a point of knowing that. Northwest, the same direction three miles away where his father lived with his new family.

I'll never play the drums, Dad ... He stood and moved to the window, mesmerized by the darkness, by the vastness of it. Why was he here, anyway? His dad didn't want him. The trade-in was over and done with. New wife, new kids. And his mother? She worked all those hours because of him, right? If she didn't have a kid to feed and clothe, maybe she'd have time to go on a date.

He thought about Monday morning, and the pain slashed at him like so many times before. How many people had heard Jake Collins shout at him tonight? Calling him gay and queer and telling the whole world that he played the flute. How many kids would sneer at him Monday morning, whispering about the gay kid who played the flute like a girl?

He used to feel sorry for kids like Holden Harris. Jake's crowd never let up on Holden—especially since Ella had become his friend. But here was the thing … Holden didn't know the difference. In his private world, the pain couldn't touch him.

But what about Michael Schwartz? Skinny, cheaply dressed Michael Schwartz? Where was his private world? The place where pain couldn't touch him? He looked around his room again… the single bed, the worn-out cork bulletin board with a math paper from last year still tacked onto one corner. Tickets to a Georgia Tech baseball game he and his mom had gone to a couple years back. An invitation to a 5K race from a year ago. Back when jumping rope seemed like it could lead to a passion for running. The empty black night on the other side of the window… the flute lying on his bed …

Where was his relief? He closed his eyes and he could see them still, hear them shouting above the roar. "You're gay, right? Just come out and say it, already. Guys who play the flute are gay … Guys who play the flute are gay."

How was he going to tell everyone at Fulton that Jake Collins was wrong? That the flute calmed the bear—if only for a little while?

Relief … he needed relief. He didn't want to play the drums. He wasn't that little boy sitting next to his dad, dreaming for the first time about sharing something like drums with his daddy. No more. He loved the flute, and he wasn't gay. No matter what Jake said. Michael closed his eyes tight. The pain was gaining on him, and if he didn't find a way out he would be ripped apart, piece by piece. Any minute that would happen. Then … like a single safe place in the darkest of forests … Michael opened his eyes and saw it. The only other thing in his bedroom besides the furniture.

His jump rope.

From there his eyes darted across the room to the chin-up bar that hung on the backside of his bedroom door. He didn't do pull-ups often, but it held his weight. Michael already knew that. The possibility ran like wildfire, like the craziest intoxicating drug—through his heart and mind and maybe even straight through his soul. Who would miss him? The kids at school wouldn't notice he was gone. His dad could stop feeling guilty— if he ever felt guilty—about not sending money. He had a new family, and kids who would probably grow up to play the drums.

And his mom could quit working doubles.

It was a way out, for sure. The only one Michael could see. He had to move quickly before he changed his mind. He stood and grabbed the rope, looped it around his neck in a hurry. The fibers scratched against the skin around his throat and he coughed a few times. It would be over before he could get scared and stop himself. Here was his relief, a way to stop the onslaught of pain. This way pain wouldn't have the last say for Michael Schwartz. He wouldn't have to defend himself to anyone Monday morning.

Boy Scouts had been another bust for him—without a dad it wasn't a lot of fun. But he'd been in long enough to learn about knots. It didn't take long. Less than a minute. He did a pull-up and adjusted the rope, fixed the knot so it wouldn't slide. All he had to do was let go, and that would be that. No more Jake Collins, no more dad living three miles out the northwest-facing window. No more kids thinking he was gay because he loved the flute.

The flute.

For a minute he'd forgotten about the flute. That was a way out, too, right. What had his teacher told him that evening? He was one of the best flutists she'd ever heard. *"You could play in a symphony one day, Michael. You have a very bright future ahead ..."*

Bright future ... bright future ... bright future ...

Maybe he didn't want to do this. He tried to lengthen the rope, slip it back from the knot so he could find his way to the floor. His arms were shaking... he couldn't hold this position much longer. Panic coursed through him. Just because of his dad and the drums ... because of Jake Collins? He was taking this way out because of them? He stared at the flute and tried to keep his grip, tried to pull the rope free.

But as he tried, his hands slipped and he fell, the rope jerking tight around his neck. He couldn't breathe, could barely even cough. "Mom." He squeaked out the word, but it was only a whisper. "Help me … help!"

Fear gripped at him, tighter than the rope digging through his skin, cutting off air and life and circulation. Fear bigger than the bear from earlier. "Help …"

His neck was on fire, his lungs even worse. But as the seconds passed, as the air drained from his lungs, the pain let up. Black spots dancing before his eyes. The last thing he saw — the very last thing — was his flute. The flute he should've spent a lifetime playing … for audiences all over the world.

His flute.

One day his father would've come to see him play and he would've said, "Good job, Michael. Very good job." And every Jake Collins of the world would be sweeping floors while every Michael Schwartz was making music for symphonies, and life would win. Because he wanted to live! Living would always be better than this … than … than —

Suddenly the message of the Christmas song filled his heart and he knew, he absolutely knew. There was a Savior! He had come to earth that holy night, and He had lived then. He lived still. *Please, God … save me … I'm sorry. I don't want to die … please, God … I need a Savior!*

He lurched again at the rope, but it was too tight, the knot too sure. He couldn't breathe, and he grabbed at the fibers binding to his neck. *Set me free, God … please. I believe in You!*

There was no answer, nothing but a strange, sad sort of peace that swept over the pain and stilled the roar. No more names and strange looks … no more wishes from his mother that maybe — just maybe — he would play the drums. No more longing through a northwest-facing window ... All of it ... all of it was over now. One final time the Christmas song filled his heart and he was carried away on the words ...

Truly He taught us to love one another ... His law is love, and His gospel is peace ... Chains shall He break, for the slave is our brother ... and in His name, all oppression shall cease ...

All oppression ... all oppression ... all oppression.

Ceased.

For all time ceased.

Twenty-Five

AN HOUR AFTER THE PAPER HIT THE SIDEWALK SATURDAY MORN-
ing, the news spread through the tree-lined neighborhoods and
cheerful North Atlanta suburbs surrounding Fulton High. They'd
lost one of their own. Michael Schwartz was dead. Victim of a
hanging.

An apparent suicide.

Manny Hawkins set down his morning paper and turned dry
eyes out the window at the sunny day outside. Shouldn't it be
raining, he thought? Wouldn't that be apropos on a day like this?
He stared at the headline ... let it seep into his heart and mind.

"Fulton High Junior Hangs Himself."

The air inside Manny's two-bedroom condo was stuffy. Too
stuffy. He stood and took long strides toward the patio door.
Once it was open, he breathed deep. Two breaths, three. Until
the nausea began to subside. He'd had Michael in his class the
last two years. English Comp I and II. The kid seemed normal
enough. Quiet, a little dark in the wardrobe department, but
nothing too out there. Nothing gothic or deathlike. No signs that
this past Friday night he'd ride his bike home from band practice
and hang himself in his bedroom.

Manny pushed himself back to his kitchen table and sat down
again. The breeze through the open door was good, a reminder of
life. The life that still reigned all around him. He scanned the article, catching quotes from the boy's mother and father. The two
were separated—nothing too unusual. His father commented

through a family friend stating only that the family "appreciated the prayers and support from the community."

His mother told police the teen left no suicide note, nothing but his flute on his bed and the music to "O Holy Night" open beside it. Manny narrowed his eyes and tried to look past the morning sunshine, to a place where he might find some under-standing, some rationale for Michael's death. But there was no such place, no such understanding.

Lately he'd stayed more to himself at work, kept to his office and his classes and spent little time in the hallways. But once at the beginning of the year he happened into the space outside his classroom in time to see Jake Collins and a bunch of football players laughing and pointing. Not a group laugh or a good-time laugh, but the sort of laugh that was directed *at* someone. As the memory came back, it settled like rocks in his gut.

The kid was Michael Schwartz. Slinking out of the build-ing at the other end of the hallway, his face downcast, shoulders slumped. Flute case tucked beneath his arm. In that moment back in September, Manny had known that whatever he'd just missed, it had to do with Michael. Call it mockery or bullying, but it had happened.

And Manny had done nothing about it.

He looked back at the paper, at the school photo beneath the headline. The face was the same one he'd seen at the end of the hallway that day. Michael Schwartz, the kid being laughed at. Manny stared at the eyes of the kid he'd failed. The kid they had all failed. There was no sign, no way of believing that behind those eyes was enough suffering to make the guy put a rope around his neck.

Manny stared back out the patio door. He had a reason for not saying anything about the incident in the hallway. He was busy... his next class was arriving... he had notes to review and lessons to tend to. Besides, kids had changed since he first started teaching. Bullying was normal now. Jocks like Sam and Jake picked on everyone… it was practically understood. There were exceptions, but most of them were mean. Plain and simple.

Manny sighed and folded up the newspaper. Who was he kidding? He couldn't expect the kids at Fulton High to turn out for the spring musical. These kids were rich and privileged and completely self-absorbed. They didn't care about anyone but themselves. In fact, most kids at Fulton made teachers long for retirement. They were bad enough to make the staff seriously worry about the future. Last year two kids had killed themselves. This year it could be more.

A breeze wafted through the apartment and brought with it the single exception, the reason he would return to school on Monday, to a building with one more empty seat… the reason he would keep teaching theater and plodding through rehearsals for a program that would be nonexistent after this year. The reason was strong and sure, because he'd seen it with his own eyes. Seen the kindness and the transformation. The miracle, even. He couldn't write óff the entire student body, because the reason for his hope fell on the shoulders of two of his very own students.

Ella Reynolds and Holden Harris.

ELLA DARTED DOWN THE STAIRS, CHECKING HER BLUE LEATHER purse as she ran. She needed her wallet and her phone. She was supposed to meet LaShante in fifteen minutes. The two were buying Christmas gifts for kids at Holden's church. Last Sunday the church had placed a giving tree in the foyer, chock-full of paper ornaments. Each one represented a boy or girl in the community who wouldn't have Christmas presents unless someone stepped in to help.

This year, Ella wanted to be one of those people.

She'd called LaShante an hour ago and explained her idea. LaShante's dad was president of a bank. She and Ella never wanted for anything. "But I've never thought about buying presents for strangers," she told her friend. "What do you think?"

"Girl, are you kidding me? That's the best idea ever." LaShante's smile was audible in her voice. "I'll be ready."

As Ella reached the kitchen, she saw her mom reading the newspaper at the long stretch of brown granite that made up the kitchen bar. Her mom looked small and frail, less confident all the time. Ella breezed into the kitchen and grabbed an apple. "Bye." She still had no interest in talking to her mom at length. They had nothing in common. "I'm going shopping with LaShante."

Her mom looked up. "Michael Schwartz ... you know him, right?"

Ella stopped and turned toward her mom. The water was running, her apple poised above the sink. "What about him?"

Her mom looked down at the open paper and then up at Ella again. "Did you know him well?"

Images from last night flashed in Ella's mind. Michael with his flute case tucked under his arm, struggling with his bike lock and bearing the brunt of Jake's meanness. Ella set the apple down on the counter. "What about him?"

"I'm not sure if it's the same Michael you know ..." Her mom hesitated. "But a Michael Schwartz from Fulton High ... He killed himself last night."

It was like someone had pulled a plug on all the blood in her body. She grabbed onto the counter and opened her mouth to speak, to say there wasn't any way Michael Schwartz—her Michael Schwartz—had killed himself, and that there had to be a mistake because he had a performance coming up with the school band and LaShante wanted to hear him play the flute.

But no words would come.

She bent over a little and found a single breath, enough to push her around the kitchen counter to the place next to where her mom was still sitting, a sad, uncomfortable look on her face.

Ella slid the paper over and stared at the headline. And there he was ... there was Michael, with the warm brown eyes and hopeful half smile. "No." The word came quietly at first. "No!" She dropped her purse and raked her hand through her hair. A few quick steps toward the stairs and she spun around again and returned to the newspaper. "Not Michael!"

"Ella ... I'm sorry. I thought—"

"No!" She didn't want her mom's pity. How could this happen? She forced herself to focus on the newspaper, on the headline above Michael's photo. *"Fulton High Junior Hangs Himself."* "No, Mom ... no, this can't be real." She shoved the newspaper and clung to the nearest bar stool. Why hadn't she pulled over and forced him to take the ride? She could've talked to him, told him not to worry about Jake Collins because the guy was a jerk and Michael wasn't. Michael was a kind soul—he was one of the only friends Holden Harris had, right? And now ...

Now he was gone, and there was nothing she could do about it.

The tears came in a rush, and she squeezed her eyes shut. "Why ...? What's wrong with people?" The question came out as a wail, and before she knew what was happening, she felt hands on her shoulders and the smell of her mom's perfume filled her senses. "Ella ... I'm here."

Ella wanted to fight her mother's comfort. She hadn't cared about Ella's senior year ... hadn't asked about her participating in the school play or wondered why Jake didn't come around anymore. And she didn't care about Holden Harris. But here ... now ... more than anything in the world, Ella wanted her mom to love her. She couldn't bring Michael back, couldn't give him a ride or hug him or tell him everything would be okay at school on Monday. It was too late for that.

But it wasn't too late for this.

"Mom ...?" Ella turned and for the first time in longer than she could remember, she clung to her mother, clung to what little life they still shared together. And then — like she'd done once in a while when she was a little girl — Ella buried her face against her mother's shoulder and wept.

HOLDEN LIKED HAVING HIS COUSIN KATE LIVE WITH THEM. SHE was happy, always happy. And she treated him like a friend. The way a friend should be treated. Plus he liked that Kate loved pancakes with whipped cream for breakfast. Even on a rainy Monday-morning school day like today.

"Can I sit beside you, Holden?" Kate tugged on his sleeve when he was already sitting at the kitchen table looking at his PECS cards.

Kate had pretty, light blonde hair and blue eyes, and sometimes Holden thought that looking at her was like looking into a mirror because he had the same exact shade of blue eyes and tan skin too. From the Atlanta summers. Holden smiled at his little cousin. *Yes, Kate. You can sit by me, and we can share our whipped-cream pancakes together.*

"Okay." Kate pulled up the closest chair and sat down. "It's a happy Monday, know why?"

Why? Holden heard the music begin to play. Pretty strings and melodic harps. This was a happy day, Kate was right. The music was already more beautiful than on most days …

"Because I'm living with you now, and that means I won't miss my mommy and daddy that much." Kate's eyes twinkled because they had a mix of happy girl and Jesus love tucked inside. Twinkly eyes. "Know what else?"

What? Holden put his PECS cards to the side. His mom was making the pancakes. He could smell them, warm and sweet, and the smell mixed with the music. A happy day for sure.

"I've got a SpongeBob lunch box. And that's the best kind of all."

I like SpongeBob. He's always smiling.

"Right." Kate giggled. "Just like you, Holden. Even when you're not smiling, I can see your smile. Know why?"

Why?

"Because it's in your heart all the time." She leaned closer and her voice fell into a whisper. "I can see your heart, Holden. I always could see it."

Yes, that was the other thing he liked about his cousin Kate. She could see his heart. He nodded. "I thought so."

Too bad his dad wasn't here to share the day with them. But his dad would come home one day and until then if he needed his dad then push-ups would happen. Because *"That's right, Holden, just like that. That's a push-up, except when you're older you'll keep your back straight. Very good ... like the big boys. If you can do that at three years old, you can do anything. Absolutely anything, Holden. Push-ups will make you big and strong like me, buddy. Thatta' boy. Keep doing that and no one will mess with you ever ..."*

They were going to pray in a minute for the warm, sweet pancakes, but first Holden wanted to pray for Kate. *Dear Jesus, I really like my cousin, Kate. She sees the smile in my heart. And so, if You could, please take care of her real good, and make sure she stays safe and healthy. I know You can hear me, and I know You're here at the table with us. You love me, this I know. Thanks for that. Your friend, Holden Harris.*

The music played soft and soothing through breakfast and pancakes and extra whipped cream. When it was over, Holden smiled at his mother. His wonderful mom. *Thanks, Mom. That was the best ever.* He patted Kate's blonde little head. *Plus having Kate here was the best ever.*

It was 8:10 and that meant school, because school meant leaving at 8:10 whether Kate was here or not. But at school something was different this day. He prayed for the kids as they got off the bus. Cheryl with the crutches and Dan in the wheelchair and the other kids and the bus driver. Because the sign at the church said "Pray in the Spirit on all occasions with all kinds of prayers and requests. With this in mind, be alert and always keep on praying for all the saints." That's what the sign said. And then "Ephesians 6:18." Keep on praying …

So Holden would keep on. Every hour.

But after all the praying and after walking to his class in the special-ed wing, Holden noticed something. The rain wasn't only outside, it was inside. And it was on all the faces of everyone in the halls. Rainy eyes and wet cheeks. By the time Holden met up with Ella for lunch, the drums were beating. Slow and steady in the background, but ready to get louder all the time. Drums meant he needed his dad, and maybe push-ups would help.

Something was wrong. Kids were at lunch at 11:53, and usually no one came to lunch until 11:56 and that was off schedule, so something was definitely wrong.

He walked beside Ella toward the hamburger line, because Monday was hamburger day. The drums were quiet, not too loud. So he started to sing. Just to himself and Ella, but it was music that made the drums go away most of all.

"Jesus loves me, this I know …" The words came fast and they bumped into each other like a train wreck.

"Holden …" Ella stopped walking and looked at him. Her eyes looked rainy too. "Do you know something's wrong today?"

Yes, Ella, I know. Because everyone's rainy today. But I'm not sure why.

"Are you singing?" Ella's lips turned into the beginning of a sad smile.

I'm singing our favorite song. Can you hear the words? Holden looked at her, and he could see the little girl she used to be. *Sing with me, okay, Ella?*

"'Jesus Loves Me.' That's what you're singing." Ella didn't look around to check if anyone watching her. She just looked into his eyes and sang along. "Jesus loves me, this I know ... for the Bible tells me so."

The song lasted all through lunch, even when they weren't singing. Later Holden walked to Theater and he passed Locker No. 3447 at 2:02 p.m., but no Michael. Something was wrong because Michael was always there, coming out of Algebra II and passing Locker No. 3447 at 2:02 p.m. Every day he was there, because that was the schedule, except days when Mr. Wiggins went late and then it was maybe 2:04 or 2:06. Holden stopped and looked at Locker No. 3447.

What was the problem? Where was Michael today? He was never sick, except once in September, and that was only after he had a cough for three days. So maybe he was sick and maybe that's why he wasn't here. Holden checked his watch. Two-oh-five and getting later all the time. Michael wasn't here today.

Holden lifted his face to the window. It wasn't rainy anymore. Sunshine was spreading through the clouds and suddenly Holden could imagine Michael plain as if he were here next to Locker No. 3447. He was happy today, Holden was almost one hundred percent sure. Yes, Michael was happy and spending the day with people who loved him.

Because this was a happy day, and the music was happy even with all the rain. "Jesus Loves Me" happy all through the halls and the classrooms and all through Ella and him. He was the Prince, after all. Not the Beast. And this was a happy Monday.

Just like his cousin Kate had said over pancakes that morning.

DAN HARRIS HAD BEEN OFF THE ROUGH SEAS OF THE ALASKAN Peninsula for five hours. Long enough to get back to port, gather a suitcase full of clothes, and head to the airport. Holden needed him. That's all Tracy had to say in her phone call yesterday, and since they were headed into dock for supplies anyway, he informed his captain he needed a week and he booked a flight.

One of Holden's friends had committed suicide over the weekend.

"I'm not sure how much he understands. Ella told me he was singing 'Jesus Loves Me' all day at school." Tracy sounded weary and hopeful all at the same time. "And this morning—before he knew anything about the suicide, I caught him talking to little Kate."

"Talking?"

"Yes." A ripple of forgotten laughter slipped into her voice. "He was talking, Dan. She was telling him about her Sponge-Bob lunch box, and Holden said, 'I like SpongeBob. He's always smiling.'"

"With actual words."

"Yes. I know." She laughed again, the unbridled girlish laughter of a mother no longer consumed with fear. "He's changing, Dan. You have to see for yourself."

Ella would bring Holden home that afternoon, so Tracy could pick Dan up at the airport. Between Kate's arrival and the loss of a classmate, and the renewed friendship with Ella, Holden had a lot going on. As a father, Dan had missed much of Holden's life. Most of the time he didn't mind, because he didn't think Holden noticed, and because his limitations only broke Dan's heart.

A son who wouldn't look at him? Who couldn't talk or make eye contact or laugh with him? A son who was unreachable, untouchable, no matter what Dan tried, no matter how he begged God?

Better to stay at sea praying for the boy and making money, so that one day the therapy and treatments and training sessions might by some miracle pay off. But now... now maybe God was answering them, after all. And every hour at sea, every dollar hard fought from the depths of the ocean, would all be worth it. If only Tracy was right. If they were really getting their Holden back.

Whatever changes were happening in their son, Dan could hardly wait to be home. In ten hours he would see for himself.

Twenty-Six

ELLA MET WITH PRINCIPAL RANDI RICHARDS AFTER LUNCH ON Tuesday and together they set up the memorial for Michael Schwartz. No one else had come forward and Ms. Richards said it was the first time anyone had suggested holding an all-school memorial for a victim of suicide.

"This is a nice thing you're doing, Ella." Ms. Richards seemed compassionate enough. "I think it's time for a meeting like this."

"It's too late for Michael." Ella was angry with herself, angry at her classmates and the administration. Michael had been bullied to death and they were all to blame. She set her jaw. "But we have to do this. To save the next Michael Schwartz."

The memorial would take place in the gym Friday morning —first thing—and would be mandatory for all students. The choir and school band would perform, and Michael's parents would be in attendance. One of the girls in the band would play a flute solo in honor of Michael, and Ms. Richards would say a few words. But the main message would come from Ella.

She had a lot to say.

Today, though, belonged to Holden.

Before he arrived at the drama classroom, she was setting up the stage, preparing for rehearsal, when Mr. Hawkins entered the room from his office. He looked different, less jaded somehow. "Ms. Reynolds?" He sat down at his desk and motioned to the chair across from him. "Do you have a minute?"

She hesitated, but only for a few seconds. "Sure." She hadn't talked to the drama teacher about Michael. On Monday everyone was too much in shock to say much, and rehearsal had gone by in a blur. But today she had a feeling Mr. Hawkins was processing Michael's loss. She took the chair and waited.

"I had Michael in class for two years." Mr. Hawkins looked past Ella, to the open classroom door and the kids walking past in the hallway. "I feel ... I feel there was more I could have done. More most of us could've done."

"Yes, sir. I feel that too." Ella's throat tightened. Michael's loss was so final. There was no way to go back and change a thing about how he'd been treated or how he felt about himself. It was the hardest part for all of them.

Mr. Hawkins breathed in deep through his nose and looked at Ella, renewed purpose in his expression. "I've thought about Holden. If you'll help me, I'd like him to play the Prince. I think ..." He paused, and his chin trembled a little. "I think it's the right thing."

Tears flooded Ella's eyes and she wanted to jump up and hug the teacher. Instead she clasped her hands and nodded. "Yes ... yes, I can help you." She wiped at a couple of happy tears as they spilled onto her cheeks. "He can do this ... I know he can."

"Yes." Mr. Hawkins cleared his throat. "If there was something we could've done for Michael ..." His voice trailed off. He coughed, struggling for composure. "We'll start today. We can ... adjust the script so he can sing. Whatever works." He nodded, his eyes damp. "We can take it slowly."

"Thank you." Ella dabbed her fingers beneath her eyes. She thought she probably understood the way Mr. Hawkins felt. Holden was still here, still alive and with them. They couldn't do anything for Michael, but maybe they could make a difference for Holden. Before it was too late.

Mr. Hawkins slipped back into his office then, and a few minutes later Holden appeared at the classroom door. He hadn't talked to her since last week. All day Monday he did nothing but hum and quietly sing "Jesus Loves Me." He might not have understood suicide, but he knew Michael was gone, and he knew the kids around him were sad. Ella could tell.

Lately she didn't wait to start the music. Holden was best when the song was playing, so she started his favorite piece — the theme song. With the melodic instrumentals playing softly in the background, she called to him.

"Holden, can you come here for a minute?"

He looked up, straight at her. "Okay."

Relief filled her heart. She was afraid if he understood about Michael, he would withdraw again. They might've lost the ground they'd gained. But he was talking again, which meant God was still working a miracle for Holden. *Please, God … Today's a big day.* Ella breathed the prayer silently in her heart. She waited until Holden was on stage with her. "Mr. Hawkins says you can be the Prince in the play. That can be your part, okay?"

Holden twisted his hands together and rocked for a few seconds. Then he turned toward the music and his agitation eased. His eyes found hers again. "I am the Prince, Ella."

"I know." She stifled a giggle. "That's what I told Mr. Hawkins."

"Can I sing?"

"Yes, Holden." The part didn't call for a solo. In the script, the Prince simply said a few lines and then danced with Belle and the cast finished with a reprise of the theme song. "You can sing the whole song."

"And we can dance?" A smile tugged at his lips and his beautiful eyes shone brighter than ever.

"Until the very end."

"We used to dance, Ella. Me and you on a green field with the sun shining on our faces and laughter and 'Jesus Loves Me.' I remember that."

Just when Ella allowed herself to believe she was having a normal moment with Holden, he would say something that reminded her of the truth. There was nothing ordinary about him. Dancing on a green field? Did he really remember that or was the idea something from his imagination, a figment of the world he was emerging from? Either way, she wasn't about to challenge the concept. "That's nice. I'm glad you remember."

She moved to mid-stage. "You know the end of the play?"

"Tale as old as time ..." Holden sang his response.

"Okay, right." Ella would have to pray constantly. Holden wanted the part. He believed he was the Prince. But making it work for an audience was going to take God's help. She gathered her resolve. "So the Beast will be on stage with me, and it'll seem like he's dying. Then there will be fog and a curtain and the Beast will get up and leave. But no one in the audience will know. And you'll come in and it will be a happy ending." She wondered if she'd given him too much information at once."

Holden sang a line from *Beauty and the Beast*, a line about finding friendship when it seemed least likely.

"Right." Ella bit her lip. Holden's voice made her weak at the knees, but it did nothing to convince her he understood the instructions. "Let's run through it." The music was still playing in the background as she pointed to the spot in front of her. "Be my prince, Holden. Okay?"

He nodded. "I'm your Prince, Ella." He stood across from her and held out his hands.

Ella grinned. This was a victory, because Holden had to understand at least a little of what she'd said. Otherwise he wouldn't have held out his hands. Tentatively, she took hold of his fingers and waited until the song was just about to start. Then she found her most professional stage voice. "It's ... it's you! You're alive!"

The script called for a kiss here, but Ella would never push for that. Holding hands was enough of a stretch for Holden. He maintained eye contact with her and at the exact right moment he began to sing. "Tale as old as time … True as it can be."

Ella listened, caught up in the song and the message. If Holden could pull this off, it wouldn't be a traditional ending to the play. It would be better. She was wondering how to get him to start dancing with her, but as he reached the part about "ever a surprise," he began dancing her in a sweeping circle, full and beautiful, as if he'd been dancing all his life. He kept to the beat and continued to sing even as he led her around the stage.

Somewhere near the end, Mr. Hawkins entered the room. He stayed back, but he watched and Ella was pretty sure he was fighting tears. When the song ended, Ella hit the Replay button, so that the music kept playing. Holden stopped, slightly breathless, and he looked at Mr. Hawkins. The first time Ella could remember him ever looking at the teacher. "I'm the Prince."

"Yes, Holden." Mr. Hawkins chuckled, and again he seemed to struggle with his emotions. "I believe you'll be the best prince we've ever had."

Holden nodded. "I will." Then he stepped off the stage and took his seat at the back of the room.

They were running that scene today, so later when the class was in progress, Mr. Hawkins took the front of the room. "I'd like to announce a casting decision." He waited until he had their attention.

Ella glanced at Holden. He was looking at his hands, rocking slightly in his back-row seat. *Please, God … let him understand what he has to do … Let this work for him.* Never before had their classmates seen what Holden was capable of. She was pretty sure none of them would understand what Mr. Hawkins was about to say. "In light of my recent discussions with Ella Reynolds, I've decided that the role of the Prince will go to Holden Harris."

The class sat quietly, probably too stunned to move or speak. But from the back of the room, Holden began to clap. First softly, and then with more vigor. He finally stood, looking from Mr. Hawkins to Ella and clapping with great enthusiasm. Ella wanted to rush to his side and protect him from the sneers and mean comments that were bound to come. But before she could move, three girls in the second row began clapping, too, and at the same time a guy in the first row and a couple kids in the third row started to clap. In seconds, the whole room had erupted into raucous applause.

Mr. Hawkins seemed to catch what was happening about the same time as Ella. Holden wasn't clapping for himself. He and every other student in the room were clapping because Mr. Hawkins had done the right thing by giving a kid like Holden a part in the play.

So many wondrous moments had already happened this day, Ella was only a little surprised when they ran the scene and right on cue Holden came up onto stage and played his part—same as he'd played it before when the room was empty. As long as she lived, Ella would remember the astonished looks on the faces of her peers. Because she already knew what Holden Harris had inside him. But for them, this was their first time to see it. The truth was Holden wasn't a beast after all. No matter how strange or awkward or different he seemed.

He was a prince.

ELLA HAD NEVER TAKEN HOLDEN HOME FROM SCHOOL BEFORE. She'd stopped by his house and visited with him and his mother. But today his mom and his cousin Kate were at the airport picking up Holden's dad. Holden's mother had explained about his routine.

"Snack is first—it's in the fridge, all ready for him. Then the movie." She explained that Holden would know the timing of each step, and that he'd get worked up if the schedule was changed in any way. "The movie is in the player—it's the same one he watches every day. The same one he's watched for the last decade."

Being a part of Holden's routine was something Ella had looked forward to all afternoon. Already this had been a day full of milestones — moments she couldn't wait to share with his parents. She found Holden's snack in the refrigerator, just like his mom had promised, and she sat next to him while he lined up his raisins and ate them one at a time.

"You're going to make a very good prince." She folded her arms, watching him.

He didn't look up right away.

"The whole class was proud of you."

He sang another line, this one maybe most poignant of all, the part of the song that explained how it was possible to change, possible that first impressions could be wrong.

Ella studied him, amazed. This wasn't some random part of the song, the way it might seem to someone who didn't know Holden. He was telling her something deeper than his love for music, his love for the play they were performing. The idea of Holden Harris having so much inside him was probably bittersweet and strange to their classmates. But the truth was, people could miss the beauty inside someone. The way they had missed it with Holden.

"Yes, Holden." She nodded, her eyes watery. "That's exactly right."

When snack was over, they walked to the living room and Holden went to sit on the floor, the place where his mother said he always sat for the movie. But this time he stopped and instead took the place on the sofa beside Ella. He didn't say anything, just focused intently on the blank screen and waited.

Ella used the remote and started the movie. She hadn't asked Mrs. Harris what movie Holden liked to watch, but she assumed it was a cartoon or a Disney film. Something comforting to take the edge off a long day at Fulton. But instead, the pictures that came to life on the TV were clips of home movies. Ella might not have known who the children in the film were, except that she'd found their old photo albums a few months ago.

A little boy and a little girl were running around, chasing each other, and it took only a minute for Ella to understand what she was seeing. The children were her and Holden. She leaned forward, her elbows on her knees. This was the movie Holden watched every day? Home movies of the two of them as children? Every day for the last ten years?

A rush of tears made her throat tight, and she blinked so she could see clearly. The images changed, and now she and Holden were holding hands and singing. They were singing "Jesus Loves Me." Holden turned and looked at her. "Our favorite song."

"Yes." Tears ran onto her cheeks, but Ella barely noticed them. The film clips changed again and now she and Holden were on a sunny green hillside and they were laughing and singing and Holden stopped and took her hands and ...

And they were dancing.

She and Holden with the sun shining on their faces and laughter and "Jesus Loves Me." Just like Holden remembered. This was the friendship they had shared when they were children, the friendship Holden had replayed in his mind every day for ten years. The life he lived locked away deep inside him.

Again he turned to her. "That's our dance when—" He stopped and searched her face.

She felt embarrassed, not wanting to disrupt his routine. He couldn't possibly understand why she was crying, how she was processing all that this movie told her about the past and about the friendship they'd both lost. There was more to Holden than anyone knew, but the complexity of her broken heart was beyond him. She was sure of that.

But even as she was convincing herself, Holden reached out

and took hold of her hand. For a long time he looked at her, the way he had only just learned to do. Not at the Ella Reynolds she was today, but at the little girl who had lost her friend when she was three years old. He held her hand for the rest of the movie, and by the time the film came to an end, Ella knew she was wrong. Holden understood.

Maybe more than anyone else in her life, Holden understood.

Twenty-Seven

NOW THAT HOLDEN WAS WILLING TO SING, ELLA FIGURED OUT quickly that his ability to perform knew no bounds, no limits. Music was in Holden, where it had always been. And now—in their quest for a miracle—they had found it in a song. For that reason, Ella and Holden worked with the school band Wednesday and Thursday after classes, and by the time Friday's memorial service for Michael came around, she and Holden were ready to surprise the entire student body.

Ella arrived early and greeted Michael's mother. The woman wore dark gray, not quite as dark as the circles under her eyes. She hugged Ella and thanked her for putting the memorial together. "It makes me happy… that someone cared." She sniffed, her eyes red from what had probably been days of tears. "That Michael had at least one friend."

"He had more than one." Ella remembered LaShante—and her determination to hear Michael play the flute. "People cared about him. We just… we didn't know how to show it."

The woman nodded. "Anyway, thank you." She took her seat in the front, a few feet from the podium. Ella sat three seats down, next to Holden and his parents. His father was still in town, a nice, quiet man who thanked Ella every time they were together. Holden still hadn't talked to his father, but that would come. Ella believed completely. God was only getting started where Holden was concerned.

A few minutes later the classes began filing in. Ella sat back in her seat, watching, listening. Most of them were quietly uneasy, entering the gym in a more somber fashion than usual. But some of the kids talked or texted or laughed with each other, shoving each other in the shoulder and snickering about one thing or another. As if this were any other assembly on any other day. A reason to get out of class, nothing more.

Her eyes fell on Jake and his buddies. They were whispering, laughing between themselves and pointing at a group of sophomore girls. Ella stifled her anger. *Please, God ... change them today. Let them know what they lost with Michael ... Please don't let this be a waste of time.*

Ms. Richards waited until the gym was full, until every bleacher was filled with nearly three thousand students. Then she stood and went to the podium. She thanked them for coming and explained that the next hour would be in memory of Michael Schwartz. Then she introduced the choir.

At about the same time, a man slipped into the front row and took the chair next to Michael's mother. His father, Ella guessed.

A couple dozen kids filled the risers on the stage, and two large screens lowered on either side. This was a part of the service Michael's mother had worked out with Ms. Richards. A slide show of Michael's life. The choir sang a song by Rascal Flatts called "Why." The song was about the suicide of a friend, and it asked, "Why you'd leave the stage in the middle of a song."

The music played, and around the gym Ella watched kids lower their phones and their voices and pay attention. Not everyone, but more than before. The pictures showed a smiling baby Michael, and then Michael as a young boy on a Big Wheel and then in grade school holding a hand-painted drawing of a dinosaur. Michael in a middle school track uniform, and with his dad, fishing on some scenic lake. One photo after another told the story of a boy who had hopes and dreams, happy days and milestones like every other kid in the gym. The last photo was probably taken by the band teacher. It was Michael playing his flute, standing in the front row with the other flute players.

As the song ended and quiet fell over the gym, Ella was amazed that she could still hear some kids talking among themselves. She dabbed at the tears in her eyes. If the slide show and the Rascal Flatts song didn't hit their hearts, what would? *God, please ... use me today ... If they have any ability to care, please let that happen here.*

The band was next, and the students filed onto stage with their various instruments. Ella caught herself looking for Michael. *He should be up there,* she thought. Michael and his flute. She glanced down the row at Michael's mother. Her arms were crossed in front of her and there seemed to be a wall between her and Michael's father. How often had they sat together at one of Michael's performances, Ella wondered. And were they wishing—like her—that they could have one more chance to hear Michael play?

The band performed a song selected by the band director— "Amazing Grace." It wasn't a song typically played at the public high school, but no one complained and Ms. Richards had given the okay. It was a memorial service, after all. The song ended, and Ella leaned close to Holden. "Are you ready, Holden?"

He rocked a few times, and quietly hummed the familiar tune, the one they'd worked on.

"You're next, okay?"

He glanced at her, then back at his hands.

Ms. Richards had decided that Ella would introduce the next number. She took a deep breath and made her way to the podium. In her hand, she held a folded piece of paper, and as she reached her spot on stage, she saw something that shocked her. A few rows back at the end of the row was her own mother. She had a tissue pressed to her eyes. Ella forced herself to focus. "Hello. My name is Ella Reynolds."

Someone near the back let out a loud, appreciative whistle.

Ella ignored the sound. "I'd like to ask Susan Sessner up to the stage."

A few quiet giggles came from the back of the gym, the place where the PE classes were seated. Susan was maybe a hundred pounds overweight, and her hair always seemed a little too greasy. But her eyes held a light that defied the teasing she must've taken every day here. No question Susan had spent nights crying into her pillow. But she was also an amazing flutist. With a confidence that surprised Ella, Susan walked with her flute up to the stage and waited.

More laughter came from another section in the gym.

"You know ..." Ella tried to control her fury, "I can hear you. Being rude that way." Her tone was passionate, her voice louder than before. "How about you all just be quiet for once." The sharpness of her command silenced the building for the first time that morning. Ella hesitated. "Thank you." She gathered herself, trying to find her place again. She stared at the piece of paper in her hand. "As far as we can tell, one of the last things Michael did before he died was play his flute." She looked intently at the place where Jake and his buddies were sitting. Finally they were quiet. Most of them had their eyes downcast. Ella continued. "Michael played his flute because he was good at it, and because he loved it."

In the front row, Michael's father massaged his brow with his thumb and forefinger. His composure was cracking, for sure, and Ella figured there was a story behind his emotion. Something about the flute, maybe.

"The song Michael loved most was 'O Holy Night.'" She hesitated, registering the silence throughout the gym. "He was looking forward to playing it at the Christmas concert." She unfolded the piece of paper. "This... the music and lyrics... were the only thing he left behind, open on his bed. His final song." Ella nodded to Susan, and the girl began softly playing the music to "O Holy

Night." As she did, Ella looked at the front row of seats. "Holden, you can come up and sing now."

At the mention of Holden's name, another wave of whispers and snickers ran through the gym, loud enough that it could be heard even over the haunting soft sounds from Susan's flute. Ella couldn't get mad. If she did, Holden would become frightened, and the moment would be lost. *Please, God* ... Ella exhaled slowly and kept her tone kind, but loud and clear. "You don't think Holden Harris can sing?" Her words rang out with a fresh sense of passion. "Just because he's different from you... because he has autism?"

The students fell suddenly silent again. The only response to Ella's question was an awkwardness that consumed the cavernous room. Ella let her anger pass. She smiled as Holden joined her. He brought his hands to his chin and started to flap his elbows. Ella leaned away from the microphone. "You can pray later, Holden," she whispered. "It's okay."

He nodded, a rocking sort of nod. And he lowered his hands back to his sides. Ella turned to the audience. "Yes, Holden is different." She paused and tears gathered in her voice. "Michael was different. If you look around, a lot of us are different. But we can still have a beautiful voice... a beautiful song." She paused, studying their faces. "Do you understand what's happening here?"

The students shifted, clearly uncomfortable.

"We lost Michael Schwartz because no one took time to love him." Her voice cracked, but she fought on. The message was too important to stop now. "No one took time to hear his song." She sniffed, struggling to find her voice. Couldn't they understand? Didn't they care? Michael was gone, and there was no going back, no way to make things right for him. But it wasn't too late for Holden or Susan or any of the kids at Fulton who so badly needed love and acceptance.

"We ..." She pressed her fingers to her chest, "We failed

Michael Schwartz." A few quiet sobs shook her body. She looked at Michael's parents. "It's true. We failed him." She lifted her eyes to the students again. "All of us failed him. But we don't have to fail Holden. We ... we don't have to fail each other."

Around the room, she caught a few girls dabbing at their eyes. The message was getting through—even to just a few of them. Ella didn't bother wiping her eyes. Never mind if she was crying. She wasn't about to stop now. "Holden is a very ... very beautiful person." She looked at her mother, and the heartbreak was there for both of them. The years without Holden and his family were a loss they would live with forever. "He's just ... he's locked up inside himself."

Holden's father put his arm around his wife's shoulders.

"But you know what?" Ella was barely able to speak. "Holden's not the only one." She looked straight at Jake, at his crowd of followers. Her voice rose with her conviction. "A lot of kids are locked up. And it's time we change that ... We need to love each other. Now ... while there's still time." She sniffed. "The way we should've loved Michael Schwartz."

As she stood there, as her tears overtook her, she felt Holden reach toward her. Like before in his living room, he slowly took her hand. The feel of his fingers against hers was all she needed, all it took for her to find her composure again. *Thank You, God ... thank You for Holden.* Good would win today ... it would. With God and Holden and all that was happening in his life, she had to believe that. No matter what happened with the student body at Fulton.

"We need to come together. Think about that. Please." Ella gave a signal to Susan, and the girl nodded. She took a long breath and began playing her flute louder than before, the sound crisp and full as it overtook the awkward silence and stifled tears among the students.

Ella handed Holden the microphone and stepped aside. "You can do this," she whispered again. "I'm here."

Holden aimed his eyes down at his feet, held tight to the mic, and began to sing. "O Holy Night, the stars are brightly shining … this is the night of the dear Savior's birth." Every word was clear, every note sung beautifully. Ella felt herself choke up again as all around the gym, students sat straighter, amazed at what they were hearing. *See*, she wanted to shout out loud. *Holden can sing. And he isn't the only one with a song inside him.*

As Holden's song grew, so did his confidence. He looked at Ella and then at Susan, the flute player. Then his eyes found the first row and he sang straight to Michael's mother. "A thrill of hope, the weary world rejoices … for yonder breaks, a new and glorious morn."

Michael's mother nodded, tears streaming down her face. Ella noticed Holden's parents holding hands, and she saw that they were crying too. Then her eyes found her own mom. She was as broken by Holden's performance as anyone in the room. Maybe more. Ella breathed deep, and tears fell onto her own cheeks. This was what they needed, what they all needed. Holden's song.

He looked from his parents to the kids in the audience. "Truly He taught us to love one another … His law is love and His gospel is peace."

Holden had never sounded more beautiful, not in any of their private rehearsal moments. It was as if he'd lived all his life to sing this song, to share the message of true hope and kindness with his classmates in this, one of their darkest hours. The thing with Holden was every word mattered. He didn't talk much — though Ella believed he would one day. But his heart came through in music, and the message now was unmistakable.

"Chains shall He break, for the slave is our brother … and in His name, all oppression shall cease …"

Ella felt as if God Himself was in attendance, as if His Holy

Spirit was flooding the room with a sense of awakening, a sense of understanding and compassion that before today was completely foreign on the campus of Fulton High. Holden Harris was singing his heart out. If this were *American Idol*, the judges would've been crying—Ella was convinced.

The song came to an end and Ella didn't have to worry about whether she should hug Holden. He put his arm around her shoulders and held her close for a long few seconds. At the same time, the students began to clap. First a few scattered throughout the gym, and then more kids, and finally the gym was rocking with the sort of applause they never gave even for playoff basketball games.

The sound convinced Ella that at least some of what had been shared that morning had gotten through to them. She believed that. Holden seemed nonplussed by the applause, almost unaware of it. And this time he didn't clap along. Instead, he took the music and lyrics to "O Holy Night," he stepped off the stage, and he walked back to the first row. When he reached Michael's mother, he stopped and handed her the sheet of paper. With that, he sat down beside his parents.

Ella had a longer speech planned, but in light of Holden's song and all she'd already said, she wanted to share just one more thing. "This spring, Fulton will put on a musical—*Beauty and the Beast*." She was more composed now, the tears in her eyes not enough to stop her from pushing through her final message. "It's the story about not judging anyone by their outer appearance." She caught Holden looking straight at her, and they shared a smile. "Because locked inside the less perfect people might be a prince."

The students were listening.

"This spring, I and the other theater kids need you to come see the show. Otherwise this school will cancel the drama program, and kids like Michael and Holden—kids like me—won't have anywhere to sing."

She hesitated, unabashed in her plea. "If you have any regret about Michael Schwartz, any thought that if you could do it over again you would've smiled at him or complimented him, or maybe even defended him from a bully ... then you can do this one thing. You can come see the play. When you do ... look at the orchestra, the school band. Missing will be one flute player. Michael Schwartz.

"Let's have him be the only Fulton student missing." She looked at Michael's parents. "I'm sorry. We're all so ... so sorry."

His parents nodded, and around the room Ella was pleased to hear some of the kids softly crying. She closed the service by praying. Never mind that this was a public school or that she wasn't very experienced or good at praying. God didn't care—Holden's mother had told her that much. He wanted the hearts of his people, not perfect prayers.

"We need you here at Fulton, dear God." Ella felt the prayer like a cry in her soul. "Forgive us for our indifference and selfishness, and help us learn to love. Let us look more deeply at the kids around us, because all of us are locked up one way or another. And help us listen for the song of each person we come across." She grabbed a quick breath. "Where there is meanness, let us stop it, let us be kind ... and let us be the difference. Help us carry Michael in our hearts every day from here, so that his death will not be in vain. In Jesus' name, amen."

Ms. Richards dismissed the student body, and the next few minutes passed in a blur. Ella hugged Susan Sessner, and LaShante joined her. "Girl, you have to teach me how to play the flute." LaShante squeezed Susan's hand. "I'm going to talk to the band director about joining."

"Okay." Susan looked surprised. Girls like Ella and LaShante never talked to girls like Susan. Not before Michael's death.

After she'd bid a quick good-bye to her mom and Holden's parents, after she'd hugged Michael's mother and introduced herself to his father, Ella made her way back to class. She still felt like God had worked a miracle that day. Certainly the kids understood Holden better, and guys like Jake would have a tough time returning to business as usual when it came to mocking their classmates. But the real proof couldn't possibly be seen just yet.

No, Ella wouldn't know if her peers really heard her heart, whether they'd really listened to Holden's song, and whether they wanted to change in the wake of Michael's death. Not until four months from now.

On opening night for *Beauty and the Beast*.

She and Holden left the gym together, and as they passed into the empty hallway Ella smiled at her friend. "You were amazing. And now everyone knows you can sing."

Holden seemed a little flustered, embarrassed by her compliment. He wrung his hands, keeping up with her but avoiding eye contact.

"I hope they heard us." She sighed, emotionally drained from all the morning had held. "I really hope they heard us."

Then, with the most perfect timing ever, Holden lifted his face and began to sing, the words and music speaking straight to Ella's wounded soul. "A thrill of hope ... the weary world rejoices ... for yonder breaks, a new and glorious morn."

And so it was true with Holden, with this new friendship she had found. The thrill of hope lay fresh each morning, and even in the midst of such terrible loss and sadness, Ella could see the sunrise ahead. She willed herself to believe, the way Holden believed, that one day soon would come the day they were all looking for.

A new and glorious morn.

Twenty-Eight

TRACY HAD NEVER EXPECTED THIS, NOT IN ALL HER LIFE. NO MAT-
ter how often she had prayed, or how strongly she wanted to believe
in a miracle, she couldn't have imagined Holden standing in front
of a packed gymnasium of his peers and singing "O Holy Night."
Not in a million years. And she wasn't sure whether she was happier
about that, or about the fact that Dan was here to see it happen.

Her husband held her hand through the entire memorial
service, while Tracy wrestled with her feelings. She ached for
Michael's mother, for the loss they would all take with them every
day from here. But it was hard not to think mostly about her own
family. How lonely she had been in the months and years without
Dan. Yes, he'd made a decent living for them in the waters off
Alaska. But she had been alone far too often.

Having him here this morning only reminded her how hard
it had been, how much she had needed him. This was how they
were supposed to be—holding hands, side by side—whether
Holden continued to come back to them or not.

The feel of his hand in hers, his fingers intertwined with her
own, felt as right as breathing. And she caught herself praying
silently that Dan would stay. That he would stop blaming himself
and running from the pain of losing Holden. That he would be
part of their family and get a job here in Atlanta.

Then, just before Ella took the stage, Tracy had the feeling
someone was watching her. She looked over her right shoulder
and what she saw made her heart slam into a crazy mixed-up
rhythm. Suzanne Reynolds was sitting a few rows back. Their

eyes met, and Suzanne offered the slightest smile, a smile heavy with remorse and uncertainty.

They both looked away, and the moment ended before it could become anything more. But Tracy sat there shaking, her knees and arms and shoulders trembling. Dan noticed, because he looked at her, curious. But she only shook her head. This wasn't the time or place. She could tell him later. Besides, what could she say? She'd gone fourteen years without seeing Suzanne Reynolds. As if she needed one more reason to feel overwhelmed this morning.

But all those thoughts ceased once Holden took the stage. From that point on, all Tracy could think about was the miracle playing out before her eyes. Dan was equally stunned, because in all the days since they'd lost Holden, he had always processed his pain quietly. No tears or shaking his fist at God. At first he did what he could to bring Holden back, but then their time together faded to a quiet desperation. And before too many years, Dan left for Alaska. In all the time since Holden's diagnosis, Tracy had never seen her husband cry about their lot in life.

Until today.

As Holden sang "O Holy Night," Tracy felt something wet hit the top of her hand. Dan had his fingers between hers, their hands resting on his leg. So when Tracy felt water hit her skin, she looked up and what she saw told her this was a special moment for all of them. A turning point they would never forget.

Because Dan was crying.

No question the journey ahead remained long, and normalcy was still an ideal that might never be reached. But then, Tracy could never have dreamed they'd share this moment. And in the applause that followed Holden's song, she turned to Dan and the two of them clung to each other. "Please, Dan ... don't leave us again. You can work here." There had been times over the years when she'd been mad at him for not being there, for choosing to run from Holden and the life he represented. But all that was behind them now. She pressed her cheek against his. "Please stay. We need you."

"Let's talk about it." He pulled back enough to see her eyes. "Really."

As the program drew to an end, a knot formed in Tracy's stomach. She couldn't avoid talking to Suzanne Reynolds, not here. When the students were dismissed, Tracy and Dan stood on either side of Holden. Dan said the words Tracy hadn't heard him say since Holden's diagnosis. "Holden, son ... I'm proud of you. Your song was ... well, it was perfect."

In the movies, Holden would've slung his arm around Dan's shoulders and shrugged off the compliment. "It's nothing, Dad. But thanks for being here." The two would've shook hands or hugged, and the moment would've been registered for all posterity. A memory they'd revisit in years to come.

But this was real life, where scenes had a way of finding their own endings. Holden looked down at the toes of his shoes and rocked a few times. Heel ... toe. Heel... toe.

"Holden ... can you hear me?"

Tracy willed him to respond, to give them some sign that the song was not an aberration, a fluke never to be seen again. "I'm proud of you, too, Holden. You have a beautiful voice."

He looked up and nodded, his movements quick and jerky. "Thanks ... thank you." His eyes never actually found their way to either Tracy or Dan, but his words were enough. It was another breakthrough. The first time he'd said anything to his father since he was three years old.

Dan moved to pat Holden on his back, but then stopped, clearly thinking better of his decision. "We'll, uh ... we'll talk to you later, then, okay?"

Holden nodded and walked a few feet to where Ella was

ready to head to class. She looked back and waved at Tracy and Dan. "I'll make sure he gets where he needs to go."

As they left, Dan motioned to Michael's parents. "I'm going to talk to them." He glanced the other direction, toward the spot where Suzanne Reynolds was sitting by herself, waiting. Dan kept his voice low, so that only Tracy could hear him. "Go talk to her."

Tracy sighed. "Pray for me."

"I will." He squeezed her hand and headed in the opposite direction, toward the Schwartzes. Tracy felt her palms grow sweaty. What was she supposed to say? After all this time, how could they have any common ground? She eased her purse onto her shoulder and walked back the few rows to where Suzanne was sitting. Their eyes met again, and Tracy registered the effects of time. It seemed just yesterday that they'd been sitting side by side on the swings, Holden on her lap, Ella on Suzanne's. Two young moms who had been best friends since high school.

But now Suzanne was barely recognizable. Bleached blonde hair and puffy lips. She couldn't have been bigger than a size 3, and her chest was more filled out than when she was nursing Ella. Tracy had heard rumors in the news now and then about Suzanne's husband, the fact that Randy Reynolds was washed-up. She hadn't wanted to believe it back then, but looking at Suzanne there was no denying the brokenness in the eyes of her long-ago friend. The woman seemed miserable in every possible way.

As Tracy walked toward her, she forgot every hurt in her heart, every way she'd felt abandoned and rejected by Suzanne. In this moment there were only the two of them, a couple of former best friends who had once a lifetime ago loved and laughed, and who had both lost much in the years since.

Tracy stopped a few feet away, and Suzanne stood. For a long few seconds, neither of them said anything. Then, as if it was too late for grudges or awkward beginnings, they came together in a long hug.

As they eased apart, Suzanne had fresh tears in her eyes. "Holden was amazing." She looked at the empty stage, at the place where Holden had performed. "Is this ... does he sing very often?"

Tracy crossed her arms, willing her heartbeat to slow back to normal. "Only since he found Ella."

Suzanne closed her eyes, a wave of quiet sobs hitting her.

Tracy put her hand on the shoulder of her long-ago friend. "He's... he's loved music since the beginning." Suddenly she realized that Suzanne already knew this. "Of course ... you remember. He and Ella would sing and dance all afternoon."

"Yes." Suzanne opened her eyes. Her lip quivered, but she smiled despite her damp eyes. "I remember."

"But today ... this was the first time we've heard him sing like that. The first time since ... since he was three."

Suzanne shrugged, her frame and effort equally weak. She looked like she might pass out from the emotional toll of the morning. "It's a miracle. I'm glad I was here ... to see it."

Questions poked pins at Tracy's composure. Why had it taken this long for them to have this conversation and how come Holden's autism had scared Suzanne and Randy away, and was it worth it? All they'd lost in the process? But as each question hit, Tracy set it aside. Maybe, as long as God was working miracles, they would have time for those conversations later. Nervousness raced through her veins as she searched for the next thing to say. The right next thing. "I guess Ella told you ... about her and Holden."

"Yes." Two tears splashed onto Suzanne's cheek and she wiped at them with the back of her hand. As she did, it was clear she was trembling. Worse than Tracy, this moment was hard on Suzanne. "Ella says ... he's become very important to her."

"The changes in Holden ... most of them are because of Ella." Tracy felt her heart swell as she pictured the sweet friend who had found her way back into Holden's life. "She's a very ... very special girl."

Another shrug and more tears. "I don't know, really. She ... she doesn't talk to me."

Tracy took a few seconds to grasp what Suzanne was saying. Ella didn't talk to her mother? And suddenly every bit of nervousness and angst over where the conversation would go and what could be discussed and whether this was a beginning or another ending ... none of it mattered. Clearly Tracy's first assessment of her friend had been right on. Suzanne was suffering. Long ago Tracy had learned that in a moment like this no questions were needed. Instead she put her hand on Suzanne's bony shoulder and allowed empathy to fill her tone. "I'm sorry. I ... I didn't know."

For a minute it seemed like Suzanne might gather her purse and her sweater and dart out of the gymnasium before she could give away any other details of her life. But instead she looked at Tracy and for the first time since the conversation began, her eyes looked the way they had when they were teenagers. The connection between them was that strong.

"Randy ... he's never home. His career's in jeopardy. We don't talk ... don't share anything anymore." She sniffed and held her hand to her eyes for a long moment. When she lowered it, she looked more distraught than before. "The kids know and they ... they feel sorry for me. At least the boys do. Ella thinks I don't care because ... because I spend all my time trying to be Randy's wife." Her tears dried up, and she sounded almost robotic. As if the pain of her admission was so great she couldn't register it in her heart. Otherwise it might kill her.

Tracy remained quiet, listening to every painful word.

"I'm sorry." Suzanne seemed to realize that her statements were odd in light of the years they'd missed. "This isn't the time."

"The time is fine." Tracy didn't break eye contact. "We're here, right? There has to be a reason for that."

Suzanne nodded, and a glazed look darkened her eyes. "My days are … They're empty, Trace." She shivered a little, like she might break into a panic attack right here in the gym. "Completely empty. I mean … I spend my days at the gym or shopping … getting my hair and nails and face done. I get Botox and I wear extensions and still …" She shook her head, and a glimpse of her pain broke through her strangely blank expression. "Still, it's not enough. It's never enough. He won't look at me." Her voice cracked and she hugged her arms tight around her middle. Her next words came in a broken whisper. "I don't know how I got here, Trace. I don't know how to go back. I mean … I can't remember how to be anything but Randy Reynolds' wife."

A long time ago, Tracy was a fixer, the sort of person who would spout off the first natural solution that came to mind in a moment like this. But years of living with Holden had taught her to move slowly, to let God lead when people were broken and hurting. She reached out and gave Suzanne's hand a soft squeeze. "What's Randy say?"

"Not much." She looked off to the distance, as if she were seeing her husband in her mind. "He stays married to me, but … it's a formality. Any day he could serve me with papers." She found Tracy's eyes again. "The distance between us is that bad."

Tracy didn't have to ask if Suzanne and Randy were still attending church, still praying together and reading the Bible the way they'd done when the four of them hung out. Time had been hard on all of them. From the world's viewpoint, Tracy and Dan had gotten the rougher deal. It was their healthy little boy who had disappeared into a world of silence. But until now Tracy had no idea how much the years had taken from Suzanne.

"Maybe … maybe we could have coffee Monday morning.

There's a Starbucks near my work. My shift doesn't start till eleven."

Suzanne seemed to realize that she hadn't asked anything about Tracy's life, about where she lived or what she did—other than the obvious, her earlier comments about Holden. "Where do you work?"

"Walmart." Tracy held Suzanne's gaze and watched her reaction. It wasn't quite pity, but no question she felt uneasy about this turn in the conversation. Tracy expected as much, and it didn't matter. She felt no shame about her job, or the fact that she and Suzanne were in different tax brackets. The people she worked with were nice, and her boss continued to pray for Holden. No matter what rich people thought, Tracy was a fan of Walmart. The company kept costs down for families like hers, and she was grateful for the work.

Suzanne nodded … her eyes distant again as if she were trying to process the mountain of changes that had happened for both of them since their last time together. For the first moment since the conversation started, Suzanne smiled. Not the practiced smile she probably handed out all day long, but the hesitant, broken smile of someone wracked with regret. "Coffee would be nice." She picked up her purse and her sweater and pulled out her phone. "Which Starbucks is it?"

Tracy told her, and they shared another hug. Before Suzanne walked away, she hesitated. "I was wrong … walking away when I did." Her voice was scratchy again, her emotions raw and close to the surface. "I need to say that."

"I could've called." Tracy wasn't sure where this new attempt at connecting with Suzanne would end up. But she would pray every day that God would use it. She held her ground, wanting Suzanne to hear her sincerity. "We all lost. But we can't look back. It's too late for that."

Suzanne started to say something, but in the end she only

nodded and turned away. She hurried toward the door quickly, as if she might crumble at any minute, nothing but a weeping broken-down failure on the middle of the Eagles' gym floor.

Tracy watched her leave and suddenly everything about the morning came rushing back at her. The good-bye for Michael ... Ella's desperate plea ... Susan and her flute ... and Holden. Her precious Holden and his song. Dan crying beside her and now this. A coffee date with Suzanne Reynolds. For a long minute all Tracy could do was marvel at it all, aware in the depths of her soul that this was God—all God—at work around her. Because Ella was right. There were lots of ways to be locked up. And it was clear now that God wasn't only working a miracle in unlocking Holden.

He was working a miracle in all of them.

Twenty-Nine

DAN CONTACTED HIS CAPTAIN AT THE END OF THE WEEK AND told him the news. He wasn't coming back. He'd applied at the school district—the maintenance department—and already he had an interview scheduled. The position looked promising, that's what he'd been told. The money wasn't what it could be out on the open seas of Alaska, but it was steady.

And it would keep him home with Tracy and Holden.

Not that being home was any easier than it had ever been, because the transformation they were watching with their son still hadn't happened in conversation—not between the two of them. Holden talked to Tracy once in a while, but mostly he hummed or sang. Sometimes he danced.

The holidays came and went, Christmas day special only because he and Tracy stayed up late into the night looking through photo albums, talking about years gone by. "He still won't talk to me." Dan hated to admit his frustration. After all, God was bringing Holden back. But Dan wanted him back all the way—the Holden they'd had the first three years of his life.

"He will." Tracy covered his hand with hers. Something about her quiet strength, and the daily battle she'd fought getting Holden to therapy and going years at a time without seeing even the slightest glimmer of hope, had done more than earn his respect. He was enamored with her, more with each passing day.

"Coming home … It's the right thing."

She never complained, never criticized him. But that night,

she let the loneliness show in her eyes for a few seconds. "You should've come sooner."

"I know." Dan leaned over, his forearms on his knees. The distance between him and Holden hurt as much now as when the boy was four years old. Before his diagnosis, Dan had pictured hiking and camping and Scouts and sports. A thousand ways he and Holden would grow close over the years. But autism had stolen every dream, every father-son moment that never took place. Dan shook his head. "But the truth was Holden didn't need me. He still doesn't."

"Dan ..." She raised her brow, searching his eyes. "I need you."

Something about the way she said those three words stirred up deep guilt within him. He sat up straighter, amazed by her. "Why'd you stay with me?" He looked more intently at her, searching for answers he might never find. Suddenly the weight of his absence hit him like one of the fishing cages they dropped into the ocean every day at sea. Tracy was right. Never mind his role as Holden's father. What sort of husband had he been? "You should've left me a long time ago."

"No." A smile filled her eyes, a smile that mixed patience and persistence, courage and concern. "Love doesn't leave."

They should've had this conversation a month earlier, when Dan first came home. But he'd been too afraid to bring it up, too afraid of what he'd find if he did. Now, though, he couldn't stop himself. "You ... you had to do everything by yourself. All the work with Holden ... the appointments and therapy." He felt disgusted with himself. "I didn't help you with any of it."

"You helped." The apartment's electric fireplace crackled in the background. Holden and Kate had been asleep for hours, and this was the first time they'd been alone all day. Tracy set the photo album down on the nearby coffee table and slid closer to him. "You did what you could."

"All those days … you were alone here with him and … It's just … I should've been here."

"Yes." She put her hand alongside his face. "But that's behind us. You're here now, and I love you. You love me. And God's bringing Holden back." She smiled again. "What else could matter?"

"You." He took her in his arms. "Just you, Tracy. That's all that matters." They stood then and turned off the fireplace and lights and walked quietly to their bedroom. They finished the conversation there, and later that night Dan fell asleep thanking God for his wife and making a promise to himself and the Lord. He would give Holden the attention he deserved, even if he received nothing in return. He could at least do that.

As the winter wore down and new leaves began to bud again, Dan made good on his promise. The school drama rehearsals lasted an hour after school now that the performance was drawing closer, and Dan told Tracy he wanted the job of picking Holden up. The first day Dan tried to make small talk, asking questions and making observations about the drive home. But Holden only looked out the window and remained silent. So silent Dan wanted to catch the next flight back to Alaska. But he fought the urge and the next day, after Dan made fewer observations and asked only a couple questions, they were halfway home when a breakthrough happened.

After a few minutes of silence Holden turned to him. "Dad?"

He let up on the gas pedal and glanced at Holden. If his son hadn't been looking straight at him, he would've been convinced that he was imagining the sound of his name. An overactive imagination honed sharp from years of silence at sea. But Holden was clearly waiting for his response, so Dan pulled over onto the shoulder of the road. If he was about to have his first conversation with Holden in fifteen years, he didn't want to miss a single moment.

When the car was safely parked, he shifted so he could see

Holden full on. He thought about turning off the radio, but then he stopped himself. Music was always a good thing where Holden was concerned. Dan turned it down just slightly, so they could hear each other. "Holden ... you know my name." He narrowed his eyes, trying to see all the way to the place where Holden had been hiding.

"Dad." Holden blinked. "Your name is Dad." He looked down at his hands, and for a long moment he worked his fingers together, nervous and unsure. Then, as if he suddenly remembered his train of thought, he looked at Dan again. "Dad?"

"Yes, Holden?" His heart was thudding hard against his ribs. *He's talking to me, God ... Please, let him keep talking.*

"Mom said you were fishing." His voice was monotone, and the rhythm wasn't quite normal. But that didn't matter.

Dan's mind raced. "Fishing? In Alaska, you mean?" Guilt came over him like the rogue wave. "Yes, that's right. I was fishing."

Holden rocked a few times and he looked out the window again. Was that it? Had he disappeared to his own private world again? Dan wasn't sure what to do, whether he should ask more questions or wait. But if he'd learned one thing at sea it was patience, so he waited.

Half a minute passed. Holden looked at him again and began to sing—something about both of them being afraid and unprepared.

A song? That's how Holden was going to talk to him now? Dan felt a surge of kindness toward his son. What came so easily for other people was deeply painful for those on the autistic spectrum. Music was easier for Holden, so sometimes he sang. Wasn't that what Tracy had told him. "The words always mean something," she'd said. So what were the words again? They were lines from his *Beauty and the Beast* music.

But what was Holden really saying? That this communication between them was new and more than a little frightening? Was that it? Dan remembered to breathe. He wouldn't say or do anything that would make Holden retreat. But it took everything in him to sit still. He wanted to take hold of the boy, hug him, and hold onto him so he couldn't disappear again. Instead, he waited.

More time, one minute, then two. Finally Holden looked at him again. "Dad?"

"Yes, Holden."

"So … Dad … how was the fishing?"

Joy exploded in his heart. His son was talking to him! Not just spouting lyrics or disconnected phrases. He was talking. He understood that Dan had been gone at sea, and he wanted to know how the fishing was. Dan hurried with his answer. "The fishing was good. They paid me for it, Holden. It was my job."

Holden rocked a little. "Tale as old as time …" Then he brought his hands to his chin and flapped his elbows — but only a few times before he seemed to catch himself. "I can pray like this." He folded his hands on his lap and looked down. "I can pray like this, Dad."

"Yes, you can pray however you want, Holden."

"Like this."

"Okay."

Holden stayed that way, maybe praying about the same thing Dan was praying about. That this precious, fledgling conversation would be a beginning. The digital clock on the car's dashboard ticked off another two minutes before Holden lifted his face. He didn't look at Dan this time. "We watched movies without you. In the living room, we watched movies." He glanced at Dan for a brief instant. "Without you."

When he put the pieces together, Dan couldn't deny the point Holden was making. His son knew who he was and where he had been, and that maybe he should've been at home. The puzzle was clearer than it had ever been.

Holden needed him.

Dan felt sick at the realization, like he was freefalling off the deck of a twenty-story ship. Finally he said the only thing he could say. "Not any more, Holden. I'm watching movies with you now." It was true. Dan was trying to free up Tracy's schedule, trying to make up for the times he'd missed. Holden's afternoon routine belonged to him or to both of them, but Dan hadn't missed a day. He'd been hired by the school district, but he never worked past three o'clock. So he was available for Holden. Available to watch movies.

Holden nodded. Or maybe he was rocking again. "But every time ... The drums came every time and you were gone."

Dan racked his brain. Tracy hadn't ever mentioned this. "The drums?"

"Yes and push-ups."

This he knew — that Holden did push-ups when he was upset. "You ... you did a lot of push-ups, Holden."

He rocked a few times and looked out the window. Fifteen seconds, thirty ... a minute while Dan waited.

"Push-ups." Holden looked right at him. "Because 'That's right, Holden, just like that. That's a push-up, except when you're older you'll keep your back straight.'" He caught a quick breath. "'If you do that at three years old, you can do anything. Absolutely anything, Holden. Push-ups will make you big and strong like me. Thatta' boy. Keep doing that and no one will mess with you ever.'"

Dan was too shocked, too dazed to speak. He couldn't be completely sure, but he had a feeling his son had just repeated the very words he himself had spoken when Holden was three. He'd taken Holden to the gym and he'd done a series of push-ups only to stand up and find Holden trying to copy him. His little backside high in the air, Holden spent a minute trying his very hardest to imitate what he'd seen Dan do.

And now ...

The realization was still hitting him. Was Holden saying that

… that … "So … when I wasn't there … and when you were in trouble … you did push-ups," he felt lightheaded. "Because of me?"

"Push-ups." Holden nodded slowly. "Because you were fishing."

All this time? Dan couldn't see for the tears in his eyes. All this time there had been meaning in Holden's push-ups. Because they made him feel closer to his father. The father who was fishing. "Holden … I'm sorry." He could barely get the words out, but he had to say this. No matter how difficult. "I didn't know you missed me."

Holden looked like he might say something. But instead he looked at Dan again and smiled. A smile Dan recognized, because it was the smile of the three-year-old boy he'd lost so many years ago. Holden hummed for a few seconds and then sang softly, a line about giving in to friendship even against the odds. Even here in the car, his voice was clear and powerful. No question the boy could sing.

Dan thought about the meaning in the lyrics and he smiled. "That's right, son. Unexpected and wonderful."

"Dad?"

"Yes, Holden?"

"You can drive now, Dad."

Dan hesitated, then he chuckled out loud. "You got it, buddy. Let's get back home to Mom."

"And the movie."

"Right." Dan pulled the car back into traffic. "And the movie. We can't forget about that."

THERE WAS A PHOTOGRAPH TRACY KEPT, ONE SHE DIDN'T SHARE with anyone—not even Dan. In the picture, Holden was just three, a few weeks before the trip to the doctor, a few weeks before a whole slate of immunizations and the changes that eventually led to his diagnosis.

But in the photo, Holden was holding a dandelion out in front of him, his eyes bright and alert, his smile full of love and unabashed charm. The flower had been for her. Holden had picked it during an outing to the park, and he had run up to her, calling out, "Mommy! Mommy, look what I found for you!" Tracy pulled her camera from her bag and held up her hand.

"Wait there, buddy. Mommy wants to get your picture."

And Holden had flashed the cheekiest grin ever. *He'll break a hundred hearts before he finds her*, Tracy thought to herself.

By the time she had the film developed, Holden was a different child. He would line up his cars and his toys and his building blocks. One after another. And when she'd talk to him, he wouldn't look at her, wouldn't respond. Watching her son slip away before her eyes was enough to make Tracy doubt whether Holden had ever been very communicative.

She would walk up to him and touch his shoulder, only to have him jerk away — almost as if the feel of her fingers on his arm caused him physical pain. It was the same when she and Dan tried to pick him up and take him to bed. He would kick and fight, screaming as loud as he could. From the beginning, music provided the only respite, the only calm in a constant storm.

Sometime in that first month of a nightmare that was only now beginning to end, Tracy drove to Walgreens and picked up her pictures from summer. She sat in her car and looked through them and when she got to the one with Holden and the dandelion — for the first time since he began slipping away from them, Tracy broke down and wept.

The little boy in the picture was as gone from their lives as if someone had swept into their house at night and kidnapped him. In their situation, the loss was accompanied by a child who looked like Holden and smelled like Holden and lived in Holden's room. But after that summer he was gone. And the one bit of private proof that he had ever existed was the picture.

Holden and the dandelion.

Tracy kept the photo in an envelope in her top drawer, tucked beneath a stack of summer shorts and tank tops. She didn't look at it often, only when she missed Holden so much she wasn't sure she could breathe without taking a few minutes alone with him. The boy he used to be.

This was dress-rehearsal week for *Beauty and the Beast*. Opening night was the second Friday in March — just a week away. Dan was off to pick up Holden, which left Tracy alone for an hour. Lately she'd been meeting with Suzanne, having coffee, and in the past few weeks even reading the Bible with her. They still hadn't found the same closeness they'd shared before, but their new friendship was headed that way. Suzanne was meeting with Randy today — to talk about their marriage. Tracy had been praying for her all day.

Whenever she wasn't thinking about Holden. His conversation was still quirky and stilted, not nearly what they wanted. But now that he was making strides to connect with them, there were days when Tracy wondered what would become of her son.

A year ago she figured he'd live with her forever, unable to work or care for himself. But now ... now he was showing more signs of independence. Brushing his teeth and flossing, cleaning up after himself. He'd even made his own peanut butter sandwich this morning. Did that mean he'd want to go to college and get a job? Live on his own? And what about his friendship with Ella? Once — a lifetime ago — Tracy and Suzanne had lightheartedly joked about Holden and Ella going to the prom. Ella didn't see him that way, and Tracy was pretty sure Holden saw Ella the way he'd seen her when he was three years old. She was his best friend, nothing more. Further proof that even as he was coming out of his severely autistic behaviors, he was still not the same as other kids his age. Not the same little boy they'd lost.

That afternoon, for the first time since Christmas, Tracy couldn't go another day, another hour without seeing the picture. Kate was watching a SpongeBob video, sleepy after a day of school. Tracy crept back to her bedroom, opened her top drawer, and found the envelope tucked between the clothes and the rough wood bottom. The envelope was yellowed now, the flap ripped some at the edges. She opened it and slid the photo out. It was faded a little, but Holden's smile still shone through the frozen images, his eyes still danced with life the way they'd done back then.

What had happened? Was it the immunizations, the way some people believed? Or something in the food they fed him? She'd heard specialists tell parents not to panic about getting kids their shots. The inoculations protected kids against deadly diseases, after all. But maybe not so many at one time. That was the new thinking. The schedule of shots had changed in 1989,… become more aggressive. Maybe too aggressive for some kids — kids like Holden. It was hard to know.

Tracy let the thought fade. It no longer mattered the reason, the culprit behind the kidnapping of Holden's personality. It had happened. The photograph was proof. Tracy held it a little closer. "I miss you so much, Holden …" she whispered, and as she did she heard the sound of footsteps behind her.

"Aunt Tracy?" Kate was standing there, her blue eyes so much like Holden's, so alert and full of life the way Holden's had been.

"Hi, sweetie." She lowered the picture. "Is your movie done?"

"It's boring." She flashed an irresistible grin. "I wanna dance instead." She peered around Tracy at the photograph. "Holden used to dance, right? In the movie he dances all the time."

"That's right." Tracy wasn't sure whether she should put the picture away or wait for Kate to finish talking to her. She hadn't shared the photo with anyone, and it felt strange to do so now. Like an invasion in the only private world she still shared with her son.

"What's the picture?" She came closer and hovered her little tan face over the photo. "Is it Holden?" She looked up at Tracy. "It looks like Holden from the movies."

Tracy hesitated, but only for a moment. She was being ridiculous. What could it matter if she shared the picture with Holden's little cousin? "Yes, Kate. It's Holden—back when he was three."

"Can I see?" She stood on her tiptoes.

"Here." Tracy brought the photo closer. "He was giving me a dandelion."

"Oooh." Kate grinned. "I like dandelions. They're yellow."

"They are."

Kate studied the photograph. "Yep," she nodded. "That looks like Holden. His eyes are the same."

Tracy wanted to disagree. She looked at the picture of her son and back at Kate. "You think so?"

"Mmm-hmm." She nodded. "If you look really hard at Holden his eyes are the same. And he still likes to dance."

"He does?" Kate had only been with them for a few months. But her sweet spirit and guileless concern for Holden already made her an expert. She was good for Holden, for sure. Tracy had a feeling the two talked more often than anyone knew. "How do you know, sweetie? That he still likes to dance?"

Kate giggled. "He told me. He dances with Ella when he's the Prince."

"Oh." Tracy should've guessed that. "Did he tell you?"

"A'course. He tells me everything." Kate was finished with the photograph. "Come on, Aunt Tracy." She took hold of her hand. "Let's go dance! I have energy bursting through my feet!"

Tracy laughed. Kate wasn't only good for Holden ... she was good for all of them. Joy brimmed from her heart and soul and filled their home with love and laughter. Between Kate and Ella, and Dan and her, God had Holden covered. That was for sure.

She slipped the picture back in the envelope and hid it once again at the bottom of the drawer. There were other photographs, and of course the home movie. Lots of ways to remember the boy Holden had been. But this single picture, hidden here in her room, would always be special. With the picture in her hand, she could smell the humidity in the air that summer day, see the shimmer of sweat on his little-boy forehead, hear the excitement in his voice. She could smell the faint scent of his baby shampoo and the hint of Tide in his shorts and T-shirts. And for just a few minutes she was there again, in the place where she'd lost Holden.

The photo was important because it brought her comfort, and it gave her a reason to believe. Holden was in there somewhere. They'd seen glimpses of that lately, and Kate … well, Kate had seen more than glimpses. Tracy sighed as she left the room, following a skipping Kate down the hallway. Yes, the picture would stay where it was. Tracy couldn't post "Missing" signs around the community, asking if anyone had seen the Holden she'd lost. But she could have the picture of Holden and the dandelion. A constant reminder to never stop praying for his complete return.

Or that she might see his eyes the way Kate saw them.

Thirty

ALL THE HOURS WALKING THROUGH SCENES AND PRACTICING with the school band, all the afternoons painting sets and watching the show come to life and finally ... finally it had come to this. Ella finished applying the last touches to her makeup. In half an hour they would take the stage for opening night.

They'd do the show three times this weekend — less than half the number of performances the Fulton High drama department had once done. Mr. Hawkins had gone over the numbers with a few of his leads, encouraging them to invite their friends, hand out flyers, and hang posters throughout the school.

"We need to sell out opening night." He didn't sound hopeful. "It's a great show. One of our best. If they come opening night, they'll come back and they'll tell their friends." He explained the situation, but what he didn't say was how much this show mattered to him. Not so much that they made money for the school, but that the student body might see his swan song. That they would share in the miracle he'd watch unfold through the months. And that they would remember this ... his final effort as drama teacher at Fulton High.

"If it doesn't happen ... if they don't come ..." His eyes glistened. "Don't take it personally. Not everyone appreciates theater." He looked around the room at each of them one at a time. "But that doesn't make it less profound." He nodded slowly. "And what you've done these past months as a team has been profound."

He was talking about Holden, Ella was pretty sure. Everyone

had come to see Holden as the centerpiece of the musical. He was clearly a different guy than he had been at the beginning of the school year. He still didn't talk to the other kids, but he made up for it with her. All week he'd been looking forward to opening night.

"Seven p.m. Friday night, right, Ella?"

"Right, Holden. Seven p.m."

"I'm the Prince."

Ella laughed. She had come to care deeply for Holden, and more often lately she wondered whether he would keep improving, keep finding his way back to normal. Sometimes when he was watching her, when his forever blue eyes seemed to reflect his belief that all people were kind, and no one had ever been mean to him or bullied him, when he looked so intently at her that she wondered if he could read her thoughts, Ella would almost feel herself falling for him. This handsome friend she'd known since her baby days.

But unless he kept coming back ... he would never see her as more than he'd seen her when they were three years old. A relationship at this point was out of the question. Ridiculous, even.

She slipped into her first costume — the blue dress — and took a last look at herself in the full-length mirror. Six months ago she could've played the part, but her acting would've been shallow, her portrayal of Belle only skin deep. Now, though, she felt passionate about the character. A girl willing to see the beauty in someone everyone else had pushed aside, a young woman helping in the transformation of a guy with a heart of gold.

Yes, Ella could relate to the character of Belle. She would play it with everything she had, and she would know at least this much: if *Beauty and the Beast* were the last show to grace the stage of Fulton High, people would remember it.

She hurried from the dressing room to the classroom just off the stage. The place was bustling with activity. The kid playing the Candlestick was having trouble with his flame and someone was tacking the hands of the clock onto Cogsworth. A group of moms had volunteered to do costumes, and now one of them had a needle and thread in her hand. "Velcro isn't working. It's time to sew these hands on."

Mr. Hawkins was sitting nearby, looking over the script one last time. He didn't seem to notice the trouble with Cogsworth.

"You know what they say—" The kid shrugged. "A stitch in time saves ..." He looked at a passing townsperson. "What does it save?"

"Nine." The girl giggled. "It saves nine."

"Nine what?" Cogsworth waited, but when no one answered, he shrugged again. "Whatever. As long as I get a stitch in time." He laughed at his own joke, and the volunteer parent kept sewing.

"Twenty minutes, people." Mr. Hawkins was feeling the pressure—that much showed on his face. But his tone was kind and patient. If this was their last show, like everyone in the cast their teacher was determined to enjoy it.

Ella was used to this, the chaos that took place backstage before any show—especially opening night. But she wanted to find Holden. None of this would be normal for him and Ella worried that the confusion would make him forget his song, the words and the melody. He still did push-ups every now and then. Once during a dress rehearsal. *But not tonight, Jesus ... please, not tonight.*

She had a feeling where she'd find him. More than once during the last week she found Holden in the prop room, all by himself, counting the buttons on various costumes. Ella darted down a short hallway and opened the last door on the left. Sure enough.

Holden was dressed in his costume, looking every bit the Prince. But he wasn't counting buttons. He was holding his hands out in front of him, turning in wide, graceful circles—dancing with an imaginary partner. He stopped and turned when he heard her enter the room. "Opening night." He smiled, his eyes bright. "Seven p.m."

"That's right." She held her hand out to him and Holden took it. They held hands regularly now. Ella figured he could tolerate the physical touch because it took him back to their childhood, when they held hands constantly. Otherwise, Holden was still sensitive to anything too sensory. That was the word she came across whenever she googled autism. Too much sensory stimulation and a person on the autistic spectrum would shut down or burst into a tantrum. In Holden's case, he would drop to the ground and do push-ups. His mother had told her yesterday that they'd solved that mystery too. Push-ups meant he wanted his dad. The revelation only made her care more for Holden.

She stopped near the door, their hands still linked. "You're a good dancer, Holden. You don't have to practice."

"Practice before opening night." He nodded, his eyes downcast, almost shy. "I'm a Prince. Seven p.m." He met her eyes and like so often, he began to sing. "Tale as old as time ... True as it can be."

His voice melted her. She took in his broad shoulders and tall stature, the smooth complexion and always piercing blue eyes. "Yes, Holden." She smiled. "You're definitely a prince." She led him down the hallway and out with the others. He still didn't like to be rushed, didn't like being in the middle of chaos. So Ella was careful to sit with him in the back of the room. By then people were settling down, just ten minutes before curtains would go up.

It was only then that Ella heard a sound that made her heart hesitate. The walls backstage were paper thin, and a crowd of people could usually be heard. Certainly by now if the theater was filling up, they would hear something. But that was just it.

The sound Ella heard was silence. Nothing.

Holden released her hand and squirmed in his seat. He sensed things better than other people, and this was one of those moments. Ella hid her disappointment in the deepest basement of her heart. "This will be fun, Holden. You're going to do great."

"Seven p.m."

"That's right, Holden. Seven p.m."

By now his parents would be here, and her mom. too. Her dad was even going to try to make it. Ella smiled at the picture of both her parents sitting in the audience together. She and her mom had talked more lately, and Ella had a feeling they would talk more when the show was over. But for now she was too busy. Holden deserved all her attention. This was about to be his shining moment — his second shining moment. And if her classmates showed up the way she'd asked them to at Michael's memorial, then today would mark a turning point for all of Fulton.

She'd talked to LaShante, but her friend hadn't heard whether people were coming. "I'll talk to them," she said. "Sometimes I wonder if anyone even remembers what happened to Michael."

LaShante had been coming to church with Ella since Christmas, and both of them had prayed for tonight's performance.

"I have a surprise," she told Ella yesterday. "I can't promise you anyone will be there. But I still have a surprise."

Surprise or not, Ella struggled against the disappointment flooding her heart. If no one showed up tonight, the performance would be weakened by an empty auditorium. The death sentence for the drama program and Mr. Hawkins. Maybe God's plans were different than they had hoped.

Holden shifted, more uneasy than before.

I can't do this, God ... I can't be discouraged. Holden deserves more than that. Please ... help me. She sat up straighter and found the smile that had faded in the last few minutes.

"It's okay, Holden. Everything's okay."

He nodded, rocking the way he did when he wasn't sure. Then he grinned at her and sang in his softest voice. "Ever just the same ..." His song was so soft no one but her could hear him.

Especially because the other kids were still settling down, grabbing last-minute costume pieces and adjusting their hair, finding their props. Holden found the next line about the surprises in life.

"That's right, Holden." Ella tilted her head. Could he know her uncertainty ... the fact that she feared the surprise of an empty auditorium? "Ever a surprise."

A look of hope danced in Holden's eyes. "I prayed."

"You prayed?" She loved this kid, the way his heart was so pure. "You prayed for our show?"

He hesitated, his gaze off to the distance for a moment. Then he shook his head. "I prayed for the seats."

"The seats? In the auditorium?"

"One thousand fifty-three seats." His answer came quickly. "I prayed for one thousand fifty-three seats."

"You counted them?" Ella tried to imagine when Holden had found time during the rehearsal to count each seat in the theater. "Really?"

"One thousand fifty-three."

Ella wanted to hug him, hold onto him and promise him that if he'd prayed for every seat in the auditorium, then certainly God would make sure they were filled. But she wasn't sure.

"You did the right thing, Holden. Keep praying, okay?"

He hesitated, and for a few seconds he looked more confused than he had in a long while. Then he stood and walked across the room, grabbed his backpack, and brought it back to his seat beside her. He unzipped it and began sifting through the contents. He was looking for his PECS cards, something he hadn't done in more than a month. They must've fallen to the bottom of his bag, but he finally grabbed onto them and started sorting through them. The old Holden all over again.

"Holden ..."

He didn't hear her, didn't acknowledge the presence of her voice.

"Holden, you don't need those cards ... You can do this. You can talk to me."

Slowly ... very slowly he stopped sifting through the flash cards. He took one from the deck and set the rest carefully inside his backpack. Then he handed the card to her.

She took it, surprised. This wasn't one she'd seen before. It was covered with music notes and in the center was a heart. There were no words, but the message was obvious. "You love the music? Is that it, Holden?"

He smiled, a shy sort of smile. "That for you, Ella. Because hearts are for love."

"Love for the music?" She wasn't sure she understood him. And even as the most wonderful feeling came over her, she wanted to be sure. "Hearts for loving the music?"

"Hearts ..." He looked at her, straight into her soul. "Hearts for you, Ella. Hearts are for love." For a few seconds he wrung his fingers together, fighting the nervousness that was trying to consume him. "Hearts are for love."

Ella looked at the card. She would save it forever, in a place where she could see it. Because she was pretty sure no one had ever loved her as much as Holden Harris loved her in this moment. He loved her enough to fight his uneasiness and tell her exactly how he was feeling. She blinked back tears. "Can I hug you?"

"No." He might've seen the irony in his answer, because he gave a nervous laugh. Then he reached out and took her hand. "Beauty and the Beast."

She smiled at him. They had nothing to fear tonight. The musical they were about to perform was a party, a celebration. No matter who was in attendance. They had prayed for a miracle, and God had given it to them in a song. Ella's research told her that faith alone didn't always account for unlocking a person trapped in the private world of autism. God was with Holden, whether he lived somewhere in his own world, or here with the rest of them.

In his own world he spent his days hearing the music and praying for everyone, every hour. He cherished precious memories and he had found a way to be near his father, even when the man was thousands of miles away at sea.

Yes, Holden was fine.

The miracle wasn't for Holden, it was for the people who loved him.

And in this case, God had given them music as a way to reach Holden. That, and the memory of their long-ago friendship. Ella held a little more tightly to Holden's hand. The friend beside her had changed her life. Because of him, she would never be the same again, and neither would anyone who came to see the play tonight.

Even if most of the one thousand fifty-three seats were empty.

TRACY HAD THE STRANGEST FEELING AS SHE AND DAN WALKED from the parking lot to the theater that night. Kate was already inside. She'd come early with the family of a friend so both girls could pass out programs. They were running later than Tracy liked, but she suddenly stopped short of the front door—off to the side and out of the way of other people arriving. She turned to Dan. The two of them wore their Sunday best, dressed up for a performance they never dreamed they'd get to see.

"You know how I feel?" She tilted her head, the cool spring breeze dancing in the air around them.

Dan allowed a quiet laugh. "If you're like me, you're scared to death." His smile faded. "What if he can't do this ... I hate the thought that maybe we're setting him up."

"Dan ..." A calm confidence came over Tracy. "He'll do it. He's been perfect at every dress rehearsal."

"I know ... but still." He seemed to remember how she'd started the conversation. "Okay, so how do you feel?"

She came closer to him, and looped her arms around his waist, her eyes on his. "When we lost Holden, I always had the sense that someone kidnapped him. Stole him from us."

Dan nodded. "I felt that way too."

"But we couldn't report him missing or ... or go looking for him because ..." She felt the familiar sadness rise within her. "... he was still there. Right across from us at the dinner table."

Her husband touched her face, listening. He was so much more attentive now, as if he, too, had returned from some faraway place. Somewhere farther away than Alaska.

"The thing is," Tracy tried to find the right words, "so many times ... more times than I can remember ... I wanted to get in the car and drive. Just drive. As far and fast as I could in search of the boy we'd lost."

Tears blurred her vision, her sorrow great over the missed years. But even with her tears, a glimmer of today's hope put a catch in her voice. "But here ... tonight ... I feel like I'm finally about to do what I always wanted to do all those years." She turned and nodded at the front entrance. Two tears slid down her cheeks. "Go through those doors and find my son."

His cast and crew were ready, Manny Hawkins had never been more sure in all his life. This play—if it was his final effort—would be the sweetest yet. He had no doubts. In the past months, he'd learned the value of a life and the worth of doing the unconventional.

Yes, he'd learned much from Ella Reynolds and Holden Harris—lessons he'd take with him long after the theater program at Fulton High closed down: the ability to love, for instance. And the skill of looking beyond a person's outside appearance. And he'd learned to pray. No one prayed like Holden Harris. All that flapping ... Manny understood now. Holden was praying.

No surprise that most of the cast had taken to joining in. It was common now at the end of a rehearsal or when a scene wasn't coming together to see the cast circle up and hold hands, praying to a God no one in the drama department had publicly acknowledged before this.

He thought about the administration and the warning he'd been given at the beginning of the year. His principal would be in attendance tonight, no doubt, counting empty seats. The end was at hand. But that didn't mean he couldn't go out the way Holden would go out.

"Okay, young thespians." Manny felt a sudden lump in his throat. Drama program or not, they had won something much more than a packed house this year. "Let's circle up."

The cast seemed to sense the bittersweet feeling in the room. They didn't joke or laugh or talk among themselves. It was five minutes to curtain call, and all eyes were on Manny. He waited until they were all in the circle. Holden and Ella were the last to join in, but they joined, Holden taking direction like any other student. Manny watched and for a single instant he remembered the way Holden had looked at the beginning of the school year, how Manny had fought against having Holden even observe the class. His behavior so strangely erratic, his ability to communicate nonexistent.

The transformation was nothing short of what they were about to watch on the stage tonight.

Manny nodded at Ella. Not many students had lead prayer before musicals at Fulton High. But tonight was different. Ella stood a little straighter. "Let's pray." Her voice was clear and calm. "Dear God, we know You are with us, and that You've done something very special here." She paused and Manny pictured the empty theater that awaited them on the other side of the stage door. He coughed a couple times so he wouldn't break down and cry. Ella continued, her confidence other-worldly. "No mat-

ter what ... no matter how tonight turns out, we have won. As a
team, and as individuals, and as people who believe in something
bigger than ourselves. Please ... go before us tonight. And God,
we dedicate this performance to the student who taught us how
to believe in the impossible. Holden Harris." She paused, collecting her emotions. "We dedicate tonight's performance to him. In
Your name, amen."

Manny's heart was full, and he wasn't sure how he would
speak after Ella's prayer. But as was protocol for opening night,
it was Manny's turn to take the stage first — before the first note
of the overture was played. He would walk through the door and
welcome the crowd — however sparse. He would do his best to
avoid the eyes of the principal and any other members of the
administration, and he would tell them the truth: the show they
were about to see was nothing short of a miracle.

Manny drew a deep breath. *Give me strength, God ... help
me stay positive for the kids.* He held up his hand, quieting the
students. "Scene One, be ready in the wings." He straightened his
striped tie and adjusted his best white shirt. "I won't be long."
He walked up a slight ramp and opened the door. It took a few
seconds for his eyes to adjust to the dim lighting in the auditorium, especially as the spotlight hit him. But even as his brain was
trying to comprehend the scene before him, the room burst into
applause. Not the applause of a few rows of people doing their
best to be polite.

But rousing, deafening, thunderous applause.

Manny stopped and his knees shook. He prided himself on
staying composed, on handling the real-life drama at Fulton
High even in a year like this one. But there was nothing he could
do to stop his tears. He wasn't quite to the microphone, but he
couldn't take another step, couldn't process what he was seeing.

The house was packed.

No, it was beyond packed. Students and parents filled every

seat … every single one … and more were lined three deep along the walls at the sides and back. He scanned the crowd and he saw kids who had never been to a play at Fulton High — the skaters and cheerleaders and science club … the debate team … and half-way up the right side of the auditorium was a group Manny never thought he'd see in this building.

Jake Collins and his buddies.

They didn't wear jerseys, but rather buttoned-down dress shirts. And as the applause from the audience grew, it was Jake and Sam who were the first to stand. Others joined them until the entire auditorium was on its feet. And it occurred to Manny that this wasn't the end. The drama program at Fulton High would live on after tonight. Only then did Manny's teary eyes find their way to the floor seats, the place where the band was set up, ready to begin.

One chair was empty, a chair in the front row of the flute players. The seat belonging to Michael Schwartz. But next to the empty seat was a fresh face. Manny knew about the surprise — the girl was a natural. The band director was amazed at her prog-ress in so little time. He smiled at her, a girl who never would've played the flute if this year had turned out differently.

LaShante Wilson.

She grinned and raised her shiny flute in a sort of salute. He responded with a nod and then he waved at the rest of them, at everyone who had heard Ella's talk that terrible day four months ago. Michael's death had touched them after all. They were here because they cared. Because no matter who they were or what they stood for, they needed each other.

The crowd finally settled down, and Manny moved to the microphone. As he did, he saw Holden's parents — sitting in the second row. They looked happy, but nervous. Manny could understand. But they didn't need to worry. They weren't about to see a group of kids doing a favor for a guy with special needs.

They were about to see their son.

Manny smiled despite his trembling hands. He could hardly wait to see the reaction of his drama students, to sit in the wings and watch them play to a full house. He found his voice, but only long enough to thank them for coming.

"And now …" Manny waved his arm toward the curtain, "I present to you Disney's *Beauty and the Beast*."

Thirty-One

THE SHOCK OF PLAYING TO AN OVERFLOW AUDIENCE DIDN'T wear off through the entire performance. Ella had chills up and down her arms through every scene, every song, every line. The cast and the band members delivered each moment like the rarest gift, a show of thanks to the people who had decided on this night to come together. In the name of Michael Schwartz or the name of Fulton High or in the name of God, who maybe meant more to them now.

But whatever their reason, they were here for Holden Harris — the one student who loved everyone.

She caught LaShante's eyes early in the first scene, and the two shared a smile. Maybe Michael had a window somehow, a way to see how the song had gone on, how his love of music had spread to a girl who might otherwise never have discovered her gift. They were well into the second act when she began praying for Holden between scenes. He was sitting in the wings, in a chair by himself, and when the music wasn't playing, he was rocking. Rocking the way he'd done when she first met him.

Please, God ... not tonight. Don't let him slip away.

She needed to get a message to LaShante. If the flute players could start "Tale as Old as Time" earlier than usual, during the transformation, then Holden would be okay. She wasn't needed on stage for a couple minutes, so she raced back to the classroom and scribbled a note for her friend. Then she found one of the tech guys. "Here ... get this to LaShante ... the black girl in the front row playing the flute."

The kid didn't ask questions. He was gone before she made her way back to the wings. Holden was still sitting there, alone in the darkness. "Just a few minutes, Holden. Your big song."

He kept his eyes on the stage, on the Gaston scene playing out.

"Are you ready?" She crouched down beside him, her yellow dress flounced out around her ankles.

This time he looked at her. "Tale as old as time."

"That's right." She didn't have long. She took his hand for a few seconds and then gave it a light squeeze. "I'll see you out there."

He smiled. "Beauty and the Beast."

Ella knew her part well enough to keep delivering her lines, giving her best performance ever. But she was keenly aware that the scene with Holden was drawing near. *Please God ... let LaShante get the message.* Time seemed to move into a speed warp, and suddenly the moment was upon them. Gaston appeared to stab the beast, and then fall to his death. The Beast lay on the floor, gasping for breath.

"No," Ella cried out. "Don't leave me ... please." She breathed hard and fast as she fell to her knees. Her body heaved as she grieved the loss of her friend. "You can't leave." She sat up, her attention completely on the face of the Beast. "I ... I love you."

With that the haunting sounds of transformation began. A curtain shrouded in fog came around them and made the moment magical. The Beast slid behind the curtain and lumbered into the wings. It was Holden's moment. His time to join her on the stage. But he was nowhere to be seen.

"Holden," she called out quietly into the foggy darkness. "Where are you?"

At that same instant the lilting sound of the entire flute section kicked into gear. The music was "Tale as Old as Time"—Holden's favorite song. And there in the fog, before she could waste another second panicking over what might go wrong, Holden appeared before her.

He smiled, his eyes intent on hers. "I'm here," he whispered.

"Good." She kept her voice low. The lights were coming up, the transformation complete.

Holden looked stunning, standing inches from her in his white and gold costume, his shoulders back, strength and kindness emanating from his eyes, his expression. Never in all the times they'd rehearsed this number had Holden recited the actual line, the one the script called for. But the miracles God was working tonight were still playing out. Holden touched her shoulder. "It's me, Belle ... Can't you see? This is who I've been ... all along."

Ella's lips parted, and for a long moment she wasn't sure if she could recite her name, let alone her lines. It was like Holden was no longer playing a role, but rather telling her something about himself. That this — and not the boy she'd met last fall — was who he really was. She smoothed the wrinkles in her dress and tried to remember her words. All the while the music played. LaShante and the tech guy had done what she asked and now ... now the music was giving Holden a chance to shine.

Focus, Ella ... come on. "It's ... it's really you! I can't believe it." She reached out and took Holden's hands.

And with that he began to sing. "Tale as old as time ..."

It was her turn to sing, but before she could begin, something happened in the audience — something none of them had planned for or rehearsed. Those in attendance were clapping, louder and louder. The band seemed to understand that Ella needed time, so they played the same eight bars of music again.

But what about Holden? How would he respond to the thunderous applause. She searched his eyes, but he only moved closer to her, so close she almost wondered if he was going to kiss her. But at the last moment, he brushed his cheek against hers and spoke near her ear. "It's okay, Ella. Wait for the music."

Up until this moment, Ella couldn't tell the difference between what was acting for Holden, and what was real. But now she knew. This wasn't acting ... this was Holden as real as he could be. The Holden he might someday become even without the music. Gradually the applause faded, and the band picked up by repeating where they had left off. Ella stood straighter, breathing deep before she began to sing. She smiled into Holden's eyes as he began twirling her in graceful circles.

The other cast members joined in, Cogsworth and Lumierre and Babette dancing in sweeping arcs around Ella and Holden at the center of the stage. "... Beauty and the Beast." Holden finished the song in a moment Ella knew she'd remember forever.

Ella wondered if everyone in the audience was crying the way she was, if they were processing the message Holden was singing. At the beginning of the year they'd been wrong—all of them. Wrong about Michael Schwartz and wrong about Holden. It had been tough to look past Holden's strange exterior, past his quirky behaviors and non-communicative nature. But now ...

Now everyone in the building was witnessing the miracle of Holden Harris. The music had always been inside him, only now they'd found the right song. Holden's song. And on this night they could all see the truth. Holden Harris wasn't merely a boy who struggled with autism. He was a friend to everyone at Fulton, and more than that—he really was a prince.

Ella would believe that as long as she lived.

SUZANNE COULDN'T STOP CRYING. SHE WASN'T SURE IF THE flood of emotion that had come over her was because of the very real transformation taking place on stage or because her husband had arrived at intermission and was sitting beside her. Whatever had brought him, she didn't care. Tonight she felt something she hadn't felt in years.

She felt hope.

And it was because of Holden Harris. Because of the impact he'd made on their family. As the play wound down, as Holden and the cast received a standing ovation that went on for nearly five minutes, Suzanne refused to think about all they'd lost by backing out of the friendship with the Harris family years ago. Yes, Holden suffered from a handicap. A disability.

But didn't everyone in some way or another?

What lessons might they have learned if they'd stayed connected with Tracy and Dan and Holden? Maybe the guys would've kept up their Bible study, and Randy wouldn't have drifted from their family. Maybe she wouldn't work so hard to keep up her outer appearance. Being around Holden made it painfully clear that the most breathtaking beauty came from inside.

When the play was over, after Mr. Hawkins thanked them again for coming, and as the cast members spilled into the audience for hugs and congratulations, Suzanne wanted to find just one person.

Her daughter, Ella.

She spotted her across the room and she touched Randy's arm. "I'll be back." She had to talk loud above the sound of the crowd. He nodded, and before she turned to make her way to the other side of the auditorium, she saw Dan Harris come up and give her husband a friendly slap on the shoulder. "Randy ... it's been too long."

It was another miracle — the idea that Dan would find Randy before he ducked out the back door, that the two of them might talk tonight after the emotional performance they'd all witnessed.

Suzanne clutched a long-stemmed red rose as she made her way through the crowd. Ella was surrounded by well-wishers, and standing next to her, still looking every bit the prince, was Holden. The expression in his eyes had changed, and he wasn't making eye contact with everyone pressed in near him. But he still held his head high, a protective figure at Ella's side.

Suzanne was only a few feet away, but still Ella hadn't seen her. And for a few seconds, she was grateful for the fact. Watching Ella and Holden was like seeing a vision, a figment of her imagination from back when they were three years old. Wasn't this what she and Tracy had always dreamed — that Ella and Holden would be the most lovely couple, that they would support each other and encourage each other, and be a magnet for everyone around them?

And here — against everything — it was happening almost like they'd hoped. She studied Holden, the kindness in his expression. He might never be completely out of his world of autism, and most likely the two of them would never date. But Suzanne knew as she looked at her daughter that Ella loved the friend she'd found in Holden.

She would love him as long as she lived.

A little further through the crowd and Suzanne was at her daughter's elbow. "Honey ..."

Ella turned, and with only the slightest hesitation she flew into her mother's arms. "Wasn't it amazing? Holden's miracle? Did you see what happened?" Ella barely paused long enough to take a breath. "Holden was ... he was completely with me up there."

"I saw it." Tears stung at Suzanne's eyes. She handed her daughter the rose and kissed her cheek. "I'm proud of you, Ella. It was like ... You were a real-life Belle. Your love and the music ... I think God used it to give Holden a miracle."

Ella beamed at the young man beside her. He seemed oblivious to the crowd, his eyes stuck on some quiet place in the far distance. But as Ella touched his arm, he met her eyes. The only person in the room he wanted to connect with. "You remember my mom, Holden?"

His eyes shifted to Suzanne and after a few seconds, the corners of his mouth lifted. "Yes." He had to raise his voice to be heard about the noise of the crowd still filling the theater. "You were sitting on the swing with Ella."

Suzanne was stunned, and she realized one more bit of truth. Holden hadn't missed anything. Never mind that he had gone away to live in a silent world inside himself. He still heard and saw and remembered. "That's right." She smiled at him. "We'll talk more later, okay?"

"Later." He looked back toward the far wall again, still standing shoulder to shoulder with Ella.

"Mom..." The enthusiasm in Ella's voice fell away. "I'm sorry. For not making time to talk. Maybe... maybe we can start again."

"I would like that." Suzanne felt a single tear roll down her cheek. "I love you, Ella. I'm sorry about how much I missed. I want to change. I want you to see the real me."

Ella smiled, and the light returned to her eyes. She glanced at Holden, and then back at her mother. "I guess that's true for a lot of us."

More admirers wanted a few words with Ella, a chance to take her picture or congratulate her. So Suzanne moved back through the people to the place where her husband was still talking to Dan. Tracy was standing nearby, and as she walked up the two women hugged. "Holden was amazing."

"I never could've imagined... It was like a dream."

"It was a miracle."

"Yes," Tracy looked at their husbands and then back at her friend. "God's not finished yet."

With that they turned their conversation back to the play, to the packed house and the level of emotion the final number held for all of them. This was not the place to talk about her marriage to Randy, or whether they would get counseling and try to work things out. It was enough that Tracy was right. God had worked a miracle here tonight, and He wasn't done yet. Not with Holden ...

And not with her, either.

HOLDEN LIKED HIS VIEW. HE COULD SEE EVERYONE, ALL THE people from school and the parents and teachers, and he knew God had heard his prayers. He knew so much that he'd been praying ever since the performance ended. Sometimes he was talking to Ella, but right now he was praying.

Dear Jesus, look at all the happy hearts in this room. It's exactly what I prayed for. One thousand, fifty-three seats. Only tonight there were more than one thousand, fifty-three people. Because two hundred and eleven people were standing. And that meant one thousand, two hundred, sixty-four people were happy. Every single one. The music began to play again, sweeping him away to the happiest of places.

I know, God, that You were with me tonight, and that You'll stay with me after this, too. Because You gave me my friend, Ella. And that's where my heart is. Up on stage and back in the drama classroom and there on my couch watching our movie. With Ella. And now maybe everyone will have their heart in the right place.

He was still praying when his cousin Kate walked up and tugged on his sleeve. "Kate ... you're a pretty princess tonight." He said the words, and she must've heard him because she giggled and her smile filled her whole face.

"You're the best prince, Holden. The very best."

"And you're the best cousin."

"I can hear you, Holden." Kate hugged him around his waist. "Even when no one else hears you, I hear you." She bounced off to find Holden's mother. And then she came back and his mom and dad were with her.

"I'm proud of you, son. You were perfect up there." His dad

patted his arm. It was a lot to take in, but Holden held his ground. This was his father. Home from fishing. "Thank you, Dad. Thank you for being here."

His mom didn't say very much because she was crying. But Holden wasn't sad for her. The tears on her face were happy tears. Holden knew the difference. When they left to wait for him at the back of the theater, Holden finished his prayer.

And so, Jesus, thank You for this night. Because I've prayed for this all my life. I know You hear me, because You were right in the front row and in the back and on stage and everywhere tonight. He thought for a minute. *Can You tell Michael we missed him? I know You love me. Your friend, Holden Harris.*

There was just one last thing to do, the thing he'd wanted to do since Ella asked him before the play. Less people stood around them now, so he looked at her. "Ella?"

She turned his direction. "Yes, Holden?"

"Can I give you a hug?"

Her smile turned into a pretty laugh. "Yes ... yes, of course."

Then, without any drums in the background, he pulled Ella into his arms and he hugged her. The music played, sweet and melodic, filling the room. Only now there was a difference, because Ella was swaying with him and that could only mean one thing. The thing he had known all along.

Ella could hear the music too.

READER LETTER

Dear Reader Friends,

Three years ago, my kids were taking part in a Christian Youth Theater (CYT) musical when at rehearsal one day I noticed a boy sitting in the back of the room, rocking quietly and utterly withdrawn from the other kids. We'll call him Samuel—to protect his identity. Samuel's mom sat not far from him, and later that hour she told me that her son had autism.

"He's noncommunicative," she told me. "His sister's in the play, so we'll be here at every rehearsal." She paused. "We pray for him every day, that something will unlock him."

Samuel was ten years old at the time, and over the next eight weeks all of us noticed something change with the boy. He stopped sitting in the corner, stopped rocking, stopped passing the time locked in his own world. Instead he kept his head up and he began creeping a little closer to the kids. When they would work on a song, Samuel would nod along—, clearly mesmerized by the music.

The next session with CYT, Samuel was a different boy. He was able to take direction and communicate on a basic level—so much that he was allowed to be on the backstage crew.

"We can't believe this," his mother told me. "Every day he comes out of his private world a little more. It's the music. It has to be."

A year later, after a long break from CYT, our kids took part in another show. It was Christmastime, and the production was *Scrooge*—the musical. I'd been busy with writing, so I hadn't been to as many rehearsals, but as I took my seat on opening night, I could not believe what I saw. As the townspeople filed onto the stage in old English costumes, singing and interacting with each other—there was Samuel.

The boy who hadn't been able to talk was performing on stage.

At intermission I found his mother, and we both had tears in our eyes. "It's a miracle," she told me. "God used the music to give us back our boy."

I knew from that point on that I would write a novel about an autistic boy who was brought out of his private world because of the power of a song. That's how it was for Samuel... and so that's how it was for Holden Harris.

It was with great care and a tender heart that I ventured into writing about an eighteen-year-old boy on the autistic spectrum. I learned quickly that autism is called a spectrum disorder because no two cases are exactly the same. Some people are more highly functioning—as is the case with Asperger's Syndrome. Others—like Holden in *Unlocked*—are noncommunicative and sometimes never find their way out of the private world they live in.

People on the autism spectrum struggle with sensory overload. Too much noise, too much color, too much conversation—even touch can make a person with autism explode into a tantrum or fall prey to a panic attack. Some of them experience trouble communicating from birth. Others—like Holden—progress normally and then experience a sudden, unexplainable setback. Every person's story is different.

For those of you who know and love someone with autism, I have prayed for you often. In my research something I heard time and again was that kids with autism have a special way of loving others. They are kind and sincere, and often their odd or different behaviors are very genuine expressions of emotions or feelings locked inside them.

I'm also keenly aware that not everyone who prays and loves

and works with their autistic child will experience the miracle Holden received. However, I patterned Holden after the real-life Samuel. So I do know that some kids with autism can be unlocked. Some can make amazing strides, and with today's advancements in autism, hope remains strong for everyone involved.

In addition, if you're not directly connected with autism in some way, I pray that the story of Holden made you more sensitive to people around you who might be different. Kindness can go a long way toward understanding each other, and I found myself learning as I journeyed with Ella through her patient friendship with Holden.

Another topic I've never dealt with is suicide... and it was very, very difficult. Life is God's. It is His to give and His to take away. If you or someone you love is struggling with meaning in life, or especially if you know someone being bullied, please report the situation immediately. If you don't find life worth living, you need help. See a counselor, take yourself to an emergency room, or talk to someone you trust. In the end the only way I could deal with Michael's suicide was to show his last minute change of mind.

That's one of the worst parts about suicide—it's final. But that does not have to be the outcome. God wants us all to embrace life—not because it's easy or pleasant or even always tolerable. But because life is from Him. If you woke up today and you were breathing, God's greatest purpose for your life is still ahead. God tells us in Deuteronomy that He sets before us life and death, blessings and curses. "Now choose life!" is the message of the Bible.

I pray that for each of you and for those you love.

Finally, I dealt with the idea that there are many ways to be locked in your own world. Life is too short to be anything but real with the cast of characters God has placed in the story of your life. Love well, laugh often, and find your life in Christ. Don't hide away or be a follower. Be the wonderful unique person God made you to be, and know that your purpose will always be best when defined by your faith in Him.

As always, I look forward to hearing your feedback on this book. I'll tell you something. I outlined *Unlocked* on a flight from Washington, DC's Dulles Airport to Portland, Oregon. I started writing, and hours later I had filled twenty pages in a spiral notebook. Page after page, just pouring from my heart. Along the way I caught myself loving Holden Harris and Ella Reynolds, and weeping with them at the loss of Michael.

I'm sure my seatmates thought I was a few crayons short of a box.

But when I was finished, I had the sudden, certain feeling that I was on holy ground, that God had met me in that crowded plane and given me this story as a very special gift. I saved my boarding pass and scribbled on it "Unlocked" and the date. It was the first time I'd ever done anything like that. I just wanted you to know.

Anyway, take a minute and find me on Facebook or visit my website at www.KarenKingsbury.com. There you can find my contact information and my guestbook. You could even join the Baxter Family Club—a special set of benefits for those of you who read all my books, pretty much as soon as they hit the shelves! Just one way I can show how much I care about you.

Baxter Family Club members get a limited run Collector's Signature edition of each book. This is a high-quality paperback book with a copy of my signature integrated into the cover. Club members also receive an "extra chapter" of each book sent by email, and a newsletter with each release written by John Baxter. There's no membership fee except the reduced price of the book —and you can opt out anytime. See my website—www.Karen Kingsbury.com—for details.

As for Facebook, I'm on nearly every day! I have Latte Time, where I'll take a half hour or so, pour all of you a virtual latte, and take questions. We have a blast together, so if you're not on my Facebook Fan (Friend) Page, please join today. The group of friends there is growing every day and is very special to me. I consider that my "living room" where I can hang out with my closest reader friends.

I'd love to hear how God is using these books in your life. It's all Him, and it always will be. He puts a story in my heart, but He has your face in mind. Only He could do that. If you post something on Facebook or my website it might help another reader. So please stop by.

Also on Facebook or my website you can check out my upcoming events and get to know other readers. You can hear about movies being made of my books and become part of a community that agrees there is life-changing power in something as simple as a story.

You can post prayer requests on my website or read those already posted and pray for those in need. You can send in a photo of your loved one serving our country, or let us know of a fallen soldier we can honor on our Fallen Heroes page.

My website also tells you about my ongoing contests, including "Shared a Book," which encourages you to tell me when you've shared one of my books with someone. Each time you email me about this, you're entered for the chance to spend a summer weekend with my family. In addition, everyone signed up for my monthly newsletter is automatically entered into an ongoing once-a-month drawing for a free, signed copy of my latest novel.

There are links on my website that will help you with matters that are important to you—faith and family, adoption, and ways to reach out to others. Of course, on my site you can also find out a little more about me, my faith and my family, and the wonderful world of Life-Changing Fiction™.

Another way to stay in touch is to follow me on Twitter. I give away books all the time on Twitter, and I'd love to see you there! It's free and fun, and much less time-consuming than Facebook. (Even though I absolutely love Facebook!)

Finally, if you gave your life over to God during the reading of this book, or if you found your way back to a faith you'd let grow cold, send me a letter at Office@KarenKingsbury.com and write "New Life" in the subject line. I would encourage you to connect with a Bible-believing church in your area and get hold of a Bible. But if you can't afford one and don't already have one, write "Bible" in the subject line. Tell me how God used this book to change your life, and then include your address in your email. My wonderful publisher Zondervan has supplied me with free paperback copies of the New Testament, so that if you are financially unable to find a Bible any other way, I can send you one. I'll pay for shipping.

One last thing: I've started a program where I will donate a book to any high school or middle school librarian who makes a request. Check out my website for details.

Again, thanks for journeying with me through the pages of this book. I can't wait to hear your feedback on *Unlocked*! Until then, my friends, keep your eyes on the cross, and don't forget to listen to the music.

In His light and love,
Karen Kingsbury
www.KarenKingsbury.com

DISCUSSION QUESTIONS

1. Do you know anyone on the autistic spectrum? Tell us about that person and what you have learned from them.

2. What did you learn about autism by reading *Unlocked*? Do you think Holden suffered with autism? Why or why not?

3. Holden's father Dan left his family to work on a fishing boat in Alaska. Why do you think he did this? Explain about a time when you wanted to run from a situation.

4. Suzanne and Randy pulled away from the Harris family after Holden's diagnosis of autism. Have you seen a handicap or disorder separate friends before? Tell about that situation.

5. What did you learn from the friendship between Tracy and Suzanne?

6. Have you ever had a broken friendship? What caused the break, and what did you learn from the situation? Was there ever resolution?

7. Suzanne worked hard to keep up the appearance of being the wife of a professional athlete. Do you think there is more pressure to appear a certain way in today's culture? Why or why not?

8. Michael Schwartz was a quiet kid who didn't fit in the way the popular kids did. Do you know any kids like Michael in high school? Did you befriend them? Why or why not?

9. What did you learn from the character of Michael Schwartz?

10. Deuteronomy 30:19 tells us, "… I have set before you life and death, blessings and curses. Now choose life, so that you and your children may live." What does this mean to you? Do you think a life of faith would have helped Michael? Why or why not?

11. Do you know anyone who has ever been bullied? What did you do about the situation?

12. Why do you think kids bully other kids? What does this say about today's youth?

13. Holden's mother compared autism to a kidnapping, since she felt like her son had been stolen from her. What did you like about Tracy's character? Have you ever lost someone you love? What helped you during that time?

14. Ella was first drawn to Holden because of his eyes. Luke 11:34 says that, "Your eye is the lamp of your body. When your eyes are good, your whole body also is full of light." What does this mean to you? Tell about a time when you were drawn to someone because of the light in their eyes.

15. What did you learn about the character of Ella? How are you like her, or how would you hope to be like her?

16. Why did Ella struggle with her mother? Why is it important that we show compassion not only to the strangers in our lives, but also to the ones who live under the same roof as us? Give an example.

17. Manny Hopkins was a beleaguered drama teacher on his last chance at being a success. Explain the transformation that happened in his life because of Ella and Holden. Tell about a time when someone jaded was changed by the kindness of another person.

18. Holden found great significance in watching movies from his past. What old home movie scenes or special memories do you sometimes revisit to remember who you are? Talk about some examples.

19. Did Holden's story give you hope for your own life or make you feel hopeful for someone you love? Did it affect your level of faith? Explain.

20. If you had to write the next chapter in Holden's life, what would happen? What would you hope for people with autism in our culture today, and how can you help?

ABOVE THE LINE SERIES

The Above the Line Series follows two dedicated Hollywood producers as they seek to transform the culture through the power of film.

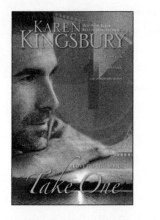

Available in stores and online!

Every Now and Then

Karen Kingsbury,
New York Times *Bestselling Author*

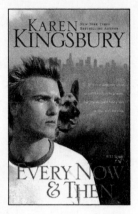

A wall went up around Alex Brady's heart when his father, a New York firefighter, died in the Twin Towers. Turning his back on the only woman he ever loved, Alex shut out all the people who cared about him to concentrate on fighting crime. He and his trusty K9 partner, Bo, are determined to eliminate evil in the world and prevent tragedies like 9-11.

Then the worst fire season in California's history erupts, and Alex faces the ultimate challenge to protect the community he serves. An environmental terrorist group is targeting the plush Oak Canyon Estates. At the risk of losing his job, and his soul, Alex is determined to infiltrate the group and put an end to their corruption. Only the friendship of Clay and Jamie Michaels—and the love of a dedicated young woman—can help Alex drop the walls around his heart and move forward into the future God has for him.

Available in stores and online!

Between Sundays

Karen Kingsbury,
New York Times *Bestselling Author*

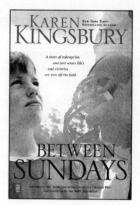

Aaron Hill has it all — athletic good looks and the many privileges of a star quarterback. His Sundays are spent playing NFL football in front of a televised audience of millions. But Aaron's about to receive an unexpected handoff, one that will give him a whole new view of his self-centered life.

Derrick Anderson is a family man who volunteers his time with foster kids while sustaining a long career as a pro football player. But now he's looking for a miracle. He must act as team mentor while still striving for the one thing that matters most this season — keeping a promise he made years ago.

Megan Gunn works two jobs and spends her spare time helping at the youth center. Much of what she does, she does for the one boy for whom she is everything — a foster child whose dying mother left him in Megan's care. Now she wants to adopt him, but one obstacle stands in the way. Her foster son, Cory, is convinced that 49ers quarterback Aaron Hill is his father.

Two men and the game they love. A woman with a heart for the lonely and lost, and a boy who believes the impossible. Thrown together in a season of self-discovery, they're about to learn lessons in character and grace, love and sacrifice.

Because in the end, life isn't defined by what takes place on the first day of the week, but how we live it between Sundays.

Available in stores and online!

One Tuesday Morning

Karen Kingsbury

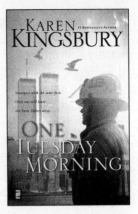

The last thing Jake Bryan knew was the roar of the World Trade Center collapsing on top of him and his fellow firefighters. The man in the hospital bed remembers nothing. Not rushing with his teammates up the stairway of the South Tower to help trapped victims. Not being blasted from the building. And not the woman sitting by his bedside who says she is his wife.

Jamie Bryan will do anything to help her beloved husband regain his memory. But that means helping Jake rediscover the one thing Jamie has never shared with him: his deep faith in God.

Available in stores and online!

ZONDERVAN®
.com

Beyond Tuesday Morning

Karen Kingsbury

**Winner of the Silver
Medallion Book Award**

Determined to find meaning in her grief
three years after the terrorist attacks on
New York City, FDNY widow Jamie Bryan
pours her life into volunteer work at a small
memorial chapel across from where the Twin Towers once stood.
There, unsure and feeling somehow guilty, Jamie opens herself to
the possibility of love again.

But in the face of a staggering revelation, only the persistence of
a tenacious man, the questions from Jamie's curious young daughter, and the words from her dead husband's journal can move Jamie
beyond one Tuesday morning ... toward life.

Available in stores and online!

Even Now

Karen Kingsbury

Sometimes hope for the future is found in the ashes of yesterday.

A young woman seeking answers to her heart's deepest questions. A man and woman driven apart by lies and years of separation ... who have never forgotten each other.

With hallmark tenderness and power, Karen Kingsbury weaves a tapestry of lives, losses, love, and faith — and the miracle of resurrection.

Ever After

Karen Kingsbury

2007 Christian Book of the Year

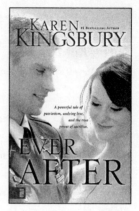

Two couples torn apart — one by war between countries, and one by a war within.

In this moving sequel to *Even Now*, Emily Anderson, now twenty, meets the man who changes everything for her: Army reservist Justin Baker. Their tender relationship, founded on a mutual faith in God and nurtured by their trust and love for each other, proves to be a shining inspiration to everyone they know, especially Emily's reunited birth parents.

But Lauren and Shane still struggle to move past their opposing beliefs about war, politics, and faith. When tragedy strikes, can they set aside their opposing views so that love — God's love — might win, no matter how great the odds?

Available in stores and online!

Oceans Apart

Karen Kingsbury,
New York Times *Bestselling Author*

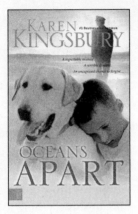

A riveting story of secret sin and the healing
power of forgiveness.

Airline pilot Connor Evans and his wife,
Michele, seem to be the perfect couple
living what looks like a perfect life. Then a
plane goes down in the Pacific Ocean. One
of the casualties is Kiahna Siefert, a flight attendant Connor knew
well. Too well. Kiahna's will is very clear: before her seven-year-old
son, Max, can be turned over to the state, he must spend the summer with the father he's never met, the father who doesn't know
he exists: Connor Evans.

Now will the presence of one lonely child and the truth he rep-
resents destroy Connor's family? Or is it possible that healing and
hope might come in the shape of a seven-year-old boy?

Available in stores and online!

Shades of Blue

Karen Kingsbury,
New York Times *Bestselling Author*

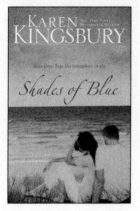

A fairytale future. A Checkered past. A decision awaits.

Brad Cutler, twenty-eight, is a rising star at his New York ad agency, about to marry the girl of his dreams. Anyone would agree he has it all—a great career, a beautiful and loving fiancée, and a fairy tale life ahead of him ... when memories of a high school girlfriend begin to torment him. Lost innocence and one very difficult choice flood his conscience, and he is no longer sure what the future will bring except for this: He must go back to the shores of Holden Beach in search of his first love, and a forgiveness neither of them has ever known.

Three people must work through the repercussions of a decision made long ago before any of them can look toward a new future.

Share Your Thoughts

With the Author: Your comments will be forwarded to
the author when you send them to *zauthor@zondervan.com*.

With Zondervan: Submit your review of this book
by writing to *zreview@zondervan.com*.

Free Online Resources at
www.zondervan.com

Zondervan AuthorTracker: Be notified whenever your favorite
authors publish new books, go on tour, or post an update
about what's happening in their lives at www.zondervan.com/
authortracker.

Daily Bible Verses and Devotions: Enrich your life with daily
Bible verses or devotions that help you start every morning
focused on God. Visit www.zondervan.com/newsletters.

Free Email Publications: Sign up for newsletters on Christian
living, academic resources, church ministry, fiction, children's
resources, and more. Visit www.zondervan.com/newsletters.

Zondervan Bible Search: Find and compare Bible passages in
a variety of translations at www.zondervanbiblesearch.com.

Other Benefits: Register yourself to receive online benefits
like coupons and special offers, or to participate in research.

ZONDERVAN.com/
AUTHORTRACKER
follow your favorite authors